Stolen
Princess

Royal Conquest Duology, Book 1

NIKKI JEFFORD

For Amber Shepherd for inspiring this story,
and
For my sister, Chelsea, a world away, but always in my thoughts.

CHAPTER ONE

Aerith

Darkness closed in on the courtyard like a giant's fist. The lanterns had been extinguished. Not even a single flame to welcome my moonlit return from the netherworld. One moment there had been fireworks and supernatural beings of every kind, and a warm, firm hand in my own. The next, a burst of blinding light had transported me back home. Alone.

Blonde hair tumbled down my shoulders to my lower back. I'd arrived at the mysterious Monster Ball by the light of the moon and returned home the same way. I still had no idea which realm the enchanted castle had been located. Faerie? Mortal? Elven? Perhaps someplace in between. Neutral ground where those chosen to attend were safe from danger and enchantment, free to revel in the splendor of the supernatural ball.

I was most certainly back in the elven realm now.

Not quite home. This had never been home. Not the estate, nor the town of Sweetbell, and certainly not the sprawling rooftop covering the scheming minds of my father and sister Shalendra.

My yellow ballgown swished over my legs like pale light in the darkness. The chill of the night's air settled over my bare arms. But nothing could crush my spirits after the magical evening I'd spent in the arms of the last elf I'd ever imagined falling for.

Jhaeros.

I could still feel the ghost of his lips ravishing mine and recalled every endearment he'd spoken with such sincerity and devotion.

"*I want to love you like this every day for the rest of my life.*"

Those lavish, hungry lips had frowned at me for so long I could still hardly believe he was smitten—with *me*. Perhaps it had all been a trick of the mind, an elaborate illusion. All part of an evening enchantment among magical beings.

The lingering ache between my legs said otherwise. I was too tired to worry about consequences. My former mate had bedded me nearly every night of our doomed union, and I'd never once felt the stirrings of life inside my womb. I could be barren. Then again, Cirrus could have been rendered impotent—with meddling from his younger brother, Liri. Or perhaps one of my sisters-in-law had put a curse on me. For whatever reason, I was unable to have children.

I shoved thoughts of my Fae in-laws to the far recesses of my mind. I'd half expected to see Liri at the ball since so many royal supernaturals were in attendance. I'd even worried Liri had somehow arranged for my invitation. It was the sort of thing he would do. But there'd been no signs of the meddlesome Fae prince, which had been a Herculean sigh of relief.

The tall French doors with sandblasted glass and wrought iron swirls swung inward without a squeak. Only the best in Sweetbell, all for the small price of leaving everything behind— my family, my home, my entire realm—to marry a Fae prince. All to save my family from starving.

If only Father had learned his lesson the first time and saved the coins Cirrus sent rather than spent them as soon as they reached his fingers.

The estate's polished wood floorboards weren't as silent as the doors. They creaked beneath my golden slippers as I followed the long ornamental rug down the hallway to the base of the wide staircase leading up to the bedchambers.

A second pair of footsteps joined mine as the soft glow of a single candle appeared at the top landing of the stairs. Father's pointed ears poked out over a long nightcap that matched his blue satin robe. He held a tallow candle in front of him like a bony finger ready to scold. "Who's there?" he whispered harshly. "Aerith, is that you sneaking in?"

Right, "sneaking" since Father had forced me to attend the ball in search of a new benefactor.

I folded my arms over my chest. "Yes, it's me."

"Shh," he hissed, glaring down at me. "Your sisters are sleeping."

I lowered my arms and took the stairs up slowly, my eyes latching on to my father's in the murky light of the single flame. Head lifted, I carried myself like the princess I'd been forced to become back in the kingdom of Dahlquist. Father scowled. He despised my high-and-mighty manners as much as he'd despised my lack of glamour and grace before sending me off to Faerie.

Nothing about me pleased him. Only one daughter held his affections.

As soon as I reached the landing, he looked me over, scrutinizing my loose hair, and wrinkled his nose as though chewing on a mouth full of pitberries.

"What happened to your hair?" he demanded, holding the candle near my head for closer inspection.

I took a step back lest he set it on fire. "I decided to let it down."

"After all the hard work Penelo put into your coiffure? Most ungracious." Father shook his head.

Even my eyes were too tired to roll in their sockets. Ever since I'd left the Faerie kingdom of Dahlquist to rejoin my family in the elven city of Sweetbell, Father had taken to talking fancy. *Coiffure?* The word made me want to cough. Why couldn't he say "hairdo" like a normal elf? I was a princess by marriage, but back in the elven realm my family had never been part of the elite. Not even Shalendra, with her gaggle of admirers, had managed to ensnare a high elf—much to her chagrin. And now, oh, *sweetberries*, I had her ex-admirer wrapped around all ten of my fingers.

I'd rather save the surprise of Jhaeros for later—like when he arrived at the front landing, pounding on the door to see me as he'd promised at the end of the ball. Shalendra had tossed him aside without a second thought—forsaken us both. It was poetic justice that her castoffs had moved on with each other.

Father narrowed his eyes at the smug smile on my lips.

I shrugged with indifference. "Things at the ball got a bit—*wild*—toward the end. You should have seen some of the other guests. At least my dress wasn't torn to bits."

Father sucked in a breath then quickly released it in a huff. "Well, I'm glad you were off enjoying yourself while the rest of us were stuck behind, worrying about our futures."

"You mean whether you'll be able to continue eating from golden spoons rather than silver?" I arched a brow.

Father's face darkened as though a shadow had passed over the harsh wrinkles around his cold eyes. "I've heard about enough sass from you, Aerith. You are no longer the lady of the house. You lost that privilege when you failed to protect your mate. Do not blame me for your misfortunes, especially when I am forced to share in them."

The candle nearly guttered out as Father spewed his disdainful words at me.

All the warmth and passion I'd experienced at the ball vanished as abruptly as the mysterious castle in which the revelries had taken place. Shadows seemed to creep off the floral-patterned walls and settle into the depths of my soul, coiling inside my stomach like blackened smoke.

"Fear not, Father. I found a suitor at the ball, just as you wished."

"Oh?" Father's voice rose and softened with interest and hope.

I looked past his shoulder, down the hall leading to my chamber. The anger and frustration from seconds before drained from my body as exhaustion took hold. I wanted to free myself of the tight gown and drown in the luxurious sheets and blankets on my bed. "He promised to call in the afternoon."

Father raised his brows. "Who is he? An elf? Fae? A supernatural being from the mortal world?"

Yes, I'm sure father would love to send me off to yet another realm far from home. And, although the sexy shifters at the ball made it tempting, the elven realm would always be my one true home, especially Pinemist, the village where I'd grown up. More importantly, I wouldn't leave my youngest sister, Melarue, again. I was surprised she wasn't up now, hiding in the shadows to make sure I returned home, demanding every detail of the supernatural ball. Some things were better left at the ball, but I had enough delights to satisfy her curiosity. It wasn't like Mel would want to hear about the kissy bits anyway. She'd much rather hear about the fire-breathing dragon shifter, badass succubus, soulful siren, and twin gargoyles whose human forms turned to stone. I'd even met a jaguar shifter who seemed to think he was someone important in the mortal world.

What Mel wouldn't care about is boring old Jhaeros from Pinemist or that we'd played my favorite strategy board game, campaigne, while verbally sparring. I could already imagine her "ew" face if I told her we'd kissed. And what we did after . . . At seventeen, she was much too young to even think about sex.

"Well?" Father asked, shoving the candle near my face

again.

I blinked several times, but my mind kept drifting off. I needed to lie down. Close my eyes. Get some rest before first light, which couldn't be too far off. "Father, I am tired. You will meet him tomorrow." When I opened my mouth to sigh, a yawn emerged instead. I started in the opposite direction of my father, eyelids heavy, and my golden slippers beginning to drag against the thick rugs covering the upper floors.

"He is wealthy?" Father asked from behind me.

I yawned again and nodded, my back to my father.

"Rest up, Aerith. We want you looking presentable for your caller tomorrow."

With my back still facing him, Father missed my smirk.

I could waltz downstairs in my nightgown and Jhaeros would still want me. Or maybe we'd both come to our senses after a few hours of sleep. One evening of passion didn't mean Jhaeros and I were destined to become mates. I'd been a bride once. I wasn't dying to do it again anytime soon.

I glided into my chamber, shutting the door behind me. The weak flame of a candle at the end of its wick cast a dim glow beside my bed. Wild red hair spilled over the pillows, and deep breaths alerted me that Melarue had fallen asleep waiting for me.

I unzipped the back of my gown, letting it spill to the floor, and stepped out—not bothering to put it away. Gently, I opened a drawer of my armoire and pulled a thin nightgown over my head before slipping beneath the covers beside Mel.

When I closed my eyes, it wasn't darkness waiting but colorful memories from the ball—twinkling lights, mystic fog, and chandeliers. Conversations and melodies played in my head, one sentence in particular repeating itself to me: "*You've captured my heart.*"

Deep brown eyes closed in on mine. Warm lips. Eager hands.

I fell asleep on a sigh and drifted into blissful oblivion

until being shaken awake.

"Aerith!"

A pair of bright green eyes peered into mine from two inches away, red hair hanging over her shoulders like thick wavy curtains. As soon as Mel saw me awake, words avalanched from her mouth.

"When did you get back? What happened at the ball? I can't believe I fell asleep. Why didn't you wake me?" She sat up and bounced in place on the mattress.

I groaned and tried to bury my head back in my pillow.

Light fingers shook me by the shoulders. "Aerith, don't keep me in suspense."

I rolled onto my back and threw my arm over my eyes.

Mel huffed impatiently.

Slowly, I uncovered my face, a grin stretching up my cheeks.

Mel's eyes widened as she anticipated the goods about to be delivered.

I propped myself up on my elbows and described the bedazzled evening to her in detail, from the enchanted castle to the mysterious host in the red dress. I told her about Dec, the dragon shifter bartender and his colleague, Imperia, the succubus with the bat tattoo. Mel's eyes lit up when I mentioned meeting a jaguar shifter named Jax.

"Not just any jaguar shifter," I noted, "the alpha of one of the biggest packs in the mortal realm."

Mel's lips formed an "O" that mirrored her rounded eyes. "What else? Did anyone shift at the ball?"

"No."

"Were any sacrifices made?"

"No."

"Did any vampires try to suck your blood?" Her eyes scanned my neck.

"No." I laughed.

Mel's mouth and eyelids relaxed to normal, not-so-impressed size. She still wanted every last detail. It wasn't enough to tell her a glowing blue light had guided me into a tunnel when entering the castle. Mel wanted to know the exact hue of blue. Light? Dark? Shimmery like the ocean? Faint like the sky? Or deep like my eyes? She wanted to know about the mysterious proprietor. Who was she? What was she? I didn't even know her name! How could I not introduce myself to the being behind the enchantments?

I chuckled again. At this rate, we wouldn't make it downstairs until lunch. Fine by me. I was in no rush for more questioning from my father.

"Did you dance?" Mel next asked, waltzing into hazardous territory.

This was one part of the story I didn't want to share too many details of. "Yes."

A second avalanche of questions cascaded from her lips, running together and knocking into one another. "With the jaguar shifter, Jax? No, wait. Was it Dec? No, he was bartending—unless he took a break. Did he take a break? Or maybe Imperia. You said she was a succubus. Oh my gosh, did she seduce you into dancing with her?"

"Mel," I said, throwing up my arms.

At this point, she was practically hyperventilating with excitement.

"I danced with Jhaeros."

"Jhaeros Keasandoral?" Mel's eyebrows pinched in confusion. "He was at the ball?"

"I was surprised too."

"And you danced...with Jhaeros?"

"Yep." Danced, that was all Mel needed to know.

"Uh, okay. Not really exciting news there, Aerith. Who else did you dance with?"

"Just Jhaeros."

Mel wrinkled her nose. "Why?"

"We bumped into one another at the ball, got to talking,

and spent the rest of the evening together."

Mel yanked her red hair back and huffed. "Talk about a buzzkill."

I narrowed my eyes and frowned.

"What?" Mel demanded. "Jhaeros is a bore. I can't believe he was invited to the Monster Ball, let alone attended. And you don't even like each other."

"Well, we do now," I said firmly, as though scolding a child. I still couldn't believe I felt defensive on Jhaeros's behalf. A day ago, I would have heartily agreed with Mel and been all too ready to cast stones on his character right alongside her. He'd always appeared arrogant and proud, except, of course, when he'd doted on Shalendra.

How could I explain what had transpired between us at the ball? I'd tried first to avoid him. He hadn't recognized me in my golden mask and yellow ballgown. The last time Jhaeros had seen me, I'd been a hollowed-out version of myself practically dressed in rags.

When our paths crossed at the ball, Jhaeros had taken me by surprise when he followed me to a private room along the castle's darkened corridor. I'd meant to best him at his favorite board game, campaigne, a match of strategy and thought. After all the years he'd disregarded me, I anticipated an opportunity to beat him in an activity I'd mastered during the lonely months in Dahlquist.

Jhaeros wasn't used to losing or teasing—or kissing it turned out. Though he'd been exceptionally skilled at the latter. Before the kissing, he'd put more effort into getting to know me than winning the game. I'd never seen such open desire nor felt such heat in a male's gaze. It had been unnerving. Dizzying. Intoxicating. Only to come crashing down when bitter memories from my past came pelting down like the pits leftover from cherries picked apart by blue jays. But Jhaeros had shown genuine concern. He'd cheered me up and made me feel safe. I never would have believed him capable of such tenderness and passion, not until the Monster Ball.

I'd given in to my desires. Nothing had ever felt so right. Jhaeros had promised to come calling. He'd offered Melarue a place in his home as well.

I must have been staring off dreamily because Mel released a horrified gasp.

"Oh my sky, do you *love* him?" Mel asked, her mouth opening wide.

Did she have to be so—adolescent? I pressed my lips together.

"You do!" she accused, launching herself out of my bed. She stood on the side, arms folded, glowering. "You're going to leave me again, aren't you?"

I slipped out of bed and faced Mel. "Of course not. Jhaeros said you could live with us."

The temperature increased in an instant, emitting heat like a furnace about to roast everything inside my chamber. I swung my head around in confusion, warmth blazing down my cheeks to my neck. I didn't realize Mel was the source until flames erupted from her open palms and threaded up her arms.

"Mel," I cried, taking a step toward her, afraid the fire would burn her up.

"Don't come any closer!" she shrieked. Her eyes widened, and it took me a moment to realize her fear wasn't for herself but for me.

I halted and watched in wonder as the thin thread of flame circled her wrists like bracelets.

Our mother had possessed frost powers. It had looked as though none of her magic had been passed down, until now. It usually appeared after an elf's seventeenth year. I supposed I shouldn't be surprised that someone as high energy as Mel had been the one blessed with abilities.

"When did you come into your elemental powers?" I

asked, marveling at the flames, which glowed over Mel's skin without burning her.

Suddenly, they were gone, and Mel's head and shoulders drooped. "While you were in Faerie, when I turned seventeen," she said, sounding as though all the fire and spark had gone out of her.

I'd only missed her birthday by a few months, but it had killed me to miss it at all.

"Why didn't you tell me as soon as I returned?" I couldn't believe she hadn't mentioned it first thing. Elemental magic was a rare and precious gift among elves.

"Father ordered me to hide it."

I saw flames again, but these were inside my head. Elemental magic wasn't something to suppress or shove away in a cupboard. It required development with an elemental master to help Mel nurture and control her powers.

"Mel, you are fire blessed," I said, awe in my voice. She should be proud of her gift. I feared father's reaction had made her ashamed. I started toward her to show I wasn't afraid—not even the tiniest bit. Mel could never hurt me. "I'll make sure to find you the best elemental master once we move back to Pinemist."

Mel scowled and backed away from me as I advanced, as though I was the one who might burn her. "You mean after you move in with Jhaeros, you'll send me away for training. How perfect," she spit out. "Well, don't bother. I can take care of myself. I did while you were gone, didn't I?" She spun around and stormed out of my chamber, slamming the door closed behind her.

I rocked back, feeling stunned, hurt, and confused.

Clearly this wasn't a great time to move forward with Jhaeros. But I did need to get Mel and me out of Sweetbell and away from Father. Hopefully she'd settle down once we were in Pinemist. I'd find an elemental master to work with her and prove to my youngest sister that I was truly back for good and not about to ditch her for a male.

My shoulders slumped. I shuffled over to my discarded dress and picked it up off the floor. I wished Mel hadn't been so harsh on Jhaeros. But this was only the beginning. Just wait until Shalendra found out. And Father. Jhaeros was rich, but not that rich. Not the illustrious suitor Father needed me to marry to keep the wine flowing and good times rolling at the Sweetbell estate.

"*What if he wants you to buy me?*" I'd asked Jhaeros.

His gaze had darkened in an instant. "*Not a chance. He's a widower. If he wants to maintain his extravagant lifestyle, he can go find himself a wealthy mate. A father should look out for his offspring, not the other way around.*"

I'd loved him for saying those words, which held more sway in my heart than sweet nothings or flattery ever could.

Father had sold me once. I wouldn't let him again.

I tossed my yellow ballgown on my bed then went to my wardrobe and selected a light blue empire-waist gown.

Father, not knowing any better, sent Penelo in after lunch to do my hair up before my suitor arrived. She arranged it much in the same fashion as she had for the ball—not that it had stayed up the whole time. My blonde locks were piled loosely on my head with wisps of hair framing my cheeks.

Once all the pins were in place, Penelo swept over to my vanity and opened a large carved wooden jewelry box. She selected a pair of opal teardrop earrings, which I approved with a nod. When she lifted a large garnet necklace circled in tiny diamonds, I shook my head. Penelo set it back down, closed the lid, and sighed.

"Such a waste holding on to such stunning necklaces you'll never wear."

I knew she thought I was being greedy, like a dragon guarding her treasure. There were plenty of pendants Shalendra would happily wear around her neck—not that she was lacking in jewelry. But the fact that I held on to these glittery pieces did not pass without comment by my middle sister, her faithful maid, and Father.

Little did they know I meant to buy my freedom with these jewels. I would secure my own little cottage with Mel in Pinemist and sell off jewels to keep us going for as long as we needed.

There was only one necklace I'd wear around my neck—the blue filigreed pendant my mother had gifted me before passing. She'd given one to each of us: blue to match my eyes, green to match Shalendra's eyes, and red to match Mel's hair.

We'd had to sell them back in Pinemist to get by, along with anything else of worth. Jhaeros had managed to find Shalendra's pendant and buy it back for her. A vision of him fastening it around her neck with that stupid adoring gaze of his flitted across my memory. Old feelings flooded in like lemonade without the sugar, leaving behind a sour aftertaste.

"A shawl will do," I said crisply to Penelo.

She stomped over to my armoire, yanked out a wispy white one, and returned to me, holding it out, not quite close enough for me to reach. I approved of the shawl she'd selected but not the method of delivery.

Standing my ground, I lifted my chin regally. "Do not forget who really pays your salary, Penelo."

The maid flushed and stumbled forward, placing the shawl in my arms. "Will there be anything else?" she asked, not quite meeting my eye.

"No," I said.

She couldn't get out of my room fast enough. I smiled to myself then sat in the brocade chair beside my bed and waited for Jhaeros to arrive. I heard the sturdy knock when it came. After it stopped, I counted steadily in my head until . . .

"Aerith!" Father bellowed. "You have a visitor."

He did not sound one bit pleased.

CHAPTER TWO

Aerith

From the landing of the stairs, I was able to look down on the foyer and survey the shocked and angry faces of my father and Shalendra. Stationed at the center bottom of the stairs was Jhaeros holding a thick bouquet of sunflowers tied in a gold ribbon. He was dressed in stiff-looking slacks and a starched white shirt—not as formal as the tux he'd worn at the ball but close.

For several seconds, my feet wouldn't move.

Being together at the ball had been one thing, a night off from the pressure put on by my father. An escape from prying eyes and judgments, including my own preconceived ideas of Jhaeros's character. I hadn't wanted to fall for him, but I had. Now that he was here, I felt awkward and unsure.

Maybe we'd made a mistake. Did we really belong together? Should we have said our goodbyes after the ball and left it at that?

I chewed on my bottom lip, unable to move.

Then Jhaeros looked up at me. His eyes devoured mine as his hungry gaze raked over me.

My knees went weak, and all my doubts were chased away by his open adoration.

He once looked at Shalendra that way too, a nasty little voice reminded me.

I straightened my body, lifted my chest, and took the stairs down slowly. Shalendra had her arms folded beneath her bosom and scowled at me every step of the way. Father's face had turned entirely red, and one eye twitched. Jhaeros's lips parted slightly as he watched every step of my progress.

When I was halfway down the stairs, the butler came forward to take the flowers. Jhaeros looked from me to the butler before handing them off.

"I will put these in a vase and have them sent to Princess Elmray's room," the butler assured him.

Jhaeros nodded slightly, gaze back on me, a soft smile on his lips—lips that had been on mine mere hours earlier.

When I reached the foyer, Jhaeros still stared but from much closer. His body twitched as though he wanted to rush to me, but propriety forced him back. I took a step forward, letting my shawl slip from my shoulders and fall to the ground.

Jhaeros rushed forward, practically diving to the floor to grab my shawl. While his head was bent, I met Shalendra's eyes and smirked. Her mouth, which hung ajar as Jhaeros threw himself at my feet, snapped shut into a severe frown.

I'd never acted catty toward her, no matter how snippy she behaved, but fifteen months in Faerie had changed me. I was no longer the obedient floor mat I'd once been. Still, I worried I'd pushed it too far. Cruelty wasn't in my nature. I didn't want my time in Faerie to take all that was left of me and twist it all up into a spiteful version of myself.

When Jhaeros stood and offered me my shawl, I smiled brightly as I took the light fabric and draped it around my arms.

"Thank you, Jhaeros."

His gaze fastened to my lips before he dragged them back up to meet my eyes. "You look lovely. You arrived home safely from the ball?"

"Yes, I appeared in the outer courtyard—the same place from which I was spirited away."

Jhaeros moistened his lips. "And you are well?" His eyes drifted to my belly, eyebrows lifting in question.

It was too soon to know if there had been consequences to our coupling at the ball, but I'd never had so much as a pregnancy scare with Cirrus. I felt certain that one time with Jhaeros would not result in a baby elf.

"Very well," I assured him.

Having had enough of our idle chitchat, Father stepped forward, demanding, "What is the meaning of your visit, Jhaeros?"

The brown eyes that had gazed on me so softly now hardened as Jhaeros turned and flicked his gaze over to Father and said, "I mean to claim your eldest as my mate, Elred."

Shalendra gasped then covered her mouth.

Father turned to me aghast. "Is Jhaeros the suitor of which you spoke?"

My eyelashes fluttered as I smiled demurely. "He is, Father."

My father chewed on the inside of his cheek and regarded Jhaeros with a raised chin. "My daughter is in mourning," he said, choosing his words with slow consideration.

I rolled my eyes, but no one was looking at me. Father's focus was on Jhaeros, and Jhaeros stared back with slanted brows. Shalendra gaped at Jhaeros as though he'd grown a second head.

Even though Father was short and stocky and Jhaeros towered over him, he managed to look upon him like he was no more than a slug he'd like to crush beneath his buckled shoe.

"You must wait the appropriate six months before I will give you my consent to court her," Father said.

"How long has it been?" Jhaeros asked through gritted teeth.

"Four months," Father announced.

And I bet he planned to have me wed within the next two.

I cleared my throat. "Cirrus told me that if he were to enter the sky realm earlier than expected, he did not wish for me to mourn him. Jhaeros may court me anytime. If he wishes, he can even get down on bended knee and—"

"What would folks say?" Father asked frantically before I could finish the last of my sentence. He softened his voice, addressing Jhaeros. "Surely you do not wish to harm Aerith's reputation, do you, Jhaeros?"

Sure, appeal to the elf's sense of honor.

Jhaeros's jaw tightened as he looked between my father and me. I could picture his thoughts darting back and forth, determining his best move. Honor had brought him to my doorstep to begin with. He'd offered to make me his life mate after ravishing me at the ball. But now my father had gone and muddled his mind with propriety—something Jhaeros seemed to be a stickler for. But this wasn't a game of campaigne. He wouldn't find an acceptable move no matter which choice he made.

I decided to make it easier on him. "Fine, we won't rush our claiming," I said to my father. "Jhaeros will court me first."

Both my father and Jhaeros looked relieved. Some of the tension eased from the room until Shalendra stomped out of the foyer into the sitting room. Guess I wouldn't be inviting Jhaeros in there for tea or coffee, hold the sugar.

I offered Jhaeros a friendly smile. "It's a little chilly to sit in the courtyard, but if you wait here, I'll get my cloak and we can take a carriage to town square and walk around."

"What was I just saying about your reputation?" Father scolded.

A month ago, he'd put me on the local market to Sweetbell's wealthiest bachelors and then pressured me into attending the Monster Ball in pursuit of a suitor. This was too much.

"Then we'll stay hidden inside the carriage," I said nonchalantly. "It will be cozier that way, anyway." I shrugged.

Jhaeros's eyes turned hooded while Father's cheeks reddened.

"Absolutely not, Aerith. Not without a chaperone. I will send Penelo with you."

I wrinkled my nose. "No, thanks. At any rate, I don't require a chaperone, being a widow."

Father scowled.

"What if we took a short walk down the lane?" Jhaeros suggested.

"Excellent idea. I'll get my cloak," I said before Father could object.

I lifted my skirts and hastened up the stairs, not wanting to leave Jhaeros alone with my father for longer than necessary. I dived into my chamber and pawed through my cloaks, selecting a hooded dark gray one.

When I returned to the foyer, it didn't look like my father and Jhaeros had spoken, so much as glared at one another, during my brief absence.

"Please, allow me," Jhaeros said, taking my cloak to hold open and help me slip into.

Such a noble male. But I knew he had another side. One I wanted to see again to reassure myself I hadn't only imagined it or undergone an otherworldly psychedelic experience at the ball.

"Don't stay out long," Father said as Jhaeros and I walked to the front doors. "It's cold," he added.

Lame.

"Don't worry, Father. I have Jhaeros to keep me warm." I smiled sweetly over my shoulder and looped my arm around Jhaeros's.

Father shot me a warning glare, but my smile didn't waver.

As soon as we were outside, alone, Jhaeros turned his head

to stare at me, eyebrows furrowed. "I know he's overbearing, but he has a point about propriety. I would never wish anyone to think ill of you, Aerith. I can wait two months."

My footsteps froze. The warm feeling in my belly cooled like cocoa left out too long. It turned to sludge inside my stomach. I slipped my arm away from Jhaeros and pressed my hands at my sides. We hadn't yet made it to the estate's wide drive with the topiary trees spaced apart just so, and already I wanted to storm back inside.

"Aerith?" he asked, trying hard to read my face.

He was overlooking the fact that my father had sent me to the ball for the express purpose of finding a mate to whisk me off at once. Time didn't matter. Two months. Two days. So what?

Jhaeros had been at that tournament nineteen months ago—seen the Fae prince I'd "won" with my bow and arrows. As a former bride of Faerie, the folks in Pinemist would already judge me as corrupted. Only a desperate elf would give up her realm to marry a Fae.

I would have found another way to keep our family fed if given the chance. I'd managed to hunt down deer in Brightwhisk Forest. I'd taken no pleasure in killing, but the meat and hides had helped support us after my mother's death left us impoverished.

When Prince Cirrus and his brother, Prince Liri, had come calling looking for eligible elf maidens to compete in a tournament for his hand in marriage, Father had forced me to participate. My performance had been utterly lacking, especially compared with two of the prettier elf warriors. I'd nearly avoided Cirrus's notice until an out-of-control ogre had rushed onto the field. I hadn't thought, merely reacted, taking the ogre down with my arrows. Too late I learned this was a final test arranged by Cirrus. My quick actions earned me a tiara and a mate in a foreign realm far from everything I loved.

At the time, I never thought I'd return to Pinemist again. If my father had his way, he'd prevent me even now.

"Two months," I repeated, "very well." My words were spoken without emotion.

"Unless—" Jhaeros stared pointedly at my belly.

"I told you I'm barren."

"And you still can't know that it wasn't your late mate who was impotent," he returned.

"Do you want children?" I asked.

His lips thinned. "I've never cared for them."

I snorted, utterly unsurprised. Lucky for Jhaeros, he had nothing to worry about.

"That doesn't mean I'm opposed to having my own," he threw in.

"Ever the diplomat," I muttered.

Jhaeros frowned as though he'd made a wrong move on a campaigne board and was trying to figure out how to get the game back on track. "Tell me what you want, Aerith, and I will gladly submit. I will wed you tomorrow if that's what you wish."

"Tomorrow but not today?" I challenged, arching a brow.

His head jerked, and his lips parted. He stared intently down the drive. I couldn't be sure if he was contemplating running for it or taking a moment to gather his thoughts. Then his gaze slid to mine, and I grinned.

It took several seconds to register that I was teasing him. I doubted anyone before me had ever taunted Jhaeros Keasandoral. A knowing look entered his eyes, followed by something I couldn't discern. He didn't chuckle. Instead, he stepped closer and took both my hands in his. Gaze locked onto mine, he stared at me with open longing.

"Aerith, I would marry you right now, on the spot, if you would consent to be my mate."

The air left my lungs. Was he proposing? He was!

For all my joking, I wasn't ready yet.

I squeezed his hands then released them and stepped back. "I've never been courted before. I think I should like to try it before I settle down."

Jhaeros pursed his lips and clasped his hands together as though he might beg for me to reconsider. Ironic when he was the one moments before speaking about propriety. "Then I would like to start at once."

"You don't want to wait the respectable two months?" I challenged.

His arms shot out, and he pulled me against him, mouth on mine in a hungry kiss that somehow managed to steal my breath and savor it all at once. My eyes closed on cue, leaving only the feeling of Jhaeros holding me in his embrace, coaxing my lips apart with his tongue.

I gave into it, my body going slack. I felt the muscles tighten in his arms all the way to his hands, which gathered me against him. Jhaeros didn't have the broad, muscular build of the shifters I'd met at the Monster Ball, but his chest was firm and toned and strong like his arms.

I moaned a little into Jhaeros's mouth, and his kiss deepened, becoming more insistent.

My insides heated and throbbed, wanting more than his tongue. I broke the kiss only to whisper, "There's a garden shed in back." Cool air answered me. I opened my eyes to find Jhaeros blinking as though coming out of a daze.

He shook his head slowly, a slight frown on his lips. "The next time I bed you, we will be proper mates."

Oh no, not this again. I took in a deep breath and released it.

Jhaeros gazed into my eyes. "It's the least you deserve, Aerith." He kept staring until I nodded.

"Very, well. I will try to behave myself during our courtship."

"And I as well," Jhaeros said, straightening his shirt, though it wasn't out of place. "Would you still care to take

21

that walk down the lane?"

"Sure," I said, slipping my hand onto Jhaeros's arm.

I needed something to cool off. My insides were still oozing with anticipation. Damn Jhaeros for being such a noble male.

But as we fell into step, an easy conversation started. At the ball, I'd thought beating Jhaeros at campaigne would be my greatest triumph over the arrogant elf, but walking arm in arm, here and now, it was making him laugh that proved to be the best reward of all.

Father was waiting in the foyer after Jhaeros walked me to the front door and took his leave. It wouldn't have surprised me if my father had been standing there the entire time, fuming while I walked with Jhaeros. The area around the foot of the stairs felt ten degrees hotter, as though Father's anger could heat the whole first floor.

"Aerith, explain yourself," he commanded as I entered.

"Explain what?" I asked saucily.

Father's eyes bulged, and his hands fisted. "You know what. Jhaeros! What happened at the ball to make him so ridiculously bewitched by you?"

I pulled off my cloak and hugged it against my belly. "We had a good time together. Simple as that."

Father scowled. "You can do better than him."

"And by better, you mean richer?"

"Yes, that's exactly what I mean." Father didn't even try to deny it. "You know we need more than a wealthy bachelor from Pinemist to maintain the family estate. We need a high elf or royalty from another world."

I dug my nails into my woolen cloak and glared at my father. "Maybe you should have thought of that before moving to Sweetbell and buying this monstrosity."

"What was I supposed to do with all the money Cirrus sent?" Father challenged.

"Save it," I replied without a beat.

"I never expected it to stop—especially not so soon." Father straightened his spine and lifted his nose, narrowing his eyes on me. "The fault lies with you, Aerith, as well as the responsibility."

A burst of laughter escaped my lips. Brittle. Bitter. Infuriated.

Still he pressed. "Or do you not think your sisters deserve a little happiness?"

"And what about my happiness, Father?"

He drew his lips back and sucked air in through his teeth. "I hardly recognize the spiteful, selfish female you've become. Faerie changed you, and not for the better."

Pushing past the anger and hurt, I kept my chin held high. "Faerie did change me," I agreed. "The Fae are always out for their best interests. You'd fit right in."

Father's eyes bulged out of their sockets. "You will not speak to me that way. I am your father."

"Pity for me," I said, rushing past him for the stairs.

"What did I just say?" he bellowed at my back.

I stormed up the first four steps before turning around. "You reminded me that you are my father. Let me take this opportunity to do the same by reminding you I am your daughter and a grown female. A widow. A princess. A lady of great wealth. I have no need of a mate, affluent or otherwise. I am moving back to Pinemist tomorrow, and I'm taking Mel with me. I suggest you encourage Shalendra to make a gainful match as soon as she can. You might try doing the same for yourself."

I raced up the rest of the stairs, afraid if I heard anymore of Father's ruthless comments, I wouldn't last another night in Sweetbell. I wanted to leave at first light and secure temporary lodgings until I could find something more permanent—a cute cottage to rent. I'd give Mel the option of leaving with me right away or joining me once I had found us a place.

Mel, of course, wanted to run off with me at once. She found me in my room, tossing gowns into trunks. She didn't linger, not after I told her to pack.

One more night in Sweetbell.

I skipped dinner to avoid Father's scathing tongue and Shalendra's venomous glare. I'd had adversaries in Faerie, too, but none of them thought as ill of me as my own father and sister.

One more night, I reminded myself.

I couldn't wait to return home—to settle into a cozy, little cottage with Mel and make up for the time we'd lost together. We could maintain the place ourselves and discuss her elemental magic further. It would give her more time to warm up to Jhaeros and see the wonderful male I'd come to know.

I hated to admit it, but my brother-in-law, Liri, had given me a second chance by poisoning Cirrus. If not for him, I might have been stuck in Faerie forever. Cirrus had been kind enough, and more attentive than I required, but he'd forbidden me from visiting my family. He was all too happy to deliver letters back and forth between the realms, but it hadn't been enough, and a dark part of me reveled in his death.

"Yes, I did us both a favor," a husky voice whispered across the room after I'd fallen asleep for the night.

My eyes flew open, and my body tensed, sensing the presence nearby.

His skin was as pale as the moon, his hair white as snow. He'd braided it back into a whiplike tail that followed him as he crept along the edge of my bed.

I tried to sit up, but every bone in my body felt as though it had turned to mashed potatoes. "What are you doing here, Liri?" I demanded.

He smirked. "I am not really here, which is a shame." He climbed onto my bed, walking on his knees toward me. The mattress made no movement, no dip or shudder. "See?" His smile widened as he made his way toward me until he straddled my limp body.

I narrowed my eyes at the pitiless face above mine. He was beautiful, but I knew better. "Why are you here?" I asked again.

"I've come to check on you," Liri said, stroking the blanket near my hip. I hated the tingle I felt even though he wasn't really here, wasn't really touching me. But my brain said otherwise with the information my eyes fed it. He smiled coyly, well aware of the fact that he didn't need to physically touch me for me to feel him.

"I would have come sooner," he continued in a lazy drawl, "but I've been busy."

"Poisoning more rivals?" I asked in a haughty tone.

Liri's next smile showed all his teeth, white and gleaming like his hair and skin. If it weren't for his pointed ears, I might think him a vampire. He was just as heartless too.

He stared at my lips, his eyes turning lambent. "My desire for you has not changed, nor my wish to have you as my bride."

"Nor have my wishes changed," I fired back. "I'm back in the elven realm where I belong—where I want to be."

Liri shook his perfectly sculpted face.

"You belong on the highest pedestal, my pet. Nothing short of a kingdom will do for such beauty, such grace, such...fire." His eyes gleamed. His long, pale fingers faded into the covers on both sides of my thighs, causing my hips to rise toward him. Sure, now my limbs worked. I thought he'd rub it in my face, but his expression brightened with hunger.

"My brother made you a princess, but I, sweet Aerith, will make you a queen."

CHAPTER THREE

Melarue

The next morning, I kicked off my covers, rolled to the edge of my wide mattress, bounced off, and landed on my feet.

"See ya, Sweetbell!" I said, lifting my arm into the air and waving it around. "I'd say it's been swell, but that would be lying, and lying isn't good . . . unless it's to your sister Shalendra about her missing jeweled comb that you used to pick fleas out of poor itchy Mugsy, the groundkeeper's dog."

I snickered to myself as I got dressed in a pair of trousers and a loose blouse, which I secured with a brown leather waist cincher. No more dresses for this elf! My trunks were already packed with items of value to sell. The gowns I did pack were for the express purpose of padding, especially around the breakables.

Not all the valuables were technically mine. Well, none of it really. Father had always given me useless stuff, like dresses, slippers, and fans.

Then again, it had all been paid for by Aerith, so really I should take one last look around the estate for more goods that were easy to transport. There was a beautifully engraved cigar box in the study. Too bad it had been personalized with the initials "E.H." But maybe I'd get lucky and find another

"E.H." out there or someone who didn't care. Or maybe I could turn "E.H." into something else.

"Expert Huntsman," I said aloud. *Good one, Mel.* "Educated Highborn," I continued on the way to my bedroom door. "Elderly Humbug." I lifted my hand to my lips to cover my snigger, even though no one was around to hear me.

An insistent knock sounded on my door before it was swung open and Aerith rushed in. Her blonde head swiveled from side to side, searching the corners of the room.

"Um, I'm right here," I said with a wave.

When her gaze met mine, a chill crawled down my spine. There were dark circles beneath my sister's eyes—the kind I remembered from before she left, when she used to get up early to hunt for our next meal in Brightwhisk Forest.

My heart plummeted. What if she'd changed her mind about leaving? What if it was guilt eating away at her?

I frowned and concentrated on pulling my lower lip back so it didn't puff out into a pout. "You changed your mind," I said, unable to hold back the accusation.

Aerith came to a jerky stop. "What? No! We need to leave at once."

My body relaxed. This wasn't what I'd been expecting when she stormed in all crazy-eyed like an elf out of bedlam. "So, right after breakfast?" I asked. I still needed to swipe that cigar case. Some Esteemed High Elf was going to want it. Maybe I could add an extra "E" after "H." I rubbed my lips together in thought and stared absently at the ceiling.

"Now," Aerith said.

I tried to meet my oldest sister's eyes, but it was like trying to catch a firefly in a jar the way her pupils darted all around the room. She'd returned from Faerie looking like a beautiful golden princess, but right now she looked bedraggled and not quite right in the head.

"Did you get any sleep?" I asked.

She twisted her fingers, still unable to hold my stare or keep still for more than a second. "Nightmare," she grumbled.

I put my hands on my hips. "Are you sure you're not having second thoughts?"

"Never." The steel in Aerith's voice convinced me. "I told you I'm ready right now."

"Okay. Cool." I bobbed my head, stealing glances at her. She'd managed to remain in place for about five seconds now and seemed calmer. "Are you sure there isn't a little extra time to, you know, look around, make sure we didn't miss anything?"

Aerith turned a sharp blue gaze on me as though she'd sleepwalked into my room and just now fully awakened. She laughed, which made me grin. It was good to see her back to herself.

"You little scamp," she said, sounding delighted despite her words. She glanced at my closed trunks. "I don't even want to know what you've squirreled away."

I stretched my arms over my head with indifference, yawned, and smiled. "Finders, keepers."

"Said every thief in history," Aerith muttered, shaking her head. She took a deep breath and straightened her spine. "Fine, whatever, we don't have time to waste putting anything back."

"Okeydoke, but I really do have to grab one more thing."

"Make it quick," Aerith said.

I smiled. "I will."

It took two footmen eight trips up and down the grand staircase to bring down all our trunks. Not exactly the stealthiest getaway.

Father sputtered and fumed in the foyer the entire time. He told Aerith that if she left, she shouldn't expect to be welcomed back. I, however, had a standing invitation to return home since I "didn't know any better." Hello? Seventeen, not seven. Sometimes being the youngest sucked. Then again, I liked the "getting away with everything" part—a lot.

Despite Father's tantrum, we took one of the estate's carriages, which would return after depositing us at Dixie's Inn in Pinemist. All but two of our trunks were following on a wagon and would be delivered to Jhaeros Keasandoral's manor home.

I wrinkled my nose. Too bad boring old Jhaeros had to be involved, but I understood we couldn't bring eight large trunks into a rented room at the inn. I definitely didn't want to leave my loot behind.

What I didn't understand was Aerith's sudden fondness for the uptight drone. Even Shalendra had blown him off the first chance she got. Somehow, I didn't think Aerith would do the same. Shalendra had been using Jhaeros until better prospects came along. Aerith would never treat another elf that way.

I sighed inwardly. It was up to me to keep them apart for as long as possible. After Aerith's ordeal in Faerie and with Father, she deserved a break, plenty of time to get back to nature, catch up on reading, and go on adventures. Several years at least.

If Jhaeros truly cared about her, he'd be willing to wait. And while he waited, perhaps they'd drift far, far apart until Jhaeros sank out of sight altogether.

Ugh, I was tired of thinking of him and the stiff way he always stood as if a wooden board, rather than bones, kept him upright. I tried to picture kissing his patronizing lips then stopped myself. Ew—ee!

Why did he have to attend the ball? It was only natural to get caught up in a magical evening. Everything and *everyone* would appear more glamorous at an enchanted ball filled with supernatural beings from every realm.

Me, I would have gone for the jaguar shifter. Jax and Mel tearing up the town. And he'd be a hot kisser, of course.

I didn't realize I was bouncing on the carriage bench until Aerith said, "Mel! Think you can sit still for five seconds?"

She sat in front of me on the opposite bench, smiling warmly, but I wasn't the only one fidgeting. She hadn't stopped wringing her fingers in her lap since leaving Sweetbell.

I lifted my gaze from the grip on her hands to her eyes and offered up my most reassuring smile. "Everything is going to be okay."

A soft airy laugh escaped Aerith's lips. "I should be the one telling you that. And yes, it will be. Everything will be great. Sweetberries from here on."

"Cool." I began bouncing in my seat again.

Aerith cleared her throat and raised a brow.

I stopped—for about ten seconds. "I haven't been back home since Father made us move," I said.

Aerith nodded. It had been longer for her, but she said nothing. Instead, she stared out the window, a haunted look entering her eyes. She twisted her fingers harder. The smile on her face soon faded.

A grin split my lips as I burst into a childhood melody that used to annoy my older sisters. "Ninety-nine feathered arrows in a quiver; ninety-nine feathered arrows; take one out; shoot it about; ninety-eight feathered arrows in a quiver."

Aerith slapped a hand to her forehead and groaned.

At least she was no longer wringing her fingers.

I told Aerith I didn't mind sharing a room at Dixie's, but she insisted on separate rooms. She was probably afraid I'd burst into song again or kick her in my sleep.

As soon as our trunks were brought up and we had a warm meal in our bellies, I followed Aerith into her room where she chewed on her bottom lip while pacing.

"We need to find a nice cottage to rent, but first we need funds, which means pawning off my jewels. And we need to find you an elemental master and a weapon. Father neglected weapons training for both you and Shalendra," Aerith continued, thinking aloud. "Mother gave me my first bow when I was seven years old. But I don't think a bow fits you." She looked up and met my eyes.

"You just don't want me to sing the feathered arrows song."

Aerith grimaced, which made me laugh. She shook her head. "No, for you I think a sword."

"Or both," I said, remembering the elf, Keerla, who had competed in the same tournament as my sister nearly two years ago. Keerla had been the only contestant to use a bow and arrows *and* a sword for her skills demonstration. She was badass. But not as badass as Aerith. The contestants had attacked straw dummies, but only Aerith had taken down a real live ogre sent charging in by Cirrus as a final test.

Yeah, my sister was the queen of badassery.

"Or both," Aerith repeated in agreement.

Seriously, best sister ever. At lunch, she'd even said I could look at cottages with her and help decide where we'd live—unlike my father, who had up and decided we were all moving to Sweetbell, despite my protests.

I did a little hop and dance in place while Aerith removed her jewelry from a beautifully carved wooden box and placed the pieces into a knapsack. Once the sack was full, she pulled in a deep breath and met my eyes.

"Okay, now for the finance part."

"Time to hock our wares?" I asked, rubbing my hands together. "Leave it to me to fetch the best prices."

Aerith winced. "I won't have you out *hocking* anything.

Neither of us will." Aerith lifted her head into the air higher than was natural.

Sheesh, I don't know if she was aware that she'd formed a habit of taking on airs since returning from Faerie. Then again, she was a princess. That title was bound to go to anyone's head, even Aerith's.

No, thank you. I'd pass on titles any day. Being plain old Mel was good enough for me. Plain old powerful Mel. I grinned. Way badass.

"Uh, right," I said. "So, then how are we supposed to turn those jewels into coins exactly?"

"Third party," Aerith answered.

"Rot on a berry." I covered my face with my hands and groaned. "Does Jhaeros have to help us with *everything*?"

"Not Jhaeros," Aerith said. "Someone else."

I pulled my fingers away from my face, intrigued. "Who?"

"It doesn't matter." Aerith tossed back her hair. "He'll do as I ask, and he'll be discreet."

Hold the lead horse . . .

"*He*?" I grinned so wide my cheeks ached. "Who is *he*?"

"Someone who can get the job done," Aerith answered in a totally humdrum, bland tone that didn't give a thing away. Torture!

"So, is he a friend or ex-lover?" I pressed.

"Melarue!" Aerith snapped, eyes narrowing.

Yep, ex-lover for sure. She almost never took a harsh tone with me.

I forced my arms to my sides and fought the urge to rub my hands together. Didn't look like smooth sailing was in Jhaeros's forecast. Such a shame. Sometimes life delivered sweetberries, other times—pits. Oh well. *Buh-bye, Jhaeros. Be sure to send us a greeting from the Isle of No Return.*

This mystery male sounded a whole lot more exciting if he was the type to engage in back-cottage dealings. I liked him already.

"I'll get my cloak," I said, spinning around and heading for the door.

"No, you're staying here." Aerith's voice halted my tracks. I whipped around, ready to argue, but she was already talking before I had a chance to protest. "This isn't up for debate, Mel. We have far more valuables than this." She held up the knapsack. "I need someone to guard the rest."

"Oh please," I said, rolling my eyes and folding my arms over my chest. "Who's going to rob us in Pinemist?"

Aerith gazed at the door, her eyes going out of focus. "We can never be too careful," she said in a faraway voice.

Well, *pitberries*, if she'd argued more, I would have fought, but when she went all drifty and ominous like that, there wasn't much I could do besides grumble, groan, gripe, and relent.

"Fine," I said, "but it would have been nice to have a sword first before you asked me to guard our treasures."

Aerith smiled. "One thing at a time, Mel." She put on her gray cloak and picked up the knapsack.

"Sure you don't want me to come along and chaperone?" I asked.

Aerith scowled. "Just wait here, and keep an eye on our rooms. When I return, we'll look at cottages."

I hopped in place. "Can we get something around the center of town? Or maybe beside the river? Or forest?"

"We'll see." Aerith opened the door and paused beneath the doorframe. "But you're going to have to pick *one*." She winked and stepped out.

Off to meet her lover, I thought wryly.

I started toward the door to follow her then stopped and looked over my shoulder at the large trunk in the corner. My heart rate kicked up like a runaway horse. Dagnabbit. Aerith had entrusted me with our riches—our futures, essentially. I couldn't leave the inn while she was away. I just couldn't.

Thin red flames unspooled over my arms like ribbons.

Now was as good a time as any to practice my fire magic . . . so long as I didn't burn down the inn.

CHAPTER FOUR

Aerith

Clear, crisp sky brightened the storefronts, cafes, townhomes, and dirt roads connecting my beloved birthplace.

I stood at the center of Pinemist, in the bustling friendly streets of commerce. There was Pinky's Chocolates and Sweets where Mom used to take us for hot cocoa and cookies. And Bella's Boutique where we shopped for gowns. Mr. Harman was still in the same location with his small shop crammed from ceiling to floor with bows, arrows, quivers, and archery gear.

Tears glossed over my eyes.

I knew I'd stepped out on an errand, but I couldn't make my legs move beyond slow steps as I took it all in.

I was really here. Really home. For fifteen long months, I'd feared this day would never come.

And now Liri wanted to drag me back to Faerie.

I ground my teeth together.

He'd given me a choice, and I'd made it.

N-O!

"Perhaps after you've returned home for a spell you will find you miss Faerie. Perhaps we will meet again, my pet, and you will reconsider my offer."

Not a chance.

I'd escaped one brother. I wouldn't sacrifice myself to another Elmray prince.

"*Whatever you wish,*" he'd said, but that was back when he believed I would reconsider. I might not have powers, but I wasn't some human pet to toy with. I'd done my time. Served my purpose. And I wasn't going back. I had to find a way to get that through Liri's snowy white head and make him leave me alone.

Leave it to Liri to take the shine off my return to Pinemist.

I loosened my jaw.

No, I wouldn't let him. He had no power over me. None whatsoever. And good luck finding me again. I'd spent enough time in Faerie to know a thing or two about their powers. High Fae had the ability to dream walk. In order to visit a sleeper, they had to know exactly where he or she was— same as they would if they wanted to come knocking at the front door. Well, I wouldn't be around the next time Liri came calling.

He could ghost hump my empty bedsheets back in Sweetbell all night long.

I made my way through town with a lighter step. The cobbled streets of town morphed into smooth dirt roads lining manor homes. My family's old home was to the west, as were the beautiful grounds Jhaeros owned. But I was headed south toward beautiful Brightwhisk Forest and the small mud cottages clustered around the edge of the woods.

Manors turned into modest, square homes, and then cute little cottages with multicolored flower boxes before I reached the ramshackle cottages. The road petered out, turning into heavily rooted dirt trails.

Children ran past me in tattered clothes. A young girl with golden curls ran right up alongside me. Before she ever brushed against my cloak, I tightened my hold around the knapsack. She looked all innocent, but Mel had taught me otherwise. I clutched the knapsack against my stomach and made my way to the cottage at the edge of the cluster—slightly separated from the rest.

Hopefully, he still lived here.

The place looked the same as I last remembered. It was modest but well kept. Fresh mud had recently been packed around the outer walls, and the roof looked like it had new thatching.

Smoke puffed from the chimney. Someone was home.

I knocked on the wood door.

"Who is it?" a deep, male voice called from within.

Yep, that sounded like Devdan all right. I sagged with relief. A familiar face was a comfort, even if the tone didn't sound particularly friendly.

"Aerith," I said.

The door flew open and Devdan appeared in the doorframe. He leaned against one side, an arm up high as though grasping for the low hanging roof. It had been nearly two years since I last saw him, and he'd filled out into a lean, muscular male. Just as he kept his dwelling, his trousers and tunic were simple but clean and free of tears. The light brown hair he'd worn messy before was cropped on the sides and thicker on top. I'd venture to say he looked dashing. Too bad he didn't have the manners to go with the looks.

A pair of light brown eyes scanned me up and down. His lips formed a smirk. "The faerie princess returns." Devdan dropped his arm and dipped into a mocking bow.

I narrowed my eyes. What crawled up his butt and laid eggs? "I have," I said, "and I'm still an elf."

He raised his brows. "What brings you to my shambles?"

The weight of the jewels pulled at my fingers. I didn't exactly want to flash them around out in the open. "Care to invite me inside?" I suggested.

Devdan grinned deviously. "Of course, right this way."

I ducked my head and stepped inside the dim, cramped

quarters.

Devdan closed the door, making it even darker inside his tiny cottage. "Allow me to take your cloak," he said. "As you can see, the bed is in the corner."

I turned and glared at him. "That's not why I'm here, and you know it."

He shrugged and slouched to one side. "Thought you might have stopped by to scratch an old, lingering itch."

I snorted. "Your itch, not mine."

"What? Too good for your own kind?" Devdan sneered.

Okay, not only had fire ants crawled up his ass and laid eggs, but they'd hatched too. Why did females always get a rap for being confusing creatures when it was males who made no sense?

Well, if he wanted airs, I'd give him airs. I straightened my spine and lifted my head. Devdan was tall, but I still towered over him by half an inch. "Too good for *you*," I clarified.

Devdan's jaw clenched. The blasé pose he'd taken went rigid, and his face darkened. He hissed. "Insult a male in his own home—how noble you've become."

"What do you expect when you proposition me the moment I step inside?" I fired back. "This isn't a social call. I'm here to do business."

Devdan pursed his lips, sulking a few seconds longer before relaxing his jaw. "What kind of business?"

I lifted my knapsack. "You still peddling?"

He eyed the bag with interest. "What you got in there?"

"Jewelry made with the purest gems."

Devdan's lips twitched, and his eyes seemed to brighten. "We're back to that, are we?" He didn't have to sound so pleased. "What's next?" he asked, prowling toward me. "Furniture? Rugs? The gown off your back?" He looked me up and down, getting even closer, within inches of my person. I held still, beyond intimidation, especially by the likes of Devdan. With smirking lips, he stopped in front of me. "How soon until you're crouching in the mud, hunting down your next meal?" He rocked back on his heels, and his eyebrows jumped almost in challenge.

Did he want me to strike him? Perhaps he envisioned us grappling—pushing and pulling at one another—before ending up on his bed in the heat of the moment.

I drew in a steady, deep breath, maintaining my composure. This was no different than a game of campaigne, only we could both come out winners if he'd stop being a pit head for half a second. With slow, deliberate steps, I walked over to the bed, feeling Devdan's eyes on my back the entire way. Once I reached the single mattress with its worn patchwork quilt, I turned my knapsack over and dumped the jewelry onto the bed.

I looked over my shoulder, pleased to see I finally had Devdan's attention where I wanted it. He stared at the jewels now sprinkled over his sheets. Even in the gloom, their brilliance caught the eye.

A smile curved up my lips. "You keep fifteen percent," I said. "Do we have a deal?"

Devdan licked his lips and walked over. He reached into the pile and lifted a large diamond-cut yellow pendant.

"Sunstone, only found in Faerie," I said. "That necklace alone could cover your bills for a year."

Devdan's eyes widened. He closed his palm around the stone and quickly schooled his expression. Little did he know it was too late. I'd seen the interest—read his answer before he voiced it.

"Thirty percent," he said.

"What?" My mouth gaped open. My eyes felt like they might just pop out of their sockets and drop to the earthen floor. That was double. Outrageous. Unacceptable. "Fifteen is more than fair," I spoke through gnashed teeth, unable to mask my frustration.

Devdan tossed the sunstone into the air. My stomach

lurched right before he caught it.

"I'm the one doing all the work," he said, tossing and catching the stone again.

"I'm providing the goods," I snapped. "You'd have nothing without me."

"Nothing?" he challenged, raising a brow.

"None of these," I said in exasperation, waving my fingers at the jewelry on his bed.

"Do you have more, or is this all?" he asked in a bored tone that didn't sound fake.

Arg, great job haggling here.

He tossed the sunstone two more times while waiting for my answer.

"I have more," I acknowledged.

"Then stop being so greedy." The stone glinted as it spun in the air. I didn't realize I'd been holding my breath until Devdan caught it again.

"Stop doing that! That's a rare gemstone you're tossing around—not a crab apple!"

Devdan pinched the bright yellow stone between his thumb, pointer, and middle fingers and lifted it in front of his eyes, smirking in amusement. "Tell you what, Aerith. Kiss me like you want me, and I'll knock my commission down to twenty-five percent."

A growl from deep in my belly rumbled from my lips. Only Devdan could make me lose my cool. "Forget it," I snarled. "My kisses aren't for sale."

Devdan fisted the sunstone and narrowed his eyes. "Only to a Fae prince," he shot back cruelly.

Tears! Angry, stupid tears formed behind my eyes. I wouldn't allow them. "Fine. Thirty percent. Happy?" I shouted like I'd turned five in the space of five seconds.

His lips twisted to one side. He gave me a hard stare before setting the sunstone on his bed with the rest of the jewelry. "You haven't stormed out or slapped me. You must really need me." Devdan shook his head in disbelief.

"We worked together before," I said. "I don't see why we can't again. And just so you know, I'd never slap a male. If I really wanted to hurt him, I'd use an arrow."

Devdan chuckled. He rubbed the bottom of his chin with his fist and looked at me with consideration. "Fair enough," he said. "Okay, twenty-five percent, no kisses necessary."

I tossed the empty knapsack on the bed with the jewelry. "You're still robbing me blind," I said as I walked to the door.

Devdan followed behind me, lingering in the frame after I let myself out. "You'll thank me once you see the coin I get for these. Maybe you'll even kiss me."

I turned around and shook my head in exasperation. "That'll be the day."

Devdan smirked. "Funny, that's the last thing you said to me before you left Pinemist."

"And I mean it as much as last time," I said, squaring my shoulders.

"You're not going to disappear on me again?" he asked.

The air around me cooled. Even beneath the thick wool of my cloak, I felt like shivering. "I'm home to stay," I said firmly.

"Well, if you do leave, don't return two years from now expecting seventy-five percent, Princess." With that, he closed the door.

My nostrils flared, and my heart sped up to a gallop as though it meant for me to run after him and pound him in the head.

I pressed my middle and pointer finger together and lifted them at his cottage in a rude gesture. "Pit head," I muttered before turning and striding away from the ramshackle dwellings.

Devdan was a scoundrel and a total snob. I just *loved* the way he made it sound like I was the pampered princess. He hadn't been so keen to kiss me back in the days when my cheeks were hollowed out and I was covered in mud. He hadn't even wanted to invite me in from the cold, as though fearing I'd track muck all over his freshly swept dirt floor.

"Ugh," I seethed, fingers curling into tight fists. I glared over my shoulder at his cottage one last time before stomping away.

Males sucked, all but Jhaeros. Right now, I treasured him even more. I didn't want to be taunted and teased. I wanted to be loved and cherished.

Mel considered him a bore, but she didn't see past his outer layers. I doubted many did. It wasn't like Jhaeros showed that side of himself openly, which made it feel more special that he had with me.

I remembered how willing he'd been to cheer me up at the ball—even offering to trade up his customary scotch for pink party drinks if it would get me to smile. It had been all his idea too. He'd given me his full attention and patience when I'd been the one to tease and taunt. He'd wanted me, but that want included the desire to comfort and claim me—to make me happy however he could. As soon as my mask had come off, Jhaeros had opened his heart in ways I'd never dreamed possible. It was as though we'd both been blind for years— never recognizing what was directly in front of our noses for so long. If the Monster Ball hadn't brought us together, I might have never known what it was to truly love someone who wasn't family.

My heart grew light in my chest, lifting like a cloud on a warm summer's wind—blissfully adrift in a wide, open sky.

My legs wanted to run to him. My arms ached to circle his waist. My lips burned to kiss his mouth.

I slowed my steps as I reached the lane of cute cottages with flower boxes. Indecision weighed down my shoulders. Tempted, so tempted to go to him. I had to make a decision before I reached the end of the lane where the road widened and manor homes rose.

My stomach churned, a riot of nerves making me feel queasy. I'd never been in love before. Was it normal to feel like barfing?

It was all so new. One evening at a ball. One brief visit at Sweetbell.

If I showed up at Jhaeros's doorstep, what would I say?

He obviously enjoyed the pursuit. He wouldn't like me coming to him.

No, I was on my own—like I'd always been.

More stupid tears prickled at the edges of my eyes as loneliness seeped inside my chest. I missed him. I'd just seen him yesterday, and I missed him as though we'd been apart for weeks rather than hours.

Mel was waiting for me, I reminded myself—probably counting the seconds in huffs, or maybe singing her silly feathered quivers song.

A close-lipped smile pressed over my teeth.

As the road widened and inclined up a slight hill, the homes grew in size and stature. I passed sprawling lawns filled with geometrically shaped shrubs and stone fountains and statues of nymphs, dragons, and centaurs. Halfway up the hill, a home had been painted pink with a purple front door and trim. Shrubs shaped like unicorns raced around the grounds as little bell-shaped pixies dangled from trees, chiming softly.

My family's old home was several lanes over to the west. I thought I would want to see it, but it would bring no comfort, return no love.

Screw it. I was calling on Jhaeros. Just a quick hello before I returned to the inn.

My heart sped up along with my steps. I swung my arms the rest of the way up the hill then took a left rather than the right that led back to town center.

The closer my legs took me to Jhaeros's manor, the more lightheaded I felt. He didn't strike me as the type who liked surprise visits. I should write first. Set up an appointment.

But it was as though I'd already stepped off a ledge and was in free fall. There was no altering my course.

The stone manors up and down Jhaeros's lane had classical elegance with standard fence-like shrubs lining the front of the properties and long pebbled, tree-lined drives. They all matched, as though all the neighbors on the lane had conspired on one humdrum, corresponding look.

"*Boring,*" I could hear Mel's voice droning inside my head.

I'd never been to Jhaeros's manor. He'd always been the one to pay calls to my family. I knew the address from sending along our extra trunks, which was the perfect excuse for popping by. I studied the numbers etched into stone pillars marking the drives until reaching number twelve-thirteen.

The contents of my stomach rolled around some more as I came to a stop in front of the drive and stared down. This didn't feel like home.

I contemplated turning back, but I'd come this far, and I wasn't one to tuck tail and run from my fears.

Pebbles crunched beneath my ankle boots as I made my way to the front door. My stomach lurched on the front step. I hurried and knocked, ready to be done with the queasy faintness. Once I saw Jhaeros, I'd reclaim my calm.

I tapped my foot on the stone stoop while I waited, and waited, and waited. With a sigh, I glanced over my shoulder. Maybe I'd worked myself up for no reason.

Eventually, the door squeaked as an old, stooped butler answered. He had long, frizzy gray hair and cloudy eyes. "Yes?" he rasped as though his lungs might collapse at any moment. He stared out vacantly past my elbow from nearly two feet below me.

I didn't want to gape at him, but I couldn't help myself. Was Jhaeros's butler blind?

"Uh, hello," I said gently, as though a heavier tone might knock him down. "I'm here to see Jhaeros."

The butler turned his head in my direction, but his eyes

didn't meet mine. "And you are?"

"Lady Aerith Elmray." I didn't want to cause the butler undue panic by announcing myself as Princess Elmray.

"Come in, my lady," he rasped, opening the door wider.

"Thank you," I said as I stepped into the foyer with its oil paintings and tapestries covering the surrounding stone walls.

The elderly butler closed the door. "Follow me to the sitting room," he said, shuffling toward an open door to the right of the foyer.

I had to take small, slow steps to keep from running into the frail elf. He led me into a drafty room with a tall ceiling and thick, partially drawn curtains that allowed in minimal light. No flames rose from the hearth, not even the remnants of recent fire. I took it Jhaeros didn't entertain very often.

"Wait here," the butler said before shuffling out.

It might be a while, but it wasn't like I could make myself comfortable in such a chilly room. I walked around slowly inspecting everything, instead. There were no rugs, only cold, bare stone. The sofa, settee, and armchairs had been carved and polished from dark wood and upholstered in deep green fabric. Everything matched and looked way too fancy to sit on.

More oil paintings covered the walls with outdoor scenes of mountains, rivers, forests, and lakes. I stepped up closer to a landscape of deer half hidden amongst trees. The artist had spared no paint, laying it on so thick it rose off the canvas.

"Aerith," a deep voice said behind me.

Every time he said my name since our time together at the ball, my toes curled. A smile sprang to my lips before I turned. Jhaeros was smiling too. It still looked so funny to see him beaming at me that way.

"You must be cold. Let me build a fire." He strode toward the hearth.

"Don't trouble yourself. I can't stay long."

He stopped in place. "Refreshment then. Hot tea?"

I shook my head. "I really do have to be on my way. Mel is waiting back at the inn."

Jhaeros's face fell, but he nodded once in understanding. He glanced at the butler, hovering near the open door. "That will be all, Fhaornik. Thank you," Jhaeros said in a firm yet kind voice.

"Very good, sir. I will leave you two alone then." As Fhaornik shuffled out, he closed the door behind him, shutting me in, alone with his master.

CHAPTER FIVE

Aerith

I raised my brows.

"Does your butler often close you in with unchaperoned ladies?" I asked in a teasing voice.

Jhaeros grinned. "This is a first. He must have liked the sound of your voice."

"He truly is blind then?" I tilted my head to the side.

"And slow as snails." Jhaeros's grin widened. Nothing made him look more handsome than that smile. He could muscle up, and it wouldn't matter. Nothing could make my heart flutter more than his elusive beam.

"What about the rest of your staff members? Are they blind as well?" I asked.

"No, only Fhaornik, but my cook is deaf."

"Who knew you were so full of surprises?"

"Speaking of surprises," Jhaeros said, stalking up to me, "to what do I owe the pleasure of this unexpected visit?"

My breath stalled as he positioned himself directly in front of me, his gaze drinking me in as though I were honeyed wine.

"I wanted to make sure my trunks were delivered earlier."

"I had them stored in the attic. You're welcome to access them at any time."

"Good," I said with a firm nod.

Jhaeros's voice dipped low. "Is that the only reason you stopped by?"

I pursed my lips and shrugged. "Maybe I missed you."

Jhaeros's pupils dilated. "Not nearly as much as I've missed you," he growled, snatching me into his arms.

My heart gave a jolt as my chest collided into him. Warm hands grasped my head and pulled me into his ravenous lips. Heat blasted from my core up to my cheeks, like a fire come to life.

I answered Jhaeros's demanding tongue with greedy kisses of my own, gasping for breath but unable to tear myself away. I'd give up oxygen for one more kiss. My nostrils flared, pulling air in, feeding the fire in my belly.

Jhaeros's hands slid down my back, circling my hips, gripping them hard.

I smiled as I kissed him. What happened to propriety? Jhaeros seemed to have lost all self-control. Didn't take much, did it? My smile widened with satisfaction.

Jhaeros backed me up to the sofa, kissing me harder with each step. He removed my cloak, letting it slide free and fall in a heap on the sofa's upholstered cushions.

My breasts strained through the bodice of my gown, aching for attention.

With all the heavy breathing we were doing, we didn't hear the light tapping at the door right away.

Then the door opened.

Jhaeros and I jerked apart. Good thing Fhaornik was blind, or we might have given the poor butler a heart attack.

I regained control of my breath and tucked my hair behind my pointed ears.

Jhaeros's chest rose and fell heavily, but his voice emerged steady, if not slightly annoyed. "Yes, Fhaornik?"

"Pardon the intrusion, sir. Lady Dashwood is at the door. Should I send her away?"

"Send me away?" a female trilled from the foyer. "Don't be ridiculous."

Fhaornik bustled to the door as though he meant to block it with his feeble body.

"My master already has company," he said in a firm voice tinged with irritation.

I really liked the elderly butler.

"Does he now?" the female purred. Her full skirts spread across the doorframe like a pink stain. Pouty, full lips were rouged along with her cheeks, and hair the darkest brown slanted artfully over her forehead, sweeping back into a wide bun with tight curls arranged at the top. She peered right over poor Fhaornik's head, her shrewd, dark eyes zeroing in on me. She grinned as though delighted. "Female company," she said, her voice rising. "Marvelous. What's one more?"

Even with Fhaornik standing in the doorway, she was able to slip past his frail frame and enter the sitting room as though she owned the space and everything in it, including Jhaeros. Her gaze slid up and down his body, as though lapping him up with her rich brown eyes.

If I had to guess her age, I'd say twenty-three, roughly the same as Jhaeros, two years my senior.

Her gaze slid to me next, and her face seemed to light up with delight. If anything, she looked like she enjoyed a challenge. With her beauty, confidence must have come easily. She was neither frail nor plump. She filled out her gown in all the places a male appreciated—particularly the bosom, and she had a low-cut bodice to showcase the rounded tops of her breasts and the valley between the tightly squeezed pair. "And who might this be?" she purred as I wondered the same thing.

"Lady Dashwood, allow me to introduce Aerith Heiris," Jhaeros said, his tone not very friendly.

Lady Dashwood looked me over with a thick smile. "Oh, yes, the girl who won the Fae prince. How could anyone in

Pinemist forget?" She stepped closer, inspecting me with shrewd older eyes. "But it's no longer Heiris. You are married now."

"Widowed," I said curtly.

Lady Dashwood clutched her chest. Pretty white ruffles circled her sleeves above her elbows. She must have disposed of her cloak in the foyer before flouncing in on us. "My dear, I do apologize for your loss." She tsked and shook her head. "As a female many years a widow, I hope I can reassure you that the grief eases with time."

"How comforting," I said, narrowing my eyes.

"How long have you been in mourning?" she inquired.

"Four months."

"Oh, dear," Lady Dashwood said, dropping her smile. "Only recently, and at such a very young age. Your grief must still be extremely fresh."

"I did not know my mate well enough or long enough to truly grieve him," I assured her.

"Well, it is still a tragedy." Lady Dashwood turned to the doorway where the butler still hovered, moving his nose around as though trying to locate the older female by scent. "Fhaornik, you must tell Mrs. Calarel to prepare tea for us." Lady Dashwood turned her attention back to me. "I suppose 'tell' is the wrong word. Mrs. Calarel is Jhaeros's cook, who happens to be deaf. Can you imagine? How does a blind male see to it that she understands a command?"

"Yes, I know about Jhaeros's cook," I said, glad he had told me before we were interrupted by this harpy.

Lady Dashwood frowned, obviously unhappy with my knowledge of Jhaeros's unique staffing situation. I found it encouraging that not everything within these stone walls was standard and boring.

I looked to the doorway to tell Fhaornik I didn't need tea, but the butler had already disappeared. I moved my attention to Jhaeros. My brows lifted slightly, and he seemed to understand my unspoken question at once.

He cleared his throat and clasped his hands in front of his nether region. "I grew up with Lady Dashwood's late mate, Theomon. We were close friends."

"I am sorry." I said it to Jhaeros, but it was Lady Dashwood who answered.

"Thank you, dear. Losing Theo was the worst experience of my life." She fanned the space over her heart as though it had burst into flames that required containing. "Jhaeros got me through the worst of it. I don't know what I would have done without his friendship. Thank goodness we live so close."

"You're neighbors?" I asked, not liking that one bit.

Lady Dashwood smiled. "I live directly across the lane."

Brilliant, straight across the way where she could keep her greedy eyes on Jhaeros's comings and goings, along with any visitors—me in particular. I didn't appreciate anyone keeping tabs on me.

Lady Dashwood clasped her hands behind her back and thrust her bosom forward. "Jhaeros was such a comfort to me after Theo's passing. I'm only happy I could return the favor. I was here when your sister broke poor Jhaer's heart." She shot me a look that said, "And I'll be here to comfort him after you do the same."

Neither of those scenarios were happening.

"Shalendra did not break my heart," Jhaeros said in a clipped tone.

Lady Dumb-Dumb ignored him. She was having too much sport to realize or care that speaking to Jhaeros in that high-handed manner wasn't winning her any points. "You must have seen a lot of Jhaer before you left for Faerie. He was always riding off to call on your sister—pining after her day and night."

A vein bulged in Jhaeros's neck, but the female was still too intent on making me angry to notice she'd hit the wrong target.

"That was a long time ago," I said calmly.

"He used to consult me on what gifts to give her—so generous." Lady Dashwood giggled.

I folded my arms, getting annoyed with how far she was pushing this.

"Flowers, pastries, fans, and shawls. It was like Solstice every week when it came to your sister. But I'll never forget how excited he was after locating a pendant that had once belonged to your sister—a very special gift from your late mother from what I understand."

Anger shot through me like a burning arrow. It pierced my gut and sent sparks erupting in my chest and smoking up my head.

Lady Dashwood had hit her mark after all.

I knew the pink ruffled wench was manipulating me, but I couldn't contain the sudden fury at Jhaeros for being such a love-struck fool for my sister. He hadn't been *generous*. He'd been blinded by desire, greedy to get what he wanted: Shalendra. What were gifts if not bribes, small investments in obtaining the object of his affections?

If he'd been truly generous, he would have bought back Mel and my pendants too. That would have shown a male of true compassion and kindheartedness. He'd wanted us to be family, hadn't he? Shouldn't he have thought of us too?

Oh no, he'd only had eyes for one female.

The room went deathly quiet as I stood silently raging, feeling as though I was no longer in control of my body. How could I have kissed this fool? When I looked at Jhaeros, my lips instantly curled in distaste. His eyes widened in confusion.

My stomach churned, and acid burned in my throat. How could I have let him inside my heart? Inside me? I'd almost allowed it again—served myself up to him like a sweetberry tart on a silver platter.

I snatched my cloak off the sofa. Another few seconds and he would have had me sprawled over the furniture, too, skirts up.

I'd made a mistake. I should not have come here.

I stormed to the door, ignoring Lady Dashwood. She might have gotten what she wanted, but that didn't mean I had to see her gloat.

"Aerith, where are you going?" Jhaeros asked in alarm.

"Mel is waiting for me," I said, avoiding his gaze.

"I will take you to her."

"No."

"Let me call for the carriage."

"I said no." I rushed toward the door, but Jhaeros dove in front of me, blocking the way.

Not this again, he'd stopped me from storming out in a similar fashion at the ball, but this time I wouldn't let him win me over with kisses, though it would serve the meddlesome Lady Dashwood right to watch her beloved neighbor ravish me in the doorway.

"Move aside, Jhaeros," I seethed, teeth clenched.

"No," he said, his tone gentle but firm.

I laughed harshly. "You mean to hold me prisoner?" I still couldn't look him in the eye, but I saw the way he stiffened and frowned.

"No, I intend to take you home."

"Home," I repeated in a hollow voice.

"Jhaeros, please, let Lady Elmray pass," Lady Dashwood said, not entirely masking the alarm in her voice.

He ignored her, trying desperately to catch my eye. "To the inn," he rephrased. "A carriage will be faster, will it not? You said Melarue is waiting. Allow me to deliver you to her. I can escort you on foot if you prefer."

Just what I needed, a long aggravating walk with Jhaeros while he puzzled out why I was angry with him. He wasn't the type who let things go. I'd learned that at the Monster Ball.

From the corner of my eyes, I saw the tightness of his jaw—the resolve.

"The carriage is quicker," I conceded tightly.

"Fhaornik," Jhaeros called, still blocking the doorway. "Have the carriage brought around."

"Yes, sir," Fhaornik answered from nearby, like he'd been waiting for a summons.

"Lady Dashwood, you are welcome to stay and drink your tea in the sitting room, but I will be unable to keep you company," Jhaeros said in a chilly voice.

I heard no answer. Maybe she was too stunned to speak. I didn't turn around to see her expression. I never planned on seeing her again since I would be telling Jhaeros the courtship was off once we were in the privacy of the carriage.

Something inside me broke at that last thought. I nearly fell forward into Jhaeros. I wanted to pound his stupid chest with my fists for making me fall for him in the first place. Losing him felt like ripping out my own heart. I couldn't breathe.

I couldn't breathe! My lashes fluttered, and I swayed.

"Aerith," Jhaeros said in concern, reaching for me.

That woke me up. I jumped back.

He pressed his lips together in a tight frown. "We can wait outside," he said. "You look flushed. Perhaps the air will do you good."

I nodded.

Jhaeros stepped aside, and I rushed out of the room with him hot on my heels. Fhaornik stood in the foyer, hands clasped behind his back, positioned near the door. His chin lifted when he heard our steps.

"May I get the door, my lady?" he inquired.

"Thank you, Fhaornik, but I've got it," Jhaeros said. "I am escorting Lady Elmray to town. I will be back later. Please see that Lady Dashwood gets her tea and leaves before my return."

"Yes, sir." Fhaornik bowed his head.

As soon as Jhaeros opened the door, I stormed out. Luckily, a small carriage, pulled by a single thoroughbred, was circling up to the front of the house—almost as though it had been prepared and waiting since my arrival.

I narrowed my eyes suspiciously at Jhaeros. This time, it was he who avoided my gaze.

As soon as the carriage halted at the stone steps, he hurried forward and opened the door. I swept forward, ignoring the hand he held out to help me up the step. I pulled myself in and sat on the cushioned bench with a plop.

Jhaeros climbed in after me, sitting on the opposite bench. His mouth started moving even before the carriage. "I told you before that I no longer harbor any feelings for your sister and haven't for some time."

I folded my arms and snorted, keeping my head turned toward the window and not him.

"What more can I say or do to prove it to you?" He leaned forward, his knees knocking into mine.

The carriage jolted forward. I let the momentum take my gaze from the window to face him.

"Oh, I know you're over Shalendra," I said testily.

Jhaeros's frown deepened, creating grooves in his chin.

"Then what is it? Lady Dashwood? I certainly feel nothing for her—other than annoyance."

I huffed.

"Aerith, I won't know unless you tell me," Jhaeros said in a scolding tone that made me want to flip him a rude gesture. Supposedly, he was so clever. Why couldn't he figure it out? Why did I always have to explain things to him?

"Why do you even like me?" I found myself asking. "What do you really know about me?" I arched my brows and stared into his eyes.

He stared right back, unblinking. "I know you're clever and brave. I know you're protective and far too charitable when it comes to your family, willing to sacrifice yourself even when they don't deserve it. Shalendra didn't cast me aside. I couldn't bear her company, or your father's, after I saw how pitiless they were about sending you off with the Fae."

My breath stalled, my heart waiting to beat again. Jhaeros captured me in his gaze, holding me in the depths of his bright brown eyes.

"I know you like silly pink drinks and winning at campaigne, perhaps even more than myself," Jhaeros continued. "I know you are kind and strong, and you don't need me. But I need you, Aerith. Life holds no joy without you." His voice dropped to nearly a whisper. "I more than like you, Aerith. I love you."

Stupid tears streamed down my face before I could stop them. I gulped in air, having forgotten to breathe the whole time Jhaeros spoke. My fingers swiped rapidly at my cheeks, but the tears kept flowing.

Jhaeros leaned forward and gathered me into his arms, pulling me back with him into his lap. My arms unfolded, hanging limply at my sides as Jhaeros embraced me. He held me while the carriage rattled along, and my tears finally dried. I hiccupped.

"I do not want to cause you pain," Jhaeros said solemnly. "Can you tell me what's wrong?"

"It's stupid," I mumbled.

"What is?"

I sighed and eased out of his lap, back to the opposite bench. "Nothing," I said with a shrug. "Just the pendant you gave Shalendra. I used to have one like it, only blue, and Mel had a red one. It meant a lot to me."

Jhaeros pursed his lips. "I only recall seeing the one at Iliphar's Pawn Shop."

"It doesn't matter," I said.

"No, it's important to you. I'll find it."

"It's probably long gone."

"I'll find it," Jhaeros repeated.

"Jhaeros," I said, taking his hands. "It's just a pendant." And for the first time, I meant it. What was a necklace to the memories I had of my mother? What was a trinket to the love Jhaeros had expressed for me? He saw me. He truly saw me, and that was more than most elves could ever hope for.

I squeezed his hands then let go and leaned back, sitting up straight, lifting my chest and chin.

"It's time to let go of the past."

After the carriage came to a stop in front of Dixie's Inn, I allowed Jhaeros to step out first and help me to the cobbled road. He kept hold of my hand, reluctant to let go.

"About time," Mel griped nearby.

I let go of Jhaeros's hand and turned in place until I spotted Mel leaning against the outer wall of the inn, arms folded.

"Hello, Melarue," Jhaeros said politely.

Mel glared at him before returning her attention to me. "What is *he* doing here?"

"Giving me a ride. Don't be rude," I scolded.

Mel huffed. "Whatever. I'm starving, and you left me with no coins or anything to eat."

Jhaeros's eyes widened. "Do you need—?"

"We're fine," I assured him.

"Yeah, we're fine," Mel parroted, using her backside to push away from the wall.

"Mel!" I snapped. I turned back to Jhaeros. "Ignore her. She's cranky."

"You mean hungry," Mel said behind me.

Ignoring her, I smiled at Jhaeros. "Thanks for the ride."

"When will I see you again?" he asked softly.

Mel made a gagging sound. I needed to send Jhaeros away

quickly so I could strangle her in private and give her something to really gag about.

"We're looking at cottages tomorrow and should get settled soon. I'll let you know once we have an address."

"I can help," Jhaeros said, moving toward me.

"Thanks, but we've got this." I stepped closer, too, attempting to back him up to the carriage, but his body was an unmovable wall of muscle. If I got any nearer, I'd only end up rubbing against him, and I doubted Mel would find the sight especially enjoyable. Maybe if she weren't being such a brat I'd care.

"Very well," Jhaeros said. "But let me know if you need anything—anything at all." He looked over my shoulder then added, "Either of you."

"Nope, we're good here. Bye, Jhaeros," Mel said in a sassy tone.

"I'll update you soon," I promised him before taking a step back.

He searched my eyes for several seconds before nodding. "Until then."

I lifted my hand and gave a little wave that felt silly. I curled my fingers and dropped my arm, watching Jhaeros reluctantly re-enter the carriage. He kept his attention on me even after he pulled the door shut behind him. He stared out at me through the glass. I stood, watching him until the carriage jerked forward and rolled down the lane, out of view. As soon as he was gone, Mel stormed over to my side.

"What were you doing in Jhaeros Keasandoral's carriage?" she demanded.

"Getting a ride, obviously."

Mel glared at me. I glared back.

"Why does he have to be involved?" Mel demanded. "You went to him, didn't you? Did you even bother seeing your contact, or did you run straight to Jhaeros asking for money?"

I spread my arms and opened my palms. "As you can see,

I'm empty-handed. I passed the jewelry on to my guy."

"Your guy?" Mel's eyes twinkled, and her brows jumped.

"Not mine," I said in exasperation. "The male I know."

"Uh-huh. Does Jhaeros know about him?"

"He doesn't need to."

Mel's teeth glinted when she smiled.

I sighed. "What are you doing out here anyway? You were supposed to stay in my room."

Mel looked up into the sky as though searching for an answer in the clouds. Her gaze drifted back down and met mine. "I needed fresh air."

I put my hands on my hips. "What aren't you telling me?"

"Nothing. I needed fresh air," she repeated more firmly. "And I really am starving, so are we going to eat or what?"

"Yes, let's eat supper then go to bed. And next time, try being nicer to Jhaeros."

"Why?"

"Because I'm extremely fond of him."

"Oh, puke on a pitberry. Bleh," Mel said, sticking out her tongue. "Thanks for making me lose my appetite."

I rolled my eyes. "One day, when you meet the right male, you'll understand."

"He'll have to be a heck of a lot more interesting than Jhaeros Keasandoral."

"Jhaeros *is* interesting," I informed her. "Way more than you realize. He's also really good with his tongue." I threw in the last part as a little sisterly revenge. Mel had it coming.

Her face twisted up in disgust. "Oh, ew."

I burst into laughter, which grew louder as I stared at the revulsion on her face. As soon as I regained my breath, I tapped my lip with my finger and added, "Yes, a most excellent kisser."

"Bleh, ick, yuck, my ears." Mel covered her ears then promptly yanked her hands away. "My brain. The images. Scarred for life." She squeezed her eyes closed.

"So mature," I said with an eye roll. "Let's eat, if your poor, sensitive stomach can handle it."

"My stomach is fine. It's my brain that's scrambled," Mel informed me.

"No argument there."

She stuck out her tongue, which made me laugh again. Scamp.

But I was relieved she wasn't interested in males. She'd filled out during my time away. I doubt she realized she had the body of a grown female with hips, curves, and breasts. Her thick, red hair caught the sunlight in a fiery glow that a male would have to be blind to miss. Fhaornik aside, Mel was a vision of beauty.

We went inside the taproom and ate our suppers slowly, in no hurry to be stuck in our rooms. Mel couldn't wait to move to our own cottage, and I shared her eagerness.

When the hour grew late, we retired upstairs to our separate rooms.

After bidding my sister goodnight, I lit a lantern and closed my door. My nose immediately wrinkled. I sniffed the air. Something was burning or had burned. I glanced at the lantern, but I'd just lit it and it wasn't smoking. I sniffed harder. The smell had definitely originated in my room. I hurried to my trunk and opened the lid, but everything inside looked fine. Closing the lid, I looked around until spotting singe marks on the bottom of the drapes.

Oh, Mel, I thought.

No wonder she'd needed fresh air.

With a deep sigh, I undressed, replacing my day gown with a thin, white nightgown.

The sooner I found Mel an elemental master, the better. For tonight, I'd take smoke-filled dreams over ones that reeked of Faerie.

CHAPTER SIX

Melarue

The beautiful warrior elf's sword sliced through the air, catching the early afternoon sun, which had parted the clouds only an hour before.

I lunged at her, and our blades met in a clash of steel that hissed until sliding apart. In case Keerla tried to jab at me, I jumped back, bouncing on my toes, ready for her next strike. The trajectory of her following thrust was so obvious I had time to deflect and get around the elf in her tight leathers.

Feeling cocky, I struck out, jabbing low. Keerla whipped around, long brown hair flying like a wild horse's mane. She nearly knocked my sword out of my hands with the force of her rebound. The clash of steel reverberated all the way into my fingertips.

She pulled back quickly and struck again. I immediately blocked her sword with my own. Keerla came at me again and again. She'd been allowing recovery time in between strikes before. I guess she didn't like me taking on the position of offense when she was the instructor, but after two weeks of training, I felt like it was time to kick things up a notch.

I blocked each strike, going into a kind of trance. It was as though my body had been made for swordplay and had awakened the moment a blade was placed in my hand. Our blades met. On the next strike, I dove onto one knee, clasping the hilt of my sword in both hands, and used my momentum to strike back hard. A loud clang rang out, and Keerla's sword hand shook.

I leaped back to my feet and tossed my hair back, grinning.

Keerla nodded and lowered the tip of her blade to the ground. "Very good," she said.

I puffed up my chest, feeling pretty badass. In addition to an elemental master, Aerith had hired a sword instructor to begin training me two weeks ago. As luck would have it, Keerla had moved from Bluespark to Pinemist since our family's departure. Aerith wanted only the best, and that was Keerla. Even my sister was taking lessons from her. She watched from several feet away, awaiting her turn. She insisted I go first. The three of us stood in a peaceful meadow near the cottage we'd found to rent two and a half weeks ago.

Aerith smiled proudly at me, which made me puff up more.

Keerla frowned as she looked me over. "Just hold off on the embellishments," she said in a scolding tone. "We're practicing sword fighting, not putting on a show."

It was as though she'd punctured the happy bubble I'd been floating in with the tip of her blade. My mood deflated, and with it, my lower lip puffed out.

Keerla was one to talk. She'd competed in the tournament with Aerith and been the showiest of all the contestants. Keerla had been the only elf to charge into the clearing as though her enemies truly awaited her punishment. She'd high-kicked a dummy before gutting it and launched her sword through the air at the last one. I was no swords "expert," but I'd bet every sweetberry in Pinemist that relinquishing one's weapon was never a smart idea. What if more dummies had come along? What if an ogre had? Uh-huh. Burn.

Yeah, Keerla was amazing, but not as kick-ass as Aerith.

My sister gave me a warm smile when she stepped forward for her lesson. She fisted the handle near the blade.

I winced inwardly. Okay, Aerith was badass with a bow—not so much with a sword. I wasn't even sure why she was so intent on learning to wield a blade when it was clear from her expression she didn't enjoy swordplay. It wasn't the same as when she shot an arrow from her bow and a look of calm confidence washed over her features.

Keerla advanced on Aerith, sword at her side. My sister stood in a wide-legged stance, watching the approaching female elf intently.

Several feet in front of Aerith, Keerla stopped, dropped her gaze, and stared pointedly at Aerith's grip. "You're holding it wrong again."

Aerith, for her part, didn't take her eyes off Keerla.

"Right," she said, repositioning her grip so it was centered on the true handle. The sword lowered slightly as though it had grown heavier in her hand.

My jaw relaxed.

Good to see there were no hard feelings between past competitors. If Keerla had wanted, she could have knocked Aerith's sword out of her hand. But Keerla wasn't a pit head. If anything, she and Aerith had formed an almost instant friendship.

I stuck around the meadow, practicing swinging my sword, and glanced over at Aerith's progress every so often, trying to not let it go to my head that I was so much better than my big sis. Aerith could still whoop my ass with a bow and arrow, and I wasn't too proud to admit it.

At the end of their practice, Aerith invited Keerla for sweetberry tea at our cottage.

"Make it sweetberry wine and I'll throw in an extra half hour lesson at no charge next time."

Aerith snorted and tucked her blonde hair behind her ears. "You think I want to hold a sword longer than I have to?"

"You don't have to at all," Keerla pointed out. She fell into step beside Aerith, walking across the meadow with her toward our cottage. I ambled a couple feet behind them.

"I should know how," Aerith said.

Keerla's voice changed into a teasing tone she only ever used with Aerith. "I would think you'd already know plenty about *handling* a sword."

She and Aerith laughed then abruptly stopped to look over their shoulders at me. They turned forward again, missing the roll of my eyes. Like I didn't know what they were implying. Ew! I liked my sword sharp and pointy, thank you very much. And I wanted to be the one thrusting it.

"What about you, Keerla? Meet any nice males here in Pinemist?" Aerith asked.

Since I couldn't see Keerla's facial expression, I stared at her back. She had wispy, long brown hair that was pulled back at her temples and braided into a long, thin tail over the rest of her hair. She wore a short skirt with a big-ass metal ornament on the front and leather boots so tall they almost looked like pants. On top, she had on a skintight earthy green tank top cinched in the middle with some kind of special armor that seemed to have been designed to fit her torso like bark on a tree. Her arms, like her legs, were covered in tight fabric.

"Nah," Keerla said in answer to Aerith's question. "I have more important things to do than getting kissy faced."

Yes! If only she could convince Aerith to do the same. We were badass warrior elves. No room for males in our happy trio. Cirrus had stolen my sister from me. Jhaeros wanted to do the same. Greedy bastards. I bet Jhaeros wanted Aerith to stay home hosting tea parties and behaving like a proper mate to him. There would be no more swordplay in the fields or laughing with friends. I'd seen what happened after Aerith married Cirrus. I hadn't even been allowed to visit her. I didn't want to lose her again.

Dark clouds clogged my mind until laughter broke through.

"Besides, I have all the swords I can handle," Keerla said.

She and Aerith laughed again. This time they didn't look back, almost as though they'd forgotten me traipsing after them.

"I'd ask you the same," Keerla said to my sister, "but I'm sure you're ready to lay down the sword, so to speak. Once was likely enough."

Aerith cleared her throat. "Actually—"

"No!" Keerla said, turning to her. "Don't tell me you're sweet on someone?"

"Well, yes, in fact, I am."

My nose wrinkled, and my tongue lulled out of my mouth as though I'd swallowed a bug. Things between my sister and Jhaeros were moving much too fast, and nothing I said seemed to get through to her.

"Someone in Pinemist?" Keerla asked.

"His name is Jhaeros."

"It's a strong name. Did you know him before you were taken to Faerie?"

"Yes," Aerith answered slowly.

"Were you sweethearts before?"

Aerith's next answer took even longer. "No. Not at all."

"We'll talk more over sweetberry wine," Keerla said.

I slowed my steps, letting them get ahead. Fisting the sword handle, I stabbed at the mossy ground every few feet.

I really didn't want to think about my sister and Jhaeros. When she'd taunted me about his tongue, it had led to images of the two of them getting kissy, which then led to disturbing daydreams of Jhaeros kissing *me*! And the more I didn't want to imagine it, the more I did. "Mmm, mmm. *Melarue*," his stupid mouth had moaned in my head. "Mmm." Ew! Ick! Barf in my mouth!

I'd finally managed to scrub him from my brain and pretend like he didn't exist. Once we'd moved into the cottage, I'd hoped Aerith would settle in and decide she didn't need Jhaeros after all. I mean, we had good money coming in thanks to the sales her contact was making. Our cottage was super cute and ideal for two sisters. We each had our own room. There was a little kitchen with a window overlooking the meadow, a snug dining space, and a cozy living room with a reading nook we'd piled with thick pillows and soft blankets.

We'd mounted wooden pegs into the wall beside the door where we set our swords for storage and display when we weren't using them. It was our own happy space and a chance to make up for the fifteen months I'd lost my sister to Prince Cirrus and his stupid Fae family in Dahlquist.

Inside the kitchen, Aerith pulled out two shimmery wineglasses. Gold specks glittered inside them.

"Mel, you want a little sweetberry wine?" Aerith asked.

"No, thanks," I answered as I set my sword in the mount below my sister's.

"Tea?" Aerith tried.

"Nah, I'm good."

She poured rosy-colored wine into the glasses and brought them into the living room, setting them onto gold threaded coasters on top of an old trunk with a flat top that served as a small table.

Aerith bent down to plug in our little white lights that were strung all around the cottage. There was still daylight outside, but the cottage windows were small and few between, keeping it more cavelike even during the day.

Keerla took a seat in an armchair upholstered in purple fabric with a dark gray fleur-de-lis pattern. Aerith grabbed a charcoal-colored blanket from a stack in our alcove and offered it to Keerla, but the warrior elf shook her head.

"Thanks, I'm fine."

Aerith kept the blanket, tucking it over her legs when she sat on the sofa. They lifted their glasses in salute and tipped them back while I retreated to my room, closing the door behind me. I wasn't sticking around to listen to my sister gush over lame ass Jhaeros. Aerith said he'd invited me to live with them. I had my own room, thank you very much. Plus, I bet he was the disciplinary type who would try to father me. Oh hell no!

Our bedrooms had no windows, so I called forth a small spark of light to my fingertips and lifted them in front of me, making sure I didn't trip over anything as I walked to the center of my small, dark room.

My bed was pushed against the cooler outer wall. My body temperature tended to run hot, which my elemental instructor, Master Brygwyn, said was normal for an elf with fire magic.

Small throw pillows covered my bed because lying on top of a bed of pillows never got old. A dresser and an armoire were pushed up against the opposite wall. Beside my bed, I had a narrow vanity with a mirror above it. The vanity housed my hair combs and brushes. My father's cigar box was currently holding my hairpins, ties, and barrettes.

I walked over to the vanity so I could watch my fire magic in the reflection of the mirror. Aerith didn't want me practicing inside, but unless something caught fire, my flames produced no odor, which came in way handy.

I held my right hand up in front of the mirror and willed the rippling threadlike flames to circle my fingers. When the flames obeyed, I nearly let out a loud "whoop!" I clamped my mouth shut quickly before I gave Aerith any reason to rush in and check on me.

Concentrating on the flames in the mirror's reflection, I instructed them to spread up my hand, forming a fiery glove. I lifted my left hand and touched the tips of my fingers, igniting flames to my other fingers. Both hands now danced with fire. "Wicked," I breathed, staring at myself in the mirror.

I backed up, careful not to touch or bump into anything, which tended to be problematic when I had live flames on my fingers. I moved my hands around slowly, watching the flashes of light in the dark. I allowed the flames to travel up my arms to my elbows, then practiced bringing them back down, making sure I maintained control.

I lost track of time until there was a knock at the door. Startled, I extinguished the flames entirely. Good thing, too, because Aerith walked in before I gave her permission to enter.

Soft light spilled in from the small hallway.

"What are you doing in here in the dark?" my sister asked.

"Nothing."

"Mel, were you practicing magic?" Aerith pressed in a chiding voice.

"I was resting," I said defensively.

"You? Resting? In the middle of the afternoon," Aerith said with disbelief. I couldn't see her expression very well with the dim light at her back. She looked more like a shadowy figure peering into my room.

"Keerla pushed me hard today," I answered.

"Okay, well, I need to run a quick errand before supper. Think you can hold down the fort—without burning it to the ground?" she added wryly.

I stepped toward the doorway. "Where are you going?"

"To collect payment from my contact."

"Why won't you tell me his name?"

"It's better if you don't know."

"Why?"

"Because."

I put one hand on my hip. "Because why?"

Aerith sighed in exasperation. "Mel, please just stay here and try to keep out of trouble. You know what would be even better? If you get the stew started."

"I might burn it if you're not around to help supervise," I said moodily. She always expected me to wait around at the cottage while she went out and did the fun stuff.

"Then wait for me, and we'll make it together once I return," Aerith said.

"Or I could come with you."

"Not happening."

"Fine." *I'll follow you then.* I smiled as the thought entered my brain.

Aerith narrowed her eyes. "No going through my things while I'm gone either."

"I promise," I said, lifting both my hands.

Aerith frowned. "Believe me when I tell you there is nothing fun about this errand. Once I collect our coins, I'm headed straight back. The male is a total pit head." She scowled.

Aerith sounded a little too eager to keep me from meeting this elusive elf, and it made me want to know why.

"Okay," I said with a nod. "No fires and no treasure hunts. I promise." I stood up tall and serious.

"Thanks, Mel," Aerith said, her tone gentling. "I'll be back soon."

"Okay."

I left my door open, listening as Aerith put on her cloak and rustled across the living room.

"See you in a jiff," she called from the doorway.

"See ya," I hollered back.

As soon as the front door snicked shut, I fished out my green cloak, which blended well with the surrounding greenery in Pinemist, and yanked it over my shoulders, pulling the hood over my head and wild red tresses.

I hurried out the front door, following Aerith from a distance as she headed south toward Brightwhisk Forest. Was she meeting her contact in the woods? This was getting more interesting by the minute.

Thank Sky Mother she hadn't headed into the neighborhoods, which would have offered me little cover. Her chosen route followed patches of woods from which I could duck behind trees and shrubs, peeking at the trail of long blonde hair moving south.

I followed Aerith to the edge of town to an open area of crude, mud cottages. Elves in tattered clothes cooked outdoors over open fires. My mouth gaped open. I'd never seen this side of Pinemist before—hadn't known it existed.

I nearly lost sight of my sister as I gawked at the lopsided dwellings and families hunched around their fires outdoors.

Aerith moved with so much intention I doubted she'd look back and notice me, but to be safe, I pulled the hood of my cloak down lower over my forehead.

She passed the dwellings until there was only one cottage left. I began to suspect she really was meeting someone in the woods when she slowed at the final cottage and disappeared around its other side.

I jogged over, coming to a halt near the outer circular wall. Small step by small step, I inched my way around the structure. The sound of arguing halted me in my tracks.

"What do you mean you have nothing for me?" Aerith demanded.

"I had other business to attend to, Princess, so I didn't get a chance to make the rounds," a deep male voice rumbled.

I couldn't make out the next part, so I hunched down and moved in closer until I could hear them clearly.

"I'm going to market tomorrow. I'll fetch you your coin then," the male said.

"And *your* coin," Aerith huffed. "Lest you forget."

"Hey, I don't run a charity for princesses, in case you've forgotten," the male shot back.

My cheeks heated in outrage and sparks nearly erupted from my fingertips. Oh, yes, he was most definitely a pit head as Aerith had warned. I had to get a look at the snake.

Making my way back around to the opposite side of the hut, I looked at the surrounding woods until I spotted a good place to dive in between a tree and a shrub. I pushed through the foliage, making my way along the edge of the forest until I was facing the front of the male's cottage. I saw the back of Aerith first, her beautiful blonde hair nearly reaching her backside.

Then I saw him.

And he was so dang cute, which seriously sucked given his sour mouth.

I'd expected a male in tattered clothes like the elves outside the huts, but his trousers were clean and tidy, hugging his hips—a perfect fit. Strong arms hung from a fitted tunic. And then there was his face. He had a strong jawline, a lean, elegant nose, unblemished, slightly tanned skin, and beautiful brown eyes. His light brown hair was neatly styled, cropped close on the sides while thicker at the top.

I fixated on his lips, which were moving, but I no longer cared what they were saying. I just wanted to kiss him, and that thought wasn't even punctuated with an "ew." More like a "yum."

I shook my head to try to clear it. "Get a grip, Mel," I whispered to myself, eyes still trained on the handsome elf. "He's trouble."

Then again, so was I.

I locked him in my gaze, memorizing all of his features before backing up into the woods. I pushed branches out of my way and hopped over tree roots, hurrying home before Aerith realized I'd left.

Tomorrow, I'd go to market. It wasn't stalking. I just wanted to make sure Errand Boy here got the job done. I wasn't going to let him get away with giving my sister lip. Someone needed to put the pit head back in his place.

And that someone was me.

Mel.

Pit buster.

If Sweet Lips didn't watch his mouth, he was going to get burned.

CHAPTER SEVEN

Melarue

The bright flame of my lantern lit up the mirror above the vanity and my red tresses as I brushed my hair the following morning. When I took extra time to brush my hair thoroughly, it looked thick and shiny.

I smiled at myself in the mirror, lifting my chin to admire my strong pose, which expressed self-confidence and spirit.

I donned snug pants that my tall boots fit over and a fresh white blouse with my brown leather stomach cincher tied securely but not too tightly. I wasn't into the corset look or lack of oxygen. Outfit complete, I pulled out my favorite long fitted blue coat with gold trim. The coat was far more beautiful than any dress. Wearing it made me instantly feel elegant, but in a "better not mess with me" kind of way.

I extinguished the flame on my lantern and stepped out to the kitchen where Aerith was mashing something inside a large pottery bowl. She wore a pink apron with blue polka dots and a ruffled hem. At my approach, she glanced up from her mashing and blew some loose strands of hair out of her face.

"Are you headed somewhere? I'm making banana pancakes with sweetberry syrup."

Mmm, that sounded good, but it would take a while

before they were ready from the looks of it. "No, thanks. I'm going to check out the market."

"Do you need something?" Aerith asked as she added a dash of vanilla extract to her bowl of mashed banana.

"I want to stretch my legs."

"We can stretch them together in the meadow after pancakes."

I wrinkled my nose. Even if I weren't on a mission, that offer didn't tempt me much—beyond the pancakes. I groaned. "I'm tired of the meadow. We train there all the time. I want a change of scenery. I want to be around some of the hustle and bustle."

Aerith looked up from the bowl and stared at me a moment before sighing. "I suppose the tranquility gets rather dull. How long will you be gone?"

I shrugged. "I dunno. Maybe I'll get bored at the market and head right back."

"Do you want me to come with you?"

"No, finish making your pancakes," I said. "If you want to be really nice, save me some."

"I'm always nice when it comes to you," Aerith huffed.

"Good, so I'll look forward to those pancakes when I return." I skipped to the front door, several coins jingling in my coat pocket. "See ya, sista," I called behind me.

"Stay out of trouble," Aerith half-scolded/half-pleaded as I slipped outside.

Uh-huh. My philosophy was to be the trouble. Hardworking, well-intentioned elves like Aerith spent their lives trying to do the right thing, keeping trouble away, but trouble always had a way of finding them. If I caused trouble, at least it was on my own terms.

Morning mist swallowed my ankles as I walked along the edge of the meadow. The usually vibrant green grounds were all puffy white and light gray. I kicked at the mist, willing it to part and make an open trail through the haze for me to walk through. That would have been cool, but it wasn't my element of control.

Oh well. Fire was by far the coolest of all the elements. It could be used for light and heat—or as a weapon against an enemy.

Not that we had any enemies in boring old Pinemist.

I'd been so excited to leave Sweetbell that I'd forgotten how dull Pinemist had become the older I got.

Aerith and I should take some of the coin from the sale of her jewelry and go on an adventure. It was the least she could do before settling down with Jhaeros and having his baby elves.

I swung my leg harder through the mist.

I could just picture them in their daily routine, all kissy behind closed doors and polite in public. They'd be patient yet firm with their children, and at the end of every evening, after tucking the little tykes in, they'd sit in silence playing a game of campaigne. And that would be that. Repeat. Repeat. Repeat.

No, thanks. Not me!

Just thinking about it made me want to pull my red hair right out of its roots.

Aerith was still young. Only twenty-one. She owed herself an adventure—on her own terms. The Monster Ball didn't count. It had only been one evening—one ruined by Jhaeros. It should have been an escape from everything familiar.

Well, I was going to make sure we got the proper funds for the adventure of a lifetime. Maybe we could visit the mortal realms. Definitely not Faerie! But the human world could be loads of fun. I'd done my homework when it came to planet Earth—especially the paranormal element. They had cool supernaturals like shape-shifters, sirens, vampires, wizards, demons, and gargoyles. What did we have in the elven realm? Elves, of course. Ogres. Trolls. And some exiled Fae. Lame!

In addition to wicked cool Sups, the mortal realm had all

kinds of sights I wanted to see and activities I wanted to try. Who needed wings when humans offered such wild, fun diversions as hang gliding?

Back in boring Pinemist, elves crowded the streets as I approached the village green near town. The market took place the sixth day of the week. The square patch of grass sat atop a slight hill and was free of the fog that clung to the lower areas of Pinemist.

Vendors were crammed together selling their wares from carts, tables, and small tents. Some laid out thick blankets over the grass and set out artwork, jewelry, carvings, and other curiosities on top of their rugs.

The square was already bustling with activity. Arriving at the opening meant first pick of produce and fruits.

I wound my way through the throng, edging my way back to the goods laid out from one stall to the next. I looked closely at the jewelry, searching for familiar pieces, but I had yet to see any of Aerith's sparkling treasures from Faerie.

The sweet smell of freshly baked bread grew strong, making my mouth water. A baker across the aisle pulled a fresh tray of sugared sweet buns from his portable brick oven. I pushed my way over to the front of the line. Someone shoved me from behind. I turned around and snarled, "Wait your turn," to an adolescent boy.

Gray eyes glowered at me from beneath thick sandy-colored bangs. "You cut," he whined.

"Did not."

"Did too."

"Did not."

"Did too."

I stuck my tongue out at him, which shut him up, but only because he was trying not to cry. Tears glossed over his eyes. Oh, *pitberries*. I was just funning around. Now I felt like a total pit head.

I was about to give the crybaby my spot when an older

female in an outdated wool gown and graying hair pulled halfway back hurried over.

"Castien, what did I tell you? No sweets," she admonished.

The boy's lower lip quivered as he stared up at the matriarch. "But it's not sweets, Grandmammy. It's bread."

"*Sugared* bread," the female said, her nose squishing into her face as though the very smell of it offended her.

What was her problem? Sugared bread was the best kind of bread!

She grabbed the boy's hand and yanked him from the line.

"Next!" the baker hollered. I was still staring after the boy being led by his grandmammy to a produce stall when the baker barked out, "You, Red! What do you want?"

I turned slowly and glared at him. He was lucky he had something I really wanted.

"Two sugared buns," I said in a clipped voice.

I pulled a coin from my pocket and pushed heat into the metal through my fingers. The baker held out a meaty palm, which I dropped the hot coin onto.

"Yowch!" he cried, dropping it to the ground.

I forced a blank expression over my face, though laughter gurgled in my throat. I held out my hands and lifted my brows in impatience.

With a grumble, the baker placed a sugared bun into each of my hands before bending over to pick up the coin, which had now cooled enough to be handled. He stood up and glared at me.

I smiled back sweetly. "Nice doing biz with ya," I said before whipping around and striding off.

I watched Castien and his grandmammy carefully, waiting until the old female was preoccupied with commanding the produce vendor to sift through his vegetables and dig out the biggest, greenest, freshest of his harvest and pack it carefully in her woven basket.

While her back was turned, I stepped up to Castien and

held one of the buns out to him.

He stared from the bun to me suspiciously.

"Hurry up and take it before I change my mind," I said.

He snatched it from my hand with a glare.

"You're welcome," I said, biting into the warm, chewy, sugared goodness. I nearly moaned in ecstasy.

Castien still glared at me, not taking a bite. Did he have pits for brains? "You cut," he accused again.

For the love of sky, kids had such a stubborn hang-up of right and wrong, fair and unfair.

I squatted down, so we were closer to eye level. "Yeah, well, you weren't really a customer, so it doesn't count, does it?"

"You still cut," he insisted.

I straightened up and huffed. "Fine, I'm sorry I cut. Happy now?"

Castien nodded and lifted the sweet bun to his lips. Once he'd ripped into it, he devoured the whole thing within seconds then set to work licking sugar off his fingers. "It's important to say please, thank you, and sorry," he told me.

Great, I was receiving a lecture on manners from a mini elf.

"Funny, I'm still waiting to hear a thank you." I polished off my sweet bun, taking my time savoring each bite, unlike Mr. Manners here.

"Thank you," he said.

"You're welcome," I said and walked away, returning to the opposite aisle of goods.

I brushed the sugar off my fingers and bumped shoulders with elves crowding in for a closer look at the trinkets lined up for purchase. I made my way down the aisle and into the next one, then the next, but nothing stood out.

Had the snake even bothered to show up? What a sack of pits! Well, I knew where he lived now, and I intended to get enough coin to take an adventure with my sister. I'd sell the jewelry myself if this jerk couldn't be bothered. Then we could pocket all the profits ourselves and take a trip sooner.

Father had never wanted Aerith to sell our goods directly during the dark days after Mother's death when we were scrimping to get by. He didn't want our family to be seen as peddlers. But so what? Look at all these vendors selling their goods. Folks had to make a living somehow, and there were plenty of elves eager to purchase their offerings.

Besides, Father was out in Sweetbell. He didn't have to know I was hocking wares, and neither did Aerith.

I cut through the market, heading south toward Brightwhisk Forest. It was easier to walk through the crowd down the middle of the path than to push my way up to the stalls. I was crossing the final aisle when I saw him standing in the center of the path, whispering to a beautiful brunette in a fur-trimmed beige cloak.

Flames burst around my fingers.

An older male elf gasped, eyes expanding at my hands.

I curled my fingers into fists, extinguishing the flames, and strode toward the fiend who was flirting rather than peddling.

As I approached, he pulled an emerald necklace from his pocket and dangled it before the female's face as though holding a carrot in front of a horse. The female's eyes expanded on the glimmering emeralds.

Okay, maybe I'd been too hasty in my assessment of the situation.

Slowing my steps, I turned my attention to the stalls as though looking the goods over from a distance, while keeping my ears open to the pitch he made.

"It's gorgeous," the female gasped.

"And would look even more gorgeous around your delicate neck," he returned.

I nearly snorted. *Real smooth, pit brains.*

But the female giggled. Truly, I didn't understand my own sex sometimes.

"Where did you get it?" she asked.

"Does it matter?"

She cleared her throat gently. "I mean, is there any special story that goes with it?"

"Oh, a story," he drawled. "I'm glad you asked. This piece comes from Faerie. It once belonged to a princess."

"A princess of Faerie," the female said dreamily. Then her tone changed. "Did this belong to Aerith Heiris?"

The male sighed. "Everyone assumes that. I have contacts all over Zaleria *and* Faerie."

The female put her hands on her hips. "I heard Aerith recently returned to Pinemist. The timing is rather fortuitous, is it not?"

"So what if it was hers?" the male asked, not masking the ire from his voice.

Yeah, so what? I moved closer to the pair, nearly inserting myself in their conversation and the female's face. I didn't appreciate her tone about my sister.

The female lifted her nose high into the air. "Aerith Heiris is not a true princess."

"She married a prince. That makes her a princess."

The female huffed in disgust. "She won a contest. Everyone knows any Fae who comes to our realm in search of a bride is deranged; and any female who competes for him is desperate." She looked at the emeralds and turned her nose up as though they'd turned into a strand of pitberries.

"I guess we're not all born with a golden spoon in our hand," the male said with a sneer.

"Don't give me that tone, Devdan. You're only nice when you want something."

Devdan. Finally, a name to go with his fetching face.

Before Devdan could answer, I widened my eyes and stepped in front of the pair. "What a gorgeous necklace!" I gasped. "Are those real emeralds?"

Devdan's glower, aimed at the fancy wench, softened as it

turned to me. Our eyes met, and in that gaze, we shared a hundred smiles. My belly softened, and my heart warmed as though an eternal flame had burst to life inside my chest.

Devdan's smile widened, showing teeth. "One hundred percent real," he said slowly. "A rare beauty, ain't she?"

Forget butterflies. Birds were flying around in my stomach, diving and swooping, singing songs of sunshine and sweetberries.

I stepped in closer. "And you said it belonged to a princess?" I made my voice all breathy and eager, which wasn't too difficult when I was staring into the face of the cutest elf I'd ever clapped eyes on and he was smiling back as though I'd just offered him a sugared bun.

Miss Snoot-Face stomped her foot.

"It belonged to an elf. A couple years ago, she competed in a weapons tournament for a chance to wed a Fae prince. She killed an ogre. That's how she became a princess of Faerie."

"Whoa. Wicked," I breathed, eyes expanding. "Now I really want those emeralds. Name your price, Dev."

He chuckled, which was the most joyful sound. "Well, let me see. Normally it's five gold coins, but if you throw in a kiss, I'll knock it down to four."

My breath stalled as I glanced at his lips, which I totally wanted to latch on to. I don't know what kind of response he expected, but he looked surprised when I rubbed my lips together and grinned eagerly. "What about two kisses?" I asked. "How much then?"

His mouth gaped open.

"Are you kidding me?" Miss Snooty demanded. Her fingers, covered in cream gloves with decorative little gold buttons, formed tight fists.

"Run along, Nueleth. I've got business to conduct," Devdan said without sparing the wench a look. His eyes were right where I wanted them, locked on mine.

Miss Snooty huffed and turned to me. "A little friendly

advice since you're obviously new to these parts. He'll kiss anything in a fancy dress"—she looked me up and down—"or coat. You obviously come from a good family, so you'd be wise to stay away from Devdan."

I lifted my head regally. "Actually, I come from a family of warriors and rebels—a lucrative and exciting life. And best of all, I can do whatever I want, and no one gives a pit." I smiled smugly into her stunned face.

Miss Snooty twirled around, picking up her skirts, and stormed away without another word.

I puffed out my chest, watching her hurry away. *That's right. Run along, you stupid skirt.*

"Warriors and rebels, huh?" Devdan drawled beside me.

His voice threaded through my ears and curled around my heart. I pulled a gold coin from my pocket and turned to face him, rolling the coin across my fingers again and again while watching Devdan. Momentarily distracted, he stared at the flash of gold. Who was dangling the carrot now? I smirked.

He blinked and turned his attention back to me. "Thanks for stepping in. Nueleth can be a real pain in the ass."

I shrugged as I moved the coin across my hand. Any activity, even a coin roll, helped keep me from fidgeting too much, especially now that I had Handsome's full attention.

Devdan leaned in closer, and I nearly dropped the coin.

Concentrate on moving the coin from one finger to the next, Mel! Do not think about his sexy lips or how much you want to kiss them.

Is that offer still on the lawn? Do I have to buy the damn necklace to get the kiss? Or can we just kiss?

Stop thinking about kissing! Kissing is gross, remember?

How would you know when you've never kissed anyone? Devdan would be the perfect first kiss. I bet he's really good at it with all the kissing he supposedly does.

The next time the coin reached my thumb, I squeezed and fisted it before dropping it back into my coat pocket.

"I haven't seen you before," Devdan said, squinting at me.

"I would have remembered."

"I moved to Pinemist a few weeks ago," I said.

He didn't need to know I'd lived here before. I didn't want him putting two and two together too quickly, not before I had a chance to get to know him as myself, not "Aerith's little sister." Unless Aerith had mentioned me? On one hand, I hoped she had. On the other, I enjoyed maintaining an air of mystique.

"What's your name?"

Time to find out.

"Melarue."

"Melarue." Devdan's lips puckered on the last part as though he could taste the syllables. There was no recognition of my name, only delight in the smile on his lips. He cocked his head to the side. "So, Melarue, you don't actually know who Aerith is, do you?"

I tossed my hair back. "She sounds totally badass if you ask me."

Devdan shrugged. "More tolerable than that one." He nodded in the direction Nueleth had stomped off. Then he returned his attention to me. "You don't really want the necklace, do you?" He glanced at the emeralds dangling from his fingers.

"I'm not into jewelry. I prefer swords." I grinned.

"Yeah? You buying? I've got excellent connections. If there's anything you want, I'm your guy to procure it." Devdan puffed out his chest.

"Oh yeah?"

"Ask anyone," he said. "Even Nueleth."

I rocked back on my heels and pursed my lips, giving him a once-over before settling my gaze on his face. "I've got what I need for now. Except for that kiss." *Did I just say that last part out loud?*

Devdan's smile was like sunshine after months of rain. Its warmth radiated over my entire body. My cheeks warmed, as though my fire magic was as drawn to this male as I was.

These feelings were all new, a kaleidoscope of wonders I never dreamed for myself.

It didn't change anything, of course. Having a crush didn't mean I wanted to settle down and go all gooey over a guy. Maybe I'd feel this same way about a shape-shifter once Aerith and I traveled to the human realm. I wouldn't know until I had a chance to experience other worlds.

Devdan looked around suspiciously. "You got a father or boyfriend or big brother around who's gonna pummel me if I kiss that smart mouth of yours?"

"No. No. And no," I answered. "I mean, I have a father, but he's not even in Pinemist. No boyfriend and no brothers, big or small."

"Uh-huh," Devdan said, still looking around unconvinced.

"Anyway, I'm the one to worry about."

"Oh, are you?" Devdan asked in amusement. He slipped the necklace into a plum velvet pouch. "How about you follow me to the fountain, away from so many prying eyes?"

"Yeah, okay," I answered, sounding totally calm when my heart was knocking all around my rib cage, probably trying to whack me in the head.

We walked side by side as though we were old friends, which was so weird when we'd only just met. The crowd thinned out as we left the market, following a wide cobbled walking path to a large circular fountain with a thirty-foot stone dragon in the center. Water sprayed from beside his back and poured from his mouth, which made no sense at all. It should have been flames bursting from his stone lips, not the splash of water. It was stupid. I nearly shared my thoughts with Devdan, but my nerves made my throat go dry. Suddenly, the water gushing from the dragon's throat looked a whole lot better. I ran my tongue over my teeth, not wanting my mouth to be as dry as the cranberry scones Father served guests with tea in Sweetbell.

Devdan led me to an empty bench behind the dragon's head. We were far from alone, but the folks gathered around the fountain were eating, reading, or talking on the benches—some were even smooching.

Oh. Sweet. Berries. Was this really happening? I was about to receive my first kiss from the cutest elf ever.

We sat side by side, leaving a couple inches between us. Devdan clasped his hands together in his lap.

"Tell me something, Melarue."

"Yes, Dev?" I asked sweetly.

"Have you ever kissed a male before?" He grinned at me in amusement.

"Why would you ask that? Of course, I have." I sat up taller.

He laughed and scooted against me so our thighs were pressed together and legs were brushing against one another. A shiver ran through me right before heat flowed through my veins as though my fire magic was trying to protect me from a chill.

Devdan's eyes became hooded. "Don't worry, Melarue. I'll make sure you enjoy it," he whispered.

Before I could retort that maybe he'd enjoy it more, his mouth was on mine, pressing a warm, moist kiss over my lips. He didn't pull back or break contact. His mouth moved over mine, parting my lips, making room for his tongue. The wet tip darted in and out, making me dizzy with want. I felt giddy and hot, as though I'd chugged down an entire bottle of sweetberry wine in one sitting. I closed my eyes and gave in to the delirium of his never-ending kiss. I could feel the smile on his lips and the vibration of his chest along with his faint chuckle. No wonder he'd been so cocky. He knew how to deliver.

His hand moved to my thigh. He didn't stroke me or squeeze. It almost felt like a taunt, leaving that light pressure on my leg, making me want him to do more. He stroked my tongue with his, sending more shivers and heat through my body.

Fire erupted along my fingers, blazing like candles at the tips.

Devdan drew back. My heart hammered, worried what his reaction would be to my elemental powers. I wasn't expecting his chuckle.

"My kiss is so hot it set you on fire." He smiled smugly.

"You wish," I said, giving him a slight push.

He rubbed his lips together and stared at me hard. I tried not to fidget under his scrutiny.

"Do you know how unique you are?" he asked. I was really digging the awe in his voice. It was so much better than Father's irritation when my fire magic had flared up for the first time five months ago.

"One of a kind. I know. I know," I joked to hide the slight shake of my hands and pounding of my heart. Could we get back to kissing now?

As though reading my thoughts, Devdan's eyes became hooded. He leaned forward. Right before his lips touched mine, I closed my eyes.

His mouth made demands of mine that I attempted to answer as quick as I could.

Oh, Sky Mother, above. Or below? I didn't know up from down any longer. I was afraid if I opened my eyes, he'd stop. I didn't want him to stop. Ever. This might have been the longest I'd managed to sit still my entire life.

Never one to be idle and let others have all the fun, I pressed against Devdan and slid my tongue into his mouth, which was only fair.

He groaned in pleasure, and I felt the smile on his lips widen.

"Minx," he whispered through our kiss.

That made me smile. I leaned closer, demanding more of him with my mouth. I'd show Dev how quickly this first-timer could learn. Kissing wasn't about quantity but quality, and I was all about performance.

His hand slid up my thigh, nearing my nether regions. I opened my legs slightly, giving him access to an ache which, like an itch, needed rubbing.

"What in the seven hells is this?" a female screeched.

At first I thought it was Nueleth who had followed us and was freaking out for some inexplicable reason. I certainly didn't recognize the hysterical voice as my even-tempered sister's. But when my eyes fluttered open, there she was, spitting mad—kinda like the stone dragon behind her.

Aerith's cheeks were flushed, her fingers curled like claws extending toward Devdan as if she meant to strangle or rip him to shreds.

Devdan smirked, his full attention now on Aerith. "You're sorta interrupting something here, Princess. You had your chance, so why don't you save your dignity and stop making a scene?"

"You snake," Aerith hissed. "I'll deal with you later." She turned her attention to me. "Mel, we're going home. Right now."

Devdan's smile faded. He turned to me with expanding eyes. "You know her?"

About time he looked at me—the female he'd been kissing seconds before! It was like he'd forgotten all about me the moment Aerith showed up. I'd been so blind, thinking he didn't like her when it was the exact opposite. He was one of those stupid males who used insults to hide his true feelings.

"She's my big sis," I said in a bored voice. I got to my feet with an air of nonchalance, stepping over to Aerith's side, ready for her to march me home so I wouldn't have to stick around as the third wheel, yet again, any longer than I had to.

I thought I saw Devdan trying to catch my eye, but I refused to look at him, as though he was beneath my notice. I stuck my hand in my coat pocket and fingered my coins, concentrating on the hard bits of metal.

Devdan stood up and folded his arms.

"So, this is why it's taking so long to sell my pieces," Aerith said with disdain. "You're too busy corrupting young girls."

"Hey!" I said, glaring at her. "I'm a grown elf, and I can look out for myself."

"Clearly you can't," Aerith snapped. She turned back to Devdan. "I will be by later for my jewelry, and it better all be there."

Devdan sneered. "And who's going to sell it for you?"

"I will." Aerith puffed out her chest.

Devdan laughed humorlessly. "I've got news for you, Princess. No one wants to buy from you. Little Sis can tell you."

"Hey—" I started to say, but he wasn't finished.

He took a step closer to Aerith and smiled cruelly. "You're tainted. Ruined. Damaged goods."

Aerith's mouth gaped open as though she'd been knocked in the head and was still processing what had happened.

Flames erupted in my stomach, scorching me from the inside. I would have liked them at my fingertips to really put the fear into the scoundrel standing before me, but they'd chosen this moment to remain dormant.

"Don't talk about my sister that way," I growled with each step I took up to the stupid pit head I wished I'd never kissed. I grabbed him by the shoulders and kneed him in the groin.

Devdan doubled over, clutching his genitals, and groaned in pain.

Aerith blinked several times before taking me by the arm. "Come on, Mel. Let's go," she said in a hollow voice.

We walked swiftly away from the gurgling fountain and the cursing male. My jaw ached with tension as we skirted the market before heading down the hill. Elf folk passed us, headed up to the market. It wasn't until we'd left behind the last of the lingering crowds and were nearing the meadow that

I allowed the tears to flow freely down my cheeks.

I didn't sob, though. Sobbing was for babies.

I swiped angrily at my cheeks.

"I hate Devdan!" I proclaimed.

Aerith's body lurched as though she'd been startled. I didn't know why she looked so surprised. She knew what a stupid jerk he was. "How do you even know him?" There was no more anger in her voice, simply curiosity. When I remained quiet, she drew out my name, "Mell?"

"I saw him selling your necklace," I said, thinking quickly. "Well, *trying* to sell, anyway, and doing a pit-poor job of it. I tried to help him out, but the elf he was trying to sell to was a total bitch."

"Mel!"

"Well, she was."

Aerith chewed on the inside of her cheek a moment before speaking again. "What did Devdan mean when he said no one wanted to buy from me?"

I shrugged.

"Mel—" she prodded again. "Why did he say you would be able to tell me?"

"I don't know. He's stupid," I said with exasperation. "I don't feel like talking about him anymore—ever." I folded my arms across my chest and clamped my mouth shut into a tight frown.

Experiencing my first crush and my first heartbreak all within the same hour felt like galloping through a field of daisies for five blissful minutes before getting bucked off, trampled, and crushed into pollen—the kind that gave everyone itchy noses and watery eyes.

It was the pits. The absolute pits. Just like my heart. It felt shriveled, dry, and picked clean of all the sweet stuff.

"I'm sorry," Aerith said. "I should have told you about Devdan—should have warned you."

"I can look out for myself," I huffed.

"I know you can," she said softly.

The love in her voice made my heart beat anew. Who needed males, anyway? There was no bond more sacred than sisterhood. Well, depending on the sister, of course. Shalendra wasn't part of the sacred circle.

"And I'll find someone else to sell the jewelry," Aerith said firmly. "Someone actually motivated to sell and who doesn't insist on keeping twenty-five percent."

"Twenty-five percent?" It was my turn to screech. "That's insane!"

Aerith snorted derisively. "At first he was insisting on thirty."

I turned around abruptly and began marching back the way we'd come.

"What are you doing?" Aerith asked in alarm, jogging to catch up to me.

"I'll do more than knee his nut sack for taking advantage of us."

"It's okay. We'll find someone else."

I slowed my steps. "Damn straight we will," I said, lifting my head. "Me." Before Aerith could argue over the impropriety of me peddling our wares at market, I tried to reassure her. "No one knows who I am."

Another benefit of being the youngest daughter. I was easy to overlook or dismiss. Easy to forget when beautiful, golden, blonde Aerith emerged like the sun.

I just wished I could forget Devdan's honeyed kisses the way he'd forgotten me the moment Aerith appeared.

CHAPTER EIGHT

Aerith

Mist cloaked the meadow when Keerla rode up bareback on her painted horse the following morning. I saw her from the kitchen window where I flipped pancakes on a cast-iron griddle over a two-burner stove. After giving the pancakes another flip, I moved briskly to the front door.

I was cooking up yesterday's batter, which I'd set inside the fridge and covered with a cheesecloth to save for later. Some gut instinct had warned me Mel would get into trouble, but I'd never dreamed I'd find her with Devdan.

Luckily, I didn't have to warn Mel to stay away from him. She wanted nothing to do with the snake. The relief of that helped ease my anger. At least I had interrupted before he had a chance to invite her back to his hovel. At least it had just been a kiss. At least she wasn't "ruined" and "tainted" like I was.

Well, Devdan and the rest of Pinemist could take their ruthless remarks and shove them right up their elf holes.

I opened the door and grinned at Keerla as she dismounted and left her horse to graze. "Good morning," I said.

"Morning," she replied, answering my smile with a pleased

one of her own.

"Did you get it?" I asked.

She pulled a knapsack out of her black cloak and held it up with a wide grin. "Every last piece."

Relief filled my chest. I hadn't trusted myself to collect my jewelry from Devdan. It would have been too tempting to fire an arrow into his rotten pit of a heart.

"Thank you so much," I said, taking the knapsack from Keerla. Too bad the weight in the bag wasn't coins, but I'd find another way to sell the pieces—without sending Mel out to haggle.

"My pleasure," Keerla answered, still grinning.

"Please, come in." I set the knapsack on the trunk table and took Keerla's cloak from her, hanging it from a copper unicorn horn peg beside the door.

"Nice apron," Keerla said with a smirk.

Which reminded me the pancakes needed to come off the griddle. I dashed into the kitchen and scooped the pancakes one by one onto a large pink-and-blue-pastel-flowered serving dish. I added more cooking oil to the griddle and poured out four more pancakes.

"Tea?" I asked.

"I'll get it," Keerla said, striding into the kitchen in her usual tight dark leathers.

She was tall enough to reach the mugs on the top shelf of the cupboard without the help of a stool. She pulled out two pottery mugs with pastel swirls and poured hot water into them from the steaming kettle. I'd left a variety of tea bags out in a small open wood box on the counter.

"What kind do you want?" Keerla asked.

"Sweetberry, thanks," I said.

"You and your sweetberries." Keerla shook her head. "Please tell me they're not in the pancakes?"

"Nope, but I do have sweetberry syrup."

"What a relief."

"What elf doesn't like sweetberries?"

"Me," Keerla said firmly.

No surprise she chose one of the dark teas. To each their own.

Keerla set my mug of aromatic sweetberry tea beside the stove as I flipped the pancakes over. I leaned my back against the counter and sipped my tea while the pancakes finished cooking through on the other side.

Keerla took a gulp from her mug before setting it down.

"Thanks for taking Mel out today," I said.

In addition to reclaiming my property from Devdan, Keerla had agreed to take my sister out horse shopping. We never traveled far, but I figured it would be a welcome distraction for Mel. We had plenty of grazing area, and taking care of an animal was another way to keep Mel busy.

But this outing was as much for my youngest sister as it was for me.

After Keerla agreed to take Mel for the afternoon, I'd invited Jhaeros to call on me.

I missed him and the way he made me feel like the most treasured elf in all the realm. But no way was I going to call on him with Lady Dashwood spying from her windows. I needed good vibes only—and an uninterrupted kiss.

"Uh-huh," Keerla said as though reading my thoughts.

I'd told my friend everything—from the kiss between Mel and Devdan, to the request for a quiet afternoon in which to spend time with my sweetheart.

"I hope this gentleman caller of yours appreciates what he's got."

"He certainly does," I said, scooping up the cooked pancakes before pouring the last of the batch over the griddle. "He's nothing like that prick, Devdan."

Keerla picked up her mug and lifted it to her lips, nodding before taking another gulp and setting it down. "He's got spunk, like your sister."

I scowled.

"Keerla?" Mel's sleepy voice called out from her room. She traipsed into the open dining-and-kitchen area a few seconds later in a long blue bathrobe. Her hair looked like it had doubled in volume, tumbling down her shoulders in a tangled mess. Mel rubbed her eyes.

"Look at what the cat dragged out," Keerla said, amusement in her voice. "Morning, Mel."

"Have you been here long?" Mel asked, looking at her tea mug.

"Nope, just arrived."

"You got the jewels from Devdan?" Mel asked.

"Yeah, no problem."

"Did he say anything about me?"

"Uh—" Keerla glanced at me as though looking for help.

I stared back and nodded. I didn't need the particulars of the exchange—getting the jewelry back was all that mattered to me—but if Mel wanted details, she deserved to hear them. Devdan had merely insulted me, which was nothing compared to toying with my sister's emotions.

"I didn't really stick around to chat," Keerla said before gulping down more tea.

Mel's face fell.

"Plus, I did all the talking," Keerla added. "You know, demanding the return of your sister's jewelry and threatening to cut off his genitals if he ever so much as looked at you or your sister again."

I snorted and took a sip of tea.

Mel's mouth hung open. "Keerla," she whined.

"Don't worry," Keerla said, straightening her spine. "He received the message loud and clear. He won't be bothering you again."

Mel's lower lip puffed out.

"Who wants pancakes?" I asked a little too loudly and cheerfully.

Mel glowered, and Keerla raised her brows.

"Well, I, for one, am starving." I carried the plate of warm pancakes to the small wood table by the kitchen and set it in the middle. I'd already put out three plates, knives, and forks.

I untied my apron and hung it from a cute little button mushroom peg on the end of a cupboard.

"I'm not hungry," Mel grumbled.

"You should eat something now, or you will be later," I said.

"It's okay," Keerla said as she sat down heavily at the table. "Mel and I can get a bite in town later. I know I'll be ready to eat again this afternoon."

I took the seat in front of my friend, who wasn't shy about piling pancakes onto her plate. I did the same then grabbed the small ceramic pitcher and drowned my pancakes in sweetberry syrup.

Keerla's upper lip curled.

I chuckled and said, "More for me then."

She scoffed and rolled her eyes before cutting off a piece of pancake and stabbing it with her fork prongs. Keerla handled her dining ware as though they were weapons.

I sawed into my oozing pile of pancakes, nearly moaning when I took my first bite. My lashes fluttered and closed briefly.

Keerla snorted, and I opened my eyes to find her smirking at me with a wicked smile.

"Looks like your gentleman caller has some competition." She pointed at my plate of pancakes with her knife. "He might have to slather some of that sweetberry syrup on his lips to stand a chance with you."

I laughed. It felt good. "I'd choose Jhaeros over sweetberries any day."

"Must be love," Keerla said. "I don't get it, but I'm happy for you."

"Thanks. I'm happy for me too." I grinned and proceeded

to dig into my pancakes.

Today, I got to have both sweetberries and Jhaeros. I hoped one day Mel would meet someone who treated her the way Jhaeros treated me. I wanted her to know that not all males were pit heads like Devdan.

After devouring every last drop of pancake and sauce, I cleared our plates and set them in the sink. While I was doing dishes, Mel tromped out, talking with Keerla. I looked over my shoulder. She'd brushed the tangles from her hair and had on her usual pants and blouse. A black cloak was balled up and bunched under her arm as though she planned on attending a funeral along the way.

"Ready to find yourself a mighty steed?" Keerla asked.

Mel slid a glance my way. "I don't understand why you aren't coming." Before I could answer, Mel's eyes narrowed suspiciously. "Unless you plan to call on Jhaeros again."

"I'm not calling on him," I stated, turning my attention back to the soapy water and the mugs, which were the last of the dishes. I scrubbed and rinsed them before setting them on the draining tray.

When I turned around, Mel had her arms folded around her cloak and was glowering at me.

"Is he coming over here?"

"Just for tea and a game of campaigne," I said, feeling my cheeks heat as I thought of all the other things I'd like to do with him.

Mel huffed. "So that's why you're getting rid of me."

"Seriously, Mel?" I said, feeling my patience strip away like a banana peel. "You should be happy to spend an afternoon picking out your own horse."

"I don't want a horse," Mel snapped back. "What would I do with a horse? Ride over to the exciting village of Bluespark?" She made a loud snoring sound, briefly shutting her eyes as she did.

"It is pretty boring there," Keerla said of her former home.

"I thought you'd enjoy a companion," I said.

"A companion horse, oh sure, that makes sense," Mel snipped. "Me and my horsey are going to have such meaningful conversations." Mel rolled her eyes skyward. "I'd rather have another sword."

"We could look at swords instead," Keerla said with a shrug.

My shoulders slumped. "It doesn't sound like Mel wants to go at all. Thanks for offering, Keerla, but I think it's better if Mel stays home."

Keerla folded her arms over her chest and shot Mel a menacing glare. "Nope, no way. Mel and I are spending the afternoon together. I don't care where we go or what we do, but she's not backing out"—Keerla slid a glance my way—"and neither are you." Her fierce gaze meant business.

I nodded in thanks.

Though Mel pouted about it, she went without further argument. I watched my sister and Keerla from the kitchen window as first Mel and then Keerla mounted the horse. Mel sat in the front and patted the horse's chestnut and white neck. Maybe she'd warm up to the idea of a horse by the end of the day and I'd see her riding back on her own steed. I certainly would have been excited to have my own horse at her age. But Mel wasn't me.

As soon as they'd ridden off, I got to work making my chewy pumpkin, oat, walnut, and raisin cookies. While they baked, I rushed around the cottage, making sure everything was put away. I grabbed a miniature board of campaigne from my chamber and set it up with the tiny pieces on top of the trunk table. My miniature set was made of small wood carvings—sixteen pieces painted blue and sixteen painted red. The squares on the board were about a fourth the usual size. This was a travel set. I hadn't gotten around to buying a full-size set.

Soon, the smell of sugared pumpkin filled every crevice of

the cottage. The heat from the oven helped warm the living space and cozy up the place. Once all the cookies were baked and set out to cool, I changed into a light blue gown with a low, loose bodice. I didn't want to be tied up all tight, and besides, I had no one to secure a bodice. I loathed the things, anyway.

Everything, myself included, was ready for Jhaeros's visit, but I could not relax. I checked my reflection in my vanity mirror a dozen times. I'd taken to wearing my hair down—every last strand free from pins or ties of any kind. It flowed light and bright down my shoulders. Light blue ballerina slippers that matched my dress covered my feet. I was all but dancing in them as I flitted around from room to room. There wasn't a whole lot of ground to cover in the small space of the cottage.

When the hour of Jhaeros's arrival neared, I thought I might faint into a heap of spent nerves. I would have thought that knowing he loved me would have made things easier—no pining or agonizing over a male's true feelings. But my heart was going haywire as a cyclone of emotions spun through me: excitement, passion, love, desire, need, hunger, and longing.

I heated the water in the teakettle for the fourth time, wanting it to be ready to pour as soon as Jhaeros stepped inside.

This afternoon we'd be truly alone for the first time. No crowded ballroom outside of a castle sitting room. No meddlesome father waiting impatiently inside the estate. Not even a blind butler in the foyer.

I leaned over the kitchen sink and peered out the window. No sign of Jhaeros yet. My skirts rustled as I ran into my room to check my reflection one last time. Nope, my hair and eye color hadn't mysteriously changed during the past few minutes. Same face. Worried expression. Why did I look so worried? This was Jhaeros! I forced a smile over my lips, which appeared as more of a grimace.

A faint sound had me rushing out of my room and back to the kitchen window, but I didn't see anything. I stood stationed behind the small square of glass until a dark gelding appeared, Jhaeros riding atop with a bouquet of pastel flowers in his left hand, the reins in his right. He looked so handsome on his steed. Well, he always looked handsome.

The smile lifting my cheeks felt genuine. I could finally relax a little now that Jhaeros had arrived. I fisted a handful of oats from a bag I kept in one of the lower pantry drawers and walked outside as Jhaeros rode up.

His face lit up when he saw me, and his smile stretched to his eyes. "Hello," he said with a warm eagerness that curled my toes inside my slippers.

"Hi." I beamed up at him as though he were a knight who'd stolen my heart.

Well, I wouldn't be as forthcoming at campaigne. I could promise that much.

I offered my open palm filled with oats to the horse. His lips tickled my fingers as he gobbled them up. I swept my fingers clean while he munched on his snack. Jhaeros slid out of the saddle, landing in front of me. He held out a bouquet of pink chrysanthemums interspersed with delicate white candytuft and purple heather.

"They're beautiful. Thank you," I said, taking the flowers.

Jhaeros followed me to the shade behind the cottage where he secured his steed at a hitching post beside a water trough I kept clean for visitors—mostly Keerla. I still hoped Mel would return with a horse. I wouldn't mind having a little more life around the cottage.

Once the horse was comfortably situated, I led Jhaeros back around and inside.

"Welcome to my humble home," I said, feeling proud despite its size. I'd never had a place of my own until now.

I pulled out a blue-tinted vase with frosted white flowers etched into the glass, filled it with water, and put the lovely bouquet inside, taking a moment to admire the fall flowers. "Can I get you tea?" I asked.

When Jhaeros didn't answer, I turned and caught him staring at my backside. He looked up quickly and cleared his throat.

"I'm fine right now. Thank you."

"It's not spiked or anything. I plan to beat you fair and square," I teased.

Jhaeros's eyes danced with amusement. "We shall see."

I puffed up my chest. "The only thing you're going to see is me whooping your ass."

Jhaeros winced. It wasn't the kind of language he was accustomed to. Well, he needed to get used to it.

I smirked and swished over to the living room, taking a seat in the armchair. Jhaeros followed slowly behind and lowered himself onto the sofa. When he looked at the campaigne board, his brows nearly touched.

"I need to get you a better game set," he said.

"But this one is so cute."

He looked up and met my gaze. I smiled, which made him smile, which made my smile widen, then his, until we were grinning at one another like a couple of love-struck fools.

"I think *you're* cute."

Amused laughter burst from my lips. Had Jhaeros really just said that out loud? I was totally corrupting him.

"Okay, Keasandoral, no more stalling," I chided. "Today we find out who is the true campaigne champion."

"Ladies first," Jhaeros drawled in a soothing deep tone that warmed my belly.

I moved my first piece, a shrub, and started the game, but Jhaeros's attention kept drifting to my bosom rather than the board. My breasts ached and nipples hardened to points beneath his gaze. I shifted from one thigh to the other, trying to get comfortable in my seat. When I moved to pick up another shrub, I accidently lifted my mage.

"I meant to grab a shrub," I said in alarm. When I looked up, Jhaeros smiled and shook his head.

"These game pieces are too small. I don't know how anyone plays on them . . . unless they're only in their fifth year."

I snorted. "Just what every five-year-old wants to do—spend hours staring at a game board."

"I did," Jhaeros said, straightening his spine.

I could picture him as the dignified little elf boy, sitting ramrod straight as he contemplated the campaigne pieces and where he planned to move them. Hours of entertainment for someone as straitlaced as Jhaeros.

He looked down at the board. "Do you have a pair of tweezers? Maybe then we could move our pieces."

I laughed. "They're not *that* small."

Jhaeros raised his eyebrows at me then got up and began a slow tour of the living room, inspecting every nook and cranny.

I swiveled around in the armchair, as much as it would allow. "Hey, we're in the middle of a game."

Jhaeros kept looking around, moving from one spot to the next.

I got out of my chair and put my hands on my hips. "Still afraid to lose to me?" I questioned.

Jhaeros pulled his attention away from the stack of pillows in the alcove, sliding his gaze smoothly across the small space until locking eyes with me. His expression was very serious at the moment.

"You've already won," he said softly.

Tingles of electricity sizzled through my blood. I blinked.

He took a step toward me.

"You have my heart."

Another step.

"My soul."

Another.

"My undying devotion."

The breath left my lungs when he filled the space directly in front of me.

"You have all of me."

My body shivered in anticipation and need, spiraling out of control. But Jhaeros stood as still and immobile as a king on the campaigne board. It took me several seconds to realize he'd made his move—several moves—and was waiting for me to make mine.

Without further hesitation, I threw my arms around his neck and pulled his mouth to mine. Jhaeros grabbed me by the ass and jerked me against him. He might not be able to say the word "ass," but he most certainly knew how to handle one. I yanked his head closer, running my fingers through his silky hair as his tongue thrust its way inside my mouth.

Jhaeros lifted me several inches off the ground and carried me to the hallway before setting me back down. One hand left my backside as he pawed at a door handle.

I broke off our kiss, gasping, "No. Mel's room."

Jhaeros jerked his hand away from the knob, and I swallowed down a chuckle at the thought of us defiling my sister's personal domain.

Mel would just *lovvvve* that!

We stumbled to the next door, nearly tripping along the way as though we'd entered a three-legged race and the finish line was only a hop, skip, and a jump away. Jhaeros twisted the knob on my door before we shoved our way to the cavernous space within.

Faint light spilled in from the door, which neither of us bothered to close. I grabbed Jhaeros between the legs and squeezed. He groaned and retaliated by yanking my bodice clear down to my waist. I gasped as cool air rushed over my breasts.

Jhaeros growled at the sight. His thumbs brushed over the tips, teasing them into tighter peaks. He stared with lambent eyes as though seeing a sunset for the very first time. When it came to Jhaeros, I wouldn't be surprised if these were the first pair of tits he'd ever clapped eyes on. He'd probably planned to save himself for marriage . . . until a certain widowed elf (me!) went turning his sense of propriety all topsy-turvy, upside down.

Jhaeros groped greedily before licking, tasting—sucking the tender flesh until I could only breathe in pants and gasps. Heat bloomed between my legs. I grabbed at his pants, but Jhaeros captured my wrists, unwilling to relinquish my breasts so soon.

He backed me up to my bed. We fell over the side onto the mattress—me on my back, Jhaeros on top. I moaned as he bathed my breasts with his tongue. My hips arched, rising off the mattress, as I tried to rub against him so he'd hurry up and fill the aching need between my legs.

"Jhaeros," I pleaded.

The warmth of his tongue on my right breast made the left one tighten and peak in the cool room. Jhaeros caressed my free breast with measured strokes.

When I moaned, he drew my nipple in and sucked.

"Jhaeros," I pleaded again.

How could he torment me this way?

He slipped a hand up my skirts, fingers gliding up my leg, beneath my shift. When he reached my thigh, I opened my legs. He slipped a finger inside me and, feeling how molten I'd become, added a second finger and began to stroke.

My body shuddered, and my eyes squeezed shut as though I was in unbearable pain. But it was ecstasy, and it was blinding. My moans could have been those of a dying warrior's, feeling too much at once. If Jhaeros had a kind bone in his body, he'd stop torturing me and end my suffering.

Jhaeros yanked my skirts up to my waist with the rest of my mangled dress. I might as well have been naked with everything on display in the wide slice of light spilling in from the hallway.

Finally, Jhaeros seemed to understand that the fire he'd stoked was burning out of control and only he could put it out.

He released my breast and tore down his trousers before yanking my hips into position, driving his entire length inside me in one thrust. I nearly exploded, which I'd never dreamed was possible for a female.

The wooden headboard thumped against the wall as Jhaeros rode me into the mattress.

I threw my head back and moaned.

Jhaeros growled, which was appropriate when I felt like I had a beast between my legs.

I felt gravity slip away and my body float, hips rising with his as I tightened around him. I could no longer think, speak, or breathe. Sobs of ecstasy filled the room, followed by a wail of release. Sun, moon, and stars flashed over my darkened ceiling. I floated atop the mattress as though on a cloud.

When my body went limp, Jhaeros let go with a groan that made his body tighten and his head jerk back. Once freed from the throes of release, he scooted behind me and wrapped me in his arms, rocking me gently as he kissed my neck.

"I need you, Aerith," Jhaeros said in a breathy whisper.

I chuckled silently. "You just had me."

"I need you to be mine. I need to see your smiling face every day. I need you in my bed every night."

A soft ringing filled my ears and made my head dizzy. Something was off, pulling me from the present.

The room went arctic. My body turned cold as Jhaeros and his warmth slipped away, leaving me alone in an empty, cavernous space. All the brightness and joy were sucked from the room.

Jhaeros faded away, replaced by the last male I ever wanted

to see again.

"Lucky male, my brother," Liri drawled, "to have you in his bed every night."

How did he find me?

He couldn't be here!

He wasn't.

And neither was I.

Somehow I'd been sucked into the quicksand of treacherous memories.

My body stiffened in the tight corset of my blue ballgown. Symphony music swirled around us as beautifully dressed Fae danced in feathered and jeweled masks. Crystal chandeliers sparkled overhead, projecting shimmers of light that reminded me of broken glass.

"You shouldn't say things like that to me," I hissed at my brother-in-law, not taking my eyes off my mate and the petite brunette in the shiny silver mask he spun on the dance floor.

It was my duty to watch out for Cirrus, which meant always being wherever he was like a damn guard dog trotting after her master. Watching. Waiting. Ready to attack anyone who meant Cirrus harm, which mostly consisted of his siblings. Always on pins and needles. Welcome to the glamorous life of a princess.

"You deserve better," Liri said in his haughty royal voice.

I narrowed my eyes and turned to him. Only, it wasn't his face I looked into but that of a black mask with a long nose. He looked every bit the dark Fae prince—the one the rest of the Elmray siblings were careful not to provoke.

I glanced back at Cirrus in his white with silver glittered mask.

"I don't mean *him*," Liri said. "He's already been dealt with. I'm referring, sweet Aerith, to the male you just slept with."

The music stopped.

My bejeweled slippers remained on the polished floor of

the ballroom, but the gathered assembly dissolved, leaving me alone with Liri.

Dread spread through my veins like icy tentacles, squeezing the last of the warmth from my body. I might as well have been miles under water where no sunlight reached.

I turned once more to face the dreaded black mask.

Liri lowered it from his face. Amusement appeared in his smile and mirth in the shimmer of his deadly eyes.

"What is this?" I demanded, jerking my head around, searching for an explanation and, more importantly, an exit.

"No need to flee, love. You're not really here," Liri said, his smile widening. He reminded me of a boy poking at an anthill then standing back to watch the ensuing confusion he'd caused.

"Then where am I?"

"Wish I knew where you've run off to since Sweetbell. I don't suppose you'd tell me?" Liri smirked. I glared at him. "You're with *him*, whoever *he* is," he said, wrinkling his nose.

The fact that he didn't know my location was the only thing keeping me semi-calm.

"If you don't know where I am, then how did you find me?"

"Just a little enchantment," Liri said, circling around me as he twirled his finger. He looked me up and down as though searching for something. "I placed it over you right before you left Faerie. The enchantment was fabricated to bring you into a dreamscape with me the first time you laid with another male."

Ugh. Good thing outside magic had no way of penetrating the Monster Ball in its neutral zone, or this unfortunate reunion would have taken place a whole lot sooner.

"At least you've moved on from my brother. Pity it wasn't with me, but I'd like to think its progress," Liri drawled on. "Did you enjoy yourself?"

"It's none of your damn business!" I snapped. "Now

release me from this hellscape."

"You are free to leave anytime, sweet Aerith."

"How?"

Liri leaned in close, eyes latched on to mine. "Take off your mask."

His voice sent shivers through me.

I touched my face and felt that it was, indeed, covered. My fingers curled around the edges of my mask right before ripping it off.

"Aerith!"

I blinked several times until Jhaeros came into focus. He leaned over me, gripping my shoulders, panic in his saucer-round eyes.

"What? Happened?" I gasped, still coming out of the haze of the dreamscape. I sat up slowly, noticing my gown had been righted and a throw blanket draped over my legs.

Jhaeros sat on the edge of my bed, frowning with concern. He squeezed my hands in his. "Thank the Sky Mother above you're okay," he said.

I searched his eyes as though he held the answers.

"One moment you were here. Then you were gone," he said.

My heart beat erratically against my chest. "What do you mean?" I asked, afraid he knew where I'd been.

Jhaeros shook his head. "Your eyes were open, and you were breathing, but you were unresponsive."

"I'm okay now," I said, attempting to get to my feet.

Jhaeros stopped me with one stern look. For a moment, I felt like I'd traveled back in time, back when he used to look at me as though I were Shalendra's silly, irresponsible sister, when I was actually the one doing everything I could to provide for my family. But it was concern, not censure, that pulled his lips down.

He ran a hand through his hair. "I apologize for behaving like a barbarian. It won't happen again. Not until we are properly wed."

I snorted, coming back to myself. "Nothing about this is proper," I said, glancing from my bed to Jhaeros's rumpled hair.

Poor Jhaeros. I'd corrupted him. Who knew such a feat was possible? I might have smirked if I wasn't still reeling from the dreamscape. Jhaeros couldn't know. Nor Mel. There wasn't a thing either of them could do besides worry.

I'd treat it like a nightmare.

I'd awoken.

I was okay.

The monster couldn't get me.

For now.

CHAPTER NINE

Melarue

Despite my sister's protests, in the end I convinced her to let me have one day at the market with the jewelry to show her how much I could sell.

"I'm coming with you, and we need to rent a stall," Aerith had said.

"If you come with me, you'll scare customers away, and renting a stall means less money for us," I'd reasoned. "One day, that's all I ask."

"One day, then we'll see."

She'd probably relented out of guilt for sending me away to look at horses with Keerla while she got kissy with Jhaeros in *our* cottage. He'd still been there when we returned late in the afternoon. They'd been sitting in the living room, eating cookies and playing campaigne while he'd stared at her all dopey-eyed. Why didn't he draw a picture? It would last longer! He used to stare at Shalendra that way. If Jhaeros could transfer his affections from one sister to another, maybe there was hope for Devdan.

Arg! Shut up, brain! I despised Devdan. He was the biggest pit head of them all. The king of pit heads!

The only reason I was thinking about him at all was because I'd come to the market to hock the jewelry he'd failed to sell. Glittering necklaces, bracelets, and rings were stuffed inside my coat pockets. I couldn't imagine Aerith having worn any of the heavy jewels. After she'd left, I'd held on to my last memories of her all badass on the field when she'd killed a rampaging ogre. I'd pictured her in Faerie the same way—with her bow and arrows, taking down beasts who threatened the kingdom. I had not thought about her all gussied up in gowns and jewels.

While my thoughts wandered, my eyes kept on the lookout for a target—er, I mean customer. I leaned against one of the few trees in the square, watching elves funneling through the grassy aisles between stalls.

My eyes lit up on a middle-aged pair of elves in fine clothes, but my gut told me not to engage. Although clearly rich, they looked like the uppity type who would turn up their noses at a peddler. Shortly after Mr. and Mrs. High and Mighty, a young couple wandered into view. The blonde female was dressed in white muslin and a white shawl, and she carried a white lace parasol. Yeah, real practical. The stupid lace canopy wouldn't block rain or sun. The young male trotted beside her, clearly besotted.

Here we go.

I pushed away from the tree and wound my way around the crowd until I was several paces behind them.

They whispered to one another, making it impossible to hear what they said. The more I followed, the more I noticed they weren't looking at any of the goods—only at each other. So annoying. I doubted the love doves would appreciate being interrupted, so I gritted my teeth and continued following the pair, inching my way as close to them as I could without plastering myself against their backs.

"Elincia, my love, in another few months I will have saved enough to get us out of here."

Ah, pits!

This couple sounded like they were saving up to elope.

While I cheered on rebels, they wouldn't help me and Aerith make our own escape into the unknown.

I stopped so abruptly someone bumped into me from behind and huffed. I turned around and glared into the face of a male roughly my age.

"Watch where you're going," I said.

"Don't stop in the middle of the aisle," he returned as he strutted past me with a scowl.

I stuck my tongue out at him behind his back.

Arg! My good mood was dissolving faster than powdered milk. Now it was curdling inside my stomach. The day was still young, but patience wasn't my middle name.

I returned to my tree and folded my arms, glaring into the crowd. After what felt like an eternity but was more like a few minutes, I spotted a finely dressed male in his early twenties strolling through the market, checking out the jewelry booths. He wore a tailored coat and trousers and, best of all, had a thick coin purse tied in a pouch at his waist.

I pulled my hair over my shoulders, grateful I'd brushed it to a shine that morning—which had nothing to do with possibly running into Devdan at market. Nothing. At. All.

I trailed Money Bags through the crowded aisles, waiting until he reached a less congested area before sauntering toward him. "Hello there. You seem like you're looking for something special," I called out as I approached.

The male turned to me, a smile creeping up his lips. His hair was a sleek dark brown, and he had broad shoulders. I supposed he could be called cute, just nowhere near as attractive as Devdan.

He raised his brows. "What did you have in mind?"

"This," I said, pulling out an enormous ruby pendant.

The male frowned briefly in confusion as though he'd been expecting something else.

"I saw you checking out the jewelry earlier. None of those stalls offer the kind of rarities I do." I laid the ruby pendant across my palm and cradled it as though it were a delicate baby cardinal.

The male grinned again. "You were watching me?" he asked, stepping closer.

"Observing," I said with a shrug.

"You're very pretty, you know," he said flirtatiously.

"And I have very pretty items for sale." I returned his smile. I so had this fish on the hook. "Wouldn't you agree?" I asked, dangling the ruby in front of him.

He glanced from me to the pendant and chuckled. "Yes, very pretty and rare, indeed. How much are you asking for it?"

I schooled my expression to one of serious thought, even though I was grinning inside. "Nine gold pieces," I said after some deliberation.

"Nine?" The male laughed. "Your prices are high."

"Only because what I have to sell is high quality—the best."

"Nine," the male repeated uncertainly.

I had to go in for the kill. Close the deal. "Make it ten and I'll throw in a kiss," I blurted.

The male's eyes widened before turning lambent as his gaze drifted to my lips. My heart raced. Almost. I nearly had him until—

"I'll pay twelve!" another male voice announced.

I hadn't noticed Devdan sneak up while I was busy haggling. My heart burst with happiness. A second later, it broke into tiny jagged shards. I glared into his stupid handsome face right before turning my back on him.

Money Bags squinted at Devdan in confusion.

"Pay no attention to him," I said. "He's not a real customer."

"Thirteen," Devdan said louder.

"Go away," I hissed.

Money Bags twisted his lips to one side and scratched his head.

"Fifteen!" Devdan yelled in the other male's face.

Money Bags shook his head and sighed before turning to me. "It sounds like this one *really* wants your ruby."

My cheeks flamed at the suggestion in his tone. Suddenly, I didn't care if he'd offered ten purses of coins.

"Yeah, well, he can't have it, and neither can you!" I stuffed the ruby inside my coat pocket and stormed away.

Pitberries! I screamed inside my head as I stomped off. Maybe there was someplace else I could sell. Door to door? Local shops? They'd take a cut, but at least we'd get something back in return.

I knew I could move the jewelry if stupid pit-headed males would leave me alone. Why were males such perverts? They all just wanted kisses and other—stuff. Heat returned to my cheeks. I wrinkled my nose.

"Ew," I said aloud, even as little tingles rang through my body like wind chimes in a caressing breeze.

I walked out of the market in defeat, just as I had last time. Clearly Sky Mother wasn't smiling down on the square—at least not on me. It was time to come up with Plan B. I kicked a pebble on the cobbled road leading down the hill.

"Mel!" a voice hollered.

Aw, pits. I picked up my pace, not looking behind me.

"Mel," he said again. I heard his huffs of breath as he jogged up to my side.

"Go away," I said, still not looking at Devdan. "You cost me ten gold pieces."

"Yeah, right. More like saved you from fish lips. You can't go offering kisses to every potential customer."

I spun around to face him, planting my hands on my hips. "Why not? You do."

"I'm a male." Devdan had the gall to smirk.

"And I'm a female. Do you realize how stupid that sounds?" I dropped my arms and started walking again.

"Hey, hold up. You're not running from me again, are you?" The challenge in his voice brought me to an abrupt stop.

I turned slowly, glaring with venom. "I don't run from anyone. Certainly not you."

Devdan shoved his hands into his pockets. "That's what I figured. So, why are you leaving the market? Don't you have pieces to sell?" He nodded at my coat pockets.

I pressed my arms over my sides and the treasures my coat held, as though Devdan might try to lift them off me. "Well, I could sell if you didn't interfere."

"I promise not to interfere," he said, pulling his hands from his pockets and lifting them up in surrender, "as long as you don't bargain with kisses."

"What do you care?" I demanded.

"Hey, it's for your own good. After my kiss, everyone else is bound to be a huge disappointment. Life has enough of those already."

I laughed despite myself.

Devdan's smile reached his sparkling eyes. For a moment, all I saw was a sweet, young male who genuinely liked me. It made my heart hurt all over again.

I pressed my lips together and clenched my teeth.

"I was surprised to see you again so soon," Devdan continued. "I thought for sure Big Sis was keeping you under lock and key."

I narrowed my eyes. "Well, if you're hoping to see her again, you'll be sorely disappointed. She agreed to stay home and let me do my thing. In fact," I said, taking a step closer so I could poke Devdan in the chest, "you better hurry up and tell her how you really feel about her before she goes marrying Jhaeros Keasandoral. Your time is running out." I took a step back, removing my hand from his chest.

Devdan's head had turned down to stare at my finger on him, but he now looked into my eyes. "I'm not sweet on your sister. Maybe I'm a little too hard on her, but it's not like she can't handle it. Things always have a way of working out for

Aerith. Why is she sending you out to sell jewelry if she already has a new fiancé?" Devdan scoffed. "Didn't take her long to find another caretaker."

I kicked Devdan in the shin. I meant to go for his kneecap, but he was tall.

"Ow!" he cried. "What was that for?"

"You really are a pit head," I snarled. "You have no idea what Aerith went through to keep our family fed. She sacrificed her own happiness for us. And she can fend for herself, way better than most elves or any other supernatural being in any world. She doesn't need anyone to take care of her."

Before I could storm off at a full run down the hill, Devdan snatched my arm and pulled me to him. My stomach somersaulted while my brain raged.

"Hey, I'm sorry." It was only the soft sincerity of his tone that kept me from stomping on his foot. Devdan frowned. "I never had a family, so I don't know what it's like. But I admire the way you so fiercely defend your sister and the way she looks out for you—even when the timing isn't ideal." He smiled cheekily and released my arm.

I huffed even though the smoke clouds in my head had begun to dissipate and my breathing had returned to normal.

Devdan smiled as though it was a great triumph to stop a female from running away. He nudged the toe of my boot with his. When I took a step back, he moved forward and did it again, chuckling as I scowled.

"You're really annoying, you know?" But my tone came out sounding more amused than irritated.

Devdan smirked, ignoring my comment. "So, you need to move some jewels?" he asked.

"That's the plan."

"How much you got on you?"

Rather than tell him, I showed him what I had. In addition to the ruby pendant, I'd brought an amethyst bracelet, a diamond choker, and an assortment of whimsical rings. I wasn't dazzled by sparkles or shiny objects, but I did like one particular ring—a silver tortoise with tiny emerald eyes. Aerith had told me I was welcome to pick out and keep anything I wanted, but she was the one who'd earned the pieces and she wasn't keeping any, so I wouldn't either.

Devdan let out a low whistle as he studied the jewelry in my hands. I tried not to fixate too much on his lips while he was distracted. Once I'd shown him everything, I slipped the pieces back into my pockets.

"The diamonds will be the hardest to move but not impossible." He grinned at me. "Not with my help."

I snorted. "No, thanks. I heard about your twenty-five percent extortion."

Devdan smirked. "A fellow has to eat. We don't all have coins piling up like ol' Fish Lips."

I snorted.

Devdan puffed out his chest. "But for you, I'd do it for fifteen percent."

"Ten," I countered.

"Twelve and a—"

"Don't you dare say *kiss*!" I said, even though that's exactly what my pointy ears wanted to hear.

"Twelve percent," he said in a firm voice. "You're getting a great deal, you know. Fifteen percent is standard."

I folded my arms loosely beneath my chest. "Yeah, but we'd be working together, so really it should be ten."

"Is that a yes?" Devdan asked, a grin splitting his cheeks.

"My sister wouldn't like us teaming up," I said slowly.

Devdan folded his arms over his torso, mirroring my stance. "Now who's the one hung up on Aerith?"

I rolled my eyes skyward and huffed. "Fine, let's get going while there's still time."

Devdan fell into step beside me. "I bet you the bracelet goes first," he said as we re-entered the market together.

"And I bet you I get a gold coin for this gold Ferris wheel ring," I said, taking out the aforementioned piece and slipping it onto my pinky. Aerith's fingers were more slender and delicate than my knobby knuckles.

Devdan and I both won our bets and made new ones as morning turned into afternoon. When the ruby necklace sold to a wealthy older widow for eight gold pieces—and no kisses— we stopped to celebrate with sweet rolls and apple cider.

"I must say we make an excellent team," Devdan said, grinning widely between sips of cider.

I downed mine. It was so delicious. All the sugar made me feel giddy. It certainly wasn't the cute male who kept laughing and joking with me. Nope. Pure sugar rush.

"What do we have left?" Devdan asked, getting back down to business.

I pulled out a handful of rings.

His head bent as he peered down. "The turtle's going next," he said.

"Aw, he's my favorite."

Devdan's eyes snapped back up to mine. "Let me get him for you." His eager tone caramelized the sugar in my blood stream.

Oh my gosh, he is so sweet!

Get it together, Mel. You're mad at him, remember?

But that's so sweet!

Not to mention he was so adorably cute.

I considered his offer for several more erratic heartbeats before clearing my throat. "Nah, save your coins. Aerith already told me I could have it, but I don't want anything that reminds her of the time she spent in Faerie."

I was ready to let go of the turtle. I could make sacrifices too.

Devdan nodded. "That's thoughtful of you."

I shrugged. "She buys me swords; it's the least I can do."

We sold all the rings quickly, mostly on account of an

indecisive female gushing over each one. Her doting dad ended up paying for the whole lot of them. Devdan and I waited until they weren't looking to high-five.

"Sweetberry pie!" I exclaimed. "That was awesome. I hope she takes good care of Kuronos."

"Kuronos?" Devdan asked with a chuckle.

"The turtle," I clarified. He'd been living inside my engraved cigar box, but it was time for him to venture forth into the world—even if it was from the finger of a silly female. I patted my pocket. "You were right. We're down to the diamonds."

Devdan's lips slid into a sideways smile, and one brow rose. "You still game?"

"Of course," I said, tossing back my hair. "The market's still open. Customers are still shopping. And we've still got merch."

Laughter erupted between Devdan's lips. He flashed me a look I couldn't quite decipher. I shifted my weight from one foot to the other and pretended the sound of a squawking crow had caught my attention. But his gaze lingered in my mind. It reminded me of the way Jhaeros looked at Aerith with all eagerness and delight, as though she was a sweetberry amongst pits.

He just wants his cut of the profits, I warned myself. *And another kiss.*

"Okay, let's unload this clunker already," I said, all business.

Devdan laughed again, but at least his nod told me he was ready to get back in the game of selling.

We flashed the diamonds at several well-off-looking couples and a few males shopping alone, but the late-afternoon crowd was a lot more fickle than earlier.

I unclasped the choker and was just about to put it on my neck to show it off to a young female who looked interested when Devdan brushed against me and whispered, "Abort.

Abort. We gotta go. Now."

Before I could ask him what in the seven hells he was talking about—or glare at him for interrupting my sales pitch—he yanked me by the arm and dragged me away from the potential buyer.

"What the pit?" I demanded.

"The market commissioner is headed our way," Devdan hissed, pulling me along as though I was a stubborn mule.

Oh pit! He no longer had to yank me. I hustled alongside him until Devdan once more gripped my arm and changed course, pulling me between stalls.

"Hey!" a vendor yelped as we barreled through his hanging scarves in every shade and texture.

Ignoring him, we made our way to the back of the tent and pulled back the canvas, letting ourselves into a stall filled with wood carvings on the other side.

"Hey!" another vendor said, seeing us come in through the back way.

"Don't mind us," I said sweetly, picking up the pace.

Once we reached the grassy aisle, we took off running toward the courtyard and fountain beyond the market. I didn't realize we were holding hands until we reached the gurgling dragon. The laughter on my lips halted. I let go of Devdan's hand and stuffed mine in my pocket, rubbing my fingers over the wide diamond choker.

"I guess the diamonds are coming home with me after all," I said.

"Not a bad day, though." Devdan's cheeks were slightly flushed from our getaway. I'd rather touch his face than the hard gems or gold coins in my pockets, but as much as I wanted to, I still didn't trust him.

"Right. We need to divvy up the coins," I said, all business again. My heart had begun to sink inside my chest like the sun at dusk. One moment I was having the time of my life; the next I felt all achy and sad that the time had come to part ways.

Devdan led me to a spot behind some trees. I counted out his twelve percent, which Devdan casually pocketed. He smiled and opened his mouth to speak, but before words could emerge, I grabbed him by the shoulders and kissed him on the mouth with a loud *smack*.

It wasn't a deep, lingering kiss, but his eyes lit up as though he'd bitten into a sweet bun when I pulled away.

I hurried away from him, coins jingling in my pocket. A smile spread over my lips, and warmth blossomed in my belly. What a wonderful day it had turned out to be—better than I could have ever imagined. I nearly skipped away from the square, until I reminded myself that skipping was for children, not badass warrior elves. I altered my pace to a powerful stride.

My boots hit the cobbled street when heat flared up my spine in warning. I whipped around, but there was no one behind me. When I turned forward again, I nearly ran into two towering males with long blond hair pulled back into ponytails. They wore light gray tunics over matching trousers, black leather beaded bracelets, and thin silver chains around their necks. Matching pale blue eyes stared at me. The males were twins, and their energy caused my fire magic to flare up.

"Where did you get the diamond choker?" the one on the left demanded.

Oh pitberries. Were they with the commissioner? Were they his personal enforcers? Somehow I doubted that.

"Why?" I asked suspiciously. "You two in the market for diamonds?"

The one on the right surprised me by saying, "Yes." He sounded a little more relaxed than his brother. He even pulled out a white coin purse tied with silvery thread.

Instead of paying attention to the way my fire magic roared up inside my chest, my stupid eyes latched on to the purse, and my brain bounced up and down like a rubber ball.

Score! I might sell every piece after all, including the elusive diamond choker.

Who was the best? Mel was the best!

And no sharing commission with Devdan. He wasn't here. He missed out. Ha!

Long, pale fingers loosened the silver tie from around the purse. I watched transfixed.

"And where did you say you got the necklace?" The voice on the left had taken a melodic tone, one that lulled and soothed my mind.

Flames roared up inside my belly. *Ouch. Stop that.* Master Brygwyn needed to help me get better control.

"Chill," I said as much to the inquisitive male as to the fiery beast inside me. "I'm selling it for my roommate."

The male's eyes narrowed to slivers. "Does she know you're selling it?"

His twin cleared his throat and gave a slight shake of his head. "Doesn't matter."

This time it wasn't fire magic raging up my throat but my own fury. I squeezed the necklace in my palm.

"Of course she knows! She's my—" Dozens of warning bells went off in my head like wind chimes in a storm, but an invisible force seemed to pluck the truth off my tongue. I couldn't stop myself from finishing my sentence with, "Sister. I wouldn't steal from her if that's what you're implying," I added indignantly.

"She's telling the truth," the one with the coin purse said.

"No kidding. Do I look like a thief and liar to you?"

The one with the money snorted in answer. Sounded like a yes to me. He was about to find out I refused to do business with assholes. I slowly slipped the diamonds back into my pocket.

"Wait! How much?" the one with the coins asked.

"Five rhodium cubes."

I lifted my chin in the air and smirked, naming a price so

sky-high he'd take the hint I was no longer interested in selling. It was hard not to snicker. And harder still when the male pulled the first reflective cube of silvery rhodium from his purse.

My jaw dropped to my neck. I'd never actually seen a real piece of rhodium. It was so shiny and smooth despite the lumps in the precious metal. I'd never wanted to hold something in my hands as much as that piece of rhodium. I stared transfixed as the male plucked out a second piece.

"Two should be sufficient, don't you think?"

I found myself nodding as though my head were attached to a string. It was insane enough to offer me one piece for diamonds, let alone two. I forced my gaze off the two dazzling pieces of rhodium and stared into the pale blue eyes. "You drive a hard bargain, but it's the end of the day, so you're in luck."

Neither of the males chuckled or even cracked a smile. Tough crowd. I supposed I would be grumpy, too, if I was parting with two cubes of rhodium in exchange for a diamond choker. I was afraid to ask what was so special about these particular diamonds, lest they change their minds.

With those two rhodium pieces, Aerith and I could travel three worlds over. We could leave tomorrow.

A small pit formed in my stomach at the thought of leaving before I got a chance to partner up with Devdan again. I might have held off on the trip a little longer if it weren't for Jhaeros closing in on my sister. Once he married Aerith, there would be little chance the two of us would get to travel together.

I pulled the choker back out of my pocket, not releasing my grip on it until the rhodium cubes were in my other hand. As soon as the exchange was made, I jumped back as though the twins were the ones who might burn me.

"Nice doing business with you gents. Enjoy your diamonds," I said in a rush, scurrying away before they realized what they'd done and changed their minds.

I ran down the hill as though I really was a thief trying to evade capture. I didn't slow down until I reached the bottom of the hill, but when I glanced back, the twins were gone.

I gave a whoop of relief and excitement, squeezing a piece of rhodium in each palm. The rare metal warmed in my grip.

"What a day. What a day. What a day," I sang out.

Like totally unreal.

And kinda weird.

But whatever.

We were rich now, and we were going places.

Heat flared through my veins, fire flickering along my bones in a fury. My fire magic seemed to have a mind of its own today. Too bad I wouldn't be around for Master Brygwyn to teach me to control it. I'd just have to learn on the road.

Go away. Settle down, I tried to tell the internal flames on my walk home. Even though it was late fall, going on winter, the air around me seemed to heat to the scalding temperatures of summer. Sweat broke out over my hairline and dripped down my sides. I would have taken off my coat if I weren't afraid of coins and precious metals spilling out and getting lost in the cracks between the cobblestones.

I swiped the back of my hand over my forehead, slicking sweat over my clammy skin.

What was going on?

With every step closer to heatstroke, it became clear I needed to see Master Brygwyn before I went anywhere.

By the time I stumbled up to the cottage, my entire body felt like it was on fire. I didn't even have the energy to open the door. I bumped into the wooden barrier, slumping against it before stumbling backward.

Aerith opened the door with a smile—one that dropped when she looked out and saw me. "Mel, what's the matter?" she cried.

"Burning. Up," I managed.

Aerith's eyes widened in alarm right before she rushed out and helped me inside the cottage. Leaning on Aerith, I made it to my room and fell to my bed, amazed the sheets didn't catch on fire.

I felt like I was dying. The injustice of it angered me, feeding the flames in my body. I was only seventeen and never stepped foot outside Pinemist and Sweetbell. It was so unfair.

At least I got to kiss a cute male before the fever took me.

CHAPTER TEN

Aerith

C old numbed my fingers as icy water ran from the faucet over the rag in my hand. I waited until the cloth was saturated before turning the water off and wringing it out. I folded the cloth in half on my way to Mel's bedroom then knelt down beside her and placed the cold, wet rag on her forehead.

"Thank you," she rasped.

"I'll take care of you. You'll be fine," I assured her. "Just rest."

I remained at my sister's bedside all night—through her fevered dreams and whimpers. I wished I could trade places with her instead of watching helplessly from the side. At least she slept most of the night, even if it was in fits and starts.

In the morning, Mel managed to sip down a bowl of mushroom broth in her bed. By afternoon, she was drinking the broth at the dining table, and as evening approached, she begged for solid foods. I chuckled with relief.

"I'd say you're feeling better. You're lucky, Mel. I thought that fever would take you down for a week."

"One day was long enough." Mel sat cross-legged in the reading nook, lying against pillows in her brown-and-purple mushrooms jammies, reading an illustrated book. "And I think maybe it was my fire magic. I need to speak to Master Brygwyn."

I nodded from the kitchen. "I'll fetch him once you're feeling better, but until you are, I'm not leaving you alone."

I opened the fridge and pulled out root vegetables to add to a stew I was preparing. Mel returned her attention to her book while I chopped onions, rutabaga, celery root, parsnips, and carrots. I threw them into a large pot with oil. Once the vegetables had softened, I added in thyme, curry powder, and chopped tomatoes.

My eyelids felt heavy with the lack of sleep, but my relief at seeing Mel's quick recovery helped keep me going. I had half a loaf of crusty bread that was going stale. Using a trick the baker had shared with me, I ran the bread under the faucet then put it in the hot oven for ten minutes, after which it came out soft and chewy—almost as though fresh baked. I closed my eyes briefly, inhaling the scent of warm bread and stew.

Feeling in lighter spirits, I poured myself a half glass of sweetberry wine, taking large sips as I set the table.

Once the food was out, Mel set her book aside and sat cross-legged at the dining table where she devoured her bread and stew before requesting seconds.

I'd finished my wine but was only halfway through my stew. I laughed. "Looks like someone's feeling a lot better."

"I feel like I haven't eaten all day," Mel said. She put her feet down and started to get up.

"No. You stay put," I said. "You should still take it easy."

Mel shrugged. "If you insist."

I grabbed her bowl and my wineglass and filled them both in the kitchen before returning the few short steps back to the table.

Mel looked from her steaming bowl to me. "Is there any more bread?"

"Hang tight," I said, happy her appetite was back.

As soon as I handed Mel another chunk of bread, she ripped into it and stuffed pieces inside her mouth, saying a muffled, "thanks," as she chewed.

"Uh-huh," I replied, taking a sip of the sweet wine. "I hope you didn't catch anything while you were at the market."

Mel stopped chewing and glanced down at the table.

I set my wineglass down and stared at her. "You didn't see Devdan again, did you?" I expected a scowl, not the dreamy smile that appeared over her lips before she tried to cover it up with her hand and a cough.

My jaw tightened. "Melarue," I said, not masking the frustration in my voice. I should have never allowed her to go back to the market alone. If Devdan had touched my sister, I was going to pay him a personal visit that might very well end in bloodshed.

When Mel looked up, her smile morphed into a pout. "The market commissioner was about to bust me. Devdan helped me get away. End of story. He felt bad about the other day and wanted to make amends. He even helped me sell some of the jewelry."

"So, not end of story," I said angrily. "Did he kiss you again?"

"No." Mel pulled her hair over her shoulder and played with the ends.

"Did you kiss him?"

She stared at the tips of her hair and shrugged, not meeting my eyes.

I sighed in utter exasperation. "No wonder you got sick. I thought you were smarter than that. Devdan's a snake who preys on impressionable young girls."

Mel dropped her hair and glared at me. "You think me naïve and gullible."

"I didn't say that."

She shot up from the table. "You didn't have to. I'm not stupid, Aerith. I know what Devdan's after—what all males really want. And I'm not about to roll over and give it up just because he's really cute and funny and nice when he's not being irritating and unbearable. Arg!" She threw her hands up in the air. "I don't want to talk about this anymore. It's giving me a headache." With that, she stomped off.

Mel's door slammed shut a few seconds later.

Well, good to see she was feeling better—though not well enough to help clear the table and clean the dishes. I sniffed with amusement before grabbing my wineglass and tipping it back over my mouth, taking a large gulp.

Mel was spirited, stubborn, and no ninny. I trusted her to a certain extent, but I still worried. If she truly wanted to spend time with Devdan, she'd need a chaperone—one with a bow and arrow or sword, preferably both.

Mel would love that about as much as Devdan. I snorted and took another sip of wine, feeling the muscles in my body relaxing.

After polishing off the last of the sweet alcohol, I cleared the table, rinsed the dishes, and left them in the sink to clean on the morrow. Between the exhaustion and wine, I didn't trust myself not to break something in the soapy water.

I gave my hair and teeth a quick brush then called out a "good night" to Mel as I passed her closed door.

"Night," she said moodily.

I left my door open in case she needed me during the night; I wanted to be able to hear her. Once I'd traded my day gown for my white night shift, I snuggled under my covers and pressed my face into the soft pillow.

Sleeping is such a wonderful thing, I thought as I drifted off. Waking up in the middle of the night was a whole other matter and not nearly as pleasing.

I thought I felt hands around my neck, which woke me with a jolt. I kept my eyes closed, pretending to be asleep as my head finished clearing away the fog of lethargy. Once fully awake, my arm shot out of the covers and reached for the dagger I kept hidden beneath my bedframe. After my fingers curled around the hilt, I swung my legs over the edge of my mattress and jumped to my feet.

Staring into the empty darkness, I felt slightly foolish. My heart continued hammering in my chest, on high alert. I evened my breaths as a quick scan of my room confirmed I was alone. Hopefully I wasn't catching a fever and beginning to hallucinate. With my free hand, I felt my forehead, but it wasn't overly hot.

Something scratched my neck. My heart and breath stilled at the same time. I lowered my hand, fingers touching jewels fastened tightly around my neck.

"No," I breathed.

I rushed to my vanity, and even in the dim light I saw the sparkle of diamonds at my throat.

"Breathtaking," Liri drawled from behind me.

My fingers tightened around the dagger. It would do me no good in a dreamscape, but it gave me a small semblance of comfort to have it in my hand in case I wanted to slash at his unwelcome projection. Whatever magic he'd used on the choker was very strong. The diamonds felt like they were really around my neck. I couldn't wait for him to leave and for the damned thing to disappear. It was like a collar on a fancy pet. I hated this necklace more than the rest because Liri had been the one to give it to me.

"I knew it would shine brightest around your neck," he said.

I cursed silently. I had hoped he wouldn't find me again so quickly, but I'd been uneasy ever since his enchantment sucked me into a Faerie dreamscape—no matter how brief.

When I turned, Liri's eyes lit up as though the diamonds had somehow entered his eyes and sparkled within them.

"What will it take to get you to leave me alone?" I demanded.

For some reason, Liri kept his distance, keeping near my

far wall. Maybe seeing the dagger in my hand reminded him I wasn't some obedient pet who would blindly obey.

The top half of his white hair was pulled back in a thin ponytail and his toned, muscular chest jutted out. He'd always carried himself like a king, even when he was second in line to the throne. At one time he'd been fourth, but Cirrus's and Liri's older brothers had already been disposed of before I ever heard of the Elmrays.

"All I ask is that you give me a chance," Liri said. "Much has changed since you left Dahlquist. You would have freedom and power. You would no longer be a bystander but the center of attention."

I groaned in frustration. "I don't want to be the center of attention. I want to be left alone." But my words fell on deaf ears.

Liri frowned. "You must give me a chance, Aerith."

My breath stalled as Liri's twin guards, Galather and Folas, entered the room—through my door—as in, they were physically here. No wonder Liri had kept his distance. He was really here, which meant I could do him real harm with my dagger.

Before the twins could reach me, I launched myself at Liri, dagger raised. I aimed for the twisted organ he called a heart. Liri spread his arms wide open as though we were about to embrace. The blade went straight through him, flying through his projection and *thunking* into the wall at his back. I wasn't expecting to hit stone. My fingers yelped on impact, and the dagger fell from my hand, clattering to the floor.

Dammit! He wasn't here after all. Blackguard! Coward!

Liri wasn't present, but his guards were. I was surprised they'd left his side, being the twins were his most loyal and trusted sentinels.

They each grabbed one of my arms and held me in front of Liri's projection. I glared into his face.

"You see, Liri. You don't really want me back in Faerie. I

am a danger to you. I can't be trusted."

Liri pressed his lips together and studied me a moment before answering. "At least you are honest. You have always been . . . honest." There was no emotion in his voice.

Maybe honesty would work in my favor. I stopped trying to yank out of the twins' grips and looked Liri in the eyes. "I wish you no harm, Liri. Truly. I want only to be home."

"Then you shall be brought home where you belong." Liri lifted his head and looked from one of the twins to the other.

When the meaning of his words registered, panic shot adrenaline through my limbs as I tried to yank out of the twins' grasps.

"A princess of Faerie belongs in Faerie," Liri said as I struggled.

The grips on my arms tightened. A cool hand clamped over my mouth. The other twin blew a silvery shimmered powder into my face, causing my body to go limp.

"You belong with me, Aerith." Liri stalked toward me, and there was nothing I could do but watch his approach. "I set you free. If not for me, you'd still be under my brother's thumb, forced to share your mate with countless other females. I am old-fashioned. I believe in loyalty and devotion. And I am not feeble like Cirrus was. I do not require the protection of a female." He hissed then relaxed his jaw and smiled. "I will do the protecting: of me, of you, of our children, our people, and our realm. Yes," he said, nodding. "I made sure Cirrus was incapable of producing heirs, but you, my lovely sister-in-law, have nothing to worry about. I would never do anything to harm you. There is nowhere safer than by my side. I know you, Aerith. You are strong and brave. You will be angry at first, but you will overcome your emotions as you did for my brother. You will step into line, come willingly to my bed, and value my life above all others."

My mind screamed, but I couldn't move my mouth. Even my lips were numb.

He stopped inches from my face and smiled down at me. "Your obedience will be rewarded in ways you can't begin to imagine. You will be the envy of all of Dahlquist and kingdoms beyond."

No! I screamed, but no sound emerged.

I tried to yank out of the twins' arms and run for the door, but my limbs didn't respond.

Then Liri walked right through me, and the world turned dark.

CHAPTER ELEVEN

Aerith

Light penetrated my closed eyelids, seeping in brighter and brighter. *Go away, sun.* I groaned, wanting to sleep in a little longer. My lashes fluttered open then closed when sunlight streamed in.

What was daylight doing inside my room anyway? I had no windows.

I pried my eyes open and stared into a room with large picture windows partially open to let in the warm valley air. Gauzy white curtains billowed gently, lifting like twirling skirts during a dance.

I sat up slowly, leaving the comfort of the large mattress that had hugged my body in its soft embrace.

This isn't my room! My heart leaped to my throat in panic until I noticed my campaigne board on the small round oak table where I always kept it. The pieces were made from blown glass and set atop a mirrored board with squares that alternated from reflective to frosted white surfaces.

This *was* my room. But something wasn't right.

I peeled back the white blanket with gold embroidered swirls. My thick, fluffy white rug awaited my bare feet. Cream slippers were set on the rug in the spot I left them every night before turning in.

I nudged a foot into each slipper as I'd done four-hundred-and-fifty-six times before. Leaving behind the soft rug, I walked around the grand, familiar room. A long, deep mahogany armoire took up over half of one wall, holding my luxurious collection of gowns.

In the center of the room, I had my own sitting area furnished with a tan cushioned chaise lounge and matching armchairs.

Light reflected from mirrors placed all over the room. I caught my reflection again and again. A lacy cream negligee hugged my curves, spilling down my legs. A slit ran up the fabric all the way to my hip. Cirrus liked easy access, and he liked his females wrapped in pretty packages.

It was the past staring back at me through the reflection—Princess Aerith Elmray.

Diamonds glittered around her neck. That was new.

Another dreamscape then.

"Show yourself, Liri."

The curtains rustled in the wind, but my brother-in-law made no appearance.

Terror struck through my chest like an arrowhead made of ice. It didn't matter that the breeze wafting in was warm. My body shook as though racked with chills.

What if I'd never left Faerie? What if returning home had been the dream? What if I'd made it all up? The Monster Ball. The estate at Sweetbell. The cottage in Pinemist with Mel. Jhaeros.

My heart pounded in protest.

No. I most certainly had not made up my love affair with Jhaeros. There'd been many times I'd taken mental escapes during my fifteen months wed to Cirrus, and in all that time, I never would have made Jhaeros Keasandoral a part of those fantasies.

That had been real.

What we had was real.

Maybe if I removed the diamond choker as I'd removed the mask in the last dreamscape, I'd be returned to my own realm and reality.

I reached around my neck, fingers searching for the clasp, but all I felt were the smooth polished rows of diamonds. Frowning, I walked up to one of the full-length mirrors and attempted to twist the choker around my neck to bring the clasp to the forefront.

The thing wouldn't budge, as though the diamonds had embedded themselves into my skin.

My heart beat in a wild panic like a caged bird. I clawed at my throat.

A light tap at the door stilled my fingers. I heard the tap, a little louder this time. I spun around, searching the room for anything that could be used as a weapon.

The door opened and a familiar head of brown hair and green eyes peeked inside before entering.

"Hensley?" I asked in a daze, not yet believing my eyes.

The human's lips split apart into a wide toothy smile. "Princess Aerith!" She ran toward me as gracefully as she could in her peach cotton gown. Upon reaching me, she threw her arms around my waist and squeezed. "I'm so happy to see you! I missed you so much!"

"I missed you too."

Hensley, my favorite lady-in-waiting, had been one of the few things I hadn't been allowed to bring home with me. Not that she was a thing. Plus, she loved living in Dahlquist, serving the Elmray family. Hensley hadn't told me much about her past life in the human realm, only that it had been ugly and that a kingdom in Faerie, even a corrupt one, was paradise compared to where she'd come from. She was a lovely young woman and had been my closest companion in Faerie.

Hensley pulled back and looked me over. She sucked in a breath before releasing it. "You are so beautiful. No wonder

King Liri wants you for his queen."

Air stopped flowing from my lungs. My throat tightened and clogged as though I'd swallowed a lump of coal. I made a choking sound.

Hensley's green eyes grew wider. Her mouth moved, but I couldn't hear what she said. My ears were plugged too.

She slapped me on the back, and I coughed so violently tears streamed down my face.

Hensley rushed to the water pitcher placed with crystal glasses on a sideboard near the door. While I blinked away the tears and wheezed in air, she returned with a glass of water. I took a sip then went over to my nightstand and set the glass down.

"Did you say, *King* Liri?"

When had that happened? How had that happened? Had Liri killed his father after Cirrus? In the first dreamscape, he'd told me he'd make me a queen, but I'd been so disturbed by his appearance I had not given it any thought beyond getting out of Sweetbell where he wouldn't find me.

Hensley nodded and smiled. "I can't believe he didn't tell you." She put her hands to her cheeks and squealed. "I can't believe *I'm* the one telling you! Liri is the new king of Dahlquist."

I narrowed my eyes. "What happened to Merith?" I asked of my father-in-law, not that I'd ever cared for the old windbag. If there was one thing the Elmray siblings agreed on, it was that Dear Old Dad should retire into the realm of no return.

"Liri dispatched him." It was a testament to her time in Faerie that Hensley said it so matter-of-factly, as though announcing roast duck would be served for dinner that evening.

Becoming indifferent, like Hensley, had been one of my greatest fears in Faerie. The fear I'd lose myself over the years and become not only obedient but resigned. My campaigne board had kept me grounded and my mind sharp, watchful for opportunities and the best played moves for navigating life in the royal palace where Merith had forced all his children to live, as though keeping a close eye on them would make him safer.

Yeah, that had worked out really well for him and his three eldest sons. Cirrus had refused to speak of how his older brothers died, which had always made me suspicious that he'd had something to do with their deaths. Since Liri had poisoned Cirrus, I wondered if he'd used the same method on his dad.

"How did he do it?" I asked numbly. "Poison?"

Hensley shook her head. She wore her hair as she did before—thick, long bangs, and a braid in back.

"Slit Merith's throat with a jeweled dagger right in the middle of a family dinner," Hensley said.

Tasteful. I was glad I hadn't been around for the horrifying scene.

My fingers fluttered up to my own throat. "Can you get this thing off me?" I turned my back to Hensley, lifting my hair.

"Uh, I'm sorry, Aerith, but King Liri wants you to wear the diamonds at the ball this evening."

My stomach twisted. "Ball," I repeated softly, dropping my hair.

"Your welcome home ball." Hensley clapped her hands in excitement. "But first we need to move you to your new room and get you fed and then dressed. Oh, Aerith. It's going to be just like old times, only way better."

I stumbled against my old bed, head spinning.

"Oh! Oh no. Are you okay?" Hensley squawked.

I squeezed and unsqueezed my fingers into fists. As much as I wanted to freak out and throw things, it wouldn't do a lick of good. The game had changed, and the sooner I figured out my position, the quicker I could figure my way out of this colossal mess.

"This is no longer to be my room?" I asked carefully. If Hensley told me I was moving in with Liri, we were going to have a real problem.

"You've been moved to the king's royal wing of the palace. We both have. But King Liri wanted you to wake up somewhere familiar. He's so thoughtful!" Hensley's smiled dropped. "Well, he is when it comes to you. Others aren't so lucky." She gave a nervous little laugh. "You must be eager to see your new chambers. I'll take you there."

"Perhaps I should put on clothes first," I said, staring at the plunging V-neck that every mirror in the room threw back at my face.

Hensley slapped her forehead. "Oh my gosh, sorry about that. I got so excited I got ahead of myself. King Liri ordered a new wardrobe for you, which is in your new chambers, but let's see what we can dig out in here."

She strode over to the long armoire and pulled open one of the doors. I'd packed what I could, but there'd been a lot leftover to leave behind. Hensley plucked a light blue empire-waisted gown and brought it over to the bed.

"I realize it's simple, but it's only temporary until we have a chance to dress you up for the ball."

I was glad for simple and glad to strip out of the negligee. I tossed it onto the bed like a used linen napkin. Hensley helped me pull a fresh white cotton shift over my head, followed by the gown.

"Shall we?" she asked eagerly, leading the way to the door.

I cast a longing look at my campaigne board. It had kept me sane before. I hoped it could do so again until I found a way back home.

Hensley followed my gaze and smiled brightly. "Anything you want from your old room can be delivered to your new chambers."

I nodded, taking tentative steps to the door. The wide

hallway was silent. Mirrors lined the walls, reflecting sunlight from overhead windows. Cirrus loved his mirrors. He loved looking at his reflection and those of the court, sizing everyone up from every angle. It made me feel as though I couldn't even escape myself. I was trapped everywhere, moving from room to room—one mirror to the next.

We met no one along the way, almost as though the palace had been cleared for my arrival. Hensley tried to walk beside me, rather than lead, but as we neared the king's wing, my steps faltered. I'd never been to this part of the palace.

Two royal guards in green and gold tunics stood outside massive double doors. At our approach, they moved in tandem, each taking a door and opening it for us.

Hensley nodded at the guards before ushering me into an open hallway. Warm air breezed over us, and my mouth gaped open at the sight of the shimmering lake that lapped right up against the south side of the castle. The hall didn't need mirrors with the sunlight reflecting off the lake's surface. The air was as fresh and sweet as an eternal summer.

"It's beautiful," I couldn't help but murmur.

Hensley clutched my arm and squealed. "And we get to live here. I keep pinching myself, thinking I'm dreaming."

If only I could pinch myself and wake up back in Pinemist. I kept the thought to myself and forced a smile. Hensley was as close of a friend as I could get in Dahlquist, but I never lost track of the fact that she faithfully served the Fae.

She threaded her arm around mine and tugged. "You have an entire suite of your own. It's massive, just wait and see."

I didn't have to wait long for a tour of my new prison. It was, as Hensley had said, a massive suite with interconnecting rooms. We entered the bedchamber first, stepping onto white carpeting covered in thick gray swirls. The walls were tinted mauve. The emperor-size bed was draped in a deep purple quilt and covered in sleek white satin pillows. A tall quilted headboard lifted into a gold-tinted wooden crown as though the bed were a member of the royal family.

Matching deep purple curtains were gathered and tied over transparent white curtains. Through them, I could see the green of the distant rolling hills. Crystal chandeliers hung from the ceiling while potted plants bushed out from the corners of the rooms. All the side tables were adorned with large vases filled with fresh flowers.

Hensley led me through a set of ornate double doors that took us through a private sitting room and back to an entire room filled with armoires and shelves for clothes and shoes.

After looking everything over, we returned to the sitting room where a pitcher of lemonade, along with sandwiches, had been laid out alongside gold-rimmed porcelain plates and crystal glassware with gold stems.

Hensley stood behind one of the high-back purple cushioned chairs, waiting until I'd sat before she did. Once seated, Hensley poured us each a glass of lemonade. "So, what do you think of the new digs?" she asked eagerly, leaning forward in her seat.

"It's decadent."

And obnoxious. Busy. Gauche.

I missed my cottage.

"Sumptuous, isn't it?" Hensley winked. "You'll never want to leave your rooms, except you will because the palace is basically yours. Well, it's King Liri's, but that makes it yours. I always knew he was sweet on you." Her next smile looked forced.

"He didn't exactly hide the fact," I said, not masking the ice from my tone.

Hensley ignored it. "We all thought that was just to goad Cirrus."

"Who is 'we all'?" I asked suspiciously.

"Well, his sisters," Hensley said in a tone that indicated it should be obvious.

Teryani, Jastra, and Sarfina. How could I forget?

I groaned. My sisters-in-law were another reason I'd never wanted to return to Faerie. They made me miss Shalendra. The Elmray sisters were the worst.

Cirrus had claimed they'd despised one another since birth. But on one front they were united. They all hated me.

"Hensley," I said carefully as not to alarm her. "Are my weapons still around?"

Hensley took a gulp of lemonade then set her glass down, lips pursed. "The king doesn't want you to have weapons."

I snorted. Yeah, he was ruthless, not stupid.

But if he wanted me around, he better allow me a way to protect myself from his sisters, or I'd end up a corpse before he ever had a chance to persuade me to be his queen.

CHAPTER TWELVE

Aerith

Shortly after finishing our refreshments, there was a knock at my door—just loud enough to be heard from the sitting chamber. The lemonade soured in my stomach as Hensley sprang up and flew out the double doors to answer from the bedchamber.

She returned moments later, holding a square box with a red bow on top and announced, "A gift from King Liri."

"Is he out there?" I demanded, getting to my feet.

Hensley shook her head. "A servant delivered this." She set the box on the edge of the table, looking from me to the box then back to me.

With a sigh, I ripped off the bow, tossed it beside the platter of leftover sandwiches, and opened the box. At least it was too big to contain another necklace or jewelry of any sort. I peered inside.

No, not jewelry. A campaigne board.

I dropped to my knees in front of the box, sinking into the thick rug. A game of campaigne was my happy place. My escape. My connection to home and, now, Jhaeros.

No matter what happened, all I had to do was move the pieces to find my place of calm.

"Your favorite game," Hensley said, sounding as excited as

if the gift had been presented to her. She was the one person who showed genuine pleasure on my behalf. I swear my happiness meant more to her than her own, as though our emotions were connected.

"Let's see it. I can help you set it up if you want me to."

"Yes, thank you, Hensley."

She beamed. "Let me clear off the table first and make sure it's wiped clean."

When I tried to help, Hensley insisted I sit back and wait. I kept my place on the floor while she carried the trays out to the hall. My hair curtained my face as I stared inside the box, pretending the room around me didn't exist.

After Hensley wiped down the table, I pulled out a heavy purple-and-black board. The squares were made out of tiles while the pieces were carved out of marble and onyx. Once the board was set up, Hensley got to her feet. "I will leave you to rest and will return in a couple hours to help you dress for the ball."

"Who is attending?" I stared at the campaigne board rather than Hensley.

"Tonight's ball will be an intimate affair with nobles from the realm and immediate family: Teryani, Jastra, and Sarfina."

"What about Prince Ryo?" My eyes flicked up to Hensley's face for this question. I noted the hesitation before her reply.

"The prince will not attend tonight."

I snorted. "Liri threw him in the dungeons, did he?" Wouldn't want his younger brother to take him down the way he'd taken down Cirrus.

"Ryo has been sequestered to his room. He is quite comfortable," Hensley assured me.

I rolled my eyes.

"Can I get you anything before I go?" she asked.

"No, thank you, Hensley."

Out of the corner of my eyes, I saw the peach-colored curtsy of her skirts before Hensley swept out of the sitting room. I listened for the sound of the door as it clicked shut behind her.

I stared at the polished marble and onyx pieces on the campaigne board, my vision going in and out of focus.

I thought Liri might come by to gloat, but that wasn't his style.

King Liri.

I plucked the onyx king piece from the board and stared at it. Teryani, Jastra, and Sarfina weren't the only ones who'd assumed Liri's attention to me had been to goad Cirrus. I'd been dumbfounded when Liri offered to make me his mate after Cirrus's death. Perhaps the idea of taking his brother's bride for his own had brought him delight. Perhaps as time passed the novelty would wear off. Maybe without Cirrus around Liri would tire of me.

I rubbed the king piece between my fingers, a plan formulating in my mind.

If one good thing could come out of my captivity, it was for Liri to open his stony eyes and see what a bore it was to try enticing me without Cirrus around to watch.

I set the onyx king in the center of the board then picked up an onyx mage. There were no princess pieces, so I used the mage to represent my sister-in-law Jastra, sticking her beside Liri since she was his devotee. Next, I picked up a marble mage, representing Sarfina, who had fawned over Cirrus as though he was a divine being. I set her piece several squares to the left of the onyx king and mage. I skipped over Teryani, Liri's twin sister, going for a marble shrub. Ryo was easy. I placed him near Sarfina before returning to the puzzle Teryani presented.

Teryani had always made herself out to be neutral, queen of her own camp, treating all her brothers as though they were juvenile and unworthy of her devotion. One would think that as Liri's twin, she would naturally align herself with him, but the pair had always acted indifferent—almost as though the other didn't exist. Even if Liri were out of the picture, Dahlquist had an antiquated law that a female could not inherit the crown unless there were no males to rule the realm. Which was unlike the neighboring kingdom of Ravensburg where Liri's Aunt Naesala ruled as queen and could pass her throne on to any family member of her choosing since she had no heirs of her own. She'd made no secret of her preference for Cirrus or intention for him to inherit Ravensburg. I assumed she would leave her kingdom to Liri since she'd always expressed deep disgust for Liri's cousins on her younger brother's side of the family.

Three of Teryani's brothers were now in the realm of no return with only two left. She could be playing the long game. I had no trouble believing that, which made her piece become crystal clear.

I grabbed the marble king and set it in a corner of its own.

And who was I? An archer, for sure, but what color?

Liri was my opponent, which made me marble.

I plucked the marble archer off the board and set it near Liri.

I'd survived Faerie the first time by keeping my wits about me, and I would do so again.

I was no longer Aerith Heiris of Pinemist, nor Princess Aerith Elmray of Dahlquist. I was a piece on a campaigne board—a game I knew how to play well.

A game I knew how to win.

But could I take my skills off the board and into the ballroom and halls of the palace?

At my insistence, Hensley and I left my chambers an hour after the ball had begun.

Liri had picked out my ballgown: a deep wine-red sleeveless gown with twinkling diamonds in the full tulle skirt.

From the box of jewels in my dressing room, I'd selected a multi-stranded diamond bracelet and teardrop earrings to match the choker plastered to my neck.

For my first move, I dressed up the way Liri wanted—in the gown he'd chosen, dripping in jewels. I had a theory that my resistance excited him. By playing along, he might find I'd become less intriguing—less of a challenge.

Everyone knew I didn't care for flashy jewelry, but tonight I'd blind them with sparkles. They were about to meet the new Aerith. The independent Aerith. I might be a captive, but I was nobody's bride.

"Princess Aerith, you are a vision," Hensley gasped after she finished pinning up my hair.

Instead of looking at myself, I stared at Hensley in the mirror's reflection. She'd changed into a simple pink satin ballgown and pinned her hair into a twist. Her rounded ears looked out of place, as did the sweetness in her smile.

We walked from the king's wing to one of the palace's smaller ballrooms in the east wing. Instrumental music echoed down the hallway the closer we approached, spilling out of double doors left open.

Two guards stood at the entrance. They nodded at me.

Entering the ballroom was like stepping through a portal in time. I recognized the faces of the realm's richest nobles. They'd shown up dressed in their finest gowns and suits. I wasn't the only female draped in jewels. Gemstones flashed off all the females present, dripping down plunging necklines and circling wrists like bedazzled cuffs.

I'd seen it all before. I half expected Cirrus to step out of the crowd, dressed all in white with gold embellishments, and wave me over to his side.

All eyes turned to me, making me grateful for the loud music playing. Otherwise, the hush would have been deafening. No one had been dancing. If they had, they would have surely stopped and turned to gawk.

I lifted my head, strolling in with an air of superiority and boredom, though my heart beat wildly inside my chest. It didn't matter that Hensley was by my side. I was entirely alone, left to fend for myself.

I hadn't loved Cirrus, but he'd been a barrier between me and the treacherous world of Faerie, court life, and his sisters.

It struck me all over again that he was gone. Dead. I was the mate who'd failed to protect him.

No one approached me. They waited and watched.

"Let's get some refreshment," I said to Hensley. I needed a drink on the double, and Faerie had the best wine. It wasn't something I'd ever imbibed on. I'd had to keep ever alert on behalf of Cirrus. Now I needed to keep a clear head for myself, but if I didn't drink something, I would lose my courage. One glass, that was all.

"Oh yes, of course, Princess Aerith." In that moment, Hensley's cheeriness brought a small dose of comfort, a spot of warmth in a cold, cruel sea of Fae.

We made our way to a long table covered in a white linen cloth, silver trays, and flutes of bubbling sweet wine.

Servants attired in silvery tunics and stony expressions stood at the ends of the tables, handing flutes to anyone who walked up. There was no friendly dragon shifter or sassy succubus to serve up signature drinks here. A pit formed in my stomach, growing with each step.

Before we'd made it to the table, Sarfina pushed through the crowd and stormed over as though she wore breeches rather than a sheer white gown with a gold bikini underneath. Long, light blonde hair spilled over her shoulders with golden highlights that shone beneath dozens of overhead chandeliers.

The assembly appeared to lean forward on their toes.

Let the spectacle begin, I thought with a sigh. *Remind me to thank Liri for pushing me into the deep end without a dagger.*

Sarfina marched straight up to me, nearly stepping on my slippered toes. "You have a lot of nerve showing up here," she yelled in my face.

Even with the shriek of the instruments, anyone within thirty feet could hear what she said. Those who couldn't were quickly informed as guests turned to repeat Sarfina's biting words.

"You'd do well to be nice to me, Sarfina," I answered coolly.

Her gray eyes hardened. "Why? Because you're Liri's new plaything?"

The pit in my stomach turned to burning coal.

"*King* Liri," Hensley murmured in disapproval, but Sarfina didn't hear her.

I lifted my chin higher. "You shouldn't speak to the guest of honor that way."

"Honor, my white faerie ass." Her eyes latched on to the diamond choker. "Nice collar," Sarfina sneered. "You're no longer family. You shouldn't be showing your face or wandering the halls. You're Liri's *pet*. And pets need to stay in their cages."

"King," Hensley said softly.

The air chilled as Sarfina turn her glacial look to the human beside me. "What was that, human?" she asked in a low, menacing tone.

Hensley glanced at the floor, unable to meet Sarfina's gaze. "*King* Liri," she said, eyes downcast.

Sarfina struck Hensley so quickly I gasped in horror and surprise. Her lithe white-gowned body collided with Hensley's pink gown as Sarfina pulled Hensley's hair out of its twist and ripped at her bodice.

Hensley whimpered and squealed but did nothing to defend herself.

"Stop it!" I screamed.

Sarfina spat in Hensley's face and stepped back. "Never speak to me unless I give you permission, human. Next time I won't be so gentle."

Hensley's head hung, her messy hair falling over her shoulders like tattered rags.

"Now apologize to me." A wide grin traveled up Sarfina's cheeks. When Hensley didn't respond, Sarfina yelled, "Speak!"

"I'm sorry, Princess Sarfina. Please forgive me. It won't happen again."

Sarfina huffed. "Very well. Dismissed." She flicked her wrist toward the double doors.

Without looking at me, Hensley hurried out of the ballroom, nearly tripping on the pink hem of her gown as she rushed out.

My stomach twisted. I wanted to follow her out, make sure she was okay. I also felt like throwing up. But to run after a human servant would be viewed as a weakness.

"Looks like you lost your one friend here," Sarfina said in a low tone meant only for me.

I kept my regal stance, schooling my expression and answering in my own low voice. "You forget I have the most powerful friend of all. *King* Liri," I said, enunciating "king" as Hensley had done.

Sarfina lost her smile. "You'll pay for betraying my favorite brother, bitch. That's a promise," she hissed and stormed off.

Before I could regain my bearings, a female chuckled beside me. Teryani. Oh, sweetberry pie served à la venom.

She wore her long, straight white hair unbound, the way Liri did. It was scary how much they looked alike. All of the Elmray children were gorgeous, but Teryani had an otherworldly beauty that made it hard not to gawk in her presence. Her hair was parted down the middle, covering her ears and framing her pale oval face. Gold liquid shimmer rimmed her eyes, bringing out the cool blues of her irises. A willowy frame and light pink lips that often parted with a look of angelic wonder gave her a childlike appearance. Her dress was made of coppery fabric leaves that clung to her chest and torso then flared out from the waist over a shimmery copper slip. Thin straps left her arms bare and brought attention to the fact that she wore no jewelry—not even a single ring circled her elegant pale fingers.

"Bravo, Aerith. A most spectacular entrance," she said sweetly, passing alongside me as though I were a pedestrian on the street.

Sarfina. Check.

Teryani. Check.

That just left Jastra.

And *King* Liri.

I turned to the table and reached for a sparkling flute.

"Princess Aerith, please allow me," a server said, leaping forward.

I was closer to the table, but whatever. I took the flute from his outstretched hand and began sipping it at once. Eventually, eyes began to turn away from me when it became clear nothing more exciting was taking place between me and my in-laws. I finished the flute and traded it for another full glass, drinking until my head buzzed.

Ready. Steady.

Well, not so steady, but good enough to get through the evening, which was about to get started.

The music stopped when a Fae dressed in black coattails strolled in with a trumpet. He lifted the instrument to his lips, blasted through the tube, then lowered the trumpet and announced, "King Liri."

Murmurs arose as Liri strolled in looking resplendent in a high-collared capelike coat that was black with a golden shimmer. A crown of gold-and-red branches and leaves sat atop his snowy white hair, which curtained his wide shoulders. It wasn't *the* crown—the thick heavy gold one I'd seen my father-in-law wear on official business. I imagined Liri had as many crowns to choose from as the royal females likely had necklaces.

Jastra entered behind him, her head of teal, wavy hair held high and regal. Her attire wasn't so much of a dress as blue flowers strategically placed to cover her breasts before cascading down into a multilayered ruffled mesh skirt. A circlet of dark blue flowers crowned her head. Light blue armbands attached to wispy long scarves draped from above her elbows.

Liri's twin guards hovered nearby, ever watchful. I glared at each of them, but their focus remained on their king.

Jastra didn't spare me a glance as she trailed after her brother, who smiled smugly as nobles rushed over to greet and fawn at his feet.

Yech!

I turned and walked slowly in the opposite direction, scanning the crowd for anyone I could talk to rather than appear to be standing around waiting for His Highness to notice me. But the finely dressed Fae avoided eye contact and moved away as I passed, as though I were a leper from the mortal world.

I returned to the refreshment table and downed another flute of bubbly wine. It soothed my insides, made me feel like laughing at all the ridiculous couples avoiding me as I moved around the ballroom.

Some welcome "home."

Fucking Fae.

Laughter bubbled up my throat. I swallowed it down with a smile. Cursing them, even in my head, made me grin.

"Princess Aerith, how lovely you look." Liri's voice caressed the nape of my neck.

I spun around, diamonds winking from my choker, wrists, and skirts.

"A vision, isn't she?" Liri asked his sister, though he kept his eyes fastened on me.

Jastra had drifted to his side and flicked a gaze over me. She twirled several of her teal curls around her fingers before flipping them back. "Stunning," she said.

Liri's smile widened. "Bold colors suit her. Cirrus was always putting her in creams and pastels." Liri momentarily drew back his lips.

"I am not a doll to be dressed up," I hissed.

Jastra glared at me, but Liri chuckled.

"No, you are not. Give us a moment, Sister."

Lifting her nose in the air, Jastra spun around in a cloud of teal and blue and strode into the crowd.

"I am pleased to see you back in Dahlquist," Liri said. "But why are you alone? Where is your lady?"

Narrowing my eyes, I snarled. "Your sister brutalized her."

"Which sister?" Liri's voice dropped an octave.

I folded my arms. "You really have to ask."

"Sarfina," Liri beckoned. Despite never having raised his voice, she appeared before him as though out of thin air, hands clasped in front of her.

"Yes, Brother?"

Liri looked down at her. "You are not to harm Aerith *or* her lady-in-waiting."

Sarfina unclasped her hands and stomped her foot. "But she's *human*. And she was insolent."

"You're the one who was insolent—to me and to your brother," I interjected.

Sarfina's jaw tightened. She ignored me, staring at Liri. "Are you going to let this whore of an elf speak to me that way?"

"Careful how you address my intended, Sarfina," Liri said between clenched teeth.

My heart squeezed in panic, but I had no time to react before Sarfina was back to yelling.

"I knew it!" she cried. "The two of you plotted Cirrus's murder together."

I was speechless. Liri, on the other hand, brandished a smile that lit up his eyes. He *would* find delight in the idea of me conspiring with him to end my mate then take him in Cirrus's place.

I needed another flute of wine. I needed an entire bottle.

"As delightful as that story sounds, sweet Aerith is innocent of your claim." When he looked at me, his gaze softened. "Pity."

The skin around Sarfina's eyes crinkled, and her eyebrows pinched together. "I hate you!" she yelled at Liri.

The light in his eyes dimmed as his entire face darkened. "Careful, Sister. You are lucky you are a female, but that will only protect you so far."

Sarfina sucked in a breath and had the good sense to look scared.

"Return to your rooms," Liri said. "Your presence offends me." He turned his back to her, offering me his arm. "Take a turn with me, Aerith."

I nodded, wrapping my fingers around his arm, holding on as though he were a lifeline, even though I knew he was the very opposite—an anchor who would sink me to the bottom of the oceans if I didn't let go soon.

Liri's twin guards, Galather and Folas, followed from a distance.

"I apologize for my sister. Father always indulged her too much. Well, he indulged all of us." Liri grinned fondly of the father whose throat he'd slit. "I would also like to apologize for my actions last night—sending my guards into your bedchamber. It was most uncouth."

I looked sideways at him, surprised by his apology. The crowd glanced our way as we strolled through the ballroom, but everyone kept their distance. It was as though we were traversing a colorful tunnel of suits and gowns.

"Being cornered that way, it's no wonder you struck out at me," Liri continued. "I should have knocked on your front door first. I promise you, sweet Aerith, I will never enter your bedchamber unannounced or uninvited again."

My jaw relaxed a little. "I have your word?"

He inclined his head. "You have my word."

"What about this choker?" I asked, poking at the diamonds digging into my throat.

Liri stroked the back of the choker. "The clasp is back in place. You may remove it at any time."

He watched me as though half expecting I might rip the diamonds off in the middle of the ballroom. I left them untouched. Liri grinned.

"I understand that you are not a doll to be dressed, nor a pet to be collared." He took my hand and lifted my fingers to his lips. "Enjoy your ball, Aerith," he said huskily before kissing my hand. He released me and lifted his arm into the air.

At once, the music began anew and the crowd surged to the center of the ballroom where they spun and twirled. Liri strode forward, disappearing into the throng.

Well played. I had to hand it to Liri for offering compliments, apologies, and promises before making a well-timed retreat. He was clever, crafty—a skilled opponent.

My heart fell like an egg rolling off a table before cracking open on the floor.

How would I ever beat him?

Shrill laughter assaulted my ears. I knew the crowd wasn't laughing at me, but they might as well have been. They were all against me. My only champion was a Fae devil in a crown. Sobering thought. I didn't want to be sober. I wanted the sweet relief of faerie wine to make it all fade away, even if only for a night.

Diamonds flashed in my dark red skirts as I returned to the refreshment table. I tried to pace myself with the bubbling wine, but the more I drank, the more I wanted. Every sip brought jubilation to my head, making it hum and buzz. If I'd been human, I would have been tearing off my clothes, dancing naked in the middle of the ballroom, but being an elf, I was able to handle the faerie wine for much longer.

"Can I offer you some water, Princess Aerith?" one of the servants inquired politely.

I giggled in response.

"Princess Aerith?" He sounded so monotone, so boring.

I mimicked his voice in my head and laughed. The servant retained his neutral expression, ready to serve.

I hiccupped and blinked several times. "I need sleep, not water," I said.

"Can I fetch someone to escort you back to your chamber?"

I narrowed my eyes. "I am quite capable of walking to my rooms."

"Yes, of course, Princess Aerith." Still no emotion in his voice.

I needed someone more interesting to talk to. I took a step toward the dancers then stopped. No, I needed to get out of this den of debauchery. A game of campaigne. Yes! That was what I needed. Drunk Aerith against herself. It was sure to be a disaster. Bed sounded better. I'd recoup on the morrow.

I gathered myself up and walked out of the ballroom perfectly poised—and proud I was able to pull it off. Once in the hallway, I stumbled along, reaching out for the wall to steady myself. The oil paintings spun on the stone walls, their colors mixing into a kaleidoscopic blur. Marble statues spun as though they'd joined the dance. My reflection in the mirrors was the only thing that didn't spin, but it seemed to fade like the sun at twilight.

My feet led me to the north wing and my old room on instinct. It was where I was accustomed to retiring at the end of the evening. I shoved my way through the heavy door, entering the chamber of mirrors.

The first thing I did was remove the diamond choker and fling it at a mirror. When it struck the glass, I laughed. Next, I tossed off my bracelet and my earrings one after the other.

The gown was more difficult to remove without help, but I managed to burrow my way downward, exiting from the skirts. My hair came unbound in the struggle. Once freed, I plucked out the last of the pins, dropping them onto the floor. I kicked the gown aside and twirled naked in front of the mirrors, laughing harder and harder until the first sob escaped.

The sound undid me. I crumpled to the hard patch of floor and hugged my legs to my chest. Tears leaked from the corners of my eyes. I swiped them away, trying to take back control. I couldn't let anyone see me with red-rimmed eyes in the morning. I couldn't let them win.

Slowly, I pushed myself off the floor and took wavering steps to my bed. It wasn't made—like no one had expected me to return. The cream negligee was in the same heap I'd left it in on top of the covers. I pulled it over my head, preferring lace to nothing.

Warm air still wafted in. The perfect temperatures in Dahlquist never changed, not even at night. I wouldn't have minded a cool breeze over my flushed face.

Damn faerie wine.

I lay on my side then on my back, staring up into my own reflection in the oval mirror Cirrus had ordered attached to the ceiling above my bed.

I closed my eyes, but the spinning was worse with them shut. My stomach churned while the bed seemed to rock as though I'd been transported onto a ship at sea.

When I opened my eyes, the spinning stopped. So much for a good night's rest.

Consciousness was highly overrated.

Instead, I was left to relive distant memories. My body yearned for something I didn't want to think about but couldn't escape. With the exception of my monthly cycles, Cirrus had come to me every night. I hated to admit it, but making love to him had been my only relief in Faerie—intense pleasure followed by sweet slumber.

I breathed in and out, waiting for the spinning to stop. When it began to fade, my lashes fluttered closed and more memories of Cirrus flooded in. He was there on the bed with me, spreading my nightgown apart at the slit before entering my body. We were intertwined, pulsating in the reflection of every mirror.

I moaned and spread the lacy slit apart. I could give myself my own release. My own sweet slumber.

"Yes, that's it, my love. Spread your legs for me," a male voice said huskily.

Rage replaced yearning. I clamped my legs together and sat up.

"You promised not to—" The rest of my words were swallowed up by the shock of seeing not Liri lurking in the shadows of the room but Cirrus.

CHAPTER THIRTEEN

Aerith

This couldn't be real. Cirrus had been poisoned. Dead. Or was he?

No. No. No.

This meant we were still married. That I was bound to him again. My temporary freedom had been nothing more than an illusion. I'd resigned myself before, but I couldn't go back to the way things had been. I didn't think this nightmare could get any worse, but here was my golden-haired mate devouring all my hopes with hungry blue eyes.

My mouth gaped open, and I blinked over and over, but Cirrus didn't disappear. He was dressed in his white and gold-trimmed robe.

"How is this possible?" I asked, scrambling to my feet. I nearly fell getting off the bed as the faerie wine reminded me it hadn't fully left my system.

"I might as well be a captive like you." Cirrus made a growling sound at the back of his throat. "Liri poisoned me, though not fatally as he'd intended. Father ordered my physician to tell everyone I'd died so Liri would think he'd succeeded. I was still recovering when he slit Father's throat. I've taken refuge with my aunt in Ravensburg. We are readying an army to take back my kingdom—and crown."

My bones went slack, and my body turned leaden. I leaned against the edge of my bed to keep from fainting.

Game over.

Cirrus was the rightful heir, and I his lawful mate.

Liri had been right about one thing. I would become the queen of Dahlquist. But it wouldn't be by his side.

I wanted to scream. To cry. To wail. But that could bring guards running to my room, and I didn't want to be responsible for Cirrus's death a second time. We'd made a bargain—one in which I'd do everything in my power to keep him safe. More than a promise, it was binding, sealed by magic the day I wed him.

"Isn't it dangerous for you to be here?" I asked in alarm.

Cirrus moved toward me. "Perilous, but when I heard my brother had captured and brought you back to Dahlquist, I was willing to risk it all to see you, be with you, even for a night."

I hadn't noticed him reach me, not until his smooth, soft hand was on my thigh. I glanced down in confusion, still shocked. "But—"

"We don't have much time, my love." Cirrus eased me back onto the covers, my limbs dangling over the edge. He stepped between my legs and opened his robe, pushing it over his shoulders. The white silk spilled to the rug on the floor like milk, leaving my mate naked and hard.

"Cirrus, please," I begged, panic rising up my throat.

"Yes," he whispered. "Yes, my love, I will give you what you want."

But this wasn't what I wanted.

Please don't do this.

He spread my legs wider. Stepped closer.

Jhaeros! The name screamed through my head like the screech of an owl.

It didn't matter that I was mated. My heart, soul, and body belonged to only one male.

I jerked up and shoved Cirrus away from me.

His mouth opened in shock. He came toward me again. I slapped him across the face and scrambled for the glass lantern on my nightstand.

"You dare defy me? Your mate?" Cirrus roared.

"Shh!" I hissed. "Do you want to get yourself killed?" The fury in his eyes told me death was nothing compared to my disobedience. But he was still hard and still coming toward me.

I lifted the lantern. "Stay back," I warned.

"You have three seconds to get on the bed, Aerith," Cirrus snarled.

I narrowed my eyes. He'd never spoken to me this way before, but he'd never had any reason to. I'd never denied him until now.

When I didn't obey, Cirrus ran at me. I screamed and threw the lantern at him, but I missed. It crashed over the floor a couple feet behind him. Cirrus reached me and shoved me against a mirror on the wall.

"Let me go!" I screamed.

Cirrus's face wrinkled in anger. He opened his mouth, but a voice bellowed behind him.

"What is this?" Liri stood near the door, his three sisters and twin guards flanking him. They were all still dressed in their evening attire, unlike Cirrus, without a stitch of clothes, and me in the lace negligee.

Cirrus released his grip on me. His eyes went round in terror, and his body shook. He stepped away from me and turned slowly.

Liri stormed up to Cirrus and snarled in his face. "Who is this imposter?" he demanded before snapping his fingers. "Seize him."

Galather and Folas grabbed Cirrus. I might have pitied him if he hadn't tried to force himself on me. It wasn't like Cirrus to be violent or stupid.

"Show yourself," Liri commanded.

Cirrus grimaced right before the air around him shimmered and bent in on itself. Blond hair turned brown, blue eyes turned green, and the face morphed into one more round than oval—a face I did not recognize. Without thinking, I slapped the unfamiliar face then spit into it. The stranger snarled at me, and I hissed back.

Liri looked at his guards. They twisted the imposter's arms until he yelped. Liri prowled up to the restrained faerie, speaking in a low, dangerous tone as he did. "You dare take on the form of my dead brother?"

"I meant no offense to you, my king," the male said. "I was sent here for her." The imposter's nose wrinkled when referencing me.

I shuddered at the memory of his hand on my thigh and what would have happened if I hadn't stopped him.

"Well, that didn't take long," Teryani said, turning her head of moonlit white hair to the teal curls on her sister.

Jastra huffed. "Don't look at me."

The two sisters moved their gazes to Sarfina, who scowled. "So naturally you assume *I* arranged it."

"Didn't you?" Jastra challenged. As if she cared.

"Certainly not," Sarfina retorted. "If I were behind the attack, I would have instructed the intruder to kill her, not bed her."

"Enough!" Liri bellowed. He grabbed the imposter by the chin in a bone-crushing grip that made the male's eyes squeeze together in pain. "Who sent you? Tell me now."

The male pressed his lips together. A second later, he gasped out a name. "Jastra."

Liri released the male's jaw and nodded at his guards. "Take him to the dungeons."

The male's eyes expanded. "But, my king—"

"Leave him for me," Liri spoke over his head. "I'll castrate him myself."

Jastra sucked in a horrified breath.

Beside her, Teryani smirked. "What did you expect, Sister?" she asked in a voice as sweet as her pale pink lips. "He tried to hump the king's favorite pet."

I glared from Jastra to Teryani. I didn't know which of them I hated more. Equal hatred. Magnified. I wanted to do much more than spit in their faces. I wanted to plot their demise.

Ignoring Teryani, Jastra stomped up to her brother as her co-conspirator was dragged out of the room pleading pathetically. She stuck her teal head in front of his face. "You should be thanking me, Brother."

Sarfina snorted.

"And why should I do that, Jastra?" Liri asked in lethal tones.

"I meant Aerith no harm. This was a test to see where her loyalties lie—with you or with Cirrus. You should be pleased. She fought off the male she believed to be Cirrus."

Liri's jaw twitched. A smile twisted up his cheeks. "I am pleased," he acknowledged. Before Jastra could finish her sigh of relief, he added, "But Aerith is not. Apologize to her."

I couldn't see Jastra's face, but I saw the way her body stiffened.

"Well?" Liri said impatiently, raising a brow.

Jastra turned, chest lifting when she faced me. "I'm sorry," she said, looking over my shoulder rather than meeting my eyes.

"Address your sister-in-law properly," Liri said behind her.

Jastra's eyes flashed with anger, but she did as he asked. "I am so *very* sorry, Princess Aerith." This time she looked me in the eyes, narrowing them.

Liri looked at each of his sisters when he next spoke. "Aerith is not a pet. She's royalty, and, more importantly, a member of this family. She is not to be toyed with. Do I make myself clear?"

"Perfectly," Sarfina said with a sneer in my direction.

"It won't happen again," Jastra promised.

"Clear as mud," Teryani said.

Liri narrowed his eyes at his twin but made no further reprimand. "Very good, now leave us."

"Why?" Sarfina looked from Liri to me suspiciously.

"Why do you think?" Teryani asked in a tone of boredom. "Come along, Sarfina. Jastra. Give these two their privacy."

My face heated at her suggestive words, or maybe it was the faerie wine warming my cheeks like lanterns.

Jastra stormed out ahead rather than be led from the room by her white-haired older sister.

Sarfina followed, grumbling on the way out. "He better not fuck her in Cirrus's bed."

"He can do whatever he wants. He's king," Teryani returned. She closed the door on the way out.

As soon as they'd gone, there was only one person left to focus my glare on.

Liri wasn't looking at me. He was frowning at the silk robe puddled over the rug beside my bed. Storm clouds gathered in his eyes. He ripped the crown from his head and threw it at a mirror. Unlike the mirror that had taken a hit by my necklace, this one cracked apart and shattered over the floor.

My body jerked at the sharp noise.

"I am going to gut that deceiver," Liri bellowed. "He dares expose himself to you. Touch you." He snarled, his teeth clenched.

My shoulders slumped. "How did you know I was here?" I asked.

Liri lifted his head, huffing at the overhead mirror. "Jastra informed me she'd seen you wander out drunk and that she was worried." He lowered his head and shook it. "I should have known from the start that she set this up. Probably intended for me to walk in on you and—*him*." His upper lip curled. A second later, he schooled his expression and turned to me. "Why did you come to your old room?" He didn't look angry, merely perplexed. Curious.

"Old habit," I answered honestly. I winced. "And too much faerie wine."

"Ah, yes," Liri said, cracking open a smile. "Lucky for you I have a potent elixir that will help clear up the effects within a quarter hour. I'd already ordered its delivery to your rooms in the south wing. May I take you there?"

"Yes," I said, eager to escape the room of mirrors. I was even happy to accept the elixir from Liri, anything to settle my roiling stomach.

Liri strode to my armoire and retreated with a short cream robe. "This will have to do for now," he said, helping me slip into the arms.

Unfortunately, we had to pass the ballroom on our way to the south wing. Guests were beginning to take their leave and stared openly as Liri escorted me past them in my lace negligee and short silk robe. By morning, everyone would think I'd succumbed to him. I stole a look at Liri, whose eyes were trained forward as he steered me toward the south wing. He didn't gloat or acknowledge anyone we passed.

He didn't speak again until we'd passed through the double doors into the silent open hall overlooking the lake now reflecting the moon and stars.

"My sisters are all terrors. You are the only female I've ever trusted."

The truth and fervor of his words hit me like meteors. I felt like I was drifting through space the rest of the way to my room. Outside my door, Liri put his hands on my shoulders and gently turned me to face him. I was afraid if I looked into his eyes I would fall into their bottomless depths. Affection wasn't a feeling I could afford around Liri. But without the crown he looked more sincere, less imposing.

"Do you trust me, Aerith?" he asked in a whisper.

"Yes." I breathed out the truth. I despised him, but I

trusted him. He'd always been honest with me—overly honest, but it was the best attribute a Fae could offer.

"May I come inside and see that your rooms are safe?" he asked.

The thought of another Cirrus look-alike made me shudder. "Yes," I said again.

While Liri inspected each room, I hurried and changed out of the cream negligee into a long black silk nightdress that was left draped across the purple bedcover. I had to admit I liked the cool feel of the silk more than the itchy lace, and I especially liked the complete skirt with no slit. I wanted to burn the negligee and spread its ashes over a tar pit.

Liri returned to the bedroom holding a blue glass vial between his fingers. "Drink the whole thing, and you'll feel better. No side effects," he added, handing it to me.

It was a testament to my trust of him that I plucked a small cork from the top and swallowed the bitter liquid. Liri had, after all, poisoned his brother. I wrinkled my nose, but the bad taste quickly dissipated.

Liri smiled.

"Why did you do it?" I found myself asking. "Why did you kill Cirrus?" I nearly crushed the empty vial in my fist. I didn't mourn Cirrus, but what kind of monster killed his own brother and father? I knew why he'd taken out his father—to become king—but Liri and Cirrus had seemed close in the beginning—friends even.

The smile vanished from Liri's lips. One of his eyes twitched, making him appear annoyed. "He left me little choice. The fool made an attempt on my life."

"What?" The word flew from my mouth. This was the first I'd heard of Cirrus going after Liri. "But he was already heir."

"I imagine he wanted to keep it that way." An amused smile pushed at Liri's lips. "I also imagine he wanted to keep me from you. Perhaps he wasn't such a fool after all."

"When? How?" I demanded.

"The evening of the spring ball shortly after we danced a waltz together." His eyes lightened as though delighting in the memory of our dance, then darkened to gray clouds when he continued. "A footman brought me a glass of sparkling wine, which I offered to a noble female who prattled on about her family's three-day journey by carriage to Dahlquist. I offered her my glass to shut her up. Little did I know how effective it would be." Liri's wide grin showed all his teeth.

A gasp worked its way up my throat. "Lady Bryus?"

I remembered hearing of her death, but no details. Cirrus's demise had followed so closely behind the noble female's that it had been all but forgotten.

Liri nodded.

I shuddered. "That's horrible."

"Yes, who knew Cirrus could be so pitiless."

But that wasn't what I'd meant.

Liri ran his fingers through his silky white hair, brushing it back over his shoulder in an idle motion. "After the noble lady was found dead inside her chamber the next day, I tracked down the footman and made him confess the plot to end me. I had Galather take the servant to the lake and drown him. Then I repaid my brother with his lethal method of choice: poison."

"What about your father?" I knew why, but I still wanted to hear Liri confess since he was in such a sharing mood.

"Naturally he wasn't pleased I'd sent Cirrus off to the sky realm. He believed he was next and became excessively paranoid. In the end, it was either him or me." Liri's lashes fluttered on a sigh. "But let us not speak of the past. How do you like your new campaigne board?"

I regarded him for several seconds before offering the bland answer of, "It's nice."

Liri stood several feet from my bed, but he didn't glance at it once. Now that we were closed inside the room together, he kept his distance, giving me plenty of space.

"Interesting setup you laid out," he said. "We do not play this game in Faerie. Perhaps you will teach me sometime."

The faerie wine still buzzed in my veins, but I trusted the elixir to do its work soon. I tossed the empty vial in the waste receptacle beside a tall potted plant and stared at Liri. He raised a brow.

"I'm not unique," I blurted, ignoring his question. "You can trust other females. You just have to look for them. You'd probably have better luck outside of Faerie."

"You are more unique than you realize, sweet Aerith," Liri said. "My brother was a fool, but not when he went to the elven realms and chose you to be his mate."

"You could do the same, you know." When Liri's eyes turned lambent, I hastened to add, "You could search for a bride in the elven realms. A female untouched, worthy of the role of queen."

"A virgin?" he asked with amusement.

I nodded. Yes, exactly. He should find himself a doting, trustworthy virgin elf.

"I don't want a virgin. I want you."

"I am nothing special," I tried again.

"Sweet Aerith, the more you say that, the more special you become to me."

I scowled, which made him laugh.

"I will leave you to slumber in peace," he announced, sweeping by me toward the door. "And I will station a guard outside. You needn't worry about being disturbed."

"Thank you," I said.

Liri paused at the door, meeting my gaze. "Rest up, Aerith. Tomorrow I request your council on a most urgent matter."

"Oh?"

Rather than elaborate, Liri took his leave, closing me in alone.

Cryptic much? Well, I'd find out soon enough. With a loud sigh, I padded toward the purple bed, but before I could pull back the covers, I felt a nagging sense to check the campaigne board.

Picking up a single lit candle, I walked into the sitting room and held the flame near the game, noticing it wasn't as I'd left it. I knelt down and studied the changes Liri had made. My heart skipped a beat when I noticed he'd switched the marble archer for one carved out of onyx and placed it beside the dark king. I glanced over my shoulder, half expecting to see him standing behind me—a Cheshire grin on his lips.

Verifying I was still alone, I returned my attention to the board. In addition to switching the marble archer for onyx, he'd placed two dark shrubs in front of my piece, as though they were protecting me. He probably meant for them to represent Galather and Folas. I would have used two dark towers for the twins and placed them with the king, not the archer.

I huffed out a breath. Not only had he taken over my life, now he was trying to take over my game board.

One by one, I set the pieces in their rightful spots to begin afresh. Tomorrow was a new day. A new start. One step deeper into purgatory.

I'd underestimated Liri's resolve.

He wasn't just out to capture me.

He wanted to make sure I remained on the board indefinitely.

CHAPTER FOURTEEN

Melarue

Shopkeepers were opening the doors for the day when I arrived at Bilkin's travel shop in my favorite blue coat, sword sheathed at my side, and a pack stuffed to the gills with clothing and five full money purses hidden at the bottom.

The sign outside boasted: *No Realm Out of Reach.*

I was the first-and-only client to enter the travel shop this early. Faded posters papered the curved walls at odd angles. A yellowish one with exotic striped and spotted animals announced: *Africa. Take a trip on the wild side in the human realms.* Beside Africa there was a poster of a tall gray tower that shot up like an arrow into the sky. It read: *Paris. The most beautiful city in the mortal world.* And beside Paris: *Australia. For an unforgettable adventure a realm under.*

If my sister hadn't been kidnapped by Fae, I would have totally gone to any of those amazing destinations. All of them!

Below the posters, there were shelves filled with travel essentials such as fake rounded ears to slip on for visits to the human realms. The shop also offered a variety of hats from knitted ones that slipped on over the ears to baseball caps and safari hats.

There were very few items for traveling to Faerie besides a

metal tree that dangled with charms meant for protection. A bright, vibrant poster, four times the size of the mortal realm ones, showed a scene with lush, green rolling hills, a shimmering lake, and bright ribbons tied from branches of trees. A castle could be seen in the distance. I almost felt as though I could step into the poster and walk toward the castle. There were no words on this poster, but it was obvious the scene was from Faerie.

I passed all the curiosities that called out for fun amongst mortals, striding straight back to where Mr. Bilkin bent beside an electric kettle atop a stool next to more stools covered with tea bags and mugs.

"Good morning, sir." My voice boomed out in the quiet.

He remained bent over, not standing until he'd finished with his kettle. Mr. Bilkin's bones looked like they were groaning as he slowly rose and turned around. He wasn't tall enough to straighten much. He peered at me from behind thick round spectacles with wire rims.

"Good morning, young lady. You are calling early," he said as though I'd disturbed him during the breakfast hour at his cottage.

"Yep, all ready to head to Faerie," I chirped, patting the sword on my hip. "Dahlquist, to be specific. Round trip with passage for a second elf on the way back."

Mr. Bilkin grimaced, squeezing his eyes shut in his old wrinkled face. "My agent to the Faerie realms never returned from his last trip," he grumbled.

"I don't need an agent. Just point me to the nearest portal."

This time, Mr. Bilkin groaned aloud. "How about a trip to the mortal worlds? I have several reliable agents that regularly take travelers to the human realm." He leaned forward, smiling a little. "I bet you'd enjoy London and New York. I can book you the big city package."

"I want to go to Faerie." I stomped my foot.

"But—"

"Name your price. I'll pay it."

Mr. Bilkin glowered from behind his spectacles. "I cannot snap my fingers and send you to Faerie. You have to wait until a portal is opened, and those are rarely scheduled."

"So when's the next one?" I demanded.

"There are no portals currently scheduled." Mr. Bilkin growled in frustration.

I growled back. "Fine, then at least tell me the location of the portal."

"It changes all the time."

"Then how am I supposed to get to Faerie?"

"Believe me; you're better off not going. It's highly overrated. If it's castles you want to see, try Europe."

"I don't care about castles," I snarled. "I need to find my sister."

"Sorry, can't help you right now. Try back next month or next year."

I was too stunned to even be angry at first. "What kind of travel shop is this? Your sign says 'no realm out of reach.'"

Mr. Bilkin lifted his chin. "It isn't—when the timing is right."

Done with the useless codger, I stomped out of the shop, tempted to knock over the messy stack of rounded rubber ears on my way out. I shoved the front door open and stepped outside into the chilly morning. My breath fogged the air as I grumbled. "Oh pits." *Now what?*

"Going somewhere?" a husky voice drawled. Devdan leaned against the outer wall of the shop. He ran his hand through the thick patch of hair on the top of his head, which didn't even muss it up. So unfair.

"Trying to," I said as I headed back in the direction of my cottage.

Devdan fell into step beside me. "Where?"

"Faerie, but the old geezer can't get me there."

The playful smile on Devdan's lips turned over the moment I mentioned the "F" word. I didn't blame him there. Faerie definitely wasn't where I wanted to begin my grand adventure. Give me lions and tigers over Fae any day. When I was little, my mom had given me a book of Earth's most exotic animals and I'd dreamed of seeing them all ever since.

"Why?" he asked in a low voice.

"Because the Fae stole my sister, *again*, and this time it's all my fault!" I kicked a pebble off the ground. It sailed through the air and landed in the cobbled street roughly six paces away.

"What do you mean?" Devdan asked.

I continued toward the cottage, explaining everything I knew to Devdan along the way, starting with the twin faeries who had approached me after we parted ways at the market. Okay, so I didn't tell him absolutely *everything*. He didn't need to know how much they'd paid me for the diamond choker, only that they'd bought it from me.

"They were after Aerith. I know it," I said. "And even though I didn't see them, I know the bastards followed me home. I had this burning sensation in my body. I even broke out into a fever by the time I reached the cottage. Master Brygwyn told me that was my fire magic warning me of personal danger to me or my family. They took her the next night. I didn't even hear them."

That's what angered me the most. I'd been in the next room, and I hadn't heard a thing. I'd led the damn Fae straight to my sister and slept soundly while she struggled to fight them off. The next morning, when she hadn't risen as usual, I'd gone inside her room and seen the bedcovers tossed aside and the dagger lying on the ground. I'd known right then that she'd been kidnapped, but it wasn't until I'd gone over every detail leading up to her abduction with Keerla and Master Brygwyn that I'd put two and two together.

"Why would the Fae take her?" Devdan's face pinched in

worry. He sounded genuinely concerned, which made me want to kiss him, only I wasn't going to get smoochy until I rescued my sister and had her safely home.

"I'm not sure," I admitted. "I've reread all of the letters Aerith sent me during her time in Dahlquist, looking for clues. I always got the feeling she was careful with her words, like she was afraid her mate was reading them before he had the notes delivered, or our Father was, or both. Probably both." I scowled at my hands as though they were pages Aerith had taken painstaking care to write to me without giving too much away. She'd been imprisoned on so many levels, and now she'd been dragged back to that pit hole.

"May I try reading them?" Devdan asked.

I stopped in my tracks and narrowed my eyes at him.

"Those are private."

He rubbed his chin. "But I might be able to read between the lines. A fresh pair of eyes could help." He raised his brows, making them look like double question marks asking for permission. "You said her letters were guarded. If she wrote them to go through her mate and Father, what would it hurt for me to take a look?"

I tapped my fingers against my thigh. Devdan made a fair point. And it wasn't like I was headed through a portal to Faerie today—no thanks to Mr. Bilkin and his "some realms out of reach" travel shop.

"Fine," I said.

Twenty minutes later, Devdan sat on the sofa with the stack of Aerith's letters. "They're in order?" he asked.

"No," I said.

He sniffed in exasperation and without another word unfolded each piece of parchment and began arranging them in date order.

While he read, I paced around the cottage. At some point, it occurred to me to offer him sweetberry tea, but he declined. I paced some more, stealing glances at Devdan with his head bent over the letters in concentration. The only movement he made was when he turned a letter over or set it down and grabbed a new one. Watching him helped calm me, but I didn't want to stand there staring like some kind of love dove, so I went back to flitting around from room to room. I tried tidying up so the cottage would be shipshape when I returned with Aerith. Really, all I was doing was moving objects from one location to another.

Ten hours later, or maybe just two, Devdan set the last letter on the pile and stretched his arms over his head.

"Well?" I asked, hurrying over.

"I'll take that glass of sweetberry wine now," he said.

I scowled. "I offered you tea."

"Yeah, but that was in the morning. It's afternoon now." He grinned in his maddening way.

"So you didn't learn anything new from the letters."

"Oh, I learned a lot. I'm fairly certain I know who is responsible for kidnapping your sister."

"What? Who?" I demanded.

Devdan got to his feet and stretched again, this time more languidly, like a damn cat. He lowered his arms, taking his time to answer. "My coins are on the brother-in-law, *Leer-ee*." He leered at me as he said the name then chuckled.

"It's not funny," I said with a pout. "What makes you think it's him?"

Devdan dropped his smile and began fishing through the stack of letters. "His name comes up frequently." Devdan continued shuffling through the letters, eyes scanning over the parchment. He lifted one of the letters to his face and read aloud. "'Cirrus arranged for Lady Dearing's eldest daughter, Ialantha, to stay at the palace as a special guest during the harvest festival. He meant for Liri to woo her, but Liri scoffed as he always does when Cirrus tries to set him up. When Ialantha tried desperately to catch Liri's eye at the harvest dance, Liri insisted I dance with him so that Ialantha would not be able to bother him.'" Devdan looked up and met my eyes as though he'd just shared something noteworthy.

"So, he danced with Aerith? He just wanted to get away from Ialantha." I tried not to huff in frustration. Having Devdan read back missives I've already looked over wasn't helping me solve anything.

He smirked at me as though charmed by my lack of understanding. Undeterred, he read from another letter. "'With the extended family attending the winter ball, Cirrus and I decided it would be best for me to watch the festivities from a distance and keep an eye out for any odd behavior. When Liri found out, he raised a stink, as always, saying I was a princess, not a sentinel, and should be allowed to join in the dance. I tried to tell him I didn't care, that I was perfectly content to observe from the sidelines, but Liri wouldn't hear of it. Behind Cirrus's back, he had his twin sister, Teryani, glamour herself to look like me and for me to look like a visiting young High Fae female. I wanted to inform Cirrus, but the winter ball had already started and I knew telling him would put him into a rage that would ruin everyone's fun, including his own. The winter ball is one of Cirrus's favorites. I even suspect Liri was trying to ruin it for him, and you know how much I like to prevent Liri from getting his way. The scoundrel did give me every assurance that Teryani would watch out for Cirrus far better than I, a mere elf, ever could. And yes, he said it just like that. *Mere elf.* He underestimates me. Cirrus trusts me to protect him, and I plan to until my dying breath.'"

I groaned and gripped my neck in a strangling motion. "Bleh."

Devdan laughed, eyes shining, then continued reading. "'Despite the glamour, I watched out for Cirrus all night, much to Liri's disappointment. The following day, I told Cirrus what had happened, and we agreed it would be best for

Liri to claim a mate and spend less time at the palace. I do so hope he finally deems a female acceptable. He's trouble. A thorn in my side.'" Devdan lowered the letter. "He's obsessed with her is what he is."

"No, he's not," I said automatically, not because I was certain, but because I'd never come to that conclusion reading Aerith's letters. I put my hands on my hips. "Maybe you're the one who is obsessed with her."

Devdan set the letters down on the trunk table before looking me up and down, a smile lingering on his lips. "I told you she's not my type. I like redheads with sexy green-eyed glares."

I narrowed my eyes.

"Just like that," Devdan said, moistening his lips.

He could stop puckering up because I wasn't about to kiss him, even if he might possibly have gleaned something from the letters I'd totally missed.

The parchment crinkled as Devdan flipped through the pages. "Letter after letter talks about Liri hounding Aerith to join in the dances and faerie fun." Devdan snorted disdainfully. "He shows no interest in other females."

"According to Aerith," I said.

Devdan paused his shuffling of the letters to look up at me with raised brows.

"Who is a reliable and trustworthy source," I hastened to add. "I think you're right about Liri," I acknowledged. "I remember Aerith telling me in one of her letters that he had twin guards who followed him around like shadows, almost as if it was his life that needed guarding more than Cirrus's. I bet those were the same twins who approached me outside the market. I didn't trust them from the start." I wrinkled my nose.

"Yet you still sold them jewelry." Devdan laughed, the skin around his eyes crinkling in humor.

My mouth flew open to yell at him, but he was already

saying, "I would have done the same thing."

I nodded, I had more important things to do than discuss whether it was ethical to sell necklaces to nefarious faerie guards.

"So, we know who's most likely behind Aerith's abduction, but I still don't know how to get to Faerie."

Devdan's gaze became serious. "You can't just show up there expecting to grab your sister and get out. The Fae have magic."

"I have magic," I said, calling flames to my fingers. I lifted my hand to give him a closer reminder of my powers.

Devdan shook his head. "What about the male you mentioned here in Pinemist—the one your sister intended to wed? Shouldn't he go after her?"

"Jhaeros?" I snorted derisively. "Sure, he'll just waltz on up to the palace gates and politely inquire after my sister." I rolled my eyes. "He can't help Aerith. He'd only get himself killed by her obsessive brother-in-law."

"Glad we're in full agreement about Liri." Devdan grinned triumphantly.

I shrugged. "I don't know what his deal is, but I don't like it. He already killed at least one of his brothers."

Devdan's eyes bugged out of his head. "He murdered a member of his own family?"

"Yeah, just another Tuesday afternoon in Faerie."

Devdan's eyes remained wide. I'd had time to absorb the shock after Aerith filled me in on what led to her early release from Faerie. I wasn't a very good sister-in-law because I'd felt nothing short of ecstatic that Cirrus's death had brought my sister home. I only wished he'd been poisoned sooner. It was after Aerith returned that I started hearing the darker aspects of life in the palace at Dahlquist. I'd listened with rapt attention to the details Aerith had left out of her letters.

Her letters had made it sound as though she and Cirrus were of one mind, but after her return, it had been clear she despised him. Well, maybe not despised. I certainly despised him. Aerith had resigned herself to him. Would she submit to Liri too?

No, I couldn't believe it.

She'd entered an agreement with Cirrus on behalf of Father. What if Liri had made arrangements with Father? I wouldn't put it past the bastard. If Father had anything to do with Aerith's abduction, I might be tempted to consider family murder the way the Fae were known to do.

"I need to go to Sweetbell and speak to my father," I said, hastening to the door.

Pits, I should have gotten a horse while I had the chance. I wanted to take off at a gallop for Sweetbell.

"I'll go with you," Devdan said, catching up to me easily with his long, smooth strides.

Before I could tell him he'd already helped and I could take it from there, a knock shook the front door.

Devdan and I looked at one another for half a heartbeat before drawing our weapons. I hadn't noticed the dagger hidden beneath Devdan's tunic. He held it ready at the same time I'd pulled out my sword.

"Who is it?" I demanded.

"It's Lyklor," came the squeak of what sounded like a boy.

"Who?" I asked, focused intently on the door.

"I've been instructed to deliver an announcement to all the homes in Pinemist."

A messenger boy with an announcement for the whole town—that was rare. I sheathed my sword and opened the door. An elf of maybe fourteen years stood outside the door, clutching a cap in his hands.

Devdan stepped by my side, dagger still in his hands, staring mistrustfully at the boy.

"What's your news?" I asked impatiently.

"There is to be a tournament tomorrow at midday in the glade," he announced.

I narrowed my eyes. The Fae liked to hold tournaments when selecting brides from the elven realm. "A tournament for the Fae?" I demanded. This could be my ticket to Faerie.

The boy nodded.

Beside me, Devdan snarled. "How many brides do they intend to steal from us?"

The boy blinked. "It is not a bride they seek but two warriors to guard a Fae king's fiancée."

My heart skipped a beat. Could it be Aerith?

"Who is the fiancée? Is she an elf? What does she look like? What is her name?" With each question, I took a step toward the boy until I was in his face, gripping him by the shoulders.

His head bobbled as I attempted to shake the answers out of him. "I. Don't. Know," the boy said with each lurch.

I released him and scoffed with impatience. "I suppose it doesn't matter. I will be competing regardless—and winning."

The boy looked at me wide-eyed like he believed every word. He should. Winning the tournament was my ticket to Faerie. I wasn't about to lose my best chance at reaching my sister.

Devdan pursed his lips and regarded the boy carefully. "Do you know who this Fae King is?"

The boy nodded. "Oh yes. He visited Pinemist a couple years ago as a prince. The tournament is for King Liri of Dahlquist."

My heart slammed against my chest. "*King* Liri?" I squeaked.

The boy nodded.

I spun around, facing Devdan, seeing the shock on his face as well.

When had Liri become king? More alarming still, *how* had he become king? And most frightening of all, did this mean Aerith was his fiancée? Had she succumbed, or had he forced her hand?

"I *will* win that tournament," I growled. I only wished it was tonight.

CHAPTER FIFTEEN

Aerith

Purple covers slid from my arms as I sat up and stretched on the first morning in my new room. I'd slept dreamlessly, as though drugged. Maybe the elixir had made me extra drowsy. At least I awoke free of any head or stomachache. I still felt slightly queasy, but I attributed it to another morning waking up in Faerie.

I walked to the end of my apartments to brush out my hair and select a frock for the day.

Once dressed in a midnight blue gown, I pushed open my door and strode into the hallway. Not surprisingly, one of Liri's twin guards stood outside. Galather? I had a fifty-fifty chance of being right.

"Take me to Hensley's room," I commanded.

He sniffed at my order before grudgingly answering, "Follow me."

We headed for the open hallway, and Galather stopped outside a narrow door. It was a fair distance from my own, but given how deep my apartments ran, Hensley's room looked to be situated next door to mine.

Before I could knock, Galather stepped in front of me and pounded on the door. "Wake up, human. Your mistress beckons you."

"That's unnecessary," I snapped, glaring at him. "And I can speak for myself."

He folded his arms and grunted.

The brass knob turned as Hensley opened the door and peered tentatively into the hallway.

"May I come in?" I asked.

"Of course, Princess Aerith," Hensley said, widening her door.

When Galather made to follow me inside, I blocked his path in the doorframe.

"Not you," I said. "This is Hensley's private quarters. You can wait in the hallway."

Galather's lips folded over when he frowned. I stepped inside the room and closed the door behind me.

The room didn't lead off into adjoining apartments. It contained a single bed with a light purple quilt, similar in color to the dress she wore. A thick gray rug covered the stone floor below the bed. An armoire, dresser, and vanity lined the wall opposite her bed with large windows across from the door. Gray curtains had been pulled aside to let in the light.

It was sparse and simple yet cozy.

Now that we were alone, I inspected Hensley from head to foot. Despite Galather so rudely yelling for Hensley to wake up, she was dressed in a fresh lilac gown—a simple thin cotton frock with an empire waist. Her hair was neatly braided and her thick bangs smoothly combed.

"Are you okay?" I asked.

Appearances could be deceiving.

Hensley nodded. "I'm sorry if I spoiled your evening."

"You didn't spoil it. Sarfina did!" And Jastra. And Teryani. I was glad Liri could admit what terrors they were.

"Don't worry about me." Hensley smiled slightly. "I made it sound worse than it was so Sarfina would tire of tormenting me quicker."

I put my hands on my hips. "Did she plague you this way

while I was gone?" I hated to think of Sarfina toying with Hensley when the poor human didn't have a single ally to speak up on her behalf.

She shook her head. "No. She ignored me after you left. They all did. Don't worry about that."

But I did worry. I worried Hensley had been better off without me. I was the real reason Sarfina had attacked Hensley. If she weren't my lady-in-waiting, Liri's sisters would treat her with the same indifference they showed all the human help.

My frown had no effect on Hensley, who seemed to smile brighter. "The joke's on Sarfina. After I left the ballroom, I took advantage of the empty halls to fetch you a surprise." Eyes shimmering, Hensley hastened to her dresser, opened the bottom drawer, and tossed aside several layers of clothing before pulling out a dagger with a jeweled handle.

I hurried over and crouched beside her. "Where did you get that?" I whispered.

"Cirrus's old room. King Liri hasn't bothered to clean it out yet." Hensley glanced at the door before dropping her voice. "I'll sneak it into your room after the coast is clear." She tucked the dagger back into her drawer, placing garments over the blade.

After she closed the drawer, I threw my arms around her so tightly we nearly fell over onto the floor from our crouched positions. We burst out laughing at the same time.

Hensley's laughter was cut off when she said, "Just promise me you won't use it against King Liri."

The smile shriveled from my lips. "I promise," I said. "I don't believe he means me any harm."

"I know he doesn't," Hensley said. "He wants to keep you safe, but his sisters are another matter."

I knew that all too well.

A fist pounded at the door. I whirled around, imagining my glare chopping through wood to reach Galather. As

Hensley started for the door, I hastened in front of her and opened the door for myself.

Galather stood rigid in the hallway. "Princess Aerith, King Liri requests your presence in his throne room."

My heart jumped into my throat, blocking the flow of oxygen as my first fear played through my mind. I saw Liri asking—or rather commanding—me to marry him, to be his queen. I needed more time to figure my way out of this twisted maze.

My limbs turned to stone, locking me in place with the same immobility as a statue.

"I'll come with you," Hensley said behind me.

"Family only." Galather said the words slowly as though Hensley was dimwitted.

I took Hensley's hand in mine and gave her a reassuring squeeze. "I'll be fine."

Without looking back, I followed Galather to the double doors leading through the open hall, past the lake, through the next set of doors, and into the palace's wide main halls.

The throne room wasn't a place I'd frequented during my marriage to Cirrus. When I followed Galather into the grand open room, I half expected to see Merith still sitting on his red-cushioned throne. The ceilings were as high as a cathedral. There were even stained-glass windows beaming down colored light with the rays of the sun.

Centered at the end of the grand room were three stairs leading up to a platform on which the great wooden throne was placed. Leaves were carved into the wood. They curled around the legs of the chair as though trying to consume the chair. The thick red cushion had been removed, leaving behind a heavy polished wood seat.

Liri stood on the dais in front of the chair, as though to sit would mean strangulation by carved wooden vines. His sisters stood below him, keeping at least three feet apart from one another. I headed toward them, my heart still lodged in my throat. Galather did not follow me.

As I neared, the thick golden crown on Liri's head of white hair gleamed. He wore a midnight blue suit that matched the color of my dress.

When the three terrors turned their heads to look at me, I noticed the way they appraised my attire. Jastra and Sarfina scowled. Teryani smirked.

It wasn't like I'd coordinated with Liri that morning. I'd randomly grabbed this gown. Or had I?

I squinted at Liri's suit, trying to remember what had made me decide on the midnight blue gown. It had been the first one I'd seen when I opened my armoire. I wouldn't put it past Liri to have done more than rearrange my campaigne board. As soon as I returned to my room, I was mixing the gowns all around. He'd promised not to enter my chamber without permission, so hopefully we wouldn't end up matching like bookends again.

"Good, we're all here." Liri's voice filled the room as I stopped at the dais, doing like my sisters-in-law and keeping my distance. "I've called you all here to discuss the fate of our brother."

"And what do you mean by that?" Sarfina demanded, fists jamming into her hips. She wore another transparent white gown, this one over a tight baby blue slip. Her blonde-and-gold hair had been pulled into a high ponytail and tied with a light blue ribbon that matched her slip.

Teryani placed a delicate hand over her mouth and yawned, her lids briefly closing.

"Can he be trusted to live, or should I dispose of him now?" Liri asked stiffly.

My heart eased out of my throat, and I felt as though I'd lost fifteen pounds. My fate had yet to be sealed. This meeting wasn't about me; it was about Ryo. Perhaps I should have felt more horrified at what Liri proposed, but Faerie had a way of making such nefarious matters seem almost normal.

"You wicked brute!" Sarfina cried. "What did Ryo ever do to you? How can you even consider such a thing?"

Liri pursed his lips before calmly replying, "You are allowed your opinion and vote, Sarfina. From now on, I wish to consult with you, my closest family, on decisions regarding the realm, including its safety. Can Ryo be trusted not to attempt overthrowing me?"

"Too risky," Jastra said, flipping her teal hair from her shoulder to her back. Today she wore a sky blue gown with light green sequins. "Wiser to take care of him now before he gets a chance to make an attempt on your life."

Sarfina whirled on Jastra. "You'd forsake your own brother?"

Jastra straightened and narrowed her eyes at Sarfina. "I aim to serve my brother, the king. His safety and the stability of the realm matter above all else."

"You conniving bitch!" Sarfina started toward Jastra, her fingers curled like claws.

"Hold it right there," Liri commanded. "We haven't heard from Teryani yet."

Ah, yes, the twin terror. Dressed all in white, Teryani looked much as she had the night before with the same misleading angelic air. She never raised her voice, put her hands on her hips, or tossed her hair back like a filly whipping her tail. Her lips pressed together in a smile as tight as a pale pink rosebud before it blossomed.

"With Ryo out of the running, that might tempt our cousins to go after the crown," she said.

Liri scowled heavily.

"It is for you to decide, Brother," she added with calm ease.

He raised his brows—a silent command.

Teryani blinked once. "If I were in your position, I would either imprison him or marry him off to someone loyal to you." Teryani smiled serenely at the end of her proposal.

"And you, sweet Aerith, what would you have me do?" Liri asked, smiling for the first time.

His sisters all turned. I kept my eyes on Liri rather than meet their glares. I had my answer ready.

"This is no matter for me to speak on," I said.

"Of course it is," Liri insisted. "Tell me; should I allow Ryo to live?"

I'd never been fond of the raven-haired little monster, but that didn't mean I wanted him dead. I didn't want anyone dead, with the exception of the three sisters present. Could we vote on their disposal instead? What if I could pick only one? That would be the hardest choice of all.

I shook the fantasy away and answered, "Yes. You should allow Ryo to live. He's your younger brother."

Jastra snorted rudely. "That's the whole problem," she said as though I was daft.

I glared at her. "Ryo is Liri's responsibility to protect. Don't you think there's been enough death already?" I hissed.

Liri clasped his hands behind his back and paced the dais, no longer looking at any of us.

"I can think of one more I'd like to see," she returned, eyeing me pointedly.

Sarfina's pupils darted back and forth, following her brother's movements. "Liri, if you condemn Ryo, I will never forgive you."

Liri stopped pacing, looked down at Sarfina, and laughed. "You'll never forgive me for Cirrus. What's one more unforgivable act?"

Sarfina scowled and folded her arms beneath her breasts.

"Two of you advise me to show Ryo mercy," Liri drew his words out carefully. "And two of you advise that I take precaution and dispose of the poor bugger."

Teryani hadn't cast a solid stone at Ryo, but she didn't correct her brother either. She merely waited with the same angelic indifference that was her trademark.

Liri looked over our heads and nodded at his guard in back. "Folas, send in my brother."

Whoops, I'd guessed wrong on the twins.

We all turned and watched as Folas opened one of the arched doors. Ryo strutted through the door, head of thick, black hair held high as though he'd been summoned for knighthood. Folas's twin, Galather, walked in behind him—a tall moving wall that Ryo would smack into if he tried to flee. But Ryo moved swiftly toward the dais. He'd dressed in a midnight blue tunic and simple yet elegant cotton trousers. I didn't know how he'd guessed what color Liri would be wearing. Copying his brother was either extremely smart or dangerously foolish. Liri could see it as a show of solidarity or one of challenge.

Galather stopped beside his brother and the two twins remained, keeping their distance from the family gathering.

"Bro!" Ryo called out, adding a swagger to his step as he got closer. "And lovely sisters." He flashed a grin at the three females. "And Aerith. I heard you'd returned. Couldn't stay away from Faerie? Or maybe faeries couldn't stay away from you?" He winked.

Rather than snap at him, a fond smile played at the corner of Liri's lips. With graceful ease, he sat on his throne and homed in on his younger brother. "Step forward, Ryo."

Ryo walked to the edge of the dais and bowed.

Liri smirked as Ryo straightened. "Do you know why I've called you here this morning?"

"To determine my fate, I imagine." Ryo shrugged. "What's it to be? Banishment? The dungeon? The guillotine?"

Sarfina shuddered.

Liri steepled his fingers, eyes gleaming as though taking delight in Ryo's unruffled tone. "Perhaps there is a fourth option, little brother."

Ryo raised his dark brows.

"Marriage," Liri said.

Ryo glanced uncertainly in my direction, causing Liri to leap from his throne.

"Not to her, you imbecile!"

Ryo narrowed his eyes and clamped his jaw shut as though to stop himself from lobbing back a return insult.

Liri's chest rose and fell rapidly. His anger appeared to have interrupted whatever announcement followed the one of Ryo's betrothal.

"And who is to be our brother's lucky bride?" Teryani asked sweetly.

Liri's shoulders relaxed as he momentarily locked gazes with her before he returned his attention to Ryo. "Someone who has proven her loyalty to me. A woman I can trust not to conspire or make trouble. Someone who has been with us for some time now." When Liri didn't share a name, we all leaned forward. Was he going to tell us or make an announcement another time? An amused smile spread over Liri's lips. "Hensley."

Arctic air filled my lungs as dread prickled down my spine. I thought I might be the one coerced into marrying back into the Elmray family. I never dreamed Hensley would be in danger of such a tumultuous fate. The Elmrays would eat her alive.

Sarfina screamed. Jastra gasped in horror. Teryani was perhaps the most terrifying of all with her unreadable calm.

Ryo's lip curled in disdain. Before he could protest, Sarfina stepped in front of him.

"You cannot marry our brother, a prince of Dahlquist, to a human," Sarfina said, her nose wrinkling in disgust.

Jastra grabbed her teal hair at both sides of her head and tugged, her eyes squinting as though she caused herself physical pain. "How can I possibly call that human my sister-in-law?"

"At least marry me to a pretty elf," Ryo said. "Host a tournament like Cirrus did. I cannot marry a human." Ryo stuck his tongue out halfway as though he'd bitten into a lemon.

Liri's face turned to stone and his eyes to steel when he cut a look at Ryo. "Perhaps you'd rather marry the sky," Liri said in a low, ominous voice.

A shudder went through me, a reminder that Liri was a ruthless killer. Ryo seemed to remember this too.

"I will do as you command—marry the human," he said grudgingly. "May I be excused now?"

Liri nodded. "Galather will return you to your rooms." As Ryo stormed from the room, Liri grinned. "We made our first big decision as a family." He sounded genuinely pleased.

"*You* made it," Sarfina grit out between her teeth, only loud enough for those of us standing below the dais to hear.

"At least the little monster gets to live," Teryani sang back, facing forward as though she'd never responded to Sarfina's complaint.

"No thanks to you," Sarfina hissed. She cleared her throat and spoke up. "May I be excused as well, Brother?"

Liri flicked his wrist at her. "You may. And try remembering that ultimately you got your wish for Ryo's safety."

Sarfina's smile looked forced. As soon as she turned her back to Liri, I caught the murderous expression on her face. The loathing in her eyes momentarily stole my breath.

Liri looked at Jastra and raised one brow. "Do you wish to be excused as well?"

Jastra shook her head. "I'd rather stay with you, if I can be of service."

Liri nodded, moving his gaze to Teryani. "And you, Sister?"

Her smile was the kind that brought no warmth, like the sun back home during winter solstice. It was beautiful and blinding but transmitted no heat. "With your permission, I would like to accompany Folas on his assignment and observe tomorrow's tournament."

I looked at Teryani, willing her to divulge more—a fruitless endeavor. Tournaments made me think of my own ill-fated competition back in Pinemist, the one that had landed me in Faerie the first time. It wasn't like Liri was holding one on Ryo's account. He'd already chosen his brother's unfortunate bride.

Liri stared at Teryani for so long I thought he might never respond. Finally, he nodded. "You are there to observe only."

Teryani puckered her lips as she grinned, then turned and fluttered out of the room.

"That leaves you, sweet Aerith," Liri said, fixing me in his gaze. "Perhaps you would like to deliver the happy news to Hensley?"

I nodded numbly. For all I knew, Hensley would squeal in delight to be chosen to become a princess amongst the family she'd so readily served.

"Folas will escort you to Miss Allen's room."

"Who will guard you?" I blurted. Old instincts weren't so easily abandoned, especially now that I was back at the palace. I was used to worrying about Cirrus. He'd never wanted to be alone with any of his siblings—not without a guard or me. Preferably several trusted guards and me.

Liri wasn't one for soft expressions, but the usual steel in his eyes appeared to drift into wistful gray clouds.

Jastra stepped in front of her brother and shot me down with a contemptuous glare. "There is no one in all of Faerie my brother is safer with than me."

Ignoring the teal-headed nuisance, I stepped around Jastra to speak to Liri. "I will deliver your news to Hensley." I left out "happy." There was never happy news in Faerie, which was why this time I had to find a way to spirit Hensley away with me. No matter how adamant Hensley was to serve the Elmrays and call Dahlquist home, I had to get her out for her own good. Liri's sisters would eat her alive. I didn't trust Ryo for one hot second either. I wouldn't put it past him to take out his aggravation on poor, innocent Hensley. Helpless Hensley. She was human and, unfortunately, didn't stand a chance against Fae.

When I stepped into the corridor with Folas right behind me, I nearly ran into an apparition that turned out to be Teryani. With her pale skin and otherworldly beauty, she'd fit right in with a nest of vampires in the human realm. I had no doubt she could be as vicious as any bloodsucker.

"It is not time to leave yet," Folas said, mistaking Teryani's reason for lingering outside the throne room.

"Yes, I know. I wish to speak to my sister-in-law before we leave. I can walk her to her rooms." Teryani didn't sound so sweet now that her brother wasn't within earshot. Her tone was clipped—like chips of ice being hacked away from a glacier.

Folas frowned. "My orders are to escort Princess Aerith to the royal wing."

"Then follow behind us but not too closely." Teryani stared at Folas, unblinking until he nodded.

"Very well, Princess. You won't do anything mischievous?" he pleaded more than asked.

"Not today," she answered, which made Folas visibly relax but not me.

As soon as we were out of earshot of Folas, Teryani walked close enough for her arm to press against mine. I resisted the urge to pull away.

"I don't think it was loyalty to my twin that caused you to refuse the Cirrus glamour last night," she said matter-of-factly. "And it certainly wasn't out of love for Liri either."

I said nothing, wondering what she was getting at. Perhaps she was merely trying to frighten me. It wouldn't work. My fears had already come true. I'd been stolen from Pinemist, taken from my sister and my true love. Being back made me numb.

"Liri told me about the enchantment he placed over you," Teryani continued, "the one that would transport you to a Faerie dreamscape the first time you were bedded by another male."

My legs kept moving down the corridor. My feet pattered over the flagstones. I didn't respond.

"I think this male you were with is the real reason you fought off the one you believed to be your mate."

Speak or don't speak? Every reaction felt like one that could lead me straight off a cliff. If she'd known his name, she would have spoken it so she could watch my reaction. I could no longer allow myself to even think his name in case she managed a way to worm inside my mind using Fae magic.

And so I kept walking until somewhere along the way Teryani drifted off like smoke from a distant fire that had been carried away on a wind that could shift at any moment to return with choking finality.

CHAPTER SIXTEEN

Melarue

Clouds hovered above the glade, and fog curled two feet from the ground. The foggy breath of participants and onlookers added to the haze. All told, only a dozen elves had shown up at the glade. I imagined the rest of the townsfolk nestled comfortably inside cottages, drinking sweetberry tea beside crackling fires.

This tournament felt nothing like the summer spectacle my sister had competed in twenty months ago. But I wasn't here for the glory; I was here to win.

My sword felt as much a part of me as a limb, its solid, comforting weight at my hip.

Devdan had insisted on competing for the second spot, so I'd lent him a sword. We'd practiced the night before and early that morning. He'd stayed the night–sleeping on the couch. No funny business.

Now we were at the glade to show off our skills, along with three other elves. The turnout was pit poor, but competing to become a personal guard wasn't as glamorous as being made a princess.

One of the competing elves was a boy barely thirteen whose sword had rusted. I overheard him telling another shabbily dressed elf that his family had sent him in hopes he'd win and send home a healthy amount of coin for his services. Their situation reminded me of my family's after Mother died. I felt sorry for the young elf but not enough to give up my spot. This was a rescue mission.

A trumpet sounded, and two figures strode through the mist—one a petite female, the other a tall male. The female had long white hair and a white dress, making it appear as though she was dressed in the fog. The tall male with his blond hair bound in a low ponytail set my teeth on edge. I recognized the bastard as one of the twins who'd purchased the diamond choker.

One by one, I wrapped my fingers around the hilt of my sword.

"All those competing, gather round," he said.

Five of us strode forward, forming a semicircle around the blond Fae. The beautiful female in white stood just outside the circle, lips puckered, looking disappointed. Just wait until she saw my moves.

"Not you," Blondie said gruffly.

I looked around to see who the grumpy Fae had addressed only to find everyone looking at me. My lips parted in protest before any words emerged. I snapped my attention to Blondie, who looked straight at me. Fire threatened to flame through my coat sleeves.

"Why not?" I demanded.

"Yes, Folas. Why ever not?" the female in white purred, drifting closer to our group.

"She's Princess Aerith's sister," he said as though that was answer enough.

Blue eyes lit up in the female's face. Her irises seemed to contain the only color on her person. She appeared as delicate as a white rose with loose petals. The dainty female looked me over with as much scrutiny as I gave her. I'd say she looked impressed, which meant she had good instincts.

"Who better to guard Aerith than her own flesh and

blood?" the female asked.

I grinned. She made an excellent point.

Puffing up my chest, I announced, "Plus, I'm the best warrior you'll ever find even if a thousand elves showed up to compete."

Folas grunted.

"Hey, no fair," the boy with the rusty sword whined. "You can't choose her just because she's family."

I didn't feel as sorry for him now that he was bellyaching. I turned and stepped up to his face. "I'll fight all three of you right now," I said.

"No," Folas said. "You'll fight in the order that I call."

"Why not end this charade once and for all?" I challenged.

Folas narrowed his eyes. "You'll shut your mouth and do as I say."

"This isn't Faerie. You can't order me around," I snapped.

The female chuckled. A hand flew up to her mouth, and her eyes widened as though she couldn't believe she'd been the one to laugh.

Folas huffed out a breath of foggy air and turned to her. "You find this amusing, Teryani?"

"Don't you?" she asked sweetly.

"I have a job to do." He returned his attention to me, showing none of the amusement of his companion. "If you wish to compete to become one of your sister's guardians, then you will wait patiently and do as I instruct."

"Fine," I said, "but you'll be choosing me and Devdan here as Aerith's guards."

The female, Teryani, jerked her head in Devdan's direction, her eyes drinking him in as though he was sweetberry wine. Up and down her gaze ran, lingering in places where I'd never looked. I narrowed my eyes. She'd seemed cool, but she better not be entertaining any fantasies of elf-on-Fae action in that whitewashed head of hers.

Teryani moistened her pink lips. What male would want

to kiss lips that pale? Death lips? They looked like sugar cookies without enough frosting. I hoped, rather than believed, she was mated to Folas—not that a union ever stopped the Fae from infidelity if rumors were to be believed. The Fae weren't as honorable as elves.

"Is he family as well?" Teryani asked, her gaze still fastened on Devdan.

"He's a...friend," I finished after a pause.

The female's eyes lit up brighter. "A special friend of Aerith's?" she asked eagerly.

"A special friend of *mine*," I stated, not sure why a possessive surge came over me.

Devdan didn't contradict me or say anything at all. I had no idea how he'd reacted to my claim on him since he was a step behind me.

"Ah," the female said, sounding disappointed. "Does Aerith not have a personal champion who wishes to fight on her behalf?"

"Yeah," I said, taking a step closer, "me."

Teryani returned her gaze to me and grinned. For someone with pastel lips and clad all in white, she managed to make her smile come across dark.

"Aerith is lucky to have such a devoted sister."

Teryani pronounced the word "sister" as though it were somehow sinister. Looked like the white rose had thorns.

I had a wicked smile of my own, one that always made Aerith uneasy. I flashed Teryani my teeth. "Anyone who messes with my sister pays the price."

Teryani's smile widened. "I do believe her. Don't you, Folas?"

He frowned, not at me but at Teryani, as though her approval was a strike against me.

"Are we fighting or what?" I asked. Once he saw me in action, all his doubts would burn away with a flash of my fire magic and kick-ass sword moves.

"You," Folas said, pointing at the elf with the rusty sword. "And you," he said, pointing at Devdan.

I squeezed Devdan's arm. "Make that little pit head eat dirt."

He gave me a look that could have been amusement or exasperation. It was hard to tell since he needed to walk forward and commence with the fight.

Devdan was new to swordplay, but it was clear from the start he was stronger and faster than the younger elf. Pride washed through me every time Devdan crashed his blade over his opponent's. Silver flashed and cut down the sad, rusted sword again and again. It was pitiful, really, which made me want to feel sorry for the young male again.

After Devdan knocked the elf's sword out of his hand, I applauded. I mean, I felt bad, but that was my male kicking ass.

"You, you're out," Folas said to the young elf.

The scamp picked up his rusted sword, kicked a clump of dirt, and stormed off, cursing under his breath.

"Now, you three against her," Folas said. He didn't look at me. He didn't have to. We all knew what he meant.

I smiled in delight.

"I'm not fighting her," Devdan said.

"Then you can leave as well," Folas answered, sounding bored.

"What? No." I widened my eyes at Devdan.

He sighed and nodded.

I wrapped my fingers around the hilt of my sword and pulled it out in a motion that made the steel sing. I'd been practicing the move for weeks.

The two opponents beside Devdan stared at me in awe. That was my read on their wide-eyed, openmouthed stares, anyway. The shorter one blinked then charged me, sword raised. I jumped aside and swung at the other male, determined to make my first strike one of attack, not defense.

I was so confident that it took me aback when the male held strong then struck back. I whacked his blade with mine. Keerla would have winced, but this was three against one—anything went.

Actually, it was more like two against one. Devdan made weak attempts to come at me. At least he held on to his blade. It would have been an embarrassment to us both if he'd dropped his sword fighting me.

The two other males nodded at one another and stalked toward me, one from the front and one from behind, the tips of their blades pointed at me.

Devdan's jaw tightened as he started toward the male behind me. From the determined look in his eyes, I knew he was about to ruin everything by going after one of my opponents. I had to act fast before Folas noticed.

I flung one arm behind me, and my sword arm in front, sending fire shooting from my arms to my hands. Flames rolled down my blade as though it had been dipped in kerosene and lit with a match. Behind me, my sparks flew from my fingertips to the blade coming toward me, consuming the sword in swirls of red flames.

The elf behind me shrieked and dropped his blade as though the steel had burned him, even though it hadn't had time. *Element of surprise*, I thought with a wry grin.

The elf in front of me backed away.

Devdan jabbed his sword into the earth hard enough for it to stick and stand on end. He lifted his hands in surrender, a proud smile on his lips when he looked at me. I grinned back, wanting to kiss him in my moment of triumph.

"No fair. She has elemental magic," said the elf who'd dropped his weapon.

Not this again.

"Which makes her even more capable of guarding the princess," Folas said.

Finally, the brute was coming around to my side.

"Looks like you get your way, Red," Folas said, cutting a glance my way.

"It's Mel," I informed him haughtily as I sheathed my sword.

"Very well, Mel," he said, the grumpy tone returning, "I'll take you to Faerie. Just remember this isn't a social call. The king expects you to protect the princess—with your own life if you have to."

"Duh." I rolled my eyes.

Folas narrowed his. "And that goes for you as well."

I turned to share a smirk with Devdan, but as I twisted around, I saw Folas's long, pale finger pointing at the wrong male—the one who hadn't dropped his blade when I'd sent fire after him.

"Wrong elf, genius," I said. "That one's Devdan." I pointed at Dev, who was frowning tightly at Folas. I didn't blame him. Did the blond brute think all elves looked alike?

Teryani's eyes crinkled, and a wide smile spread over her cheeks as though she were about to laugh again.

Folas glowered at me. "I know which one is your lapdog, and I also know he'd choose to protect you before the princess."

"I'm no one's lapdog!" Devdan shouted, storming forward.

My cheeks burned hot right before flames engulfed my body. Devdan needed to stay back, Blondie was mine. I'd fry him to a crisp then hitch a ride to Faerie with Teryani.

Applause startled me out of my fury and lessened the heat of my flames.

Teryani clapped her pale hands in merriment. Once she had everyone's attention, she squeezed her hands together. "Folas, I think we should keep the happy couple together," she said sweetly.

I tried not to blush as she referred to Devdan and me as a couple. Being kissy didn't make us love doves, even though I'd become territorial over him. I didn't know what we were, only that I didn't want anyone else putting their lips on Dev.

"It's not your decision to make," Folas said in a harsh tone.

Teryani narrowed her eyes, the thorns coming out. Ice seemed to form in her irises, as if she possessed elemental magic too. In a flash, the frozen look melted away into an angelic face with fluttering lashes. Teryani swept up to Folas, running her fingers from his shoulder to his elbow as she flashed him a coy smile.

The voice that emerged between her pink lips floated out like a rainbow-infused lullaby. "Wouldn't it be nice to keep these two friends together? Faerie is such a long way away and can get rather lonely. Happy guards are much likelier to want to stick around doing their duty, serving the royal family, don't you think?"

Folas's gaze turned dreamy. The fog around us felt as if it had transformed into wispy clouds that we were all floating through blissfully. I leaned forward, not wanting to miss a word of Teryani's beautiful song. But it had come to an end.

I blinked and stared at her in wonder.

Wicked.

Folas still wore a stupefied expression as he nodded. "You and you," he said, head bobbing at me then Devdan. "Congratulations. You're about to enter the service of King Liri, ruler of Dahlquist. Gather your things and meet me back here in two hours."

"We already have our things," I announced.

"Very well. Follow me then," Folas said.

I quickly grabbed my pack and smiled at Devdan, whose grin looked more like a grimace. At least he wasn't staring all dreamy-eyed at the enchantress in white.

We did it! I wanted to shout before eyeing the Fae responsible for making certain Dev accompanied me to Faerie. I fell into step beside Teryani and asked, "Why did you help me?" I would have liked her smile a lot better if it weren't the same coy one she'd used on Folas.

"I want us to be friends, Mel." Her voice sounded different when she said my name. It sounded normal, like she couldn't turn the succinct sound of it into singsong.

"And why would you want to be friends?" I asked suspiciously.

"Because your sister is my sister-in-law." Teryani smiled. "That practically makes us sisters."

I stared at her harder.

"Did Aerith not mention me?" Teryani's lips formed a pout, but her eyes were bright with amusement rather than hurt.

I shrugged and answered, "From the sounds of it, you have a large family, though a little short on males these days."

Teryani's laughter was filled with sugarcoated delight. "True enough. Still, I wish Aerith had mentioned you before. I would have liked to have met you earlier."

"Cirrus didn't want me visiting," I said, frowning.

"Good thing he's dead." Teryani winked.

I couldn't tell if she was joking. I'd never be able to understand the Fae.

She laced a soft white arm around mine. "Liri will be delighted by your presence. He wishes Aerith to be happy, and I can see the two of you have a very special sisterly bond. Once you join our household, there will be no reason for her to miss this soggy, cold, mist-covered town."

I chewed on my bottom lip, unable to stop my brain from thinking of a gargantuan reason Aerith would miss Pinemist.

Jhaeros had already come calling twice. Both times I'd pretended not to be home. He had no idea Aerith was missing. With any luck, I'd have her back before he figured out something was terribly wrong and panicked. I knew what it was like to worry, and I wouldn't wish that on anyone, not even boring old Jhaeros Keasandoral.

"I can't wait to meet Liri," I said pleasantly.

"King Liri." Folas turned his head and narrowed his eyes at me, apparently waking from the enchantment Teryani had placed over him.

"Yeah, King Liri," I fired back impatiently. I softened my voice when I redirected my conversation to Teryani. "I've only ever heard about him in letters."

"Your sister wrote to you about Liri?" Teryani asked as her delicately shaped platinum eyebrows rose.

I nodded. "It sounded like they were close."

I might not be able to enchant other beings, but I did know how to manipulate and read an audience—even a sly Fae like Teryani. She ate my words right up, grinning with pleasure.

"Is that so?" she asked, pulling me closer.

Aerith's sister-in-law said she wanted to be friends, but as far as I was concerned, all Fae were foes. The more angelic-looking, the more likely to be devious.

I could be devious too. "Uh-huh. She barely mentioned Cirrus at all. It was always Liri this and Liri that."

Folas cleared his throat.

"Well, he wasn't king at the time," I said stubbornly.

"My brother will be pleased to hear of Aerith's regard for him," Teryani said.

"You can't tell him. I shouldn't even be telling you. Those are private letters my sister wrote to me." I didn't care if Teryani went prattling to her brother. She clearly preferred Liri over Cirrus and expected Aerith to share in her fondness. I'd also made myself sound like an ally she could count on.

"Not to worry," she said with an overly sweet grin.

Clever Fae. Her answer made no promises.

The fog cleared ahead with the exception of a large round swirling mass of wispy white air that churned violently, reminding me of a tornado turned sideways.

It must be a portal to Faerie!

Everything was almost perfect until Jhaeros showed up,

203

cantering across the field like a damn knight to a battle. *A little late for that, Jhaer.* I'd already won. He could thank me after I returned with my sister. I was literally three steps closer to reaching her as he charged at us, hair windblown, cheeks rosy, and brown eyes so bright they looked like melted caramel. His mid-length coat blew open at the sides, exposing a partially unbuttoned white shirt. He looked more like a rogue in his disheveled state than his usual tight-collared attire.

"Melarue!" he yelled, jumping down from his horse.

The agile way he landed on his feet made my mouth part in admiration. It was at times like these that I got a small glimpse into the appeal Aerith saw when it came to Jhaeros.

But there was no time to gawk. Teryani had been way too keen on uprooting any males who might hold a special place in Aerith's heart.

I took another step toward the swirling mist, hoping Teryani would do the same. "Heya," I called over my shoulder. "Got places to be, but I'll drop you a line after I'm settled in Faerie."

As Jhaeros strode up to our group, Folas folded his arms, locking his gaze on Jhaeros while Teryani anchored herself to the ground as though she'd turned to lead.

"Where's Aerith?" Jhaeros demanded.

Oh pitberries!

I scowled at Jhaeros, willing him to shut his trap.

Teryani drifted over to Jhaeros, her smile thinning. "And who is this?" she asked.

"Nobody," I said quickly. No, that wouldn't do. "He's engaged to our other sister," I amended. "Our father probably sent him to try to stop me from joining Aerith in Faerie." I faced Jhaeros, beseeching Sky Mother to make him play along as I addressed him directly. "Don't worry. I'm sure Aerith and I will be granted leave to attend your wedding." I widened my eyes, as though that would help transfer my thoughts to him.

A supposed family wedding would make a brilliant excuse to return with Aerith to Pinemist.

But Jhaeros bared his teeth in misguided outrage. "What's gotten into you, Melarue? And what is Aerith doing back in Faerie?" When I pressed my lips together, Jhaeros looked around the group. "Perhaps one of you can explain?" His tone was commanding, but he was up against Fae.

"I'll explain in a letter," I said, making one last attempt to protect him. "Right now, I'm anxious to get to my new post as Aerith's personal guard. I'll be sure to tell her you said 'hello' and that you expect her attendance at the wedding. Now, good day." I inched my way to the swirling mass, halting a foot from the opening. I looked over my shoulder and groaned inwardly when I saw that Teryani hadn't budged.

"Perhaps I can explain things," the Fae princess said, her words dripping like thick, sticky honey. She turned her head to Folas. "Take them. I'll follow momentarily."

As Folas's arm shot out, and his hand gripped my wrist, my mouth flew open.

"Don't listen to—" My words were swept away as Folas tossed me into the swirling mist that sucked me backward into a tunnel of wind and blinding white light.

CHAPTER SEVENTEEN

Melarue

My hair streamed on either side of my cheeks in rippling ribbons of red. I fought to breathe through the vortex of wind. A sensation of flying took hold, except I wasn't facing the right direction.

Everything sped up right before I shot out of the swirling tunnel. I stumbled backward, barely managing to keep my footing. Grass as brilliant as cut emeralds was crushed beneath my boots as I regained my balance and breath. Sunshine blazed down over rolling hills. There wasn't a whiff of mist to be seen nor a tingle of winter's chill. My coat, which had felt too thin moments before, turned stifling in the heat.

Before I could turn and take a look in the opposite direction, Devdan appeared, as though from thin air, hurtling toward me, face forward like he'd run after me rather than been yanked into the portal. His eyes widened right before he ran into me, knocking me off my feet and onto the ground.

"Oomph!" Air expelled from my chest when Devdan landed on me.

He jumped back to his feet, dragging me up with him. "Are you okay?" he asked, looking me over with concern.

"I'm fine, but who knows about Jhaeros? Couldn't he tell I

was trying to warn him?"

Devdan opened his mouth to answer then closed it as Folas appeared. The blond guard strolled casually our way. "Welcome to the kingdom of Dahlquist," he said begrudgingly. "We must walk the rest of the way to the castle."

"What castle?" I demanded, squinting into the endless green hills.

Devdan took me by the shoulders and spun me around.

"Ohh," I said, staring in wonder at the turrets and spires rising in the brilliant sky. I'd never seen a castle until now. It looked magical and imposing. "We get to live there?" I asked, momentarily forgetting my mission. This was the stuff of fairy tales, legends, and myths. My legs were already moving faster, eager to reach the grand palace—and my sister.

Devdan jogged to my side to catch up. I couldn't stop staring at the castle. A nagging feeling at the back of my head slowed my steps until I came to an abrupt halt. I glanced over my shoulder at the endless hills. There were no homes or signs of life on them. They almost looked like a portrait that had been pasted across the horizon.

"What about Teryani?" I asked, chewing on the inside of my cheek.

"She might take a while," Folas said.

His answer set my teeth on edge.

"She won't hurt Jhaeros, right?"

"One never knows with Princess Teryani," Folas said. "Maybe she has something more pleasurable in store for him." He smirked.

I narrowed my eyes. "She better keep her hands to herself. That's my sister's future mate."

"Are all elves this possessive?" Folas didn't hang around for an answer. He strode forward. "Hurry up."

Devdan and I exchanged glances.

"He'll be okay, right?" I asked Dev, wanting him to

reassure me so I could go back to feeling excited about entering the castle and seeing my sister.

Devdan shrugged, his lips pursed, not looking convinced of anything.

Well, there was only one direction that led someplace. It wasn't as though I could create my own portal back to Pinemist to check on Jhaeros. He was a grown male. He should be able to take care of himself. Hopefully.

By the time we reached the castle's moat, sweat dotted my hairline.

"Is it always hot in Faerie?" I asked.

"It's summer," Folas said. "And the weather isn't the same in all of Faerie."

A drawbridge had been left down, almost as though waiting for us. I hurried to it, the first to step onto the heavy wood planks.

Faces peered at us from the watchtower, but no one called down. The castle gate led into a courtyard bustling with activity that reminded me at once of market day back in Pinemist—but much more chaotic.

Our path was blocked by a pair of oxen hitched to a cart with eight large barrels that were being unloaded from the back. Folas weaved around it. Devdan and I followed, turning sideways to avoid being bashed in the head by a heavy log a Fae carried over his shoulder. Behind the oxen, a wagon filled with a towering pile of straw hindered our route. Folas ducked beneath a thatched awning into a room bustling with activity and the stench of uncooked meat. *Whack. Whack. Whack.* A butcher knife hacked off chunks of raw flesh. Workers in aprons salted the pieces of meat then attached them to heavy hooks that hung from the rafters. Not all the workers were Fae—some had rounded ears. Flies buzzed around buckets filled with blood and guts.

I pinched my nose closed with my fingers, hurrying after Folas. He led us out of the stall and past a dead pig hanging upside down, its throat slit and blood draining into a bucket below. We rounded a wood partition, which took us past a pen squeezed tight with pigs.

"What time's dinner?" I asked to try to lighten the mood, but Folas marched forward without so much as a grunt.

We passed stables filled with horses, wandering goats that tried nibbling on burlap sacks, and stores of grains that a black cat watched over, tail swishing as it waited patiently for mice.

I glanced over my shoulder, mouth ajar. The castle courtyard was like a town of its own.

Gradually, the noise died down the deeper we traversed into the castle's belly. We reached another stone wall and gate, this one leading into a courtyard lined with hanging clothes drying in the sun. The women washing and rinsing garments from baskets all looked like humans.

This courtyard led into yet another one bursting with roses, sunflowers, dahlias, and lavender. Water trickled from a large circular fountain in the center of the garden. Two peacocks strutted across the stone path as we passed through.

From the courtyard of flowers, Folas brought us to a heavy wooden door that led inside.

I half expected to see Aerith waiting inside the corridor. "Where's my sister?" I asked as we entered the palace.

"First you are to report to King Liri for inspection and instruction," Folas said.

I pursed my lips, impatient to be reunited with my sister. I kept my eyes peeled for Aerith in the halls, but all I saw were unfamiliar faces in pretty clothes. Most of them ignored Devdan and me. Some cast curious glances our way.

Folas took us to a tall set of double doors where his twin stood waiting. His brows rose when he looked past his brother at me. I smiled and waved. He frowned, turning his head to his twin.

"What's she doing here?"

"She demonstrated superior fighting skills."

I lifted my chin proudly.

"I don't think it's a good idea."

"That's for the king to decide. Is he inside?"

"Go ahead and report to him. I will keep an eye on these two," Folas's twin said, stepping away from the door.

"You two wait here until you're told you can enter," Folas said as he pulled the door open and disappeared into the room on the other side of the stone wall.

"So, what's your name?" I asked the Folas look-alike glowering at Devdan and me.

"What's yours?" he said in a haughty tone filled with challenge.

"I'm Mel, and this is Devdan."

The blond Fae wrinkled his nose, showing how little he thought of us and our names.

"So?" I prodded. "Who are you?"

He pursed his lips and glared at me as though we'd entered some kind of staring contest. Only, this was a not-sharing-names contest, which I'd already lost by telling him both my name and Devdan's.

"His name is Galather," a familiar female voice sang out in merriment.

I spun around and watched as Teryani strode up to the door, fluttering to a stop in front of us. I narrowed my eyes.

"What happened back in Pinemist after I was shoved into the portal?" I demanded.

"Nothing noteworthy," Teryani said, eyelashes fluttering in false innocence.

I tried to read her expression, but it was as bland as the color of her hair and clothes. At least she hadn't been far behind us. There wouldn't have been time to seduce Jhaeros.

My shoulders began to relax.

Hold up, Mel. She definitely had enough time to kill him.

I tensed and dropped my gaze to Teryani's delicate hands,

searching for blood.

A tinkling laugh emerged from the Fae princess's lips. "Don't fret, Mel. Your sister's beloved is perfectly safe. I merely wished to assure him of your safety and Aerith's."

My fingers twitched over my thigh, unsure whether she knew the truth. "Your sister" could have meant Aerith or Shalendra, but I'd never told Teryani Shalendra's name. Maybe Jhaeros had. Or maybe he hadn't and that's why she'd said "your sister."

I pursed my lips while Teryani flashed me a dazzling smile. I'd heard somewhere that Fae couldn't lie, which meant that if Teryani said Jhaeros were safe, I could stop worrying about him and refocus on getting my sister the freak out of Faerie.

The wood door groaned as Folas opened it. He noticed Teryani and raised his brows. "Any trouble?"

"Not even the tiniest," Teryani said sweetly.

"Was he who he said?"

She nodded, grinning. "Her sister's sweetheart," she answered, inclining her head in my direction. "Though a wedding date has not been set."

I couldn't tell whether she was helping me out again. I doubted Jhaeros had wised up after my abrupt departure and gone along with my cleverly constructed ruse. If Teryani knew Jhaeros was in love with Aerith, she wasn't sharing it—for now. Nor had she lied.

"King Liri is ready to see you," Folas said to Devdan and me. "Remember to bow when you reach the dais."

I glanced at Devdan, who wrinkled his nose and shot me a look that read, "What in the seven hells have you gotten us into?"

I shrugged and strode forward, ready to get my first look at Aerith's doting brother-in-law.

The room was one of ginormous proportions: a massive space from wall to wall and floor to ceiling where light streamed in through stained glass windows. So much space, yet only one piece of furniture—a throne atop a dais on which sat the king dressed in black wearing a gold crown. He had a pale oval face and long white hair like Teryani's. In fact, aside from their conflicting choices of colors, they looked a lot alike. Aerith had never mentioned Cirrus's sisters by name, almost as though she'd wanted to pretend they didn't exist. If I had to guess, I'd say Teryani was Liri's twin.

The princess and Folas trailed in behind Devdan and me. Steely gray eyes followed our movements. Once we were five feet from the dais, Devdan and I came to a stop and bowed.

"You look nothing like her," came a sharp voice. His lips pursed as though finding me lacking. Although it was summer in Dahlquist, the king looked cold as snow.

The wintry white male shouldn't judge. Jhaeros looked like a total stud while Liri paled, *haha*, in comparison.

I tried not to glower as I met Liri's scrutinizing gaze. "We can't all be twins," I answered tartly.

Folas stepped forward. "This one has a mouth on her. Say the word and I'll dump her back in Pinemist."

"Wait," Teryani said. "I think you will find her useful."

The king narrowed his eyes at his sister. "*I* will, or *you* will?"

"Her presence will make Aerith happy." Teryani shrugged as though Aerith's happiness mattered little to her.

The king's gaze returned to me. "Do you think being blood related makes you qualified to protect Princess Aerith?"

"No. I think my sword does." I patted the blade at my hip and grinned. "Oh, and this." I turned my hands over, palms up, summoning fire that swirled into balls of flame.

"She has fire magic?" the king asked, unease lacing his words.

That's right, force to be reckoned with right here. He should be concerned—and watch his back.

I smiled smugly.

"Yes, sire," Folas answered.

I curled my fingers, smothering my beautiful flames.

"And what of the male?" The king slid his gaze over to Devdan.

"He had the best skills out of all of the males," Folas said, leaving out the part about only three other males in Pinemist competing.

"Very well," the king said. He looked down at Devdan and me. "One of you will watch Princess Aerith during the day, and one of you will guard her at night. Should any harm come to the princess, you will suffer a punishment most severe—regardless of your relation to her," he added, staring pointedly at me.

"Works for me," I said, staring right back.

"Folas, show them to their quarters and explain their duties in more detail." The king flicked a slender white wrist at Folas.

I was really beginning to understand why Aerith had gone starry-eyed with Jhaeros. He was slender yet built, with rugged good looks, especially compared to King Liri, who, like his sister, looked cold and way too pretty.

As we followed Folas out of the throne room, I heard the king command his sister to remain behind. Hopefully she wouldn't share any more insights into Jhaeros. When it came between King Cold and Jhaeros Keasandoral, I was most definitely rooting for Jhaeros. We elves had to stick together.

Out in the stone corridor, Folas nodded to his twin before setting off at a decent clip through the hall. "Royal guards sleep in the north wing," he began.

"Where is Aerith's room?"

"Princess Aerith's quarters are in the south wing," Folas answered. Before he could add anything more, my next question burst forward.

"Shouldn't our quarters be next to hers?"

Folas turned his head and snarled at me. "Can you be quiet for even a minute? It doesn't matter that your room is in the north wing. None of the guards spend much time in their rooms, besides sleeping. Princess Aerith will never be left unguarded. When it's time for the two of you to switch, you will do so outside her quarters or wherever she might be at the time. I suggest you use the remainder of our walk to decide which one of you will take nights and which one days. After we reach your rooms, you will only see one another in passing." A cruel smile jerked up Folas's lips.

For once, my questions settled into the pit of my stomach.

This had never been part of the deal. I should have known the Fae would hide important details in the fine print. Not that we'd signed any contracts. When I glanced at Devdan, tears welled up in my eyes. I blinked them away, but Dev had seen. The concern in his gaze tugged at my heart. Is this how Jhaeros made Aerith feel? I had to remind myself this situation was far from permanent.

"You take days," Devdan said gently. "It will give you more time with your sister."

Folas grunted. "Good idea. Mel, here, might not like what happens at night."

With Folas's back to us, he avoided the missiles I launched at him with my fiery glare.

"Don't listen to him. He's a pit head," Devdan said.

"With a pit where his heart should be," I added.

I glanced at Devdan, hoping to share a smirk, but his lips were pressed into a frown. I wanted to reassure him everything would be okay, but my attention kept getting whisked away peering down passages and wondering where they led. Being Aerith's guard wouldn't allow for a whole lot of exploring. I'd have to save that for nighttime.

I lost track of all the hallways we'd passed to reach what Folas announced as the royal guards' quarters of the north wing. He pushed open a narrow door that led into a tiny chamber with a single bed, wood chair, and a narrow table with a pitcher and washing bowl on top.

"The one next door is identical," Folas announced.

"You take this one," Devdan said. He'd been on his best behavior since arriving in Faerie. It was unnerving.

After we'd stuffed our few belongings into our rooms, Folas took us on another long walk to the south wing.

"You both need to know where Princess Aerith's apartments are located," Folas said. "Afterward, I suggest you return to your room and try to get some sleep." This he said to Devdan.

My heart skipped inside my chest as every step took me closer to my sister. Was she expecting me? Or would this be a surprise? Either way, I couldn't wait to see the look in her eyes.

After reaching an ornately carved door in the south wing, Folas knocked and announced himself. When Aerith answered, her mouth and eyes flew open in utter shock.

"Mel!" she gasped, as though seeing a ghost.

CHAPTER EIGHTEEN

Aerith

Even in the daylight, the dark halls had a way of playing tricks on the eyes.

It had to be a glamour. No way was my sister standing outside my room at the palace in Dahlquist. And standing beside her . . . Devdan? I glanced at him before returning my wide-eyed stare to the redhead smiling brightly, chin tilted up with pride.

Yeah, this was Mel all right.

"What are you doing here?" I demanded.

"I'm your new guard." Mel lifted her chest and grinned.

I blinked, still unsure if my eyes were playing tricks on me. "My new what?"

"Guards. Devdan and I competed and won positions as your personal guards. I'm taking the day shift, and Devdan will keep watch outside your door at night."

Horror clamped around my heart like icy fingers. Suddenly, the two shrubs Liri had placed beside the onyx archer made sense. Was bringing my sister to Faerie some twisted part of the game?

"Mel, no. You can't be here." I looked at Folas. "You have to return them to Pinemist."

"King Liri insisted you have your own guards. These two

won fair and square."

Naturally, the blond sentinel belonging to Liri was no help at all.

"It wasn't as grand as your tournament, but we still triumphed," Mel said, practically bouncing on her toes.

She had no idea what she'd gotten herself into. She acted like this was just another adventure.

Folas stepped up to Mel and shot her a severe glare. "Listen up, fireball. From here on out you wait outside Princess Aerith's rooms and only leave your post to follow behind her. You only speak when spoken to. If anyone attempts to cause the princess harm, you stop them by any means necessary. Got it?"

Mel saluted him.

Folas glared. "This is not a game."

"Got it," Mel said.

Folas stepped over to Devdan. "Same goes for you. You guard the door outside Princess Aerith's chamber at night. You and Mel will switch posts after dinner. King Liri hosts many late-night balls, which means you will be responsible for keeping an eye on the princess during the parties. Just don't hover too close." He narrowed his eyes in warning.

"I'm going to miss the balls and parties?" Mel bellyached, showing her first true frown of concern.

"Need I remind you that you are not here to participate in the revelries?" Folas snapped. "Your only concern should be for Princess Aerith's safety."

My body felt as though it might float away. As though I weren't really here. As though I were dreaming.

It all felt so wrong. I was the big sister. I was the one who should be looking out for Mel's safety, not the other way around.

I didn't even have the energy to summon up anger when Devdan clasped my sister's hands, leaned his forehead near hers, and told her to be safe.

Now *he* was looking out for her? The snake? I'd only been gone three days, but it felt like months.

Once Devdan was dismissed and dragged his feet reluctantly down the hall, I latched on to Mel's arm and pulled her into my room, shooting Folas with a warning glare. I didn't care what he'd said about Mel standing outside in the hall. I slammed my door in his face.

Whirling around, I found my sister not beside me where I'd expected but already on her way to the double doors leading to the next apartment.

She whistled. "Look at this place. It's massive!"

As she disappeared into the adjoining room, I ran after her, calling, "Mel! Stop for one sec, will you?"

She stood waiting inside the sitting room. When I walked in, she launched herself at me, giving me a quick hug before stepping back, head already lifted to take in the chandelier and painted mural of the sky with fluffy white clouds covering the ceiling.

"This is fancy," she said wistfully.

It wasn't the dungeons, but I might as well have been a prisoner. I placed my hands on my hips. "Care to explain what you're doing here?"

Mel lowered her head and almost looked at me until she noticed the open double doors leading into the dressing chamber. Her mouth hung open. "There's another room?" She took a step toward it.

"Mel! Stop!"

She turned and smiled sheepishly. "Sorry, first time in a castle. I was so worried about you when I woke up and saw your covers tossed aside and dagger on the floor. Luckily, Master Brygwyn and Keerla came right over and helped me figure it out. Well, it was mostly Brygwyn. That weird fever I got was my fire magic trying to warn me about the blondie twins. They stopped me outside the market, and I'm guessing they followed me home."

"What did they want?" I asked.

Mel's eyes darted around the room, avoiding mine. She sighed and hung her head. "They were interested in the diamond choker I was selling. I'm sorry, Aerith, I had no idea who they were or that they were even Fae."

My hand floated to my neck, fingers skimming my throat at the not-so-distant memory of Folas and Galather collaring me in the dead of the night and whisking me away against my will. Bastards, both of them. Two rotten peas in a pod.

I sighed. "They probably would have found me at some point. Liri doesn't give up so easily."

"He's totally obsessed with you," Mel said with a grim nod.

My eyes sharpened on her, taken aback at the understanding in her tone.

"That's why Dev and I are here," Mel continued. "To break you free and take you back to Pinemist, but I'm beginning to think we might need to do more than leave. If Liri's going to come right back after you, we might have to . . . you know." Mel drew her finger across her throat in a slicing motion.

Alarm screeched through my ears, a silent deafening pulse. I didn't remember stepping in front of Mel, only feeling her arms in my hands as I squeezed. "You cannot speak of such things here," I hissed. "Do you understand? Don't even think it. The wrong look can give your thoughts away."

For once Mel's full attention was on me, but her concern appeared to be directed at my mental health rather than the dangers of scheming against a Fae king. I had no doubt my expression looked half-crazed, but this situation was far more treacherous than anything we'd ever been through. For so many years we'd lived in fear—or rather, I had. I'd feared creditors would take away the last of our possessions, humiliate our family in front of our neighbors. Anxiety over losing our home had kept me tossing and turning all night.

But this fear, right now, was about something more final.

If Mel crossed Liri, he'd end her. He might spare her life on my account but only to lock Mel away in the dungeons, a fate worse than death for a spirited female such as herself.

"Then what's the plan?" Mel asked. She glanced over her shoulder at my campaigne board then back to me. "I'm sure you've already formulated one. How can I help?"

I released her with a sigh. The only plan I'd come up with so far was to stay on Liri's good side, while keeping him always at a distance, and convince him it was hopeless to ever expect he'd win my heart.

I doubted very much Mel would be impressed with my plan. I wasn't even enthused by it. If anything, Liri behaved as though things were going wonderfully and that we were somehow a team.

It could be years before he grew frustrated.

It could be forever.

I neither had years nor forever to give him. And I now had Mel to think about. And Devdan.

"How is it that Devdan is here?" I asked, recalling his soft gaze on my sister. "Did the two of you—?" I let my question hang.

Mel squinted for a moment before realization hit. "Ew, no," she said, nose wrinkling. "We're friends. Well, maybe more than friends." A sheepish grin curved her lips.

I huffed and put my hands on my hips. "I'll deal with him later."

At least they wouldn't be spending their nights together. I hated how little control I had over my life, and now my sister's, which rekindled my loathing for Liri.

"Be nice to him," Mel said. "Devdan's never been outside of Pinemist, and now he's come all the way to Faerie to help."

"Certainly not on my account," I said gruffly.

"I told you we're close friends, and friends help each other out. You still haven't told me your plan." Mel leaned forward expectantly.

With her long blue coat, flaming red hair, and sword at her side, Mel looked like the kind of warrior elf no one would want to mess with. But she wasn't invincible. She thought she was, which put her in further danger.

My job was to protect her by any means necessary. It appeared my hand had been forced.

"I will be the one to do it," I said without emotion, my eyes glazing over.

"Be the one to—oh." Mel slid her finger over her throat again. When I didn't confirm or reprimand her, she lowered her hand. "Are you sure?"

I nodded, and the motion made me feel nauseous as dread tightened inside my stomach.

The jeweled dagger that Hensley had found for me was now tucked beneath my mattress. I'd wanted it for protection, never suspecting I'd need it for killing. I'd hunted deer, fowl, and rabbits in Brightwhisk Forest, killed to feed my family but never had it been an assassination. I didn't know if I had it in me.

What other option did I have?

Marry Liri?

I'd rather die than be his bedmate, his queen.

Scratch that.

I'd rather *he* die.

Candlelight illuminated my dressing chamber shortly after the late sun had set. Shadows bloomed over my face like bruises in the mirror above my vanity as Hensley brushed my hair in rhythmic strokes.

She'd barely spoken more than a sentence since arriving at my chambers after dinner. Ever since learning the news of her impending engagement to Ryo, she'd become melancholy.

When I'd first told her of Liri's decision, her eyes had

widened in horror. She'd tried to school her expression even after I told her she was safe to show her true feelings around me. But she'd bowed her head and claimed it was an honor to serve the Elmray family however King Liri saw fit.

Tonight Liri would officially announce the union between Ryo and Hensley at an engagement ball. His aunt, Queen Naesala of Ravensburg, had reportedly arrived that afternoon to attend, despite her deep-seated hatred for Liri, who had killed her favorite nephew and brother. She'd blamed me as well when she'd arrived shrouded in a black gown and veil for Cirrus's funeral at the palace. As far as I knew, this was her first visit since then. I wasn't keen to catch up on old times with the prickly queen.

Although Hensley was to be the lady of the hour, she still attended to me like the most devoted servant. Who would fill her shoes after she married Ryo? I hoped I wasn't around long enough to find out. I didn't want either of us to. It was more imperative than ever to steal Hensley away from Dahlquist, but now I also had my sister to worry about.

Routine seemed to be the only thing keeping Hensley calm. Conversation certainly did not. I had my own dire thoughts to occupy my mind as Hensley swept my hair up over my bare shoulders.

How to kill Liri?

First, I wanted to convince him to send my sister and Devdan back to Pinemist. Otherwise, I'd worry too much about their safety. They could be punished for my actions. After they were safe, I'd need a new ally. Perhaps Queen Naesala? Would she be more inclined to help me leave Faerie if I avenged the deaths of her brother and nephew?

I chewed on my lip. Seemed too risky. But I would need to flee Dahlquist and find a Fae willing to transport me back to the elven realms. There were plenty of jewels lying around my chambers with which to entice a greedy Fae.

I glanced in the mirror at Hensley, afraid my intentions

were written all over my face, but her deep frown and absent gaze as she pinned my hair made her look as though her mind had wandered a realm away.

The changing of the guards had occurred an hour earlier, leaving Devdan outside in the hall. Unlike my sister, he was not welcome inside my chambers. I'd wanted to reprimand him for going against my wishes to stay away from Mel. More than that, I'd wanted to shake him for failing to prevent her from diving headfirst into Faerie. But Hensley had arrived, and any kind of scolding would only echo off the stone walls. I had no authority here, and I was sick to death of it.

"You look as beautiful as ever, Princess Aerith."

Hensley's soft voice startled me. In her silence, I'd practically forgotten she stood behind me. I glanced in the mirror at my updo as Hensley held a second mirror behind me. Sapphire encrusted combs glittered from a soft, wispy twist at the back of my head. They matched the rich blue of my gown.

I stood up and turned around. "You look beautiful as well."

Hensley set the mirror down and smiled weakly. She looked the part of a princess-to-be in a light-yellow gown layered in ruffles down a wide skirt. A tight bodice accented her slender waist, and thin sleeves draped off her shoulders. A sunstone plunged between the valley of her breasts. Her brown hair was swept up and entwined with golden laurel leaves. She looked stunning, but I understood the depths of her anguish. I'd felt it right before marrying Cirrus—that sense that I was giving up my life but there was no turning back.

If I dispatched Liri in time, perhaps I could save Hensley from the same fate I'd been forced into nearly two years ago.

Before we reached my door, Hensley stopped, her eyes expanding in panic.

"It will be okay," I tried to reassure her, but she shook her head.

223

"I am not worthy to marry a prince."

As unjustified as it was, it made sense that a human would feel this way about marrying a royal Fae, but Hensley had it all wrong.

"Ryo's the one who doesn't deserve you," I said, not hiding the disgust from my tone.

Hensley's eyes grew wider, but the hint of a smile twitched over her lips. "You shouldn't say such things."

"I'm a princess. I can say whatever I wish," I said with more confidence than I felt. "And the same will soon go for you." Hopefully not, but if it did, Hensley needed to own it.

"No—I could never," Hensley sputtered.

I put my arm around her. "Yes, you can. If they want to use you, it's only fair you take advantage in every possible way. The only reason I'm a princess is because I married into the Elmray family. You're doing the same." I offered what I hoped was a comforting smile.

This time, Hensley returned it. Her entire body appeared to relax, and her head lifted a little higher.

When I opened my door, Devdan's eyes immediately landed on mine, but there was nothing of the haughty male from Pinemist. His brows pinched together with worry. Begrudgingly, I had to admit Devdan appeared to have more sense than my sister.

I wondered if she'd whispered anything to him in passing of my plan to end Liri. I hoped she'd been wiser than that. The more a secret was shared, the more chances it had of being discovered—even when keeping it to trusted individuals.

Devdan didn't utter a word, doing as Folas had instructed, following behind Hensley and me as we swept down the hall toward the ballroom.

I would have delayed our arrival, but Hensley had been firm about readying ourselves in time for punctual attendance.

Orchestra music played, filling the room with more notes

than guests. The few gathered groups were older Fae who openly stared at Hensley and didn't bother to lower their voices as they expressed their censure at such an unseemly arrangement between a Fae prince and human girl. The music drowned out some of their words, but their dirty looks conveyed their thoughts as though they were shouting them directly into Hensley's rounded ears.

Her cheeks flushed, and she took a step back. "You were right. We should have waited."

I grabbed her arm, anchoring her in place. "We're here now. You can't show any fear. You're no longer a lady-in-waiting. You're betrothed to a prince."

Hensley swallowed and looked at me. "How did you do it, Aerith?"

I lifted my nose, casting a bored look around the room, staring down any eyes that met mine. "I stopped caring," I said. *I gave in.* I kept that last part to myself.

"You make it sound so easy," Hensley said wistfully. "I don't know. Maybe it's more difficult because I'm human. I'm too sensitive. Emotional. Flawed."

I snorted and shook my head. "Believe me, all beings are flawed. Some just mask it better than others. You'll get there." I patted her arm in reassurance.

Hensley's lower lip quivered. "I don't want to become numb."

I looked at her sadly, hoping she wouldn't lose herself the way I had—hoping I could prevent that future from ever coming to pass.

"Just look at her," a cruel female voice floated over the notes of the symphony. "No human should be allowed to marry a Fae, let alone bind herself to a prince. This union is a travesty."

Hensley turned abruptly. I worried she'd make another attempt to flee, but this time she rushed over to the refreshment table and grabbed a flute of sparkling wine before one could be handed to her. The servants didn't look as eager to serve her as they had me.

Hensley had gulped down half the wine by the time I reached her. When I tried to snatch the flute away, she turned from me and downed the remainder of the bubbling liquid.

"I thought you didn't want to be numb," I chided.

"I already feel numb," Hensley said. "I need something to liven me up." She grabbed another flute.

"Er, maybe you should hold off on the faerie wine," I said, recalling my own unfortunate evening imbibing on the delicious sparkling beverage. As a human, Hensley's tolerance would be even less than mine. I'd heard rumors that once a human ate and drank in Faerie, food and drink would become tasteless in the mortal realm. I'd even heard that some people ended up wasting away if returned.

Hensley's lips paused on the rim of the flute. She lowered it and cast a wistful look my way. "I wish I had your courage, Aerith. I just need a little more help getting out of my own head." At least she sipped rather than gulped down the second glass.

"It's not worth it," I said, narrowing my eyes at the flute.

When a servant offered me a glass, I turned it down.

After finishing her second flute, Hensley picked up a third.

"Hensley!" I scolded.

Her cheeks were already red, and the ball had yet to officially commence. "It's just to hold on to," she said defensively.

I was going to have to keep an eye out for her. Well, I was used to spending my evenings in that capacity in Faerie. It's not as though I had anything better to do.

The ballroom began to fill, and more and more disapproving looks were aimed at Hensley. Many times, the malevolent glances slid from her to me. Every five minutes I felt tempted to grab my own glass of bubbling wine to hold and sip. I'd learned my lesson. I would be careful and only take a few sips this time. No. I smacked the thought away and held out, unlike Hensley who'd polished off her third glass, taking sips when I wasn't looking. It wasn't until all the guests had arrived that the trumpets sounded and the royal family entered, following behind Liri and his aunt, Queen Naesala, whom he escorted on his arm. I was glad to be by Hensley's side and not part of their entourage.

I stood on tiptoes and craned my head for a better glimpse of Queen Naesala. She was reportedly in her thirty-eighth year, but she looked ten years younger. Her fair skin was flawless, blonde hair as light and airy as a lazy summer's day. Tonight she'd dressed in a red gown that clung to her body like paint—or blood. I chewed on my bottom lip, trying to determine if the color was a sign of revenge to come.

I wouldn't put it past her. The Fae loved to play mind games that kept others anxiously speculating.

Rather than a crown, Queen Naesala wore a golden headband with a ruby teardrop in the center of her forehead. Liri wore a half crown of silver that spiked out from his ears to the back of his head. His fitted tunic glimmered dark gray and metallic silver, his white hair brushed back silky smooth and straight.

Liri's sisters followed behind him and their aunt, with Ryo trudging in from the rear. Ryo had dressed all in black, as though attending his own funeral rather than an engagement party. His glower made him look like a raven-haired devil.

Beside me, Hensley gave a slight tremble. Before Mel showed up, she was the closest thing I'd had to a sister in Faerie.

"Stay strong," I told her. "And remember you're just as beautiful as any of the females here tonight. They just don't want to admit it since you're not Fae."

Liri looked around the ballroom until his steely eyes found mine. A cold smile climbed up his pale cheeks. He snapped his fingers. Ryo scowled before joining Liri at his side. Liri said something that I couldn't read on his lips. As soon as the words were out, he and Ryo walked over to Hensley and me.

"Congratulations, Miss Allen," Liri said to Hensley. "Soon you will have the honor of calling a king your brother-in-law."

"Th-th-thank you, my king," Hensley stuttered. "You are most generous."

"Yes," Liri drawled. "If only your family could see you now. I still remember when Cirrus found you in the streets, looking like a malnourished, flea-ridden stray."

Ryo's upper lip curled in distaste.

My heart hammered inside my chest. I looked at Hensley, but she was staring at Liri. A mixture of hurt and anger filled her eyes as Liri continued.

"Cirrus was always better at seeing the potential in the downtrodden. Just look at sweet Aerith here. You would have hardly recognized her before she came to Faerie."

I folded my arms beneath my chest. "Is that supposed to be a compliment?" I asked icily.

Liri turned his smile to me. "I wish only to reassure your friend. Perhaps my brother will do a better job of waxing poetic to his bride-to-be. He can start by asking her to dance."

Ryo glared at Liri, but the king ignored him as though he were beneath his notice.

"The king wants us to dance," Ryo said to Hensley, not masking the irritation in his voice.

"Uh." Hensley glanced uncertainly from Ryo to Liri then to me.

"Go ahead," I told her.

"Take Miss Allen's glass," Liri snapped at the nearest attendant. A servant in green coattails plucked the flute from Hensley's fingers and sped away. Mouth ajar, Hensley stared after him as though she was trapped in the desert and he'd just confiscated her last drops of water.

Ryo huffed and stormed ahead of her toward the center of

the ballroom where Fae couples danced closely. Poor Hensley had little choice but to trail after Ryo.

I sighed, watching the swish of her yellow ruffles. She looked like the sun chasing the night.

"I know you feel a need to toy with Ryo, but did you have to involve Hensley?" I asked the question without looking at Liri.

He moved closer to my side, the metallic of his tunic looking as cold as the Fae king beside me. "She was the only acceptable human mate for Ryo. She's served the family loyally for five years. Plus, her looks are tolerable—pretty even."

"Charming," I said sarcastically.

I watched as Hensley caught up to Ryo. He put his arms on her shoulders and held her as far away from his body as he could while they swayed side to side.

"They look ridiculous," I said.

Liri smirked. "Shall we join them?"

"I'd rather not," I said curtly.

Liri managed to look smug even after I'd turned him down, surveying his family and guests—his subjects. He stood tall and proud by my side. Anytime I tried to edge away, he moved fluidly with me as though we were, in fact, dancing. Spectacularly dressed guests stole glances at us, eyes quickly darting away as though Liri might punish them for staring too long. I didn't like the way we appeared to be together. I had no desire to be Liri's favorite.

"What a pleasing surprise it must have been to have your sister join you in Faerie," Liri said.

"Actually, I wanted to talk to you about that. I'd rather she and her friend be returned to Pinemist as soon as possible."

Liri stepped in front of me, blocking the view of Hensley and Ryo, his eyebrows slanted. "And why would you wish to send her away so soon?" he asked suspiciously.

"Because she's young and rebellious," I answered

229

truthfully. "Mel's always had a mind of her own and a propensity for trouble. I can't relax with her here. I'm worried she'll offend the wrong Fae and suffer the consequences. It was hard enough keeping an eye out for her in the elven realms." I looked Liri in the eyes and shook my head. "As much as I love and miss her, nothing good can come from her being here."

Liri pursed his lips and studied my face. He gave a slight nod and gracefully veered to my side. "I know how taxing younger siblings can be." He stared pointedly at Ryo. "You bring up a good point. Your sister shouldn't be a royal guard; she should be a guest."

My eyes widened. "That's not what I—"

"She should have been here tonight celebrating with us," Liri interrupted. "She's the sister of a royal princess—family. And you know I like to keep my family close." His teeth gleamed white.

No! This wasn't how I wanted things to go.

"Inviting her to more functions would only cause more problems," I tried to reason. Dread gripped my throat as I recognized the determination in Liri's steely eyes.

"I would think you would want to keep your sister around since this is to be your home."

Anger replaced dread, burning up the icy feeling. It hissed and smoked with my rage. "Dahlquist is not my home. It's my prison," I snarled between clenched teeth.

"It's what you make of it, sweet Aerith. Excuse me." The bastard strode off, making his way to Jastra, who smiled smugly from her curtain of curly teal hair.

I wanted to scream, to throttle the monstrous king, but I had more pressing matters to plot—like how to get inside his room and slit his throat without condemning my sister in the process.

I had to take down the king before he captured us all.

As I fumed silently, Queen Naesala approached me, filling

my vision with her snug red dress. A long, narrow V cut nearly to her navel, showing off skin slightly more tanned than her nieces and nephews. If it weren't for the golden chains linking the two sides of the dress, it would have surely popped open and exposed the other halves of her partially covered breasts.

"What an unpleasant surprise to see you back in Dahlquist," Queen Naesala purred beside me.

Well, I could cross the queen off my list of potential allies. Shocker.

I folded my arms, sick to death of all the Elmrays and their relatives. "I have as little desire to be here as you do to see me," I informed her.

Queen Naesala grinned. "Yes, young Liri does as he pleases. Such a shame you were incapable of stopping him from killing your mate. Cirrus would have made a spectacular king. And you could have been his queen." She tsked and gave her head a slight shake. "Well, there is nothing to be done now. Though, it has made me consider my lack of husband or heir. It had been my intention that Cirrus would inherit my kingdom. Since things have changed, I must reconsider." Her gaze sharpened. "Liri will not have Ravensburg." The queen pushed a smile to her lips. "Ryo is not the only one engaged. I have followed lovely Cirrus's example and selected an elven mate for myself. You might even know him. He comes from your old village of Pinemist."

The music faded away, sucked into a silent abyss, as a feeling of foreboding churned inside my gut. Queen Naesala lifted one slender arm and flicked her wrist. Horror crashed over me as a tall dark-haired male strode over dressed in a tan embroidered waistcoat and red breeches that matched the queen's dress, ending just below the knees where white stockings tucked into buckled shoes.

The queen's smile widened maliciously. "Aerith, allow me to introduce you to my fiancé, Jhaeros Keasandoral."

CHAPTER NINETEEN

Aerith

Every last spark of hope drained from my body, leaving me swaying in my slippers as Jhaeros stepped beside Queen Naesala and wrapped an arm around her middle.

I stared at his arm in utter confusion, unable to grasp that any of this could possibly be real.

Jhaeros squeezed the queen against his side and gently kissed her temple.

Queen Naesala's eyes lit up in delight, but I could tell it was my distress that made her glow, as though she was sucking my soul out of my body.

"Jhaeros, darling, you are acquainted with my late nephew's widow, Aerith, are you not?"

Jhaeros's eyes flicked briefly in my direction, nose giving the slightest wrinkle. He refused to meet my horror-stricken gaze, as though I was a sight unfit for his sensitive brown eyes.

"I was present during the tournament in which Miss Heiris, as she was then known, competed for your nephew's favor." His voice sounded as indifferent as he'd appeared that cursed afternoon when he'd stood beneath the trees fawning over Shalendra.

Old, ugly feelings rekindled themselves inside my twisting

stomach. I felt myself growing smaller by the second, my heart shriveling into a dried-out pit at his cold indifference. It was as though we were strangers. Something horrible had happened. Jhaeros would never treat me this way. His memories had to have been altered or an enchantment had been placed over him. Either way, I'd lost him, and it was taking everything inside me not to break down into a weeping puddle.

No one here would help me. No one would care. Quite the contrary. Every last one of the Elmrays would delight in my misery. It was the one thing they could all agree on. I didn't want to kill only Liri. I longed to end them all.

"You were sweet on her sister for a time, weren't you?" Queen Naesala asked.

"If I'd known you, I never would have considered someone of such inferior looks or charm," Jhaeros said, staring intently at Queen Naesala—the same way he used to gaze upon Shalendra. The same way he used to look at me. "You are my sun. My moon. My star in the sky."

"Oh, Jhaeros." Queen Naesala giggled, which sounded as unnatural on her lips as a hyena chirping a tune. "You flatter me."

My fingers curled. I wanted to rip the white lace cravat from his neck. It reminded me too much of a collar, like the diamond choker Liri's goons had forced around my throat.

"There are no words in existence eloquent enough to flatter you, my love," Jhaeros gushed, turning his back to me as if he was shielding Queen Naesala from yet another inferior ex-lover. "Would you do me the honor of a dance? Or perhaps you would prefer refreshment?"

"I believe Aerith is the one in need of a drink," Queen Naesala said with a cruel laugh. "Bring us three flutes of bubbling wine, my dear, so that Aerith may properly toast and congratulate us."

"I will be right back," Jhaeros said, giving the queen's

temple another kiss before strutting away in his square-heeled shoes.

The Jhaeros I knew would have sooner gone barefoot than be caught wearing such ridiculous footwear.

Queen Naesala grinned triumphantly as soon as Jhaeros's back was turned.

"What have you done to him?" I demanded.

"Not I, but one of your dear, sweet sisters-in-law."

"Who?" I asked between gritted teeth.

My mind raced backward, coming to a tumbling halt when I remembered that day in the throne room when Teryani had asked to attend a tournament—no doubt the one that had brought my sister and Devdan to Dahlquist. But how had she found out about Jhaeros?

I needed to speak to Mel. Shake her from sleep if I had to in case she knew anything about this, this, this...travesty!

The queen smirked, then her eyes narrowed. "You should have kept Cirrus safe. Now I will take away someone you love."

Terror twisted around my ribs, squeezing them together too tight like a corset—one meant to kill me where I stood.

I couldn't speak. I certainly couldn't remain obediently in place before Jhaeros returned with the sparkling wine—not when bile bubbled up my throat. It would rip the last of my fragmented heart to its final slivers to drink a toast to the queen's captive.

"This is not over," I snarled at her, pivoting and rushing for the ballroom doors as though rabid wolves were chomping at my heels.

If I weren't around to torment, Queen Naesala might lessen her grip on Jhaeros. She wouldn't let him go, but there'd be no reason to play with him like a malicious cat in front of a caged dog. If I did stay, his kisses might reach her mouth. I might then break my flute and use the glass shard to slit the bitch's throat. After which, Liri would inherit the kingdom of Ravensburg and see to it that Jhaeros was never seen or heard from again. At least with Queen Naesala he was alive.

I nearly tripped in my hurry to leave the ballroom.

I couldn't live in any world without Jhaeros.

It wasn't until I'd reached the empty open hall of the north wing that I remembered my unwelcome guardian.

Devdan cleared his throat. "That was the elf Jhaeros back in the ballroom, wasn't it?"

I spun around, grabbed Devdan by the shoulders, and shook him. "How do you know Jhaeros?" I asked in a high-pitched, panicked voice.

Devdan wore the same uneasy expression that had fallen over his face like a mask since arriving in Faerie. Frown lines were already appearing around his chin. "He rode up on his horse right as we were leaving Pinemist for Dahlquist."

My heart gave a lurch, as though I could reach back in time and stop them all from coming here.

"Melarue tried to convince Folas and Teryani that Jhaeros was engaged to your sister, Shalendra, and that he'd been sent by your father to summon you for the wedding." When I scowled, Devdan shrugged, the first hint of a smile flickering over his lips. "It was fast thinking on Mel's part. Your lover wasn't as quick. Too bad he didn't take a moment to assess the situation."

My nails dug into Devdan's shoulders. He hissed in pain, but I didn't let up. "It's called honor," I spit out before releasing Devdan, huffing with disgust.

Devdan rubbed one shoulder and glared at me. I glared back.

"Have your hardships taught you nothing?" Devdan demanded. "Honor is as useful as a brick is to fire."

I wanted to argue with him, to rage. The heat of my anger was so intense it shocked me when I felt tears streaming down my cheeks. From the wide-eyed look on Devdan's face, it shocked him too. He winced, as though in pain, and took my arm, leading me down the rest of the hall. "Let's get you to your rooms," he said in a soothing voice I barely recognized from the typically smug elf.

He entered the chamber with me, steering me to the edge of my bed where he had me sit before fetching a washcloth. Devdan was surprisingly gentle as he dabbed my cheeks with the cloth. He stepped back, a grim line over his lips and his head slightly bowed. "I did not mean to upset you," he said solemnly.

"It's not you," I said.

"I know, but I could have been more comforting."

I stood and lifted my chin high. "I do not want comfort. You were right. Honor won't win our freedom. To beat them, we'll have to be just as cunning and ruthless. I want to end these bastards." My fingers balled into fists. I couldn't decide who I wanted to strangle first—Queen Naesala or Teryani. The only reason the queen had a new toy was because he'd been delivered by the white witch. I'd thought Teryani above such games, but it appeared she was as vile as Jastra and Sarfina.

Devdan soon left me alone in my rooms. I had no plan to discuss, only intentions. In Faerie, I had to seize the moment when it came.

Too bad I didn't have Mel's fire magic—or elemental magic of any kind. Never mind, I had a dagger. That was something. A very sharp, pointy something. A bow and arrow would be nice too. I could bring Queen Naesala and Teryani down from across the room. Hopefully their hold over Jhaeros would end with their lives.

I lit a lantern and took it to my wardrobe where I rummaged through a drawer of scarves, selecting a thick white one. I brought it back to my bedchamber, pulled my dagger out from beneath my bed, and tied the weapon against my leg, shifting its placement, until I'd found a sturdy place on top of my right thigh that still allowed me to sit. The skirt of the gown hid the blade beautifully. I'd need to make sure to wear a similar style frock the next day and the next, until I found the ideal opportunity to dispatch the queen. I'd try to get her when no one was looking so it wouldn't blow back on me. Everyone would probably suspect Liri, and he might not care enough to investigate—not when it meant expanding his empire. He and his aunt had never been close.

Aside from Teryani, I doubted anyone would look in my direction. She was next on my list, anyway.

I untied the dagger and hid it beneath my bed again before folding up the scarf and setting it on a table beside a tall glass vase filled with sunflowers.

After changing into a night slip, I tossed and turned beneath my covers, wishing I could visit Jhaeros in a dreamscape the way Liri had invaded my dreams.

My greatest strength was with a bow. I'd shot down an ogre to save Cirrus, not knowing it was a test. It had been instinct. I hadn't even cared about the golden-haired Fae or his kingdom. I hadn't wanted any part of it, but Father had insisted. As the oldest child, it had been my duty to take care of my family.

It should have been his too.

As far as I was concerned, Queen Naesala, Teryani, and Liri were worse than ogres. While Jhaeros was the love of my life.

There was no question in my mind that I would do whatever necessary to protect what was mine at any cost.

On that thought, I fell asleep feeling more determined than ever. No one visited me in my dreams, though someone knocked at the door. The pounding came again. At least they weren't barging into my dreams. Still, I wanted to ignore whoever it was before they ended all chances of drifting back into a cloudless oblivion.

Pound. Pound. Pound.

The noise was ceaseless. Loud and intrusive.

"Pitberries," I cried out. "I'm coming." With a loud groan, I threw the covers back and weaved my way to the door as though drunk. "Who's there?" I demanded, not masking my aggravation.

"It's Hensley," came her voice.

Oh pit. Seeing Jhaeros had so blindsided me that I'd forgotten all about poor Hensley and her sham of an engagement to Ryo. A twinge of guilt fluttered through me for leaving the ball early. Normally I would have stuck around to provide moral support.

As soon as I opened the door, Hensley flew inside like a cat chasing after a mouse. She still wore her yellow ballgown, and half of her hair had come unpinned, falling over her shoulders in brown wisps.

Devdan started in after Hensley. I caught his eye and shook my head. "It's all right. I'll let you know if we need anything." I shut my door and turned to find Hensley rapidly pacing my room.

She lifted and dropped her arms, squeezed and loosened her fists. A flush ran from her neck to her rosy cheeks. I tried to determine if her eyes were shiny because she'd been crying, but there were no tear tracks on her cheeks, and her eyes most certainly were not bloodshot. Aside from her frantic movements, Hensley almost seemed to glow.

"Hensley, what is it?"

She jerked to a stop and, for a moment, looked at me as though I'd been the one to appear unexpectedly in her bedchamber. Then Hensley clutched her chest and cried out, "Forgive me, Aerith!"

Seven hells, now what?

"What do you mean?"

Quivering lips pressed together on the human's face.

I groaned in exasperation. Better to release the arrow and hit me with it rather than delay any longer. "Hensley," I prodded. "What happened?"

Shimmering green eyes looked through me dreamily before snapping back to attention. Hensley started toward me then stopped and leaned back as though I was a snake that might strike her. "I blame the faerie wine," she said. "That's my excuse, although I don't know what his is. He most definitely was not drunk."

Oh no. I folded my arms. "What did Ryo do?"

"Not Ryo. Liri. I mean, King Liri." Hensley's cheeks flushed brighter. "He, uh, took me back to his room."

"He what?" I screeched, my arms flying to my sides.

Though fully awake, my brain didn't have time to process what Hensley had just confessed before a knock sounded at the door.

Had Devdan heard my shriek? As I started toward the door to tell Devdan I was fine, the door flew open and Sarfina strode in with Devdan chasing after.

"You can't just burst into the princess's room," he bellowed at her back.

She had on her same gown from the ball, another transparent white frock with a gold slip underneath. Sarfina's blonde-and-gold hair was pulled into a thick high ponytail with a golden tiara encrusted in sunstones.

Her smile of triumph didn't vanish as she addressed Devdan without facing him. "You're new here, elf, so I'll explain things this once. I was born a princess, which gives me the right to burst into any room of the palace, save the king's, whenever I choose."

Devdan glared at her back with pure loathing.

"Now go back outside like a good guard," Sarfina said with a dismissive wave of her hand.

"Actually, I want him to stay," I said. Sarfina didn't get to dismiss my guard, who also happened to be my sorta friend. Being in Faerie certainly redefined friendships.

She shrugged. "Suit yourself, though I doubt you'll want any more ears than necessary to hear what I have to say." She lowered her voice and smiled slyly. "It's a bit of a personal matter." Her eyes slid over to Hensley, taking on a cruel shine.

Hensley paled. She turned to me. "He can wait outside, can't he?" Pleading eyes stared into mine.

I sighed. "Fine." I turned to Devdan. "Mind waiting outside while I sort this out?"

With a tight jaw, Devdan inclined his head. "Yell if you need me."

Once he'd left the room and shut the door behind him, Sarfina rubbed her hands together and grinned wickedly. "Did your human tell you about the mischief she got into with my brother, the king?"

"I don't see how that's any of your business," I snapped.

Sarfina pouted her lips, but her eyes glittered. "You're not jealous?" When I didn't answer, she grinned. "Well, you have no reason to be. Liri would never lower himself to bed a human dog." She smirked at Hensley. "I placed an enchantment to make her look like you."

I made a growling sound, half-tempted to fetch my dagger and stab it straight through Sarfina's golden slip until I pierced her black heart. But killing her wouldn't help any of us. Sarfina was only a shrub in this game—a vicious one but still a shrub.

Clutching her stomach, Hensley looked ready to double over. The thought of Liri thinking he'd bedded me made me want to pull out every golden strand of hair out of my sister-in-law's head.

"I don't know what you're smiling at," I snarled at her. "Liri will punish you severely for this."

"*Punish*," Sarfina said eagerly, pronouncing the word as though it was the start of foreplay in a game of seduction. "Maybe, but he'll end her." Her eyes gleamed like a vulture's when she looked at Hensley. "Liri will either kill her or lock her away for the rest of her life once he learns he was deceived by a human."

Hensley's head snapped up. "I didn't deceive him!" she cried.

Sarfina smiled smugly. "It doesn't matter. You, a mere mortal, dared lie with him." She snarled. "Serves him right after trying to force you on poor Ryo."

My nostrils flared. "Liri ordered you not to harm me or Hensley," I practically yelled.

Sarfina adjusted the golden tiara on her head, stretching her arms slowly back to her sides as though we were her subjects to command. "I did no harm."

"By enchanting her to look like me, you were going against your brother."

"It wouldn't have worked if she hadn't thrown herself at him." Sarfina's lip curled when she looked at Hensley.

"It was the faerie wine," Hensley sputtered, cheeks flaming. But even to my ears, her protest sounded weak. Could it be she felt an attraction toward Liri? I felt my lip curling in a mirror image of Sarfina's.

Sarfina shrugged. "I was just giving my brother what he wants. Maybe not the real thing but close enough. Elves are only a step above humans."

I started for her, but Hensley jumped between us. "Aerith, no!" she said, grabbing for my arms.

"Step aside, Hensley," I growled, not taking my eyes off Sarfina. "My sister-in-law's been begging for a beating."

"Ohh, a beating." Sarfina laughed with delight. "I'd like to see you try, sister of mine." She looked turned on by the idea of a smackdown.

"Please!" Hensley shouted. Her eyes were wide, expression frantic.

I stormed past both her and Sarfina, straight for the door, yanking it open. "Leave now, Sarfina," I ordered. "Before I make you."

Sarfina's eyes glittered, feeding off our fight. My heart pounded with anticipation, almost eager for her to refuse so I could forcibly remove her. She must have read the anticipation in my eyes.

Flicking her ponytail over her shoulder, Sarfina strutted out of the room. As she passed me, she smiled gleefully. "Have a lovely morning, Sister," came her sugary voice. She paused to look over her shoulder. "Goodbye, Hensley. I'd say it was nice knowing you, but I'm incapable of lying. I hope having my brother between your legs was worth dying over." She blew her a kiss and exited into the hall.

Devdan came forward again, and again I told him, "Everything's fine," then closed the door in his face.

It took me several seconds to clear the smoke in my head. Hensley didn't interrupt my murderous thoughts. She'd gone as rigid as a marble statue and as pale as Sarfina's gown.

"He'll kill me," she whispered, staring glassy-eyed at the floor.

"Not if he doesn't find out," I said.

Hensley's eyes expanded as she looked up at me. "But that would mean—" She didn't finish her sentence.

I shuddered as revulsion swept through me. I knew exactly what it meant. My brother-in-law would think he'd bedded me. Even worse, he'd think I'd gone to him willingly. Why did Hensley have to have such pit-poor taste in males? My skin crawled at the mere thought. I scratched at my arm as though Liri had touched me.

"What exactly happened?" I asked Hensley.

Color returned to her cheeks as she blushed. She quickly looked down and rubbed one of the ruffles on her gown. Other than her partially undone hair, the rest of her attire was in place. Lust didn't appear to turn Liri into a hungry beast the way it had with Jhaeros.

Pain shot through my heart thinking his name. I shook my head. One thing at a time.

Hensley cleared her throat. "He didn't actually bed me."

"He didn't?" My chest expanded as some of the weight

lifted off.

Hensley used two hands to fiddle with her ruffled skirt. "He, uh, pleasured me with his, um, mouth."

I wrinkled my nose. If I'd been Mel, I would have cried out, "Ew," but I kept it to myself and it resembled more of a "yech," because this was Liri we were talking about, and he was under the impression his mouth had been on me. My lips drew back in disgust.

"How did he get you to his room in the first place?"

"He invited me."

I groaned at Hensley's succinct answer. I couldn't imagine Liri striding up to my side and casually inviting me to his bedchamber for a little one-on-one action. Ugg.

"That's it?" I prodded.

Hensley stared at the floor. "Well, uh, he invited me to dance first, so we danced—and stuff."

"Stuff?" I raised my eyebrows.

"We kissed."

"He kissed you or you kissed him?" I demanded.

Hensley still wouldn't meet my eye. "Er, I suppose I started it."

I slapped my hand to my forehead. Really, I should have been slapping the sense into Hensley. How had I been so blind to her feelings for Liri? I'd always believed her to be stubbornly loyal, but never infatuated. Enraptured. Insane!

"Once we went to his room, it was hard to think past all the orgasms," Hensley said, poking at her dress.

I clapped my hands over my ears and groaned. I didn't want to picture it, but I had to know everything. I uncovered my ears. "Then what happened? Did he fall asleep?"

Hensley smiled with too many teeth. "Um."

"He didn't say my name once?" I asked. I was beginning to wonder how oblivious Hensley had truly been or whether she'd suspected the enchantment and kept going anyway.

Hensley's eyes darted to the chandelier for a moment as

she thought. "No, but he did say he could give me, I mean you, more orgasms than his brother ever did—and all before he ever properly bedded me. You!" She grimaced. "It was really confusing. I assumed he meant Ryo, but it didn't really make sense since I was drunk on faerie wine."

It looked like she was still feeling the effects. Despite her alarm at Sarfina's words, Hensley still acted giddy.

I rolled my wrist, wanting to wrap things up. "Okay, so he did the oral stuff." I winced in disgust. "Then what?"

"Then I thought it only fair I return the favor," Hensley said.

"Ew." This time I said it aloud because Liri...orgasm...pleasure. Ew!

Ugh, could this get any worse? Now, supposedly, I'd pleasured him back.

"He enjoyed it immensely." Hensley smiled proudly.

"I'm sure he did," I snapped. How in the seven hells was I going to protect Hensley when I didn't have the stomach to pretend I'd been the one to engage in these intimate acts with Liri?

The thought was so sickening I could feel my disgust rising up my throat. I barely made it to the trash receptacle in time to empty my stomach.

CHAPTER TWENTY

Aerith

Napkins shaped into white swans perched on each plate at the long table of the dining hall. Small crystal bowls filled with berries topped in cream waited at each place setting. But even my favorite treat wasn't enough to tempt me. It might as well have been a bowl of pits glazed in tar. I did not feel like eating breakfast, especially not with my Fae in-laws.

I inched my way to the table as though approaching the plank on a pirate's ship as the sharks swarmed at the surface below.

I would have preferred sharks.

"Princess Aerith, your seat is here," a short, plump, and matronly Fae announced, indicating a high-back chair in the center of the table.

A footman stepped forward and pulled back the chair. At least being in the middle meant I was as far as possible from the head of the table on either side. I wouldn't have to sit near or look at Liri or Naesala.

The king and his queen aunt had yet to appear, leaving me with Liri's sisters, Ryo, and Hensley. Since our early morning encounter, Hensley and Sarfina had changed into new frocks and were doing their best to ignore one another. Both cast looks my way, which I ignored. I smoothed my sky-blue skirts back as I took my seat, lifting my head regally. I'd had plenty of time to dress since there was no going back to sleep after the dreadful news I'd been delivered. My stomach still roiled.

Mel had changed places with Devdan but had been forced to wait outside the dining room. I'd updated her on everything with the exception of Hensley's drunken mistake, which sounded like a welcome mistake, while unknowingly glamoured to look like me. Mel had apologized profusely for Jhaeros as though his capture was somehow her fault. None of this was. We were all here for one reason: Liri's stupid obsession with me. I'd thought Cirrus's death had freed me, but the months following his death had been merely an intermission before act two.

The dining matron instructed the rest of the Elmrays where to sit. Teryani was placed across the table, one over from me, an empty chair left beside her. Next to the empty place setting, Ryo plopped down once directed to the spot. He folded his arms, bent his head, and glowered at the fabric swan as though he'd like to rip off its neck. Hensley was directed to the seat beside him. Sarfina was placed across from Hensley, which made it impossible to stare at me without having to lean over the table and crane her head in my direction. It was a small comfort. Jastra was given the spot between Sarfina and me.

Once we were all seated, the matron left the room, returning shortly and ushering Jhaeros inside.

My throat closed as Jhaeros was led to the seat directly in front of me. I couldn't swallow. I could scarcely breathe. When the footman moved forward, hands reaching for the chair's back, Jhaeros stepped between the servant and the chair.

"I can get my own damn chair," he said with a scowl.

He sounded so much like himself that my heart gave a lurch. It was foolish to hope, but my eyes wouldn't listen to reason as they searched him for any spark of suppressed feelings he might yet fight to unearth on my behalf.

Jhaeros flipped back his coattails as he took his seat. Ryo glanced over and wrinkled his nose before returning his insolent glare to his plate.

I tried desperately to catch Jhaeros's eye, but even without Queen Naesala present, he ignored me.

Tears swarmed my eyes. Only Teryani noticed. I waited for her smug smile, but she frowned. I knew it wasn't out of pity. Most of the time Teryani was incapable of any type of smile, not even the arrogant kind.

The doors of the dining room opened, and a lanky footman entered. "The king and queen have arrived," he announced.

Liri and Naesala swept into the room side by side. Three of the queen's guards followed, as did Galather and Folas. A Cheshire smile lit up Liri's face like an albino jack-o'-lantern. He looked straight at me, pinning me down with a heated stare. For the life of me, I couldn't return his smile. I was no actress. No liar. No cold Fae devoid of all emotion and honor.

A footman pulled back the chair at the end of the table nearest me. As the queen took the seat, her three guards arranged themselves several steps behind her, keeping watch over the room.

We all waited for Liri to take the seat on the opposite end of the table. When he stopped at the chair beside me, I tried not to recoil in horror.

A footman rushed forward to pull the seat back for Liri.

Liri beamed at all the faces around the table. "What a splendid morning to be king," he announced. "Please, enjoy your fruits. They were picked fresh and delivered all the way from the village of Torra early this morning." He glanced at me as though to say, "Especially for you, sweet Aerith."

I ground my teeth, refusing to meet his gaze. But Liri kept staring. It wasn't until I dipped my spoon into the cup of berries and took my first bite that he did the same. The berries were tasteless as my teeth ground them into a mushy pulp. With nothing better to do, I emptied the bowl bit by bit. I'd need my strength.

Empty crystal bowls were cleared, replaced with breakfast plates. Each serving had a biscuit, eggs, bacon, and boiled greens. The berries had been tasteless, but at least they didn't smell. The scent of cooked meat made my stomach spin.

As a footman lowered a plate in front of me, Queen Naesala snapped her fingers. "You will bring me the princess's plate and give her mine instead," she commanded.

The footman looked at Liri, who nodded with an amused smile. As the footman traded the plates, Liri chuckled at his aunt. "I have no desire to poison or harm you in any way. I am already king."

I picked up my fork, knowing that if it really had been poisoned, there was no way Liri would allow me to stab at the egg.

Queen Naesala narrowed her eyes. "Lest you get any ideas about taking Ravensburg, let me put them to rest once and for all. You will *never* inherit my kingdom. Even if I were to die this very day without an heir, I've had a contract drawn up as to who will inherit the crown."

Liri's smile didn't waver. It was disturbing. "Good," he said. "Then I hope we can enjoy the remainder of the week free of suspicion or malice. My days of debauchery are over. I want only to rule in the company of my beloved household. Now is the time to expand our family."

Beneath the table, Liri's hand slipped into my lap.

I dropped my fork. It clanked over my plate and landed in the food. Liri drew his hand away only to lift it and usher a footman forward. My fork was plucked off my plate and a fresh one set atop the linen cloth.

"Thank you," I murmured.

Luckily, everyone else had commenced eating and paid

little attention to me—everyone except Hensley, who stared at Liri and me sullenly from down the table.

Jhaeros sat with his back straight as a board, using his knife to make small cuts in his egg before taking measured bites. He used his knife and fork on the bacon while Ryo lifted the strips with his hands to chomp on.

Each bite of egg made my stomach turn. I tried to hold my breath to stop my nose from sucking in the smell. After finishing the egg, I tore off bits of biscuit and chewed on each piece until it dissolved to mush inside my mouth.

Beside me, Liri bit into the bacon and chewed. *Crunch. Crunch. Crunch.*

I gagged and clutched my stomach, trying to keep the food in, but it rushed up my throat. I only had time to turn to my right before regurgitating on the floor beside Jastra.

Scooting away from me, Jastra nearly knocked into Sarfina, her teal hair flying at the golden blonde. "That's disgusting," Jastra cried, but her words were only noise.

Even emptied, my stomach twisted as though wanting to leave my body the same way my food had. I groaned, feeling too miserable to worry about having an audience. No one rushed to my aid. I sat up slowly, grabbed a swan napkin, and dabbed at my mouth without bothering to unfold the thing. The room had gone as silent as the stars. No crunching or clink of cutlery. The Elmrays had probably never seen anything so offensive in all their royal, privileged lives.

Only Hensley looked distressed, the skin pulled taut around her eyes and lips as though she were in pain.

Nose wrinkled, a look of revulsion settled over Jhaeros's face. My composure nearly crumbled as I fought to remain in my seat, calmly dabbing my mouth, when all I wanted to do was stand up and scream at him. I quickly calculated the weeks since Jhaeros and I had lain together at my cottage. Nearly a month. This sickness could be the signs of a child—one he'd put in my belly back in Pinemist, back when he loved me.

If this didn't get through to him, nothing would.

Still, he sat immobile, frowning in distaste.

Even the footmen stood frozen.

Teryani was the first to rise from her chair. "Don't just stand around gaping. Clean it up," she commanded a footman across the table from her.

From there, the room burst into action. The queen's guards rushed forward, surrounding her.

"You *did* mean to poison me," she accused Liri, eyes bulging in outrage.

"No one's been poisoned," Liri snapped.

"She's pregnant!" Sarfina screeched, ignoring the queen's accusation. She shot up from her seat and pointed down the table. "It hasn't even been six months since poor Cirrus was murdered and already Liri has impregnated our brother's widow."

Teryani sighed. "Stop being fanatical. For all we know, Aerith simply indulged in too much faerie wine at the ball last night and is suffering the consequences this morning."

Queen Naesala pushed back from the table with a glare. "Let us hope she is either pregnant or hungover. Until that is determined, I will be dining in my rooms. Come along, Jhaeros."

Jhaeros stood and offered the queen his arm, escorting her out as the guards followed after them. The roiling in my stomach morphed into emptiness. If I was pregnant, the father of my child had just left with another female, one he looked determined to protect at any cost while leaving me behind with the Elmrays.

After the footman finished cleaning up my mess, Liri commanded him and all the other servants to leave the dining room and close the door behind them. Galather and Folas were instructed to remain behind with the family. All traces of warmth had left Liri's voice.

A crunching sound momentarily distracted everyone as all eyes turned to Ryo, who had bitten into another piece of bacon. "What?" he asked as he chewed. "My stomach is fine, and I'm still hungry."

"How can you eat anything after she spewed?" Jastra demanded.

Ryo shrugged and took another bite of bacon.

Liri stood up before facing me, his pale face looking down on me. "Are you pregnant?" There was no emotion in his voice. "Are you carrying the child of that elf from back home?"

Instinctively, my hand slid to my belly. Liri's eyes followed the movement.

"I don't know," I said.

"Don't know or didn't want to tell me until you had an opportunity to trick me into thinking it was mine?" His voice dipped, getting colder with each word.

"Trick you?" I asked in confusion.

"Is this why you threw yourself at me last night?" he demanded, his voice now rising. Color sprang to his cheeks like bruised plums. A vein bulged in his neck, and his teeth appeared to sharpen the more they flashed as he raged. "You discovered you were with child, so you came to my bed hoping to deceive me—make your bastard elf heir to the throne."

Jastra turned her chair around to face us and folded her hands in her lap, watching the show with obvious enjoyment. Her smile could not have been any brighter.

"I planned no such thing. I'm not a deceiver like the rest of you," I spat out with venom. "You know I don't want to be here. You know I was with another before you kidnapped me against my will. Last night was a mistake." Hensley's mistake, but I left that part out. She could thank me later.

"This is who you wish to make queen?" Jastra asked sarcastically.

"Shut up!" Liri snapped at his sister before returning his cruel gaze to me. "If it turns out you are pregnant, Aerith, it won't only be your baby's life you will have to fear for."

My mind went numb, my body as cold as death.

He'd never threatened me until now. Not only that, I'd lost any opportunity to end him first.

Bitter defeat pressed over my shoulders, and I sagged into the chair, every muscle in my body giving up. Whether I was pregnant or not, I felt doomed. Worst of all, my sister and Jhaeros were stuck in this mess with me.

I was at a complete and utter loss.

"It was me!" Hensley's chair fell back as she shot up and yelped. Once she saw all eyes on her, she continued with grim determination. "Sarfina glamoured me to look like Aerith. I wasn't aware of it until after the fact, but I was the one who threw myself at you, my king. It was me in your bed. I drank too much faerie wine at the ball. Please forgive me."

Jastra gasped.

Sarfina hissed.

Ryo burst into laughter. "Liri never could keep away from his brothers' females," the dark prince remarked.

Teryani showed off one of her rare smiles.

"Lies!" Liri bellowed. If he questioned Sarfina, she wouldn't be able to deny it, but he was too intent on Hensley. "You cannot protect your mistress, Hensley."

"It *was* me," Hensley insisted.

Ignoring her, Liri turned his cold eyes to me. "Get up."

I remained in my seat, glaring up at him. What did he plan to do? Throw me in the dungeons?

"I said get up." He spoke to me as though I were a stranger, an enemy—someone he loathed.

A shiver tingled down my spine.

"If you don't—"

"'I've wanted you for so long,'" Hensley said in a loud, commanding voice, impersonating Liri. It grabbed the attention of everyone inside the room as though he really had spoken. "'I've wanted to lick every inch of your body until you screamed my name. Mine, not his.'" I knew who Liri had been referring to. Cirrus. Hensley's voice rose as though emboldened, as though she was falling off a cliff gaining speed. I knew what awaited her at the bottom.

"Hensley, no!" I cried, but she was practically shouting, and everyone listened raptly as though she'd cast them all under a spell.

Hensley lifted her chest and smiled wickedly. "'I am your king now, and I will conquer you. Open your gates to me. Open them wide and prepare to be besieged by my royal tongue.'"

Someone snorted before Sarfina erupted into laughter. Tears streamed from her eyes, and she doubled over. Ryo joined her, nearly falling off his chair as he clutched his stomach. Teryani cocked her head in mild amusement but did not laugh. Jastra fought to maintain a scowl, folding her arms as though it would help prevent her from laughing at her beloved brother's expense.

My teeth clenched. There was nothing funny about any of this. In trying to save me, Hensley had sealed her fate.

Liri went rigid beside me. Tight fists pressed into his thighs. "Galather," he commanded in a calm, cool voice. "Take the human to her room and make sure she doesn't leave."

Galather swept through the room like a cold wind, promptly removing Hensley before she could utter one more damning word. But the damage was already done.

"Folas." The twin guard stepped forward the moment Liri said his name, as though expecting his summons. "Escort Princess Aerith to her rooms, and keep watch until I relieve you of your duties. Tell her guards they are dismissed from duty until further notice."

My heart dropped as Folas lifted me from my seat and

steered me to the door.

In the hall, my sister rushed toward us, wide-eyed. "Aerith!" she called. "I tried to get inside after the queen rushed out with Jhaeros, but the stupid guards wouldn't allow me through." She glared at the two guards standing outside the dining room.

"It's okay, Mel," I said in the most convincing voice I could muster.

"Hensley was dragged out of here a moment ago and now you." She put a hand on her hip and glared at Folas.

"Breakfast is over. Folas was about to escort me to my rooms." I smiled weakly.

Mel scowled. "That's my job."

"Not any longer," Folas said. "You and your boyfriend are relieved of duties until further notice."

Mel's brows pinched together. "Relieved of our duties?"

"By order of the king," Folas said firmly.

"What's going on?" Mel asked, her green eyes searching me for answers.

My mouth opened then snapped closed.

"Aerith?" Mel prodded.

"Time to go," Folas announced, pushing me forward. "Not you," he growled as Mel followed at our heels.

"Tell me what happened!" Mel demanded.

Folas stomped to a halt and swung around. "Your sister is pregnant," he announced.

My jaw clenched. How dare he deliver such intimate news to my sister? It was mine to share, and it might not even be accurate.

"Princess Aerith is with child," Folas pronounced once more like some kind of all-seeing shaman, "and the baby is not the king's."

CHAPTER TWENTY-ONE

Hensley

A lazy breeze blew in from the hills, across the lake, climbing up the castle's stone walls to my windows. I filled the frame, staring out over the lands I'd come to love. They were vibrant and sunny, unlike the gray gloom I'd grown up in. The air smelled sweet. I'd all but forgotten the stench of refuse and rot; suppressed memories of drugs and needles; violence and sex. Depression. Despair. Hopelessness.

Cirrus had saved me.

He'd saved Aerith too. When she first came to Dahlquist, she'd told me her family would have become desolate without his generosity.

I wasn't blind. I knew Aerith never loved Cirrus, but that hadn't stopped her from taking her commitment seriously. She'd served him as loyally as I had. It had bonded us, and I would sacrifice myself on her behalf ten times over. For friendship. For Cirrus. Even though Liri had been the brother to capture my fancy from the beginning. He had such a commanding presence and godlike beauty. I knew something had to be off when he'd invited me back to his room but, Lord help me, I hadn't been able to resist, and I couldn't entirely blame the faerie wine.

Aerith had done nothing wrong.

Some warped part of me was relieved she'd found comfort in another male's arms and had no intention of becoming Liri's mate. He'd always acted smooth as silk with his calm caressing tone and expressions. He hadn't been calm this morning...or last night. And it had gotten my blood pumping like lava.

It had been twenty months since I'd been intimate with anyone. Nearly two years. I felt as though I'd turned into a nun. Until Liri.

Oh Lord, his tongue.

Or rather, "Oh Sky," as they said in the elven and Faerie realms.

It was like nothing I'd ever felt. Everything in Faerie was better: from the food and wine to the music and males.

His touch had been as delectable as the faerie wine. And like the wine, it was intoxicating. He was intoxicating.

But now I would pay the price for Sarfina's deception. I hadn't been aware of the glamour, but I had most definitely been fully aware of him. It had been confusing when he first asked me to dance, but I'd believed it to be a family courtesy since I was to marry his brother. Between the wine and the way he'd gazed into my face, I'd become emboldened, molding myself against his lithe, muscular body, clutching him. And then he'd gripped me back.

I'd pressed my luck kissing him, but again he'd answered with enthusiasm and passion that made my already spinning head whirl faster.

I remembered every detail of the erotic encounter back in his chamber, every lick, every touch, every word spoken. I remembered screaming his name.

My next screams would not be ones of pleasure.

Would he punish me first or throw me directly in the dungeons?

I expected to be kept waiting the rest of the morning and likely afternoon. He'd see to Aerith first. Hopefully, he'd be gentle with her now that he knew she hadn't thrown herself at him in some feeble attempt to pass off her child as his. Was she truly pregnant? If so, who was the father? She hadn't breathed a word of him to me.

We were close and yet kept so many secrets from one another. Owning up to my part in the evening's deception was the least I could do. I'd never meant to get in the middle, though it was plain to me that Aerith held no affection for Liri and never would. My heart ached for him. For Aerith. And for myself. Happily ever after didn't appear to be in any of our futures.

My door opened and closed. It seemed much too early. The sun had yet to rise to its zenith. The breeze ruffled my skirts as though I was one of the curtains draping alongside the landscape.

"Turn and face me, human." Liri spit out the words in disgust.

So, I was no longer Hensley but "human."

I contemplated jumping out the window for half a heartbeat, but it was a fall that could break bones, possibly my neck. And I didn't want to flee. Faerie or bust. I had no place else to go. No place I'd rather be. Liri might kill me anyway, but I liked to believe it would be more pleasant by his hands than flattened against the earth below.

I turned.

Liri's arms were folded over his black fitted tunic. Long white hair streamed down his shoulders, reaching like pale fingers over his taut, muscled chest. He looked taller than I remembered, but then, we were never alone together.

Not until last night.

And early this morning.

And now.

I swallowed and kept my distance.

Liri looked me up and down, his lip curling. He sneered. "Get on your hands and knees like a dog, human."

Even as his compulsion pulled my body to the cold, hard floor, I glared at him for all I was worth—which wasn't much in his eyes. I knew he was angry, but after everything we'd shared it still hurt to be treated this way. I supposed he wanted to even the score after being humiliated in front of his family at breakfast.

Liri's eyes narrowed when he caught my daggered gaze. "Crawl to me," he commanded, pointing at the ground in front of him.

I crawled on my hands and knees toward him. I could practically hear his twisted thoughts. *Weak human. Pathetic. Powerless.*

My knees weighted down my skirt and made my progress pitiful, which likely pleased the king even more. Fortunately, there wasn't much ground to cover in my sparse room. I hoped he didn't kick me when I reached him. I tried to stop at the foot of my bed, out of kicking range, but my limbs refused to stop moving until I was crouched at his feet.

"Now lick my boot," he said cruelly, pointing at the toe of his boot.

I lowered my head, brown hair brushing the floor. No matter how hard I clenched my jaw, my tongue pried itself free of my mouth and ran up the toe of his boot. I tasted leather but luckily not dirt. Liri always managed to keep his clothes impeccably clean.

I lifted my head defiantly, hardly knowing what had come over me as the next words rose from my lips. "Is there anything else you would like me to lick?"

Liri's eyes expanded, wider than I'd ever seen them. Then they turned lambent, the desire swirling inside his steely irises turning them to liquid silver that sent a warm wave through my body. My mouth went dry. The king, realizing he'd momentarily forgotten himself, turned an angry shade of red. I'd seen him displeased before, but his pale face had never taken on the color of candied apples. Two red splotches filled his cheeks.

I didn't need compulsion to keep me on my hands and knees. Terror froze my body to the ground.

In a move so quick he seemed to blur, Liri grabbed me by the shoulders and hauled me to my feet. "You dare mock your king?" he bellowed, hot breath on my face.

I briefly closed my eyes, cursing my idiocy. He hated me, and he especially hated the reminder that a lowly human had put her mouth on his precious prick.

Warm hands wrapped around my neck and squeezed. My first thought was to wonder how someone so cold and so cruel could feel so warm, his body heating mine with the kind of fire I wanted to bask in naked.

My second thought was much more rational. *He's going to kill me.*

Liri's squeeze tightened in confirmation. He held me by the throat, his jaw clenched, and his eyes bright with anger.

Earlier he'd worshipped my body with the same hands crushing my windpipe. For years I'd tried to imagine what kind of lover he was. I never dreamed he would be so attentive, that he'd give himself over so completely, that he could be corny and turn giddy, like a little boy unwrapping presents at Christmas. It all felt like a beautiful dream now.

I didn't fight him. It would be useless. Instead, I met his eye and asked, "Have you ever killed a woman before?"

The pressure around my neck eased up, though Liri's hands remained wrapped around me like a scarf or a noose—it remained to be seen.

After several intense seconds, he released me.

"You are lucky Aerith is fond of you," he said in a bored tone as he wiped his palms over his pants as though touching me had dirtied his fingers. "But you must be punished. You will stay, standing here the remainder of the day repeating the phrase: 'I will obey my one true king, King Liri.'" He took a step back and folded his arms. "Now begin."

All the warmth and desire I'd felt for him turned to steam that hissed from my hot angry head. He'd already made me crawl to him on my hands and knees, and lick his damn boot. He should be punishing Sarfina, but I supposed it was more entertaining to humiliate the poor, defenseless human.

"I will obey my one true king, King Liri," I said bitterly.

He hadn't told me to say the words sweetly. King Liri grinned, as though delighting in my tone.

"Again," he commanded.

"I will obey my one true king, King Liri." I snarled the words, causing his eyes to light up. I shouted the sentence next—over and over while he watched transfixed.

Go away! My mind screamed. *Leave me be.*

My throat burned as I repeated his cursed phrase over and over again. Still he stayed and watched as though he was the one who'd been compelled to remain standing in place. Desire shone through his eyes. I didn't even think he was aware it had surged into his gaze—not when he had such amusing entertainment before him.

Loathing twisted my insides like poison consuming my once blindly obedient self. I wanted to do the exact opposite of my words. I'd loved him. Not many did. Aerith certainly didn't. I'd done her a favor by drawing his attention away. And I'd offered him something no one ever had. Love and affection weren't something to be stomped on, even if they were offered by only a mere mortal. All hearts were of equal value. I'd never offered mine to anyone until Liri.

"I will obey my one true king, King Liri," I rasped as my voice began to fade.

What if it left me altogether? Would I simply mouth the words like a guppy in a narrow glass vase filled with marbles?

"I will obey my one true king, King Liri." My voice turned into barely a whisper. "I will obey my one true king, King Liri." My shoulders sagged. "I will obey my one true king, King Liri." I sounded like a broken, scratchy record beyond repair. All emotion left my voice. I barely had any volume left. "I will obey my one true king, King Liri."

"Stop," Liri commanded.

Tears of relief threatened to spill from my eyes.

He stalked over to where I stood. I avoided looking him in the eyes, not wanting to have to speak in his presence ever again.

"Did my brother Cirrus ever bed you?"

The question took me so by surprise my gaze flew to his. The anger had left his eyes, replaced by mild curiosity.

"No." The answer rasped out of my lungs.

Liri narrowed his eyes. He took a step closer and spoke slower. "Did you sleep with Cirrus?"

Each word wrapped around my vocal cords and strangled out the truth. "Yes," I gasped, feeling the soreness of my throat ease up.

Liri smiled, his eyes brightening like sun breaking through gray clouds. "I knew he didn't save you merely to become a servant of the realm."

I squeezed my hands together in front of my skirt. My heart beat frantically. "It was before he met Aerith."

"And after?" Liri drawled.

I had a hard time not staring at his lips, the source of his beautiful voice. It was like watching an instrument produce a hypnotic tune.

"I refused him after he was spoken for."

It was the truth. After Cirrus brought the lovely blonde elf to Dahlquist to be his bride, I'd told him I could never lie with him again. Aerith was like a sister to me, and I'd be no man's mistress, not even a Fae prince's.

But what about a Fae king's? my mind taunted.

Liri's.

With Cirrus, the sex had been good. Better than good. Mind-blowing. But I'd never felt like I mattered much. Why would I, a human, matter to a Fae prince? Cirrus had spent more time staring at his own reflection in the mirror when we were together, as though intent on making love to himself.

I had not joined with Liri, but what we'd done together had been all-consuming and intimate on a deep, personal level. Liri had given me his full attention, worshipped my body, watched every orgasm he gave me as though he prized my pleasure above his own.

Only because he'd believed I was Aerith.

Liri's eyes were fully bright now, a wicked smile lifting the corners of his lips. "You are comparing me to my brother," he said knowingly.

"No, I'm not," I answered breathlessly. He'd released the compulsion from my tongue.

Liri's smile widened. "There's still more to compare. Get on the bed."

Horror and excitement crashed through me. His words were enough to heat my thighs. "My king, please," I said weakly.

His lips pursed into a smug smile. He said nothing as he waited.

My body didn't move. He had placed no compulsion over me. As dawning cascaded up and down my body, warming my cheeks, one of his brows hitched in challenge.

He made no move for me, but already my body was reacting, heart thumping, breath rasping, breasts aching, and nipples tightening into sharp peaks.

I opened my mouth to tell him to go, but no sound emerged. I wanted to blame his earlier compulsion of forcing me to repeat his cursed statement for stealing my voice, but it would have been a lie. He must have somehow eased my vocal cords because my mouth had worked fine when he questioned me about his brother.

"Get on the bed," he said again. Still no compulsion, and his voice promised wonders beyond the human imagination.

I backed up to my small bed slowly. Our eyes remained

locked like two dragonflies intertwined in flight. Once the backs of my legs bumped the bed, I crawled back, stopping in the center. My chest rose and fell rapidly as Liri stalked toward the bed.

"Cirrus never impregnated you?" he asked.

I shook my head. "He had a tincture sent to me afterward."

"Pull your skirts to your waist."

Don't do it, Hensley. There's still time to save your dignity.

But I'd damaged his that morning. If opening my legs for him spared me the dungeon, death, or banishment from Faerie, I would count my blessings.

I gathered my skirts and pulled them to my waist. Liri watched every inch of cloth, including my shift, as I gathered the material above my thighs. His eyes seemed to reflect sunlight and beam it back over my body.

"Open your legs," he said.

My neck burned as I did what he asked, exposing myself fully to him. I was consumed by a force more powerful than compulsion—true, unadulterated desire.

Liri's pale fingers went to his trousers, loosening them before joining me on the bed. I closed my eyes as he positioned himself over me.

"Look at me, Hensley. Look at your king."

At least he hadn't called me "human."

"Look into my eyes as I besiege you with my royal dick."

My heart thudded against my chest. Was he attempting to joke? Was all forgiven? He wanted me? Me! No glamours. No faerie wine. Just a Fae king and the human girl who loved him.

I looked at him straddling my legs and moaned, my hips arching.

There were worse punishments, and I'd wanted this last night, had ached when he hadn't given me more. I was not Aerith. He no longer had to wait for an improbable wedding night. I was his to plunder.

Once he entered me, the world turned to stardust and the laws of gravity no longer applied. He had me on the bed, against walls and the armoire. At one point, we ended up at the window, him behind me thrusting at inhuman speeds. I screamed his name across the valley and thought I heard it echo in the hills.

We finished where we'd started. On my bed. On my back, legs spread apart. When he finished, I was as wet and limp as the bedsheets below me.

Liri hadn't even broken a sweat. He straightened his tunic over his trousers, a satisfied smile on his lips as his eyes roamed my body where I lay spent on the bed. I didn't even have the energy to pull down my skirts and cover myself.

"My king," I said hoarsely. "Will you send me a tincture?" I didn't feel like speaking, but I also didn't want him to forget.

His smile was radiant and cruel. "No, sweet Hensley. I shall not."

My stomach bottomed out, and my heart lodged itself inside my throat in shock. I mustered enough strength to sit up and stare wide-eyed at my king.

His lips twitched as though holding on to an unspoken secret. The glow in his eyes seemed to brighten. I'd never seen Liri look so pleased. He looked me over one final time, as though deciding something, then started toward the door, but not before saying, "I will make my family rue the day they laughed at me. I shall make you their queen."

CHAPTER TWENTY-TWO

Aerith

The calm of my sitting room would be temporary, but I appreciated it all the same.

My mind whirled, feeling as sick as my stomach had earlier. Jhaeros's continued indifference. Hensley's public confession. The possibility that I was pregnant!

The queasiness had abated once I got away from all the breakfast smells. Now my stomach tied into knots of worry about what would become of Melarue, Hensley, Jhaeros, Devdan, and me.

While waiting for Liri, I sat in front of my campaigne board, playing against the onyx king in an endless game against myself.

At midday, lunch was delivered to my room, a meal of crusty bread, sliced cheese, and sliced turkey. At least the smell was minimal since it hadn't been recently warmed. I chewed the food slowly, giving my stomach time to digest each morsel bit by bit.

I paced the length of my apartments.

Played another game of campaigne against myself.

Waited.

And waited.

And waited some more.

The sun descended over the distant hills.

A dinner of stew and crusty bread was delivered to me to eat once more in silence. I lit lanterns as night spread across the lands, stretching its way to the windows of the castle. I changed into a night slip and lay in bed. It took hours to fall asleep, but finally, slumber came.

The following day, my first meal was delivered to my room again. Folas brought it in, and this time he stayed behind and watched as I poked at my eggs and bacon—the same breakfast as the morning before. He stood in my sitting room, arms folded, while I sat with the plate on my lap.

"How much longer does Liri plan to keep me locked in my rooms?" I demanded.

"Eat your breakfast," was Folas's reply. I stuck my tongue out at him. He shrugged. "I'm not leaving until you eat."

"Where's my sister? Was she returned to Pinemist, or is she locked in the castle?"

"Your sister is fine," Folas said. "She's allowed to move about the castle, just not the royal wing."

"No, of course not," I said moodily.

"Luckily the castle is made of stone so she can't burn it down."

When it became clear Folas truly wouldn't leave until I'd eaten the food he delivered, I stabbed at the eggs and swallowed them down, barely bothering to chew first. I grabbed the bacon with my bare hands. My nostrils flared and my stomach roiled at the smell, but I stuffed each piece in my mouth, chewing it into gritty bits before gulping it down.

I set my fork on my empty plate. "All done. May I leave my room now?"

Folas pursed his lips.

With a sigh of exasperation, I got up and shoved my plate in his hands. "Then you best be on your way."

He followed me from the sitting room into my bedchamber. As I led him to the door, my stomach turned, yanking me toward the waste receptacle where I heaved up everything I'd just eaten.

Folas stood watching the whole time, not even offering a washcloth. Instead, he stated what was appearing to be a pattern. "Morning sickness."

I was left alone to ponder my predicament. I glowered at the door. It might as well have been a set of bars.

I wanted to run to Jhaeros, tell him the news. But he was with Queen Naesala.

Had she slept with him? Kissed those handsome lips of his? Placed her bony fingers on my male?

More bile rose to my lips. I stormed to the receptacle and spit into the bin.

There wasn't much I could do besides wait for Liri's judgement. He had not sounded happy when I suspected I might be pregnant. And that was before he found out it had been Hensley, not me, who'd spent the evening entertaining him.

Maybe this would help him realize we weren't good for each other, but I doubted he'd let me off that easily.

At midday, I found out my answer when Folas returned with two footmen. He'd knocked then entered without awaiting my permission. I folded my arms from where I stood in front of the window, taking in the sight of the footmen. At least he wasn't accompanied by guards ready to haul me off to the dungeons.

"You are being moved to a new room, Princess Aerith," Folas announced.

"Where?" I immediately asked.

"The footmen will move your things," Folas said, ignoring my question. "Come with me. You don't have far to go."

Curious as to what Liri was up to, and more than ready to leave my rooms, I followed Folas into the hall. He led me toward the doors leading to the open hall. I followed right behind him, wondering which wing I was being moved to. My old room? Doubtful. No matter what, Liri wouldn't want me in the chamber I'd shared with Cirrus.

But Folas didn't lead me to the open hall. He stopped outside Hensley's door, which his twin stood guarding. They nodded at one another before Galather pounded on the door.

"Time to go, Miss Allen."

I looked at Folas. "What's going on?"

He ignored me altogether.

The door to Hensley's room opened slowly. She didn't step into the hall. All I saw was her brown head of hair bent in defeat, shoulders sagging in her cream-colored gown.

Anxiety swirled through my chest.

What had Liri done to her?

I started toward Hensley to give her a tight hug and try to reassure her everything would be okay. This was Sarfina's fault, not hers. But before I could reach my friend, Folas stepped between us.

"Are you ready, Miss Allen?" Galather asked. He sounded oddly patient and courteous.

She nodded and took a tentative step into the hallway. I tried to catch her eye, but Hensley had yet to look up.

"This is to be your room now, Princess Aerith," Folas announced.

All mental sensation momentarily left me. I gaped at him, my feet as immobile as the flagstones.

Was Liri punishing me as though I were a child? Moving me to a smaller room? Taking away the few private comforts?

My heart clenched. If this was my punishment, what was to become of Hensley? Did he think to banish her to the dungeons?

"What of Hensley?" I demanded. "I refuse to take her room if she is being sent to the gallows."

Folas and Galather exchanged a look and snorted.

"Miss Allen is being moved into your old rooms," one of them said.

I didn't see which twin spoke. I was once more gaping, my mind floating away, sucked into a tornado of intrigue and treachery.

Hensley looked up, her lower lip quivering. "Aerith, I am so sorry."

"Hensley, what's happening?"

"That is for your king to share with you," Folas said gruffly, pushing me toward the open doorway into Hensley's room.

Galather didn't have to force Hensley. She followed behind him, dragging her feet slightly.

"King Liri will speak to you soon," Folas said before giving me a final shove and closing me in.

Trapped again. My cell had just become much smaller. My nose wrinkled. It stank of sweat and sex. I spun around, lip curling at the sight of the rumpled bedspread. The servants hadn't bothered to change them before forcing me to trade chambers.

What kind of sick game was Liri playing?

I'd find out soon enough. Soonish.

As time wore on, it became apparent Liri was in no rush to explain his plans for me. Perhaps he was in my recently vacated chamber fucking Hensley on my old bed.

Sick, twisted bastard.

I walked up to the door and kicked it.

When Liri finally decided to make an appearance, he arrived with a footman who carried in the game of campaigne he'd gifted me.

Liri wore the golden crown atop his pale head. It was the only thing golden on him. The rest of his body was covered in fine black clothes with a collar that shimmered like bits of starlight had been plucked from the night's sky and sewn into the cloth. He looked deadly, unearthly—like a king not to be trifled with.

He waited until the footman left to speak. "Folas tells me

you are most certainly with child," Liri began, taking a stance near the door as though he didn't mean to stay long. "Congratulations, Sister."

I folded my arms and narrowed my eyes. He didn't sound angry, but I didn't trust him for one cold second.

"What have you done to Hensley?" I demanded.

"Nothing she didn't want me to do." Liri smirked. "Don't worry about Miss Allen. She has been made quite comfortable in your old chambers. I do apologize for the hasty rearrangement, but it is only fitting that my future queen takes the largest rooms beside mine."

"Your future queen?" I asked in confusion.

Liri's smile was as cold as his heart. "Hensley is to be my mate, and you have the honor of serving as her lady-in-waiting. Soon, I expect she will be with child. Our children will play and be tutored together. The eldest, anyway. I expect Hensley and I will have many children. My dear mother gave birth to eight of us, including two sets of twins, as you know."

I could only stare at Liri in horror. I thought I would have felt relief if he ever managed to turn his attentions to another female, but my stomach bottomed out.

"You cannot force yourself on Hensley," I said.

A menacing glare replaced Liri's smiling eyes. "Force," he said with a sneer. "You think a Fae king as beautiful as me would have to force a human to lay with him? No woman was ever so lucky as Hensley Allen from the mortal world. She will be queen of Dahlquist. Mate to the most cunning and gorgeous Fae in all of Faerie."

If I weren't so furious, I would have snorted at his overinflated ego.

"She will carry my child, my esteemed Elmray lineage. She will birth a son who will be heir to the throne. My sisters and brother will be forced to bow down before her. If you are a true friend of Hensley's, then you will be happy for her." Liri looked me up and down, pursing his lips. "You had your chance, Aerith."

Ohh! That scoundrel! If he wanted Hensley and she wanted him back, then fine. Great, actually! Freaking Fae-tastic! But forcing me to stick around was plain cruel. I wanted to slice open his neck, but of course, he'd called on me in the wrong damn room. I doubted Hensley kept a dagger stashed beneath her mattress. I didn't want to get near the wretched purple bed if she'd been making babies on it with Liri.

Good thing my stomach was already empty, or I might have spewed all over again.

"You still mean to imprison me in Dahlquist?" I demanded, stomping my foot.

Liri flashed me a smug smile. "Dahlquist isn't your prison, Sister. It is your home."

Queen Naesala made no appearance at dinner that night. Nor did Jhaeros.

Liri sat at the head of the table, Hensley on the opposite end in the chair Queen Naesala had occupied the night before. I felt as though I'd stepped into a nightmarish dreamscape. I did not bear the shock alone. The silence that fell over the table was as thick and haunting as fog over a cemetery.

Hensley had been transformed into a dark temptress. At least I hadn't been forced to dress her, despite Liri's threat to make me her lady-in-waiting. I almost hadn't recognized my human companion when she first walked in with Liri, wearing a transparent black dress that clung to her supple curves. Silky midnight leaves and vines were all that covered her breasts and groin. Her unbound brown hair shone with copper and gold highlights, while a shimmery black tiara rested above her bangs. Dark liner rimmed her eyes, making them appear seductive and exotic.

Teryani and Ryo stared at Hensley like a pair of hungry wolves while Jastra and Sarfina stubbornly refused to look at her. Liri must have spoken to his siblings before dinner. I kept expecting an outburst, an insult—something—but they all kept quiet until Teryani ventured to say, "How very delectable."

Liri's thin brows jumped, and the corners of his lips lifted into a smirk. The scene was so very different from the morning before. Liri oozed smugness. He leaned back in his chair as though it were his throne and he'd won a great victory, an exquisite prize.

We ate in silence. Jastra and Sarfina barely touched the food on their plates. I chewed slowly and carefully, pretending I was back home in my cottage, enjoying a hearty stew with Mel as we came up with baby names together.

Course after course, Liri finished his plate—the only one present with a lusty appetite. I'd never seen him eat so much. The only thing he didn't eat was the red velvet cake served last. He shot meaningful looks down the table at Hensley as though conveying that she was to be his dessert at the end of the meal.

"May I be excused?" Sarfina asked bitterly. It was the first time she'd spoken all evening.

Liri's smile faded as though soured by his sister's voice. He waved her away dismissively. With a pout, Sarfina scooted away from the table and walked out of the dining room.

"May I as well?" Jastra asked.

I looked at her in surprise. Was she really letting a human chase her off?

Liri nodded, not bothering to look directly at his most devoted sibling. "Take Ryo with you. He's stared at my fiancée long enough for one night." After they'd gone, Liri looked from me to Teryani. "The two of you may leave as well."

I hadn't taken three steps from the table when a footman

burst into the room, wheezing. "My king! The queen! She's"—
he gasped for breath—"dead."

CHAPTER TWENTY-THREE

Aerith

Blood stained the cream-and-gold embroidered bedspread. Queen Naesala's cold body, clad in a black lace sheath, was reflected in dozens of mirrors, her stony expression staring out into the guest room in Cirrus's old wing of the castle.

A deep cut ran across her neck like a ruby choker.

The queen's guards made no movement, as though awaiting orders from their new master.

Liri stood beside the bed, looking down with cold indifference. "So the bitch is dead," he said, sounding annoyed by the interruption.

In that moment, I felt certain he hadn't been the one to order her death.

I stood quietly behind the gathering. Teryani and I had followed Liri, Galather, and Folas from the dining room to the queen's chamber. I hadn't noticed Hensley get up from her seat and imagined her waiting obediently for her king to return and instruct her next move. Liri had finally found a more willing doll to dress up, instruct—mold to his every desire.

Right then, I didn't care.

Jhaeros paced the opposite side of the bed, wild-eyed,

wringing his fingers. Half the buttons on his collared shirt were unbuttoned and his thick brown hair mussed up. If the queen weren't already dead, I'd want to kill her myself.

"She warned me this would happen. She told me you were all out to get her," Jhaeros ranted to no one in particular.

"And how do we know it wasn't you who slit my aunt's precious throat?" Liri asked coldly.

The queen lay dead, and yet Jhaeros remained locked in the enchantment. I glared at Teryani, who was watching Jhaeros closely. She was the puppetmaster controlling her pet, but there was nothing I could do at the moment besides beseech Sky Mother not to allow Jhaeros to take the blame for the queen's death and meet a similar fate. Obviously it hadn't been by his hand, not when he was still besotted with the nasty Fae queen.

As though to confirm my bitter thoughts, Jhaeros gave a cry of outrage. "I worshipped the ground my queen walked on. She was my sun. My star. My moon. My life holds no light without her. No joy. No spark."

Liri rolled his eyes and huffed in disgust. "Someone get this elf out of here before my ears bleed."

"I will not leave my queen!" Jhaeros bellowed.

"Well, she left you," Liri said cruelly. He turned to Teryani and grinned. "Congratulations, Sister, the kingdom of Ravensburg is yours. As such, I trust you are capable of cleaning up this mess?" He raised a brow.

"You are making Teryani queen of Ravensburg?" I demanded. Did she think to inherit Jhaeros along with the kingdom? I couldn't figure out what she wanted with him. She'd never appeared interested in tormenting me in the past. I'd always believed her to be above such petty vendettas.

Liri turned to me and smiled coldly. "I would not give a kingdom away so easily, not even to my twin sister. After Cirrus died, my dear old aunt amended her will, making Teryani her heir."

Teryani turned her attention to the guards. "You will take my aunt's body to Ravensburg and prepare her for burial. A memorial will be held at the Ravensburg palace in three days' time. I expect all her subjects to attend, along with my own dear family."

Liri huffed. "You can hardly expect me to attend."

"Will you deny the request of your sister, a queen?" Teryani challenged.

"I shall attend," Liri acceded. "The whole family shall."

"Good," Teryani said with a nod. "Jhaeros, go with the guards and see to it that arrangements are made."

He folded his arms and shot her a foul look, one I'd seen on Jhaeros's face before. It seemed almost as though he were coming out of a trance.

"And when can I expect your majesty's arrival?" he asked gruffly.

"After I've made my own arrangements," she answered.

They stared one another down. Jhaeros was the first to look away, his eyes slipping toward me. Seeing this, Teryani coughed, regaining his attention. "She will be given a proper memorial," Teryani said firmly.

Jhaeros glared at her one last time before turning to the guards and ordering them into action. He sounded like his old self when he was annoyed, not bothering to mask his impatience—the same way he'd spoken to Lady Dashwood that long time ago in Pinemist.

"What should we do with this?" one of the guards asked, lifting a dagger with a bloodied blade from the nightstand.

It had been set there as callously as the queen had been killed.

"I will keep it for my collection," Liri said. He looked at Galather, who walked toward the guard. As the queen's guard grabbed the top end of the covers, presumably to wipe the blade, Liri snapped, "No! Leave the blood."

The guard froze. Galather reached him and snatched the

dagger from his hand.

"Is that truly necessary?" Teryani asked.

"That is the blade that killed a queen," Liri answered. "It should be kept intact to mark the occasion." At Teryani's careless shrug, Liri grinned. "Or perhaps you want it? You earned it, after all."

Teryani lifted her delicate chin. "Despite what you may think, Brother, this isn't my doing."

"No?" Liri asked, raising a brow.

But her word was good enough for the guards, who faced their new queen and bowed their heads. The Fae could not lie; therefore, she'd exonerated herself with her statement.

Then who *had* killed the queen?

I looked at Jhaeros, who told the nearest guard to wrap the expired queen in the blanket; it was ruined anyway. I couldn't decipher if his disgust was for the dead queen—that he'd somehow been playacting or recently released from an enchantment—or whether he was angry at Liri and Teryani for their lack of feelings toward their aunt's death.

"You two, take her body to the courtyard and arrange a cart to transport her back to Ravensburg," Jhaeros said, pointing a finger at one guard and then another. "Tell no one what has happened. The announcement is Queen Teryani's to make. I will follow behind in a carriage shortly."

The two guards nodded then finished rolling up Queen Naesala in the blanket until she was fully covered and obscured from view. One guard took her head, the other her feet. Folas opened the door for them to pass.

The third guard took a step forward, smacking his fist against his chest. "Shall I stay with you, my queen?" he asked Teryani.

The ghost of a smile appeared over her lips. "I am perfectly safe in my king brother's castle. Go down to the courtyard and arrange a carriage for Mr. Keasandoral. You will await him there and return with him to Ravensburg. I will send him down momentarily," she added.

The guard bowed and left the room.

"Ah," Liri said with a smirk, as though he'd figured something out. His eyes shown with love and admiration as he took in his twin. "Not your doing. Someone else's. Someone in need of a *royal reward*."

The way he said the last two words made my nostrils flare.

For all I knew, Jhaeros had already been forced to bed one queen. I would not walk away and allow him to bed another, especially not my sister-in-law. And finally, I had a weapon.

I lunged at Galather. Everyone had forgotten me, which gave me a temporary advantage. I knocked into the big lug's side and tore the dagger from his hands. I jabbed it in front of me as though it were a sword and backed up toward Jhaeros.

"Aerith, what in the seven hells are you doing?" Liri asked, sounding more amused than alarmed. It made me want to puncture his lung. He wouldn't chuckle if he was too busy wheezing.

"This elf was stolen from his home," I said, my voice shaking. I couldn't see Jhaeros's expression since he was now behind me. I had to keep my eyes on the terrible twins. "I won't stand idly by and allow you to manipulate my brethren from the elven realms."

"I assure you he came quite willingly," Teryani said calmly.

"Lie!" I bellowed.

She pursed her lips, taking me in with liquid blue eyes. "You know I cannot lie."

"I did come willingly."

My heart squeezed when I heard Jhaeros's voice.

No. I didn't believe him. I couldn't. This wasn't my Jhaeros. He must be someone else glamoured to look like him. That was a cruel specialty of my sisters-in-law. Who was this imposter? Maybe I'd worried for nothing and right now the real Jhaeros was back in Pinemist at home with his blind butler and deaf cook, pining for me. I bet Lady Dashwood stopped by daily to offer her comfort.

"That settles it," Liri announced. His eyes narrowed in impatience. He kept glancing at the door. "Now return the dagger to Galather."

Things were far from settled. My grip on the dagger tightened. "I want you to send my sister and Devdan back home."

Liri's head jerked in my direction. "You are no longer in a position to negotiate."

As though I ever was.

Teryani took a step forward. "We shall discuss it after our aunt's funeral," she said in a soothing voice. "I don't see what purpose the two young elves can serve in Dahlquist now that Aerith is no longer your primary concern."

Liri considered his sister a moment before nodding. "It will be discussed after the funeral." He nodded at Galather, who came forward and snatched the dagger from my fingers, which had turned to noodles.

Without another word, Liri marched out, his twin guards on his heels. Their footsteps faded away from the corridor, leaving me alone with the Jhaeros look-alike and the new queen.

Jhaeros—or whoever he was—folded his arms across his chest and faced Teryani with a glower.

"Close the door," she said. When he didn't move, she added, "Please," with a genuine smile of delight—the kind a mother might give to a stubborn child she couldn't help doting on.

With a low grumble, Jhaeros unfolded his arms, walked swiftly to the door, and closed the three of us inside the chamber of death.

Teryani looked from the now empty bed to Jhaeros and grinned. "Well done," she said in a pleased tone. "You upheld your end of our bargain. We don't have long, so I suggest you make haste with your 'royal reward.'" She stretched one lean arm in my direction.

My jaw hung open in confusion as Jhaeros swept up to me and gathered me into his arms, hugging me tightly against him. "Are you okay?" he asked, fury and concern in his voice.

"Jhaeros?" I asked, still uncertain.

He broke the hug to hold me in front of him, inspecting me from head to foot, wrinkles creasing his eyes the harder he looked. When his gaze settled on my belly, his eyes softened. "Is it true you're pregnant?" He slid a gentle hand over my stomach, and I wanted to bask in his warmth.

"What's going on?" I whispered, tears of relief filling my eyes.

"We made a deal," Teryani said. Somehow her soft voice magnified in the eerie aftermath of Queen Naesala's death. "If Jhaeros managed to kill my aunt, making me queen of Ravensburg, then I would see to it that the two of you were reunited and returned to Pinemist."

Hope bloomed like spring flowers throughout my body. Home. Could it be possible? A way out of Faerie? A powerful ally?

I turned to Jhaeros. "But how did you get close to Queen Naesala so quickly?"

"Oh, easy," Teryani answered for him. "I told my aunt the truth, most of it, anyway, that I'd happened upon your lover in the elven realms and that if she wanted to torment you, this was her chance."

I shook my head in disbelief. "She hated me enough to betroth herself to a stranger?"

"Oh, yes," Teryani replied in a tone I found a little too peppy. "She still blames you for Cirrus's death. I mean, it kinda was your fault. He married you to protect him and you failed."

"Thanks," I said grumpily.

Teryani shrugged. "To be fair, he would probably still be alive if he hadn't tried to poison Liri. Cirrus never was very smart. Anyway, I pretended to conspire with my aunt, telling her I could enchant your beloved to shift his affections to her. Luckily, your elf here put on a convincing show and came through on our bargain."

Jhaeros had risked everything for me.

I threw my arms around his neck, kissing him all over his face. His lips were not enough. "I love you," I breathed. "I love you. I love you. I love you."

"There is no one in this realm or the next whom I could love more than you, Aerith," Jhaeros said, his eyes filling with burning heat. He pulled me against him, caressing my back. "My heart wasn't truly beating until you made it so."

"I'll give you two a moment," Teryani said with a secretive smile.

Her footsteps were so light I didn't hear her leave until the door opened and closed. I pulled back enough to stare into Jhaeros's loving brown eyes. "You were really playacting this whole time?"

He grimaced, eyes squeezing closed for a moment. "It nearly killed me, especially when you were sick at breakfast. I had to pretend that Queen Naesala was really you and that you were the queen, but my imagination isn't powerful enough. So I kept reminding myself what was at stake. I had to free you at any cost. I nearly lost my mind when I found out it wasn't only your life in jeopardy but our unborn child's." Jhaeros's grip on me tightened.

"You really killed her?" I asked.

Jhaeros didn't grimace at this question. Jaw set, he nodded. "I would do anything for you, Aerith, without a moment's hesitation."

"Am I your sun, and star, and moon?" I asked teasingly.

This time Jhaeros scowled. "Ending her life was easier than saying those words."

I sobered at his confession. We both frowned, the mood turning somber.

"I just want to go home," I said, resting my head against his chest.

Jhaeros kissed the top of my head. "We'll be home soon."

"How?"

"After the funeral, Teryani promised to return all of us, including your sister and her friend."

My lips could not form a sigh of relief. I shook my head slightly. "He'll never let me go," I said gravely. "Even now that his attentions have turned to another female. He'll keep me in Dahlquist forever."

"I won't let him," Jhaeros said firmly. "We will return home, and our baby will be born in Pinemist. Most importantly, we'll be together."

I wanted to believe him, but even if we made it out of Faerie, Liri now knew where I lived. It didn't matter if I left the cottage to live with Jhaeros. The town of Pinemist was the first place Liri would send Galather and Folas to look. Plus, he'd seen Jhaeros's face. And Mel's. And Devdan's.

But maybe Teryani wasn't the only ally we had.

Maybe Hensley could somehow break through to Liri's cold, cruel heart.

I held back a scoff.

And maybe the sun would steal the sky, bringing light and warmth to every hour of every day.

There was no sense hoping for things that would never be.

Somehow I had to take matters into my own hands the way Jhaeros had.

CHAPTER TWENTY-FOUR

Hensley

After the dining room cleared out, I sat patiently watching the footmen clear the last of the plates before wiping the table down and leaving me utterly alone. I remained in my seat, candlelight flickering over me from the candelabra in the center of the table.

Queen Naesala was dead.

I couldn't find it in my heart to care. I hadn't known her well. What I did know is that she'd never liked Liri. I'd heard rumors that even when he was a boy she'd been hard on him.

I relished her death.

Unlike back home, in the mortal world, the Fae didn't waste time with trials. They moved forward. It was winner takes all.

Liri and I would have Queen Naesala's kingdom, as would our heir.

At least I assumed Ravensburg would be passed on to Liri. Who else? Ryo? What a disaster that would be.

It was poetic justice for Liri to take the throne from his aunt. Perhaps he'd even plotted it. I didn't want to know.

I shook my head.

No, Hensley, this is precisely the kind of thing you do need to know. If I was to be queen, I couldn't turn a blind eye to the happenings of the court, especially not my husband-to-be's affairs.

There were no clocks in the dining room, only the beat of my heart to tick away the time.

I half expected him to forget me. The queen was dead. Liri had important matters to attend to. Of course, he wouldn't hasten back to me. I should get up right now and go to my rooms.

I'd wait a little longer.

Given the shocking news of the queen's death, I was surprised when I heard Liri's voice at the door of the dining room.

"You waited." He sounded pleased, which made me happy I had waited.

"You told me to."

He closed the door behind him and walked into view, smiling smugly. "Will you do anything I tell you?"

"I don't know."

"Let's find out. Hmm?" He stalked toward me. "Push your chair aside and sit on the edge of the table."

Heat flooded my cheeks. The longer I waited, the more gleeful his look became. He already knew I'd do as he asked. It was why I'd waited here rather than fled to my chambers the moment everyone left. I wanted him. Needed him. Couldn't get enough of him. It felt as though I'd awoken from a long slumber, experienced sunlight after years trapped in a cave.

With as much poise as I could muster, I stood up and set my chair aside before sitting on the edge of the table.

"You did well tonight," Liri said approvingly. He looked me over as though I was a prized mare he'd selected for breeding.

He made me his fiancée, I reminded myself. *I'm no mistress. I will be queen.*

If only my stepfather could see me now. He'd once called

me a whore. A slut. A worthless piece of garbage who would never amount to anything.

"*I'm going to be a queen,*" I wanted to shout into his sneering face.

"Open your legs," Liri's voice invaded the storm clouds in my mind.

A queen, I reminded myself. *I'm going to be a queen.*

Even queens had a carnal duty to perform. *Especially* queens. Liri needed an heir, and I wanted to give him one. I wanted to serve the kingdom of Dahlquist and the Elmrays. I especially wanted to serve my king. Liri. I never dreamed I'd attend him in this capacity, but I was just as willing as the day I'd entered the beautiful world of Faerie.

I spread my legs wide.

Liri's eyes dilated. "I thought I preferred a female who played hard to get, but this is so much better," he said, voice dripping with satisfaction.

I nearly fell off the edge of the table in surprise when Liri dropped to his knees in front of me. He grabbed my thighs and leaned forward.

Blood rushed between my legs.

"My king," I gasped, feeling his hot breath at my entrance. Before I could say anything more, his mouth was on me.

I moaned, my lashes fluttering closed.

Why was he doing this? Was it my reward for dressing and doing as he'd said?

He'd told me to keep my head held high, that it would displease him if I cowered in front of his family. I'd done my best. It had been easier after he sent a maid to dress me. Thankfully, he'd listened when I asked that someone other than Aerith attend me. I didn't mind lording my new position over his family, but not Aerith. She'd always been kind to me. I could never make her wait on me like a servant.

Liri had sent a beautiful young Fae woman to assist me instead. After she finished my hair and makeup, I'd hardly recognized myself in the mirror, which made it easier to pretend I was someone else, a desirable woman fit for a Fae king. A king currently kneeling between my legs.

When his tongue penetrated me, I cried out his name. "Liri."

I gripped his silky head of white hair in my hands. Liri fastened his fingers around my wrists, pulling them away, pinning them to the table.

He lapped and thrust with his tongue.

"Liri. Liri. Liri." I said his name over and over again.

Sweet Jesus. It was wrong to want him this much. Did hell exist in the Faerie realm? If so, I was surely headed straight down into the fiery pits.

No, that was my stepfather talking.

"I want to be a mother," I rasped. *I want to have your babies.*

Liri paused his ministrations to look up at me with triumphant eyes of the brightest, shining silver. He loosened his hold on my wrists and stood.

"I'll give you all the children you could ever want, sweet Hensley."

I frowned. "Don't call me that. That's what you called Aerith."

Liri chuckled and freed the hair I'd tucked behind my ear, sweeping it until it covered my rounded lobe. "Jealous?" he asked gleefully.

When I pursed my lips, he chuckled again and unfastened his trousers.

Once embedded deep inside me, he leaned closer, whispering inside my ear. "You have no need to be jealous, darling Hensley. I am not my brother. I am not weak. I will not stray."

My heart beat rapidly inside my chest, pounding with longing and hope.

This was the second chance, the new beginning I hadn't dared dream of.

I would be the loving mother I never had. And Liri, for all his cruel, murderous ways, protected those he cherished. He seemed to value family above all else so long as his close circle remained loyal to him.

I trusted him when he said he would be faithful, though there was one thing he hadn't offered.

His heart.

I hoped, rather than believed, a child would change that.

CHAPTER TWENTY-FIVE

Melarue

Beautiful Fae clad in black filled the throne room at Ravensburg's castle. The males wore fancy trousers and fitted jackets. The females wore all manner of dresses that clung to their lithe bodies and shimmered with dark jewels. Black feathers, lace, tulle, and ruffles adorned their gowns. It was like no funeral I'd ever imagined.

Devdan and I stood beside Aerith near the open casket with the rest of the Elmray family. The throne sat empty on the dais just above the casket.

I wore tight black pants and a black blouse. Beside me, Aerith was dressed in an off-the-shoulder long-sleeved gown that fanned out past her knees. Her hair was parted down the middle and pulled back into a wide black hair clip adorned with black crepe flowers.

Jastra's teal hair had been tied back with black ribbons, and her flat belly was exposed beneath a tight black corset. She wore a long, wispy skirt with slits up both legs.

Sarfina's blonde-and-gold hair was pulled up and tucked into a delicate veil that covered her forehead. Her black dress had lace sleeves and a full lace skirt.

Hensley was as scantily clad as Liri's sisters. I hardly recognized the innocent human I'd first met upon arriving in

Faerie. She stood beside King Liri, who wore a shiny black crown with sharp spikes that jutted like castle spires on the sides.

I felt like I was attending a macabre costume party. In fact, there was a masquerade ball taking place after the funeral tonight. I'd never understand the Fae.

An older male with a wrinkled face and gray hair stepped onto the dais and cleared his throat, the sound rumbling around the large room. I guessed he must have been using magic. The gathering quickly quieted.

"Today we lift our heads in memory of a great queen." He paused, allowing the gathering to look up toward the tall ceiling.

I slid a glance at Devdan. He smirked and nearly made me burst into laughter. I quickly bit my tongue and stared up, which was yet another Fae novelty. Maybe it was only for royalty. Where I came from, we bowed our heads in respect, but whatever. This wasn't my realm.

"We honor the beautiful female who ruled the kingdom of Ravensburg. We give praise for her governance. We mourn her loss the way we would mourn a mother's, a sister's, a child's, a lover's. Her life meant more to us than our own existence."

"Speak for yourself," I muttered.

"Shh," Devdan scolded, but his eyes lit up with mirth.

A certain giddiness had taken hold of us the moment we learned Liri had found someone other than my sister to obsess over. Aerith said Teryani would get us back home tonight, during the masquerade ball. The new queen wasn't so bad after all. But Jhaeros impressed me the most. Aerith had filled me in on the foreplay turned to foul play. I had to admit that was some total badassery on his part. Jhaeros had killed a freaking queen of Faerie! I couldn't call him boring any longer.

He stood at the casket, his back to the crowd, playing the

part of the bereft lover until the very end.

It struck me as ironic that after trying to save him from the Fae the day we left Pinemist, he'd been the one to rescue all of us.

I mean, I would have found a way out eventually. Jhaeros's approach was simply more resourceful. Big surprise. Mr. Efficiency. Yep, my soon-to-be brother-in-law, ladies and gents.

I sorta loved him now. As a brother. Obviously.

I mean, he was making me an aunt! It made me feel so grown up.

"I'm surprised you're not saying 'ew,'" Aerith had said after I'd jumped in the air and whooped when she told me.

To which I informed her, "There is nothing *ew*, only *cu*-te, about a baby."

I planned to teach my little niece or nephew so many cool battle moves. I wondered what age was old enough to hold a sword. I was going to be the best aunt, way better than Shalendra.

In between my eager thoughts, the crusty old Fae droned on about the wonder that had been Queen Naesala.

"How come he doesn't have to look up?" I complained, to which Devdan shushed me once more. "I'm getting a crick," I said, rubbing the back of my neck.

"Hang in there, Mel," Aerith whispered without looking over.

In the past, it had seemed weird to think of her as a princess, but since observing her in Faerie, I was struck by her poise and grace. Cirrus had never deserved her, and neither did Liri, but I could understand why my sister had captivated them. She was a rare beauty and kind soul and—you guessed it—badass.

"At this rate, you'll be giving birth in Ravensburg," I said, maybe a little too loudly judging by the glare Sarfina cut my way.

I lifted my brows, silently daring the spiteful blonde to

argue with me. Her eyes narrowed sharply. Then she turned to face the droning speaker.

"And so, with heavy hearts, we send Queen Naesala's spirit to the sky realm, which will shine brighter with this royal soul we send from Faerie." The male lifted his hands above his head. Everyone around me did the same.

Rolling my eyes, I stretched my arms, yawning as I did.

Devdan kicked my boot.

"Hey," I said, dropping my arms. I kicked him back.

He smirked.

"And now it is my great honor to welcome our new queen," the old male said. *Finally.* "Teryani, former princess of Dahlquist and beloved daughter of the royal Elmray family, please step forward and accept your throne."

I lifted onto my tiptoes, trying to spot Teryani. I hadn't seen her during the service. Two guards marched out from a side entrance into the throne room, taking up places on either side of the dais. Then Teryani swept into view, commanding the attention of all those present.

I'd never seen her wear any color other than white. On this day, she wore a high-collared dress that draped down her arms and all the way to the floor. It looked like an elegant cloak with black feathers lining the inside of the wide collar framing her face. Her white hair had been braided into a crown at the top of her head. Smoky-gray powder dusted her eyelids, and her lips were stained a matted deep red.

A hush fell over the throne room as Teryani approached the casket, looking like Lady Death come to consume the old queen. She reached inside and pulled out a large gold ring with an oval sunstone that glinted as she slid it onto her finger.

Ew. I kept my disgust to myself. Teryani looked scary in black.

Next, she retrieved a solid gold crown and held it in front of herself like a shield at the beginning of a great battle.

When Teryani pivoted, her cloaklike black gown swished through the air like a raven swooping in on a prize. She handed the crown to the male officiating the ceremony, then made her way up to the dais. The male followed her, waiting until Teryani had taken her seat on the throne. She jutted her chin in a regal gesture.

He cleared his throat again. "It is my great honor to stand before the friends and citizens of Ravensburg and crown our new queen: Queen Teryani. All hail the queen." As the crown was set on Teryani's head, echoes of "all hail the queen" swept across the throne room.

The male who had crowned Teryani came down and closed the casket. Then he beckoned four guards who came forward and hoisted the coffin from its stone pedestal. An aisle formed in the crowd as they carried it out.

The Elmray family was the first to be summoned onto the dais to kiss the royal ring on Queen Teryani's finger, including my sister. A slow line formed after them.

I turned frantically to Devdan, my eyes expanding. "Please tell me we don't have to kiss the corpse ring?"

Devdan's face screwed up in disgust. "We're not her subjects. We're not even Fae. Plus, ew."

"Right?" I said.

Devdan took my hand in his and pulled me out of the line that had formed behind us. He tugged me gently, walking backward slowly. He ducked down and darted through the sea of black gowns and tailcoats, taking me with him. I stifled a giggle, reminded of the time we'd fled the commissioner at the market back home.

We weaved through the crowd, escaping into the corridor where lesser Fae waited to get inside the throne room to kiss their new queen's corpse ring.

"Teryani will be late to her own masquerade," I noted.

"What should we do while we wait?" Devdan asked.

"Explore, of course!" I gripped his hand and tugged him

down the hall. "I heard you can see all the way to Dahlquist from the watchtower."

Devdan chuckled when I pulled him behind me. The crowd thinned as we rushed along the stone corridor. When the hall bisected into three directions, I marched up to a guard positioned against the wall.

"Excuse me, which way to the watchtower?"

The Fae guard glowered at me. "The watchtower is for guards."

"We're Princess Aerith's guards," I answered, beaming.

"Guards of Ravensburg," the guard amended curtly.

"What about the queen's family?" I asked. "She's my sister's sister-in-law, which makes Teryani my—" I paused, searching my brain before casting Devdan a look for help.

"Queen," the guard furnished.

"Actually, we're not from around here."

The guard folded his arms and narrowed his eyes.

Devdan took me by the shoulders and steered me toward the hallway to the left. "But it's been a pleasure visiting this beautiful realm. Lovely scenery you have. Excellent cuisine and wine." He lifted one hand off my shoulder to kiss his fingers. After we turned the corner, he added for my ears alone, "Though the natives aren't particularly friendly."

I snickered. "I still want to find the watchtower."

"Of course you do." Devdan shook his head, but there was a smile on his lips. He totally wanted to see it too.

It felt like it took half of the afternoon—with no help whatsoever from any of the castle guards—but it was worth it when we found the steep stairs leading up and reached the tower.

It was a clear, sunny day that promised bold adventures waiting over the next horizon.

I leaned over the stone ledge, staring out toward the rolling hills of Dahlquist where we'd first portaled our way into Faerie. The castle was out of sight, but I imagined it rising grandly beyond the hills.

I pushed away from the stone wall and moved to the opposite side where forests and distant mountains sprawled out as far as the eye could stretch. To the left lay the kingdom of Ravensburg and the beautiful river district with shops and cafés lining a wide shimmering river. I would have liked to explore in town if there'd been time.

The watchtower also afforded us a view of the castle's courtyards. They were mostly empty since everyone was gawking inside the throne room or heading to their chambers to cast off their mourning clothes and change into festive frocks before the evening's masquerade ball.

Hidden in a labyrinth of tall, bushy hedges, I spotted my sister and Jhaeros locked in an embrace. Warm satisfaction filled my heart as I watched them kiss.

Devdan joined my side and followed my gaze down to the courtyard. "I'm glad things worked out for them. Aerith doesn't belong in Faerie. I'm sure she's counting the seconds until she's back in Pinemist."

Speaking of Pinemist...

I turned to Devdan. "I don't want to go home. Not yet."

Devdan frowned. "You want to stay in Faerie longer?"

"Gads, no!" I made a choking sound for effect. "But I would like to visit the mortal world before my sister becomes a mother. I want to be there for the birth. In the meantime, I want to go skydiving in Switzerland, hot-air ballooning over the pyramids, scuba diving at Barracuda Point in Malaysia, motorcycling the Great Ocean Road in Australia, hiking to the top of Mount Everest."

A smile crept over Devdan's lips. "I don't know what any of that stuff is, but it sounds like fun."

I sucked in a breath, having forgotten to take one in my excitement. "I don't want an adventure of a lifetime. I want my life to be one adventure after another." I gave his shoulder a playful push. "And I'd like to meet a shape-shifter."

I wanted to meet every kind of supernatural the mortal world had to offer.

"We're talking about a *female* shifter, right?" One brow rose over Devdan's forehead.

I shrugged, letting my coy smile answer for me.

Devdan sighed. "Just promise me no kissing."

"But what if he's a dragon shifter offering me a piece of his treasure for a kiss?"

"Mel." Devdan put his hands on his hips.

I laughed. "Fine, but you have to promise me the same."

"Done."

His immediate answer warmed my heart and made me smile wide. I felt like the happiest female in all the realm—even luckier than the new queen. A crown could be stolen, as both Liri and Teryani had proven, but true feelings could not.

Looking back down into the labyrinth where Aerith and Jhaeros remained lip locked, I was reminded my happiness was shared by my beloved sister.

"Watch out, human world. Here we come," I said to Devdan. "Besides, I think those two love doves deserve some time alone."

CHAPTER TWENTY-SIX

Aerith

Jhaeros's lips were like a taste of home and happiness as we kissed in the maze of hedges, hidden from prying eyes. He placed a loving hand on my belly. He stopped kissing me to speak but kept his lips near mine as though he couldn't bear to pull them entirely away.

"I have something for you," he said.

My eyes widening, I watched as Jhaeros reached into his pocket and pulled out the pendant my mother had gifted me before her death. I hadn't seen it in over two years. I had given up all hope of ever finding it, believing it was gone forever.

I blinked several times, not certain I trusted my sight. Jhaeros held the silver filigreed necklace with the blue stone to me in his hand, but all I could do is stare at the pendant.

"How did you find it?" I asked.

"Teryani used magic to locate the pendant. It was part of our bargain."

My gaze flew from the pendant to Jhaeros's eyes. "I'm surprised she bothered with something so trivial."

"When it comes to you, Teryani appears to be quite accommodating." Jhaeros raised a dark brow.

I pursed my lips and shrugged. "Well, I am the sweetest of

her sisters."

Jhaeros gave a grunt of amusement. "I think it's more than that. May I?" He slid behind me. The warm air of his breath caressed my neck as he unclasped the pendant and threaded it gently around my neck.

It was only when the light weight of the silver and stone touched my chest that I brushed my fingerpads over my long-lost pendant.

"Thank you," I breathed.

A grin split Jhaeros's lips. "That's not all. I asked Teryani if she could locate Melarue's pendant as well, and she did." Jhaeros reached into his opposite pocket and pulled out a pendant identical to mine, save for the red stone.

Tears filled my eyes and my heart sped up, overwhelmed with gratitude and love. I launched myself at Jhaeros, squeezing him into a hug and kissing his smoldering lips.

After we pulled apart, I touched his cheek. "Thank you from the bottom of my heart."

Jhaeros embraced me before attempting to hand over Mel's pendant.

"You should be the one to give it to her," I said.

Jhaeros nodded and pocketed my sister's pendant.

"When we return home, I want to marry you at once. I can't stand another night apart."

"I'm ready," I said, no longer craving more time alone. Being with Jhaeros filled every part of my being with joy. Besides, in another eight months or so I'd need help changing nappies. Watching Jhaeros handle a crying infant was something I very much looked forward to seeing.

I grinned wistfully into his handsome face. I bet he'd make a wonderful father—a doting dad as kind and wonderful with our child as he was to me.

Tonight we would leave the ball and return home together. I was determined never to part ways again.

With reluctance, I pulled away from Jhaeros. "I must go to

Teryani's rooms."

Jhaeros frowned but said nothing to stop me. Teryani had hastily explained the rest of her plan to us before we left Dahlquist. It was rather genius.

She'd told her guards to expect me, so when I arrived at her chamber, they allowed me inside without question.

No one guarded or attended to Teryani inside her room. The heavy crown no longer rested on her head of white braided hair, but she still wore the ghastly black gown. I preferred her illusion of goodness and innocence. Seeing the harsh angles of her high, dark collar gave me chills of unease. She looked like the queen of nightmares.

"You are not fond of my gown," Teryani said as though reading my mind.

"I prefer you in white," I answered honestly.

A smile lifted her cheeks. "I was not aware you cared one way or another." She looked me up and down. "Black doesn't suit either of us."

I folded my arms. "I had no idea you coveted a crown."

Teryani lifted her slender hands to her hair, touching her braid as though feeling for the crown. She smoothed her fingers along the woven strands. "It is a responsibility Liri and I must bear. As an Elmray and his twin, I accept this burden."

"Burden?" I asked incredulously.

She pursed her lips. "We received reports that our cousin, Malon, had begun worming his way into our aunt's life. It was only a matter of time before he convinced or, more likely, coerced her into replacing me as heir of Ravensburg."

"I'm surprised she named you at all," I said.

Rather than scowl, Teryani smiled. "I am more loveable than Liri."

I quirked a brow but ventured no further comment.

"So you entrusted Jhaeros with the task of dispensing of the queen. I know the Fae are unable to lie, but it's not as though you're required to hold up your end of a bargain.

Why are you helping us?"

"The male means nothing to me. I am helping *you*." Teryani's expression turned neutral as she stared into my eyes.

"Why?" I pressed. Despite my earlier joke, I doubted sisterhood was the real reason.

Teryani continued to gaze at me. I was just beginning to accept that she would withhold her motivation when she spoke.

"Cirrus and Liri weren't the only ones to love you, sweet Aerith. I do too. But unlike my brothers, I require love in return." My eyes nearly popped out of my head and rolled over the floor like marbles. Teryani lifted her chest and gave the barest shrug. "Your male from back home was willing to kill a queen for you, so I suppose that makes him worthy of your heart." Her gaze flicked over the pendant at my chest and a mirthful smile twitched over her lips. It was almost childlike in its sincerity. In a blink, it was gone, replaced by the cool confidence of a Fae princess destined to rule as queen.

I had no words, only utter surprise as I looked at my sister-in-law as though seeing her clearly for the first time. I knew Jastra and Sarfina had never liked me—even loathed me. I hadn't gotten the same vibe from Teryani, but I had figured she tolerated me at best. I never would have suspected that she *loved* me. What was it with Elmrays and elves? In particular, what was it with Elmrays and *me*?

Lifting her head, Teryani strode to the door and pulled it open. "Send in Ella." Teryani left her door cracked open. She swept across her chamber, taking a seat on a high-back brocade chair.

It wasn't long before a blonde female with pointed ears entered the chamber, closing the door behind her. She walked toward Teryani, stopping five feet from her chair to dip into a curtsy.

"Stand beside Aerith," Teryani commanded.

"Yes, my queen," Ella said.

Ella gave me a friendly smile as she took the spot beside me. We were the same height with similar hair and eye coloring.

"Ella is also an elf, like you," Teryani said, doing her mind-reading trick. "Serving by choice," she added with a wry smile.

"Oh yes, certainly," Ella said eagerly.

Teryani rose from the chair she'd only just occupied. She walked over and looked between us, eyebrows pinched as she studied us. "Glamours work better when the impersonator shares common characteristics. Ella, you are to be Aerith from now on. Learn as much as you can from her in the few hours you have left. I have already told my brother I wish for you to join my household. He can't keep our whole family for himself. I'll send a trusted guard at midnight to return Aerith and her friends home."

Teryani moved swiftly away from us, snatching up a black feathered mask from her vanity before striding to the door.

"Sister," I called.

She stilled but did not turn around to face me.

"Thank you."

Teryani pulled the mask over her head and swept out of the room without a word or backward glance.

As soon as she closed the door behind her, I beckoned Ella to sit as though these were my own private chambers. Words tumbled from my lips as I summarized my childhood back in Pinemist. When I reached the part about becoming a princess of Dahlquist, I tried to spare no detail, including the intimate details of my marriage to Cirrus and complex relationship with Liri. She needed to know everything if we were to pull this off. With Ella joining the court at Ravensburg, we actually stood a chance.

In several months time, Teryani would send word to Dahlquist that, unfortunately, Ella, in the role of Aerith, had suffered a miscarriage. It was easier than Ella having to pad her belly beneath gowns as the months progressed. Nor did I want Teryani stealing someone's baby as a pretend nephew or niece.

I placed a protective hand over my belly. Just talking about a miscarriage made my heart constrict.

"Who is the father?" Ella asked, leaning forward in her chair.

"Liri doesn't know, which means you don't need to either," I answered.

Jhaeros was mine and mine alone. Even a glamour of me wasn't allowed to share the memory of our kisses and joining.

The moment I was confident Ella knew enough, I dismissed her to enjoy the remaining hours of the masquerade—her last night as herself before Teryani glamoured her to look like me. Afterward, I went and fetched Jhaeros, Mel, and Devdan. We returned to Teryani's rooms right before midnight, which is where Mel shared her plans to travel to the mortal world with Devdan.

"Just until the baby is born," she added quickly.

"I don't know if the mortal world can handle you, Mel," I said with a grimace.

My sister laughed. "I'll try not to draw too much attention to myself."

I turned to Devdan and put my hands on my hips. "If anything happens to her, I'm holding you responsible."

"What if something happens to me?" he joked.

"I can live with that." I smirked.

"Nothing's going to happen to us," Mel chided. "We'll bring our swords just in case."

I snorted. "Uh, Mel. I don't think you can walk around the mortal world with a sword at your hip."

"Daggers then," Devdan said.

"They have something called a switchblade," Mel cut in. "I saw a picture of one in a book on human weapons. It's super wimpy looking but easy to conceal."

"Perfect," Devdan said.

He and my sister grinned at one another then high-fived.

I groaned. "Promise you'll be careful, and check in frequently."

"Of course. We'll send these things called postcards with a picture of where we're at on one side and a quick note on the other."

I wrinkled my nose. "I'd like more than a quick note. I want a full report."

"I'll fill you in when we return home," Mel said dismissively. "We're going to be too busy to sit in one place writing you pages."

I shook my head. That wasn't good enough. I'd just have to pop in on Mel and make sure she was doing all right—preferably on a warm sandy beach with yummy nonalcoholic beverages.

"Before you rush off, Jhaeros has something for you."

Mel's eyes lit up in her face. "And it's not even my birthday." She looked at Jhaeros expectantly.

Clearing his throat, he reached inside his pocket and held out the red filigree pendant to my sister.

Mel's mouth flew open. "Oh my gosh, my pendant from Mom!" Her eyes darted to me, lowering to my chest. "And you have yours back too!"

I nodded, grinning. "Thanks to Jhaeros."

My sister turned her attention back to Jhaeros. She stared at him for several heartbeats before tackle hugging him. Jhaeros's body jerked back, but he kept his footing and patted Mel awkwardly. I could barely contain a laugh. He'd likely received more hugs today than all the days of his life combined.

After hugging him, Mel swiped the pendant from Jhaeros's palm and dangled it in front of her face. Devdan leaned in, squinting at the stone.

"Is that a ruby?"

"Who cares? It's from my mom." My sister stuffed it into her pocket then grinned at Jhaeros. "You're not so bad, Jhaer."

He snorted. "Thanks."

Yep, Jhaeros was getting more than he bargained for with me. I'd talk to him about surprising Mel in the mortal world after we were returned to Pinemist. I'd miss her too much, otherwise, plus I wanted to keep Devdan on his toes. Just because big sis was knocked up didn't mean she was out of the picture. At least Mel had her sights set on adventure travel and not a romantic getaway. She wouldn't have the patience for sunset cruises or couple's massages.

A knock at the door silenced our group. We turned our heads and watched a tall royal guard enter.

"I am here by order of my queen, Teryani, to send you home through a portal."

Mel raised her hand then lowered it. "Can you make that two portals? One to Pinemist and one to the mortal world?"

The guard glanced at me.

"It's fine," I said. "Send my sister and her friend to the mortal world first. Can you glamour their ears to look human while you're at it?"

With a nod, the guard looked at Mel. "Where would you like to go?"

"Surprise me," Mel said, grinning eagerly.

Without fanfare, the guard opened his arms. The middle of the room seemed to wobble as the air in the center rippled.

"Wait!" I cried when Mel took her first step toward the portal. I rushed up to my little sis and crushed her in my arms. "I love you, Melarue," I whispered. "Thank you for coming to find me."

"Yeah, well, we can't all be the hero, but at least I was part of the story." She hugged me back and flashed me one last smile before sprinting toward the portal. "Headfirst this time!" she yelled before disappearing into thin air.

"That's my cue to go," Devdan said. "Later, Princess." He winked at me then dove in after Melarue.

The rippling air evened out. The royal guard lifted his arms once more, and the air swelled again.

I looked at Jhaeros and smiled. "Next stop Pinemist."

"About damn time." He took my hand in his, and together, we returned home.

CHAPTER TWENTY-SEVEN

Hensley

Fae lights twinkled from the ballroom ceiling, pulsing with the orchestra's seductive melody. Beautiful masked creatures surrounded me, a swirl of color after the gloom of the funeral.

I felt like a ballerina in my pink dress with its snug sleeveless bodice and sheer ankle-length skirt. A decorative crown that sparkled with pink and purple rhinestones was pinned securely at the top of my head while my hair flowed in brown waves down my back.

Liri wore a heavy metal crown with large sapphires and had changed from black to an only slightly less dark midnight blue suit. He twirled me around in the center of the ballroom, warm hands sliding from my fingers to my hips. The rest of the assembly could be waltzing in the outer courtyard for all the attention he paid them.

Liri gazed on me as though I was the center of his universe.

I knew it was all an illusion: as gorgeous and glittery as this magical masquerade ball. I wasn't Liri's beloved. I was his new pet.

But unlike Aerith, I liked being kept.

My body blossomed beneath the king's gaze. My

imagination ran wild. My heart yearned to become more than a servant—to discover joy with this dark king. To become a mate. A mother.

In his arms, I didn't feel trapped.

I felt free.

In the past, Liri had barely partaken in dancing, but tonight he kept me in his grasp song after song as though he meant to waltz his way into dawn. It wasn't until the band took a break that we did.

"Would you care for sparkling wine, darling Hensley?" Liri asked.

"No, thank you," I said, hoping that soon I would be pregnant. "Is there something less potent? Like water?"

He chuckled and reached a hand to my face to tuck my hair behind my ear. "We would never drink something so boring at a party, but there might be sparkling punch."

Of course the punch sparkled. This was Faerie.

My bright smile dimmed when an approaching raven-haired male sneered at the sight of me. "A human queen. That will be the day."

Liri puffed up his chest and glared at the intruder. "Sooner than you think."

Bottomless blue eyes looked at us through a snarling gray wolf mask. The male's upper lip curled, nearly touching the mask's jagged teeth. "Disgraceful," he growled. "What would your father say?"

"Nothing, since I killed him." All warmth vanished from Liri's eyes as his gaze turned to sharpened steel.

The black-haired male in the wolf mask scoffed. "Crowns are easily stolen, are they not, Cousin?" He didn't wait for an answer before spinning around and prowling across the ballroom like an animal after his next meal.

A chill clawed over my bare shoulders. My head jerked to look at Liri, hoping I'd feel better once I saw my white-haired king and lover. His jaw was locked as he glared after the dreadful male slinking away.

"Is that Fae really your cousin?" Even though I knew the answer, I willed it not to be true.

"Malon," Liri said with a sneer.

For someone who insisted on keeping family close, it surprised me to only now be learning of Liri's cousin. Though seeing what a prick he'd been, maybe it wasn't so shocking he had never been invited to Dahlquist.

"Do you have more cousins?" I asked.

"Unfortunately," Liri answered.

My heart beat erratically. "Are you in danger?"

The hard lines on Liri's forehead softened, and the steel in his eyes turned silver when he looked at me. "Are you worried about me, darling Hensley?" he asked with amusement.

I frowned, enraged by the threat on his life.

Liri leaned in close. "Do you not fear for your own life?"

"Your life is more important than my own," I said honestly.

Liri gave me a hard, unreadable stare then circled behind me. His hands snaked around my waist right before he pulled me against him. "Such an unexpected treasure," he said, hot breath caressing my ear. "I think I should like to keep you forever."

To be continued...

ACKNOWLEDGMENTS

A super special thank you to Amber Shepherd (aka: Bam) for inspiring this story. Once I created these characters for Amber's Monster Ball anthology, I couldn't let them go—or rather, they wouldn't let me go! Thank you, Amber, for being my muse and for making the online reading community a fun place to hang out.

To Najla Qamber for the gorgeous cover design. I love the way you make all the pieces come together so beautifully!

Tremendous thanks to Kelly Hashway for really digging in, straight down to the pit. Your suggestions were indispensable. I'm happy to have worked with you on this project. And thank you to Raye Wagner who first told me about Kelly!

Thanks to the kindest copy editor in all the realms, Hollie Westring. It's a wonderful feeling knowing my stories are in your capable hands and that I can follow up with questions any time and receive a swift and friendly response. You're a precious gem!

Big thanks to Roxanne Willis, a kindred spirit of the online reading community and an exceptional editor. You have a great gift for details. It really ought to be considered a superpower!

Thank you to my first readers who wholeheartedly encouraged this book: Amber Shepherd and Randi Cooley Wilson. The two of you cheered me on back when Aerith's story was just a novella for The Monster Ball Anthology, and kept on cheering when it turned into a follow-up novel. That kind of enthusiasm means a lot. Thank you both!

To my best friend and greatest supporter, Seb. Thank you for all the hugs, humor, and perspective. You have shouldered the weight of the world so that I could pursue my dreams. I dearly hope that one day soon I can repay your kindness.

To Cosmo, for being the sweetest ever, and making sure I breathe fresh air every day, rain or shine.

To my sister, Chelsea, who is a world away serving in the Peace Corps in Nepal. Thank you for inspiring the character Melarue, who likes to know all the details of what goes on when she's not around to see for herself. This book was written with you in mind. I hope it brings you some laughs.

To my mom, who is the best of the best—my own personal fairy godmother, greatest friend, and most caring human being I've ever known. Thank you for being you!

A world of thanks to Nikki's Ninjas, members of The Fantasy Fix, The Monster Ball, Monster Nation, Club YA, and the entire reading community. Thank you for getting hyped up over new books and for making me laugh out loud with your comments and GIFs. You bring endless joy and amusement to my life. I adore you to bits! (Not pits!)

To my treasured Spellbound and Aurora Sky readers, this book is especially for you! I wanted to bring you something silly, sexy, and fun in the spirit of my earlier series. I hope you were entertained.

If you enjoyed *Stolen Princess*, please let others know by posting a review. Thank you for reading!

NIKKI NEWS!

Sign up for Nikki's spam-free newsletter. Receive cover reveals, excerpts, and new release news before the general public; enter to win prizes; and get the scoop on special offers, contests, and more.
Visit Nikki's website to put your name on the list, then confirm your email so you won't miss out.
www.NikkiJefford.com
See you on the other side!

MORE PLACES TO FIND NIKKI JEFFORD

Instagram:
www.instagram.com/nikkijefford/
Facebook:
www.facebook.com/authornikkijefford
Twitter:
@NikkiJefford
BookBub:
www.bookbub.com/profile/nikki-jefford
GoodReads:
www.goodreads.com/author/show/5424286.Nikki_Jefford

SLAYING, MAGIC MAKING, AND RUNNING WILD . . .

Discover your next fantasy fix with these riveting paranormal romance titles by Nikki Jefford:

AURORA SKY: VAMPIRE HUNTER

Night Stalker
Aurora Sky: Vampire Hunter
Northern Bites
Stakeout
Evil Red
Bad Blood
Hunting Season
Night of the Living Dante
Whiteout
True North

SPELLBOUND TRILOGY

Entangled
Duplicity
Enchantment
Holiday Magic

WOLF HOLLOW SHIFTERS

Wolf Hollow
Mating Games
Born Wild

ABOUT THE AUTHOR

Nikki Jefford is a third-generation Alaskan now living in the Pacific Northwest with her French husband and their Westie, Cosmo. When she's not reading or writing, she enjoys nature, hiking, and motorcycling. Nikki is the author of the *Wolf Hollow Shifters* series, the *Aurora Sky: Vampire Hunter* series, and the *Spellbound Trilogy*.

To find out more about her books and new releases, please visit her website:

www.NikkiJefford.com.